ESCAPE FROM MATRIARCH MANOR

Copyright © 2023 by M.L. Paige

All rights reserved.

ISBN 979-8-8602609-0-0

Printed in the United States of America

10 9 8 7 6 5 4 3 2 1

ESCAPE FROM MATRIARCH MANOR

*A BRANCHING NARRATIVE FEMDOM
EROTIC NOVEL*

M.L. PAIGE

ABOUT THIS BRANCHING NARRATIVE NOVEL

Do not read this erotic novel straight through from beginning to end!

These pages include many different erotic adventures you can go on as you traverse Matriarch Manor. From time to time as you read, you will be asked to make a choice. Your choice may lead to success or disaster!

The erotic adventures you take are a result of your choice. You are responsible because you choose! After you make your choice, click the corresponding link to see what happens next.

Technically you cannot go back... but I won't tell if you do. Just make sure to keep track of your chapter number so that if you do go back, you know where to go back to.

One last note: Some of the adventures that happen in Matriarch Manor are extreme. You will be given clues when extreme situations are near, but be warned that your choices may lead you to these scenarios.

1

YOU are a mild-mannered citizen of a picturesque town with forested hills, scenic vantage points, and winding rivers. It is paradise... with a twist. Many dominant women call this town their home and have such a presence that what they can dictate how they want life to be for men in this quaint, paradisical place. YOU had a bit too much to drink this past weekend and got into an argument with a tall, domineering woman with raven black hair, a coldly cruel smile, and deep, dark eyes. When the dust had settled from your disagreement—including the entire bar siding with her, out of genuine favor and fear, she decided YOU would be locked into chastity... for the next year!

Only once you woke did you learn who she was: the terrifying, vaunted Mistress Merciless, a key figure in your town's female dominant community. That was when you knew you were truly in trouble—Mistress Merciless does not renege on her decisions, nor does she hear appeals to them. If she wants you in chastity for a year, that's where you'll be.

But not all hope is lost. You have heard about a secretive party going on to celebrate female superiority and male submission at a place called Matriarch Manor. You've never been, but after bribing someone to get directions, you find yourself on the outskirts of the manor, determined to figure out a way inside so that you can free yourself from chastity without having to wait an entire year.

You assess the manor. It looks to be three stories tall, with gothic purple-black roofing and dark brickwork. A pair of huge, carved wood doors welcome invited guests inside, while a narrow stone path seems to lead towards the back of the manor.

Try your luck with the front door (Turn to Page 8)
Go around back (Turn to Page 10)

2

You stride confidently up to the manor's carved wooden doors and slam the brass knocker against the wood. It's louder than you thought it would've been, although you can clearly hear bassy music emanating from beyond the boundary. Your heart pounds. Perhaps this wasn't the smartest idea after all.

A few moments later, one half of the double doors swing open, revealing a laughing bacchanal full of beautiful mistresses decked out in leather and latex, groveling naked male slaves, and enough food, wine, and music to last for a hundred parties. The woman who greets you has severe, arched eyebrows and seems annoyed to see someone like you during what is an otherwise bombastic party.

"Who are you?!" she asks, her voice dripping with disdain. She looks back at the rest of the party. "Anyone order a pathetic wimp?"

A few women laugh at the women, drunk on alcohol as well as their own power. Among them is the familiar sight of Mistress Merciless. She slowly swivels her head towards you and looks at you with her dark eyes like burning coals.

"Oh, I know who that is," she says slyly. "Someone who is going to stay in chastity forever."

Mistress Merciless struts over, shoving her half-filled glass of wine into the hands of a trembling, kneeling slave and reaches over to grab you by the hair. You can't think fast enough to react in time and find yourself being dragged into the thick of the party, the music and chattering deafening you from all sides. Mistress Merciless throws you onto the ground and soon dozens of hands from many mistresses are on you! They tear off your shirt and your pants and even your underwear, until you are left in nothing but your gleaming, suffocating chastity device.

Mistress Merciless puts her sharp-toed, heeled boot on your crotch and presses down, making you squirm.

"Not one for learning lessons, are you?" she asks with a sneer across her ruby red lips. "Well how about instead of a year of chastity, you have a new life—here, in this manor?"

As the mistresses cackle with spiteful glee, you see one preparing a thick leather collar with an intimidating padlock on the end of it. Your stomach drops as you realize it's for you.

"Why yes, I do believe that's a splendid idea," continues Mistress Merciless. The mistresses around her nod approvingly. "Though Matriarch Manor already has so many slaves... I guess we'll just have to get creative with how we use you, worm!"

As the mistresses excitedly conjure up uses for you in this, your shocking, horrible new life, you consider that perhaps there might've been a better way to go about getting your freedom from chastity. But alas, freedom is not something you will be experiencing for quite some time...

THE END

3

Deciding that it's probably for the best to be as stealthy as possible, you take the manor's side path, walking along a trail made of large, heavy stones that have been sunk into the mossy earth. The curtained windows of the grand house are to one side, and although you can't see what's going on in there, you can see the silhouettes of people and the muted sounds of music and laughter. To your other side is the thick woods, isolating the manor for miles around. Occasionally from the manor you hear something that might even be a champagne cork popping... or a whip cracking.

At the end of the narrow path, you step out onto the manor's expansive backyard space. It's large enough to host a party all on its own, although for the moment there only seems to be male slaves toiling in the dwindling afternoon light. Despite the growing chill in the air, the slaves are naked, save for collars and chastity devices. They work diligently and fervently to erect curious structures—cages, platforms, wooden crosses, and more are being put up and arranged, no doubt setting the stage for some later part of the evening. The slaves work with strained faces and fearful looks towards the manor, as if expecting a taskmistress to arrive at any moment to check on their work.

As you continue to observe the slaves, you see quite a few of them have old whip marks and welts across their naked bodies from days, months, or even years of service to Matriarch Manor. You shudder. Surely being kept her as livestock for the dominant women who grace the mansion is not a fate to be envied.

You also notice that a window on the second floor seems to be left open, with just enough purchase thanks to a rather hearty hedge to get you up there. You also notice that down a set of stone steps is a door leading to what looks like the basement of the manor; the door is slightly ajar. The only other entryway into the manor is a heavy backdoor that you don't dare try.

Climb up and go through the second floor window (Page 11)
Go through the basement door (Page 12)

4

Steeling yourself, you scamper up the hedge, clawing your way up the side of the manor and up to grab the ledge of the open window. It nearly takes all of your strength, but you pull yourself up and into the manor's second floor, tumbling through onto the decorative, colorful runner that lines the hallway's hardwood floor.

The second floor seems to be made up of a series of intersecting hallways, as far as you can tell, with elegant gold-and-red fleur-de-lis wallpaper. Heavy wooden doors are situated throughout the hallways, leading to who knows what. Bedrooms? Playrooms? Something more perverse than you've ever imagined? Regardless, you feel certain that this is not a floor that manor slaves are freely permitted to explore.

Sounds of partying float up from downstairs through some unseen pathway, punctuated by the occasional joyous shout or pained scream. You look back at the window, wondering if maybe coming in through this window was a mistake.

If you do stay though, you realize that to fit in you'll have to ditch your clothes to look like the rest of the male slaves. Luckily for you, there's a tall standing vase right next to the window where you can hide your clothing... though whether or not you'll have the chance to retrieve them. It's a good thing you decided to come without your wallet or keys to make sure you weren't unnecessary tied down by your personal belongings, even if might make getting into your home later a little tricky.

Your nerves get the best of you and you decide to go back outside (Page 13) You take a breath and strip and stash your clothing in the tall vase before you continue to explore the second floor's hallways (Page 14)

5

You slip into the open basement door and witness a mind-melting scene of slaves performing in little cubbies and in prison cells, the entire large space devoted to training and refining of male submissives! A group of mistresses round the corner, sure to see you any second...

Taking a deep breath, you sneak past the toiling male slaves and go down the stone steps to the open basement door. You step inside. What greets you is a labyrinth of hallways and cages and set up "stations" of a sort, outfitted with all manner of stocks and shackles and other unnerving equipment.

Many of these are occupied with male slaves and eager mistresses who are having their way with the naked, chastised men, and a near constant wailing from one man or another echoes throughout the basement's winding hallways. Signage on the walls celebrates ways to make the slaves suffer most, including helpful reminders to the women about how and where to whip and flog males.

Just as you're beginning to lose your cool, you hear a group of mistresses coming around the nearest corner! They are talking excitedly, laughing as they pull a male on all fours a leash, the poor wretch struggling to keep up with them with his arms and legs bound to emulate those of an animal. Thankfully for you, they are too busy kicking and spitting on the hopeless slave, taking turns trying to land their spit on his face.

"Let me try! It's my turn!" one of the mistresses yells. She is young, with dark hair and a skintight maxi dress on. She hocks up a wad of spit and lets it fly, catching the male right on the bridge of his nose.

"Disgusting!" another yells. She's also young, but taller than the first, walking with a willowy gait. She gives the male a sharp kick to his side. "Why are you so gross?"

A third woman, with fair skin and pale hair, glares down at the male slave. "He IS gross. Open up your mouth, you gross pig! I have something for you!" She hocks her own wad of spit and gets ready to aim for the poor male's lips.

It won't be long before they notice you.

Attempt to hide in a nearby empty cell and wait until they pass (Page 65)
Try to bluff and act like you belong down in the basement (Page 67)

6

Forget this, you think, deciding that climbing up to the second floor without a plan was a mistake. You fumble your way out the window again, nearly crashing down onto the thick, high hedge before you get back down to the backyard below.

Slaves continue to toil. There are already more of them than there were before, and you take a moment to puzzle out what they're building. It seems to be separate pieces of a larger gathering area, with a ring of stony firepits surrounding a slowly coming together platform. Next to and being built onto the platform are an array of cages and wooden stocks and crosses, which will seemingly be used to display male slaves for the female guests' amusement... perhaps some of the very males who are aching and sweating to get them built.

Perhaps one of these slaves will take mercy on you. After all, they can't all be enjoying their servitude, can they? They certainly don't seem like it. Two slaves jump out at you: one looks like he has been working since early this morning, his face flushed red and his body shaking as he pushes heavy stone benches across the grass, setting them up for mistresses to sit on near the firepits; the other looks like the whiny sort, with a furrowed brow and wrinkled nose as if he's just dying for a chance to complain about his laboring.

Of course, you could ignore the slaves altogether and try the basement.

Talk to the exhausted slave (Page 16)
Talk to the whiny slave (Page 18)
Try the basement door after all (Page 21)

7

Slinking through the hallways, you take in the decorative art pieces—vases, erotic sculptures, and vintage devices set on pedestals under glass cloches—as well as the paintings that hang from the walls, depicting scenes both placid and perverted. The floor under your feet threatens to creak with each step, but the carpeted runner helps to muffle sound... as does the thumping of your heartbeat in your ears, making your head feel full and dizzy.

There many doors in these intersecting hallways, though as you start trying knobs to see if any might be open, you find the majority of them are locked tight. Maybe those ones are bedrooms, maybe not; after all, it seems like Matriarch Manor houses endless spaces devoted to female supremacy and you try not to imagine what might be behind some of these ominous, unmarked doors.

A few do stand out, however. Down one hallway, you see a door that is painted crimson red, with delicate detailing around its frame that reminds you of winding flowers or sprawling tree branches. A smell of incense or perfume seems to be wafting out from under this door and as you ever so slowly turn the knob, you realize it's not locked.

Around the bend, there is a door that is completely black, so black in fact that at first you think the door is actually open, leading into a dark space beyond. But as you near the black door, you see that it's actually a trick of the light—or maybe the paint that's been used—that make it appear to actually suck up the light from the incandescent wall sconces that line the second floor's hallways. There is no etching on this door's frame, though it does have a silver knob, unlike the other doors, as well as a thick, gleaming lock plate. From the looks of it, it too seems to be unlocked.

Down from the black door is its opposite, an all-white door that almost blinds you when you see it. It seems to be painted with a glossy paint of some kind and when you lean in close you can see there is a fine pattern etched onto the gloss of the white door's paint. The rounded etched shapes look like horns or teeth and for some reason you can't explain, they leave you with a familiar, uneasy feeling. Looking close, you see it hasn't been closed all the way.

You wonder if you might find something of use in these rooms. More information on the manor? A master key for your chastity device? That sure would be nice. Or perhaps just a hiding spot for a bit to collect your thoughts as you wander near-naked through the second floor's hallways, the sounds of the party below still hanging in the air and reminding you that at any time you could run into wandering mistresses, with little excuse for why you're up here alone.

Go through the crimson door (Page 23)
Go through the jet black door (Page 25)
Go through the glossy white door (Page 27)
Ignore the rooms and keep looking around (Page 88)

8

You cautiously walk up to the exhausted-looking slave, a burly man whose body is shaking from the exertion he seems to have put it through all day. He wipes the sweat off his brow as you near.

"Need a hand?" you ask, pointing at the stone bench he's inching towards a nearby firepit.

The slave shakes his head. "Thanks, but if I get caught receiving help, well... won't be good for either of us." He looks at your clothing. "Who are you?" he asks.

You take a breath and explain your situation. "Well, uh, I got into a disagreement last weekend with Mistress Merciless, not knowing who she was. It didn't go well. And now—"

"Lemme guess, she put you in the ol' lock up?" he asks, resuming his straining efforts to push the bench.

You nod and the slave smirks to himself.

"Sounds about right," he says. "And she told you to come to the party?"

You shake your head. "No, I was... well, I was kind of hoping I could somehow get myself out of it. She's locked me up for a whole *year*. A year! But hey, I figure there's got to be a key to my chastity somewhere in this place, right?"

The exhausted slave looks at you like you're insane.

"You're playing with fire," he says, shaking his head in disbelief. "I started out in chastity for three months. Got caught trying to get out of it. Now it's been two years. You better be real careful..."

"I'm going to be as careful as I can," you say, looking towards the manor house. It feels incredibly daunting in the dimming afternoon light. "I just need to figure out where Mistress Merciless's room might be... and then find a way up there."

"Well the 'where' is easy," says the slave. "Third floor. Gotta be. That's where the higher up mistresses stay. But getting in there... that's rough."

"Any ideas?" you ask, trying your luck.

He gives you a cool, wary look. "I'm not your accomplice. The last thing I need is to be put in chastity for the rest of my life. And don't laugh, because some of these women have done it. Permanent chastity is no joke."

Is such a thing possible? Your mind reels.

"Sorry, I didn't mean to suggest—"

The slave cuts you off. "Someone like you though, you're probably crazy enough to sneak into the basement to look at the layout of the manor with all the mistress's rooms on it. There's room down there with just such a floorplan. Or maybe even crazy enough to pose as a scout for new slaves. You know about those right? Men who sell out other men to keen mistresses, providing them with people who will make good submissives for one reason or another."

You catch on what the slave is trying to do, offering you two options: to sneak into the basement to find out Mistress Merciless's exact room or to try to bluff your way into the manor, posing as a slaver scout... whatever that truly entails.

"Yep, bet you're crazy enough for one of those," the slave says. He turns his attention back to the stone bench, hefting it onto its legs. He starts to walk away to push another bench over.

"Thanks!" you call out, trying to keep your voice low.

The slave ignores you.

You see a trio of mistresses emerge from the basement, dragging a male slave behind them. His arms and legs are bound and he has a leash attached to his collar, making it painstaking for him to take more than the smallest of steps. One of the mistresses has dark hair and a tight maxi dress clinging to her taut curves. Another is tall and willowy, and is wearing a blouse, pencil skirt and chunky sneakers. The last has fair skin and pale hair and is dressed in a tailored blazer and tight black slacks.

Pretend to be scouting for new slaves (Page 52)
Hide and try to sneak into the basement (Page 55)

9

You trod across the backyard's manicured lawn to talk to the whiny-looking slave. He is on the short side, with rounded shoulders and a tired face, and as you approach you see him fiddling around with the metal chastity device between his legs.

"Stupid damn thing, I hate this," he mutters to himself before he sees you. But, once he does, he stands up straight and rests his hands at his side. "Yes?" he asks you cautiously.

You explain your situation: "Hi, yes, I'm in a bit of a bind. No pun intended."

You laugh, but he does not. You continue:

"See, I uh... I had a run-in last weekend with—" You lower your voice. "—Mistress Merciless."

The whiny-looking slave's eyes widen.

"Yeah. We got into a bit of a disagreement and I didn't know who she was and, well..." You knock on the front of your crotch, so that your knuckles will sound against the metal of the device you have on underneath. "She's put me in here for a whole *year*. Can you believe that? A year! All for a disagreement. Anyway, I was hoping I could find my way out early maybe by..." Your voice trails off.

The slave raises an eyebrow. "By what?" he asks, keeping his voice as low as yours. He looks around to make sure no one else is listening.

"By maybe... finding a key to the chastity cage?" you offer with a slight smile. "The way I figure it, there's got to be a key to this thing somewhere in this place, probably in Merciless's room itself."

"Mistress Merciless," the slave says, correcting you.

Your stomach turns, ever so slightly.

"Yeah, Mistress Merciless," you parrot back. "You don't happen to know where her room is, do you?"

The slave nods to himself, as if in thought. Then he says: "Hold on, I can help. Stay right there," he says. He seems to be looking towards the manor windows, looking for signs of activity. He turns back towards you. "Follow me."

You follow behind as the two of you near the manor house and, just as the slave starts to point towards the third floor of the manor, he cups his hands around his mouth and yells: "Trespasser! We have a trespasser! Mistresses, come quick!"

Betrayed! You stand in stunned silence as a half-dozen mistresses stream out from the manor's back door and the door leading to its basement. Some look like they were enjoying the party, while others are dressed in no nonsense uniform-esque wear. The group of them close in on you, demanding to know why you're here.

The slave rats you out before you can say anything.

"He's trying to get out of his chastity! He's trying to get free without Mistress Merciless's permission!"

One of the mistresses, a redhead with a perpetual smirk and lily white skin, goes over to the slave and pats him on the head. "Very good, Bootlicker, very good."

The slave seems to luxuriate in the praise.

The redheaded mistress pulls the slave towards her crotch. "You can sniff." As soon as she's given permission, the slave is taking deep breaths of her leather-clad pussy, unable to get enough, savoring each inhale with closed eyes and a blissful look on his face.

Then you are the sole focus of the mistresses.

"Trying to sneak into Matriarch Manor," says a mistress with tawny skin and light eyes. She's one of the ones dressed in uniform attire that seems more fitting in a prison than a party. "That's quite the offense."

"Indeed," says another mistress. This one looks Southeast Asian, her hair tied up in a messy bun. "What are we going to do with him?"

The tawny-skinned mistress looks at you. "What *should* we do with you? We could take you to Mistress Merciless right away and tell her what you're trying to do..."

You shudder at the thought.

"Or," she continues. "You can try to persuade us to make a good case for you. Well, as good of a case as can be made, I suppose."

The gathering of mistresses chuckle.

"Get down on your knees," says the tawny-skinned mistress. As you do, you see the whiny slave is still sucking in breaths from the redhead's crotch. She seems to be enjoying his adoration, a cold smile on her cruel face. Her hands grip his ears and force him against her, cutting off his breath.

"If you can keep from crying, we won't rat you out to Mistress Merciless," says the tawny-skinned mistress. "Sound fair?"

Before you can ask what she means by that, the first slap lands across your cheek. It stings. You turn to see which direction it came from when you feel another slap, this one strong enough to swing your head to the side. Then there's another, and another, and no matter which way you turn, there is a mistress's bare hand ready to slap your stinging, reddening cheeks. Somehow you manage to control yourself to keep from holding up your arms in defense or fighting back, but with how fast and savage the slaps are, you know you won't be able to hold out forever.

Whack! Smack!

Your vision goes dizzy with the rain of blows. You can barely catch your breath each time before another slap lands.

"Come on, you gonna cry?" one of the mistresses asks.

"Yeah, you gonna be a big dumb baby and cry from getting slapped by a couple of girls?" adds another mistress.

The slaps continue and you feel yourself reaching a breaking point. The women seem to sense this as well, speeding up their assault on your face. Finally, it is the tawny-skinned mistress who squats down on her ample, toned haunches and grabs your hair tightly in one hand while she barrages your cheek with the other.

"What's it gonna be, what's gonna be?" she asks eagerly, her light eyes wild.

The first tear is hot and salty. It rolls down your cheek as the tawny-skinned mistress bursts into laughter.

"I knew it! You fucking loser, you can't even take a little punishment!"

She slaps you again for good measure, but already the women are getting ready to drag your crying, apple-cheeked face to Mistress Merciless, where she will surely think of an even worse fate for you. Looks like getting out of your chastity is out of the question for who knows how long!

THE END

10

You start down the stone steps towards the open basement door when it suddenly swings wide open! Three mistresses are standing there, laughing and joking with one another as they drag a male slave forward on a tight leash. The male has his arms and legs bound and is only able to take small, short steps as he struggles not to fall over, much to the mistress's delight. One of them, one with dark hair, holds her foot in front of his face.

"Come on, piggy! Keep going and you can have all the stinky shoes you like!"

The other women cackle, nudging him forward by toeing his bare behind. Then they see you.

"Who are you?" one demands to know. She has fair skin and if not for her eyelined glare burning into you right now, you'd think she was actually quite your type.

You open your mouth to speak but struggle to think of an excuse.

"He was trying to get into the basement," another mistress says, this one tall and willowy. She squints down at you. "Why were you trying to get into the basement?"

The dark-haired mistress seems annoyed that she has to stop her taunting of the bound slave on all fours. She lets out a huffy, annoyed sigh. Then she looks at you, the gears in her mind turning. Suddenly she reaches out and grabs your crotch! Her hand tightens around your unyielding metal cage.

"I knew it!" she hisses. "He's in chastity!"

"Tsk tsk tsk," the fair-skinned mistress says, her lips curdling into an evil smile. "Trying to sneak away from the manor, are we? Who gave you those clothes?"

The tall mistress snatches your collar and pulls you towards the basement door. "Well, if he wants to get into the basement so badly, I say we take him inside!"

"I'll be in soon," says the dark-haired mistress, pulling the bound male forward. "Leave some for me."

The other two mistresses drag you into the basement, which is full of twisting hallways, prison cells, and all manner of frightening torture devices! They march you towards an empty cell, shoving you forward and chatting excitedly about your fate.

"We should probably let the mistresses know so we can figure out who had him caged," says the tall mistress. "After we've had our fun, of course."

"Oh of course," says the fair-skinned mistress. "And fun we shall have." She looks at you and hocks a wad of spit. With it still in her mouth she says: "Open your mouth slave, I want to see if I can land the shot."

Without waiting for you, she spits right in your face. It lands on your cheek, hot and wet. Seconds later you feel another wad of spit, this one from the tall mistress. They push you onto your ass in the empty cell and you land on a thin layer of hay.

"He's going to be our little spittoon," says the tall mistress, hocking a fat wad of spit and letting it ever so slowly drip from her lips.

"Open wide!" shouts the fair-skinned mistress.

As the phlegmy wad of spit dangles towards you, you realize your chances of getting out of chastity—and this manor—are lost. You only hope that the things the ladies decide to put in you don't get any worse than spit...

THE END

11

The room with the crimson red door. That's the one you've decided to duck into.

You pause and then turn the knob, the door easily opening inward. Inside is a room that is decorated in crimson red to match the door, with an Asiatic flair. Silkscreen prints hang on the walls, depicting scenes with women luxuriating in lush meadows and serene forests while naked males toil endlessly, some of them contorted down onto their bellies with their faces pressed between the spread legs of the women. Furniture with red leather padding is spread across the room, though most of it seems arcane to you.

But one piece of furniture is not arcane: a hefty-looking queening throne set into the center of the room. This item has a padded seat for, presumably, a mistress to comfortably rest her haunches, while an opening down below has been created for someone, surely a slave, to lie down and put his head, giving him ample access to the woman's crotch and backside.

You aren't prepared for what you see next to the queening throne. It's a mistress in a form-fitting black leather catsuit adorned with decorative silver spikes and tons of straps and buckles, with long, tumbling fiery red hair and a trim, lithe figure. She has pale, lily white skin and is busy unzipping her catsuit to expose it when you push the door open. You freeze.

She looks at you with a smirk.

"Wow, the manor's fast huh?" she asks, though you have no clue what's talking about. "I only thought the third floor elite like Merci get this kind of treatment."

Merci? Does she mean Mistress Merciless? And third floor elite... could that be where Mistress Merciless's room is located?

Opening up the crotch of her catsuit, the redhead straddles the queening throne, her lily white bottom presented like some kind of exotic pale fruit and her tender red pussy laid bare so that you can see the thick, strawberry blonde hair of her bush. The way she's sitting is so casual and so nonchalant that it's as if she's done this a hundred times before, not even needing to command a male slave on what to do. There is something truly demanding about it all, like she sees you nothing more than a thing to use...

...nevertheless, the sight and the heady smell of the redheaded mistress makes your caged cock stir. You could see yourself getting under there and servicing her with your lips and your tongue, or you could attempt to extricate yourself from this situation while you still have the chance.

Crawl into the queening throne and service the mistress (Page 81)
Apologize and make up an excuse that you are required elsewhere in the manor (Page 80)

12

Something about the black door pulls you in, just as the door seems to suck in the hallway's warm, incandescent lighting. You step to it and put your hand on its silver knob. It feels cool, yet somehow electric to the touch. You turn the knob and slowly push the door open, holding your breath as you peek inside.

It's a dungeon-like space decked out in hulking, intimidating black furniture. There's a half-covered low cage to one side, an X-shaped cross with pulleys where the arms and legs would go, a harness of some sort hanging from the ceiling, and, against the far wall, a padded whipping bench. The bondage furniture looks well-maintained and recently cleaned, as if someone had just finished using the space a little while ago... or intends to use it soon.

You start to look around for anything that might be helpful—keys, a map of the manor or a directory, business cards—anything that could help you navigate your way through Matriarch Manor and to freedom. But the only thing you find are drawers hidden into the painted black walls full of medical supplies, bondage gear, and even a few sets of fluffy dresses and garish wigs. This is definitely a dungeon space all right, one that the mistresses of the manor must retreat to when they're in the mood for some devious play.

Bending down, you look into the half-covered cage, almost expecting someone to be hidden inside as you pull away the throw slung over it. Your heart is beating hard until you see for yourself that it is truly empty, draping the throw back over it, wondering about which slaves have had to spend a day—or night—inside the cramped, demeaning cage. Across from it, on the other side of the room, is a heavy black velvet curtain you almost missed, its color and texture blending in rather well with the dark, light-absorbing walls. You pull it back with another nervous twitch, but all that's there is a window looking down onto the manor's expansive lawn. From what you can see, the slaves below are continuing to toil as they assemble equipment and seating for outdoor festivities that look still a little while off from starting.

All in all, kind of a bust you think, but at least you had a few moments to th—

You hear footsteps outside the door and muffled voices, one female, the other male. There's a shrill laugh. Whoever it is, it seems like they're about to come into the room with you! You only have a few moments to figure out a hiding place or risk being caught.

Your eyes dart over to the open cage, knowing you could pull its throw over the bars of the cage to veil yourself. Then you take a look at the heavy velvet curtain, thinking how its wall-matching look could hide you in the crook of the window.

Hide inside the open cage (Page 28)
Hide behind the heavy velvet curtain (Page 32)

13

You open the glossy white door. Much like the door suggested, the room inside is bright and clean and decorated with white furniture that gives off a Miami vacation vibe. The walls are painted light blue with abstract designs and the lighting creates a kind of low haze, late afternoon sun, the sort of light you think of at the end of a long day in southern locales. A tall white throne sits against the far wall, with a curious bench in front of it that looks designed to have a person—a male, you assume—bent over it with his rump in the air.

Soon you understand why. Fastened into the light blue walls are myriad display cases, each one having an underlit dildo or strap-on in a harness on display; the shapes and sizes vary, but their penetrating purpose is undeniable. What's more, you notice that the abstract coloring of the walls actually make up figures in lewd positions, almost all pairings where one semi-stick-figure is down on their hands and knees while the other is behind them, with a gratuitous phallic jutting from where you think their crotch would be.

A beachy smell of sea salt and ocean air hangs in the room, coming from some unseen source. You listen carefully and notice that hidden speakers are producing the gentle, relaxing sound of crashing waves and distant soothing water sounds.

But you don't feel soothed at all. You feel alarmed by this place, guessing based on the paraphernalia on in the display cases that it's a place where male slaves come—or are taken—to be ruthlessly pegged in the ass, surely by whoever would think themselves deserving of sitting on the high-backed throne against the wall.

Just as you're considering coming here was a mistake and you start towards the door, you hear footsteps outside! You desperately look for a place, but there aren't any great options.

You *could* try to crouch down under the throne, hoping that whoever comes in is tall enough not to immediately spot you under there.

Or you could just accept your fate and pray that you figure a way to get out of it later.

Hide under the throne (Page 107)
Stay out in the open (Page 108)

14

The muffled voices rise and fall and you race to the open cage, swinging its door out and crawling inside. With your hands flailing desperately, you pull at the throw blanket cast over the cage so that it creates enough cover to hide you. The blanket catches on the cage's open door, so you pull the door shut, hearing with a pang of dread in your stomach a sound like a bolt snapping into place. In your panicked haze, you test the door but it does not open again, nor does there seem to be an easy way to get it open from inside the cage! No!

You hear the doorknob turn and scramble to adjust the blanket over the cage, hoping that it doesn't move too much and give you away, even though you know your fate may already be sealed thanks to the self-locking cage door. Damnit!

A heavy smell hangs in the still, stagnant air of the dungeon space. It smells like a mix of leather and rubber, or diesel maybe, so thick you can taste it on your tongue. Underneath it all is the slight twinge of sweat and... blood?

Listening to the scene as the door is swung open and the footsteps lead inward, you surmise that a mistress has entered with a slave. As she drags the slave deeper into the room, you catch a glimpse of her through the weave of the blanket, making out a vague form of someone with her sable, wavy hair. Something about the way she moves gives off an elegant 1940s or 50s Hollywood film energy, and you notice that she seems to have full, curvy hips, teardrop breasts, and a pleasant backside that is made only more alluring by the sleeveless red latex jumpsuit she's wearing.

You shuffle in the cage to better watch things unfold as the mistress yells at the slave to "get on the bench". She has a posh English accent. Between the silhouettes you can see and what you can hear, you make out that she's strapping him down to the whipping bench at the far end of the room.

"Stop shaking," she says with a mocking chuckle. She gives his wiggling ass a sharp slap. "You'll have plenty of time for that later."

The mistress steps over to a low leather bench and flips it open. After much searching, she picks up something and tests it several times in the air to make sure it's the right choice for her. The male on the bench whimpers pitifully.

"Oh, *you*, don't worry. I have just the thing you need."

The laugh that follows is especially cruel and you can tell that this mistress truly, genuinely enjoys what she does. It's a disconcerting thought.

The mistress cracks the flogger in the air, taking small, careful steps towards her prey, who continues to shake and shudder.

"Here we go," she says, a smile in her voice. "Remember, you did this to yourself."

The blows from the flogger come quick and mercilessly. It's almost like she's painting his back with the flogger, the rhythmic thudding echoing throughout the dark dungeon space. For a bit the male holds on, but his resolve seems to actually be a kind of fuel for the mistress, making her hit him harder and faster, enough so that soon she is stopping to catch her breath.

After a brief respite, she resumes her flogging. This time she focuses on just one cheek, cracking the flogger over and over until the male begins to sniffle. Like a shark tasting blood in the water, the mistress speeds up even more, raising the flogger high above her head and bringing it down with all the force she can muster. Yes, she definitely enjoys this, you think, and in that moment you almost feel like you're listening to someone get their daily workout in.

The slave is crying now.

"Oh, my big baby is sad is he?" she says in her condescendingly posh English accent. "Learning a lesson perhaps?"

"Yes Miss Wail," says the male slave through a fit of sniffling sobs.

The mistress—Miss Wail—laughs, every bit the fairy tale villain. "Oh yes, you are learning. Although I think you might also need a reminder..."

She tosses the flogger down on the floor behind the whipping bench and the slave tries to flinch, the broad straps holding him down instead. Miss Wail smirks to herself. But as the flogger lands, some of its tails catch on the very end of the blanket covering the half-open cage. The blanket begins to slip off the cage, slowly at first, and then it tumbles off in an avalanche of dark, woven fabric.

"Hmph, I'm flogging you so hard that this place is blood falling apart," says Miss Wail as she bends down to scoop up the fallen blanket.

That's when she sees you.

Her eyes, like dark chips of obsidian, go wide—at first in shock and then in amused confusion.

"Well, well, well... what do we have here?"

You try to think of something to say but your mind is completely blank. It's a terrible time to be tongue-tied.

"A present? For me?" she asks herself aloud, laughing. "What are you doing in there, slave?" When you don't respond, the mistress adds: "Cat got your tongue? Oh there are many, many dangerous pussies around here that will do that to you..."

She stands back up, the latex of her catsuit squeaking; the shiny material clings to her long, strong legs and as she struts back to the low bench, you can't help but spy the mistress's behind through the red latex. It looks nice—very nice. It's a shame you're a million miles away from ever being able to enjoy it. It doesn't take her long to find what she's looking for. It's slender and made of a mix of plastic and metal, with a rubberized grip and a narrow, spike-like tip cast in alarming fire engine red plastic. As she revs the device's trigger, a brilliant arc of blue alights off its tip and you glumly realize what it is.

An electric shocker.

Miss Wail returns to you and squats again, ringing the tip of the shocker along the bars of the cage. She revs the shocker again, a crackling blue arc buzzing less than two feet away from your face.

"I'll only ask you one more time," she says, her eyes glittering wickedly. "What are you doing in there?"

Your mind spins through the grim calculus of having no good options as you try to figure out how you can make things *least bad*, which is a far, far way from *good*.

"I snuck in," you manage, your heart thudding wildly in your chest. "I'm not a slave here, I swear. I was just trying to get out of this."

You look down at your chastity device and Miss Wail sneers at you.

"These are all very unacceptable answers," she says, her British accent all prim and proper. She pulls the shocker's trigger and another arc bolts out from its tip; your entire body begins to quiver. "How did you get in?"

You explain the path you took, a deluge of detail spilling out of your mouth as you try to win whatever small favor you can with the latex-clad mistress. But the look on her face tells you that she isn't interested in you or your well-being, but instead in how Matriarch Manor might have unknown vulnerabilities. You can see the gears turning in her head as she considers what to do with that information.

"See, slave, I don't believe you," she says. "Not really."

You begin to whimper very, very loudly. Miss Wail ignores it.

"And I have found that when I don't believe someone, the only thing I can do is bring them to a place where all they know is how to tell the truth. It isn't easy to get there... well, not for those in your position."

Her laughter is like scalding hot velvet, rich and awful all at once. She brings the tip of the shocker towards your huddled over frame, touching your shoulder but not yet lighting it up.

"But you can at least take solace in the fact that by the time I'm done, you and I will be very well acquainted. Isn't that a nice thought?"

You try to shrink back away from the mistress, even though there isn't anywhere to go; she seems to delight in your fear, drinking it in with those cold, dark glass eyes of hers. She licks her lips hungrily.

"Shall we begin?" she asks you, just before the first agonizing shock reaches your skin.

THE END

15

You stuff yourself behind the heavy velvet curtain, trying to make yourself as flat against the window as possible. There's just a little opening in the curtain that lets you see the room, although you're painfully aware of how, if you aren't careful, the curtain might flutter forward, casting late afternoon light into the otherwise dark and dim room.

A heavy smell hangs in the still, stagnant air of the dungeon space. It smells like a mix of leather and rubber, or diesel maybe, and it's so thick that it feels like you can taste it on your tongue. You're tempted to turn around to look out the window, maybe to see what's going on outside the manor or maybe just to see if anyone can spot you from down below.

The mistress enters, dragging a naked slave behind her. Naked save for his chastity device, that is. She would be stunning if she wasn't radiating fury right now. With her sable, wavy hair, ruby red lips, and strong bone structure, there is something positively classical about this woman, as if she's stepped out of the elegant era of 1940s and 50s Hollywood films cast in brilliant, gripping technicolor. She has a figure to match this old world beauty that's complete with curvy hips, full teardrop breasts, and a pleasant backside that is made only more alluring by the sleeveless red latex jumpsuit she's wearing. Her eyes are hardened shards of black glass with long, inky lashes and perfectly manicured brows.

Somehow, you aren't surprised when she speaks with a posh English accent.

"Get over there, you filthy animal," she says, pushing the male slave towards the whipping bench.

He tumbles onto it and before he's even got his bearings, the sultry mistress is using thick, weighty straps to secure the male to the bench. He quivers as she tightens the straps so much they dig into his skin.

"Stop shaking," she says with a mocking chuckle. She gives his wiggling ass a sharp slap. "You'll have plenty of time for that later."

The mistress steps over to a low leather bench and flips it open. Inside are a dozen different whips and floggers and paddles. She runs her fingers down the line of them, going back and forth as she tries to make up her mind on what she wishes to use. After much searching, she picks up a purple flogger with at least two dozen tails, testing it in the air several times to make sure it's the right choice for her. The male on the bench whimpers pitifully.

"Oh, *you*, don't worry. I have just the thing you need."

The laugh that follows is especially cruel and you can tell that this mistress truly, genuinely enjoys what she does. It's a disconcerting thought.

You watch through the small opening in the curtain as the mistress cracks the flogger in the air, taking small, careful steps towards her prey, who continues to shake and shudder.

"Here we go," she says, a huge smile on her ruby red lips. "Remember, you did this to yourself."

The blows from the flogger come quick and mercilessly. It's almost like she's painting his back with the many-tailed flogger and then his buttocks, the rhythmic thudding echoing throughout the dark dungeon space. For a bit the male holds on, but his resolve seems to actually be a kind of fuel for the mistress, making her hit him harder and faster, enough so that soon she is stopping to catch her breath. You see the sweat roll down her elegant face; God, is she pretty.

After a brief respite, she resumes her flogging. This time she focuses on just one cheek, cracking the flogger over and over until the male begins to sniffle. Like a shark tasting blood in the water, the mistress speeds up even more, raising the flogger high above her head and bringing it down with all the force she can muster. Yes, she definitely enjoys this, you think, and in that moment you almost feel like you're seeing someone get their workout in, the mistress's sleeveless arms flexing and straining while she continues to stripe the male slave beet red.

The slave is crying now.

"Oh, my big baby is sad is he?" she says in her condescendingly posh English accent. "Learning a lesson perhaps?"

"Yes Miss Wail," says the male slave through a fit of sniffling sobs.

The mistress—Miss Wail—laughs, every bit the fairy tale villain. "Oh yes, you are learning. Although I think you might also need a reminder…"

She tosses the flogger down on the floor behind the whipping bench and the slave tries to flinch, the broad straps holding him down instead. Miss Wail smirks to herself. Then she fishes around in a compartment under the ottoman, pulling out a pink Sharpie marker. She takes it back to the male and starts to write something you can't see until she's stepped away again:

Property of Miss Wail.

Somehow, you think that there is little chance that this session is going to end any time soon. You could continue to hide behind the curtain, waiting for your chance to leave—or be discovered—or you could make a run for it the next time she turns towards the poor male slave that's the focus of her sadistic "workout".

Keep waiting behind the curtain (Page 35)
Make a run for it when you have the chance (Page 93)

16

You continue to wait behind the curtain, hoping opportunity presents itself soon.

"There we go," she says, admiring the pink Sharpie writing on the slave's ass. "Let me get a little light in here and make sure it looks exactly as I want..."

You go stiff as she approaches the velvet curtain and pulls it open. She shrieks, at first, and then realizes you are just another near-naked man wearing a chastity device. Her shock turns to anger.

"And what the bloody hell are you doing here?" she asks, her eyes dancing as she tries to work it out for herself.

You try to think of an excuse but your mind is completely blank. It's a terrible time to be tongue-tied.

She snaps her fingers angrily in your face.

"Hello? Hellllooooo? Is anyone in there? My goodness, are the slaves getting dumber and dumber around here, or is it just me?" she asks in the direction of the male bound over the whipping bench. He whimpers something in the affirmative that makes the posh mistress laugh. "Don't worry, you pathetic loser. No one will ever be as dumb as you."

"Well?" Miss Wail asks, turning back to you. "Are you going to speak or am I going to have to flog the words out of your unruly husk of a body?"

Spill your guts to Miss Wail (Page 36)
Plead with Miss Wail for her to let you go (Page 38)

17

And just like that, you crack and surrender yourself to Miss Wail, feeling a wave of terror ripple through you as you spill your guts.

"I'M SORRY!" you shriek, surprising both her and you with how loud your voice is. "I was stupid, I was dumb, I had this whole run-in last weekend with someone at a bar because I drank too much because I always drink too much and then I got into a fight and I didn't know who I was fighting with and I spilled a drink all over her and then she told me who she was and everyone else at the bar seemed to know, everyone but me, and she threatened me unless I put on this chastity device and so I said yes and then she told me I'd be wearing it for a year! And so I came here thinking maybe, somehow—I know, I know, it was stupid—I could get it off so I didn't have to go through an entire year of chastity all because I upset Mistress Merciless and—"

Miss Wail raises her hand, silencing you.

"You said Mistress Merciless?" she asks.

You try to read her tone to intuit if admitting this again will only get you in even worse trouble, but fuck it, how much worse could things get? You nod.

Miss Wail laughs to herself. "Bloody Merci," she says under her breath. "She sure does love throwing her weight around."

A ray of hope breaks through the clouds that have plagued you the last week. You try not to get too excited, but it's hard not to feel like you might just have a chance of turning this towards your favor.

"Yes," you say quietly. "I don't know why she was so angry but—"

"Stop talking," commands Miss Wail. She looks away from you in thought, "She put you in chastity for a whole year?"

Holding your tongue, you nod.

Again, Miss Wail laughs, almost unable to believe what you're saying. "You poor, sorry sod. What a terrible fate, but I'm sorry, there's just nothing I can do."

The way she says it though, it's almost like she's daring you to change her mind. Clearly, she is no fan of Mistress Merciless. Might she be willing to help you?

"I'll do whatever it takes to get out of this thing," you say, feeling sweat run down your forehead. Your hands are clammy. "Maybe I can, I don't know... amuse you, or something."

The mistress quirks an eyebrow. "Amuse me?" she says, sounding rather amused already. "And how exactly might you *amuse* me?"

You're sure there's a thousand options you could give her right now, but as fate and luck would have it, only two pop into your mind, both inspired by what you've seen during your research of Matriarch Manor. In one, you imagine offering yourself up to Miss Wail as her dog, performing whatever tricks she might request of you. In the other, you see her humiliating and emasculating you as her garish, feminine sissy, making you perform all kinds of lewd, debasing activities. You try to conjure up other ideas, but your nerves are too fraught to come up with anything else.

Offer to be Miss Wail's human dog (Page 41)
Offer to be Miss Wail's sissy (Page 47)

18

"Please," you stammer after a long comment of silence. "Please, just let me go. I know I shouldn't have been listening, that I shouldn't have been in here..."

Miss Wail snorts, like she can't believe what she's hearing. "Let you *go*? Oh, you stupid, stupid slave, I don't think you understand this place at all. Whose slave are you?"

You open your mouth to speak but no words come out. You have nothing to say.

Miss Wail snaps her fingers in front of your face again. "Slave. Who do you belong to?" There's a heavy note of genuine concern in her voice. She knits her brows and looks at you curiously. Then, as if a light has gone off in her head, she begins to smile, brows raising with her realization. "You don't belong to anyone..."

You could up your hands defensively and attempt to plead with her again.

"Please Miss, if you just let me go I promise to never come back. I'll leave the party, the manor, the whole town even, just please, please, please let me go..."

But the mistress doesn't even seem to hear you as she studies you with a cold predator's gaze. She points a pale finger towards the ground.

"Sit down," she commands.

Even as you comply, you're still begging for a way out. "You know, I can even come back and, like, you can do whatever you want to me later, just let me go home now. Okay? Please let me go home and then we'll figure out a time when we can, uh, when I can, when..."

You have no idea what you're saying or even trying to say—you're simply throwing out any idea that might give you some remote chance of getting out of Matriarch Manor.

"Shhh, shhh," says Miss Wail. She opens up the low bench and takes out several small items, including a heavy leather collar. As she wraps the leather around your neck, you notice how it curiously feels warm and snug and controlling without doing anything other than being wrapped tightly around your throat.

"Please," you whimper.

The mistress squats down in front of you, the latex catsuit stretching and squeaking against her luscious curves. Her smile is smarmy and knowing, and she strokes your cheek in a way that is almost tender.

"Please," you try, one last time.

"Open your mouth," she says.

You do as Miss Wail commands, lips trembling as she lifts a large red ball gag to your mouth. She presses it between your lips and your teeth, threading its straps behind your head and fastening them tight. No more speaking for you.

"Good boy," she coos with a smirk. "You have to understand, slaves in this do not have rights. They do not just 'go home', they do not ask for things, and they certainly don't *beg*. Frankly, it's unbecoming. Until you learn to use your words properly, there will be no more speaking for you. Do you understand, slave?"

They don't go home? Your heart races at the thought of staying in this manor forever.

"Slave, I asked you a question," the mistress says with a touch of temper in her voice.

You nod, knowing there is only one answer Miss Wail is going to accept.

"Good. Now, something must be done about your behavior, I'm afraid. Stand up."

As the mistress stands, you follow her lead, your legs trembling. She notes your nervousness with a muffled laugh to herself and then looks around the dungeon-like space, tapping her chin with her finger.

"Let us see, what does a slave lurking around the manor without permission need for his behavior... ah, yes, of course."

Grabbing your new, stiff leather collar, Miss Wail leads you over to the X-shaped cross against the wall, turning your back towards it and then positioning your arms and legs to fit into the cross's cuffs. She cinches the cuffs shut and then begins to turn the pulley wheels situated near the ends of the X-shaped cross. As she does, your arms and legs are pulled far from your body, until you are barely able to balance with your legs spread wide and your arms stretched out, your body weight leaning against the cuffs and the cross.

A helpless feeling overwhelms you. Miss Wail retrieves her pink Sharpie and starts to draw in large dots on your chest and legs and stomach, nearly ten in total that mark up your body. Then she picks up her purple flogger, thinking for a moment, and then sets it down.

"This isn't going to be pleasant," she says as she goes back to the open bench.

She pulls out a short, thick leather whip that reminds you of a lolling black tongue. Miss Wail tests her implement out, the crack terrifyingly loud in the dungeon space, making the bound male over the whipping bench flinch and shiver in fear.

"Relax, this isn't for you, loser," she says to him, turning towards you. "It's for your new friend. He's about to learn a very, very important lesson."

Miss Wail takes aim at the pink dots drawn onto your skin. As the tongue-like whip connects with your flesh, you feel a pain you've never known before. It is hot and fiery and is more like a cutting blade than a strip of leather. You shout into your ball gag and thrash against your unyielding bondage.

"Yes, wail for me, slave. Wail your pretty little lungs out."

The mistress brings the whip down again, the leather lashing your thigh. You feel another red hot slice and if you didn't know better, you'd say your leg was just cut open. But when you look down all you see is a long welt that has just missed the pink dot Miss Wail drew down there.

"Oh, drats. I missed. I'd better try again," she says.

She does not miss on her second try, the pain layering onto the long, red welt. You stomp your feet and shout into the gag, trying with all your might to pull yourself from the X-shaped cross.

"Are you going to behave and do as I say from now on?" Miss Wail asks you.

You nod frantically.

She sighs.

"I just don't believe you," she says with a cold smile. "Not yet, anyway."

As she raises the whip again, you only pray that your torment will end soon. You would give anything to make it stop—do anything, obey any command—and as you find yourself thinking this, you know deep down that your life will never, ever be the same.

You belong to Miss Wail now and to Matriarch Manor, forever destined to be a scrabbling, servile male slave for the rest of your days.

THE END

19

"I could... uh, be your dog...?" you ask uncertainly.

Miss Wail can barely hold back a laugh. "My *dog*?" she asks incredulously. "Now where in the world did you ever get a foolish idea like that? Dogs are wonderful creatures: joyful, loving, loyal, innocent. What in the world makes you think a male like yourself has anything in common with a dog?"

Her words are cutting and relentless, each one making you cringe with embarrassment. What *were* you thinking? You're overcome with a feeling of being totally out of your element; it's one thing to be a stranger to Matriarch Manor and to be stumbling your way through its halls, but it's another to try—and fail—to appeal to one of the manor's mistresses. You hang your head in shame, feeling a hot blush fill your cheeks.

"Now a puppy on the other hand," says Miss Wail in a thoughtful tone. "Perhaps a male could make a suitable one of those. Unruly. Disobedient. Dumb. And... in need of training. What do you think, slave? Do you think you could make for a suitable puppy for me to practice my training skills?"

As you lift your head, you see Miss Wail giving you a smile threaded through with mischievousness and cruelty. You nod, not knowing where this will go, only that it's one option—maybe the *only* option—of leaving the dungeon space a free man.

"Why is my puppy standing up?" Miss Wail asks sternly. "Down puppy, down!"

You drop onto all fours, down to the mistress's latex boots. She stomps her foot on the dungeon's hard floor, startling you.

"Not all the way down!" she says. "Come on, up! Beg, puppy!'

Reacting as quickly as you can, you rise up on your knees, holding your hands in an imitation of doggie paws. You look anxiously up at Miss Wail, who has on a gleaming smile and a sadistic stare in her eyes.

"That is an absolutely pathetic example of begging," she says, storming off towards the low bench. From it, she withdraws a long riding crop with a stiff leather tongue at the end of it. She motions upwards with it, like a conductor. "Do puppies stay silent when they beg?"

You almost say "no", catching yourself at the last moment, and then do your best version of a dog whine, making the whimpering noise with wrenched-shut lips. Miss Wail grins at you and nods.

"Yes, that's better, puppy." She holds the leather tongue of the crop under your chin as you continue to whine for her, the mistress nodding approvingly. "Now, sit!"

For a moment you struggle to figure out how she wants you to obey, but fear not—Miss Wail is all too happy to guide you! She swats at your shoulders and the top of your head, pushing you back and down onto your heels. Then she strikes lightly at your inner thighs, forcing you to spread your legs until you can feel the big muscles starting to cramp up. Miss Wail takes a step forward, filling the space between your legs with one latex-clad leg; the sharp toe of her boot sits right under your balls.

"I think my puppy is missing a few things," she says, inching her toe up to prod your balls menacingly. "Doesn't my puppy want to be complete?"

You nod your head, but Miss Wail tut-tuts.

"Puppies don't nod," she says in a warning tone. "What do they actually do?"

You think for a moment, as if you've been asked some arcane riddle, but the answer is obvious: they bark.

"Woof!" you go. "Woof, woof!"

"That's right!" coos Miss Wail encouragingly. She reaches down and tousles your hair and you can't believe that part of you is actually starting to *enjoy* this treatment. "Now, shall I get the items my puppy is missing?"

"Woof!"

Miss Wail toes your balls again, moving the tip of her foot in a slight circle to massage your caged cock. Despite your chastity device, you can feel yourself getting excited—trying to, anyway—at the attention this gorgeous, domineering woman is giving you. It's enough to make you not even worry about what "items" she thinks you're missing as she leans down and holds the crop out to you for you to hold in your mouth.

"You just keep that there," she says before she wags her finger at you. "And no doggie spit on it, please!"

Then Miss wail steps away to open up a well-disguised compartment in the dungeon's jet black wall. She hums to herself as she pulls out a few things, gathering them up in one hand: You see a collar and leash, a leather mask of some kind, and something else that is black and bouncy and made of rubber. With the crop still held between your mouth and you doing everything you can to not drool all over it, Miss Wail fits the collar around your neck with a rather professional, perfunctory air, letting the chain leash hang down your chest and between your legs. Then she retrieves the crop, inspecting it for unwanted spit, and sets it down so she can pull the leather mask over your head. Just before she does, you can see it is surprisingly like an actual dog's head, with little triangle dog ears made of black leather and a stiff, short muzzle over the nose and mouth.

The mask is warm and smells strongly of leather polish. Once Miss Wail has made sure it's snugly on your head and lined up so that you can see through the eye cutouts, she holds up the last item she has. It looks like a twisty, bouncy dog tail, but the other end is fat and bulbous with a flared tip. You realize where that's intended to go with a nervous, shuddering exhalation.

"You're looking much more the role now," she says. "But we still have one more *very* important puppy part to give you. Turn around and bend over, puppy."

She holds her smile, but you can see Miss Wail's eyes hardening the longer you take to follow her instructions. Smothering a reluctant sigh, you shuffle around to face away from her and then bend your head forward until it's pressed against the cold dungeon floor. The mistress pushes your legs apart and turns your knees towards each other, the positioning causing your ass cheeks to spread. You hear the soft click of a bottle top opening and then feel the spill of gloopy, cool lube down your crack. She doesn't use much.

"Deep breaths puppy," she says as she begins to tease your hole with the flared tip of the tail butt plug.

The mistress presses it against you in time with your breathing, pushing a little more with every one of your exhalations. At first it seems impossible that this thing can go in you but slowly, bit by bit, you feel your hole stretch and grip at the rubber plug, even *drawing* it inward until it's deep enough in that you can feel the bulge of it pushing uncomfortably against your tight ring.

"Biggest, deepest breath yet," Miss Wail says, her voice nearly a whisper.

There's nowhere to go but through this. You take a big breath and then let it all out in a long stream. That's when Miss Wail pushes firmly and unrelentingly, causing you to have one blind moment of panic at the size of the plug followed by a blissful relief as the largest part is past the rim of your hole and the plug's flared base is now seated surely against you. You feel a slight jiggling as Miss Wail plays with the rubber puppy tail, watching it bounce back and forth with an amused laugh.

"Turn back to me, puppy," she commands.

You lift your head, feeling the plug deeper in you now, and turn back to the mistress. She seems positively delighted at the sight of you and her big, beaming smile fills you with a curious kind of pride that you've never known before. Remarkably, it makes you forget all about your chastity and the fear of running into Mistress Merciless and you find yourself actually *wanting* to Miss Wail's good little "puppy".

She gathers up your leash and stands. "Come now, we're going for a walk," she says.

You can't help but give her a frightening look and she laughs at your wide-eyed stare through the leather dog mask. She gives a sharp tug of the chain leash and then snatches up the crop to slap your ass with it, making you let out a cry.

"Are we going to have a problem?" asks Miss Wail.

You hang your head, feeling chastised in a completely different way from the cage that is denying you an eager erection.

"I didn't think so," Miss Wail says to herself. You hear another loud *smack!* and realize she's just hit the male slave who is still bound to the whipping bench. "We'll be back, loser. Don't go anywhere."

Miss Wail leads you towards the jet black door connecting to the second floor hallway. As you shuffle out of the dungeon, feeling the plug filling you and the heat of the leather mask, your eyes dart around, praying the two of you won't encounter anyone else. Although... even if Mistress Merciless came down the hallway right now, would she even know who you were with the dog mask on?

There's a tug at your collar as Miss Wail strides forward.

"Keep up, puppy!" she says impatiently. "I don't like to walk slowly."

You shuffle after her, knees banging on the carpet runner lining the floor. The chain leash jingles as you walk after Miss Wail's striding boots and you're already starting to feel tired using up so much energy just barely keeping up. She picks up her pace, rounding the corner. You rush to follow, the sweat building up inside your mask, having to look up constantly to navigate as the mask's eye cutouts start to slip to one side. And yet, Miss Wail picks up her pace even more. You are huffing and puffing now, and feeling the burn in your arms and legs as you thump down the hallway. She rounds the next corner even faster and you bump into the wall, having to scramble to right yourself and make it around the corner too before the chain leash is pulled taut. As you turn, you see Miss Wail has stopped and is looking down at you with a bitchy look on her beautiful face.

With her crop, she points down the hallway and you see a flight of stairs leading to the third floor. Miss Wail crouches down and addresses you in a whisper.

"That's where you'll go when I'm done with you, puppy. You'll find Merci's room up there, though I can't promise you'll find what you need there," she says, her eyes searching yours. "And it shouldn't need to be said, but I did nothing of the sort to assist you. Are we clear?"

"Woof! Woof!"

Your dedication to Miss Wail's puppy training game makes her smile wide.

"Waily!" a voice cries out from behind you. Your heart starts to hammer in your chest. The voice sounds familiar, but from where?

Miss Wail notes the frightening look in your eyes and then looks past you. She stands back up and gives a curt wave.

"Hello, hello," she says with a tired sigh.

"Long day?" asks the mystery mistress.

"Oh just taking my new puppy out for a walk," says Miss Wail.

"Ohh, can I see?"

Miss Wail glances down at you with a look of surprising concern, catching the panic in your eyes. You can't place the voice. Could it be someone you saw or overhead at the manor? Or someone else that might recognize you, even with the dog mask over your head?

"Well... this puppy's a bit shy," says Miss Wail, using the crop to stroke your back. Letting the chain leash slacken, she reaches towards the back of her latex catsuit and you hear the unmistakable sound of a zipper being undone. "I was just about to give him some scent training too. You know how puppies like all those nasty, stinky smells."

The other mistress chuckles.

"Puppy, come back around behind me and make sure my bottom is all nice and clean. I feel like it's getting rather sweaty."

You keep your eyes downcast as you shuffle behind Miss Wail, grateful to have the shield of her body as you resist the urge to peek at who the other mistress is. As you lift onto your knees, you're faced with Miss Wail's creamy, lush backside through the unzipped opening of the red latex. Taking a breath, you can smell a mélange of sweat and pussy and ass, the mixture distinctly feminine and very musky. You have to adjust the muzzle of the dog mask so you stick out your tongue, and once you do you draw the tip of it along the swell of Miss Wail's ass cheek. The mistress giggles.

"Puppy! That tickles!" says Miss Wail. "I need to lick deeper. That's where I'm *really* sweating."

You push your masked face in between the mistress's cheeks as deep as it will go and flick your tongue out, tasting the concentrated sweat and musk of her. In another context, you might be horrified by it all but kneeling there, in your doggie get-up, you can't help but feel yourself straining in your cock cage while your tongue is pushed out as far as possible, the taste of Miss Wail overwhelming your senses. You rock against her with each lick, the mask and her ass muffling the sounds of conversation between her and the mystery mistress.

It's hard to tell how long you lick for, but eventually it's Miss Wail herself who nudges you away. The lights of the hallway seem strangely bright and you sway, disoriented from licking up and down Miss Wail's warm, sweaty ass crack. The other mistress is gone. Miss Wail turns and zips her catsuit back up, pursing her lips.

"My, my, puppy. You certainly can be *eager*, can't you?"

Her praise is both encouraging and embarrassing, and you're grateful for the dog mask so she can't see how much you must be blushing. She toes at your chastity device, able to feel how it bulges with your attempted hard-on.

"I bet you wish you could get out of there," she says, nodding.

You give a loud, whiny whimper.

"If you were my actual puppy, I'd let you out now and again," she says, taunting you. "Maybe once a month if you were oh-so-obedient for me. But alas, you have other things to do."

She bends down and undoes your leather collar before peeling off the mask, revealing your flushed, blushing face. With one finger she wordlessly commands you to turn around, working the plug out of you much more easily than it went in, only leaving behind slippery lube between your cheeks that is going to take a while to dry out. Holding up all the implements in one hand—and keeping the plug far from her body—Miss Wail has one more thing to say to you.

"Remember, no mentioning me should they catch you, puppy," she says with a strict schoolteacher's demeanor. Then her expression softens. "And should you decide one day that you wish to return to Matriarch Manor, I give you permission to audition to be my *actual* puppy. Though be warned, I will not be nearly as kind should you come back."

The mistress tilts her head towards the stairs, beckoning you to go to the third floor. You don't know whether to thank her or not and so you compromise, bending down to kiss the tops of her latex boots and give her a parting "Woof!" as you slowly crawl towards the third floor stairs.

Continue onto the third floor (Page 92)

20

"What if I acted like your... your..." You can't even say the words.

"My what?" asks Miss Wail. "My dumb little slave who can't even speak?"

"...your sissy?" Your voice is very quiet and you're not even sure that you've got what you're offering to her straight. All you know is you've seen pictures online of manor parties with men dressed as girly maids and hyper-feminized women, serving and pleasing the mistresses of the manor. Somehow you imagined you could, somehow, do that for Miss Wail, too.

Miss Wail can barely hold back a laugh. "My *sissy*?" she asks incredulously. "Now where in the world did you ever get a foolish idea like that? What does an oafish, brutish man have in common with a wonderful, lovely little sissy? The two are like oil and water if you ask me."

Her words are cutting and relentless, each one making you cringe with embarrassment. What *were* you thinking? You're overcome with a feeling of being totally out of your element; it's one thing to be a stranger to Matriarch Manor and to be stumbling your way through its halls, but it's another to try—and fail—to appeal to one of the manor's mistresses. You hang your head in shame, feeling a hot blush fill your cheeks.

"Now, a pretty little doll I can make look like a sissy," says Miss Wail in a thoughtful tone. "Perhaps, with enough work, I could make you into one of those. But it's going to take a transformation. Change. And a willingness to do things that might not come so... naturally, to you. What do you think, slave? Do you think you could be transformed into a sissy doll?"

As you lift your head, you see Miss Wail giving you a smile threaded through with mischievousness and cruelty. You nod, not knowing where this will go, only that it's one option—maybe the *only* option—of leaving the dungeon space a free man.

"Why is my little dolly standing up?" Miss Wail asks sternly. She walks over to the low leather bench and shuts it, pointing at its padded top. "Go sit over there, dolly."

You shuffle over to the bench and sit, feeling like you're at a perverse, macabre doctor's appointment, waiting your turn. You notice the bound slave is still waiting over the whipping bench, perhaps so used to suffering this kind of treatment that he doesn't dare make a sound to interrupt his mistress, even when she's completely changed her focus.

"Now, we will need to start by getting rid of all that nasty, ugly hair," says the mistress as she opens up a hidden compartment in the dungeon's jet black wall. She pulls out something that looks like a can of compressed air, except this can is bright pink and has a cartoon picture of a woman's smooth, long legs on it. "Hold your arms out at your sides, palms down. Oh, and this might sting a bit, dolly..."

The can has a long white stem extending out from its top and, as Miss Wail presses down on the nozzle, you feel a cool, slightly stinging sensation across your arms and then your shoulders and chest and stomach. Miss Wail withdraws the can and the cold sting becomes a hot sizzle for a few agonizing seconds before turning into a tingly numbness. The mistress wipes your arms and chest clean with a fine cloth, your skin feeling like it was just out in the sun for eight straight hours. To your shock, the hair underneath is gone! It's been wiped away by cloth—and whatever is in that pink can.

"Stand up, dolly," she says. "Now that you know what to expect, we can get to the more... sensitive spots."

You stand up, still holding your arms out, and brace yourself as the mistress begins to spray you. She sprays under your armpits, and down your ass, making sure to cover nearly every inch of your bare skin with the cool-then-hot compressed liquid spray. The armpits sting worse for sure, as do your inner thighs, but none of it is compared to what you feel when the spray hits your crotch. That stinging is like someone just dropped a hot coal on your pubic area and you start to dance your feet about in pain, wheezing and huffing at the icy-fiery pain. Miss Wail laughs as she folds her cloth over and takes away the dark hair between your legs, leaving you humiliatingly bare.

You look down at yourself with a frown.

"Oh don't be sad, dolly," says Miss Wail as she wipes away the stray hairs from your body. "You like *much* better this way. But we aren't done, oh no, no. Not at all."

Miss Wail goes back to the compartment in the wall. From it she pulls out a pair of yellow lacey panties and a matching bra, along with a disturbingly small looking shimmery purple satin dress. Lastly, she takes out a long blonde wig, first holding it up towards you as if trying to judge if the color will suit your complexion. She grins at you as she strides back, setting the wig and dress on the bench.

"These first," she says, handing you the lace underwear.

You step into the panties and pull them up your newly smooth body, the lace like crackling electricity against your skin. They fit well enough, though the bulge of your chastity device pushes against the lace, threatening to stretch it out permanently. Miss Wail taps on the cage through the lace.

"It's a shame you had to be put in such a large one," she says with disappointment. "I'm sure we could've packed you into something much more appropriate for a little sissy dolly."

A large one? Is she serious? You've spent the last week waking up several times a night because your cage is so tight and uncomfortable. The thought of being in something even smaller makes you queasy and—even though you can't believe you're thinking it—grateful that Miss Wail doesn't have the key to your device. Who *knows* what she might put on instead.

Next, Miss Wail wraps the bra around your chest, turning you so that she can fasten it in the back. It's tight across your rib cage and even though you don't properly fill it, it still feels immensely embarrassing to have the yellow bra stretched across your skin, the wiring sinking into your flesh. Before you've even done getting used to it, Miss Wail is handing you the purple satin dress, waiting with her arms folded across her chest for you to put it on.

Do you step into a dress or pull it over your head? You don't know, so you try stepping into it, only for Miss Wail to laugh in your face.

"No, no dolly, dresses go on like shirts. At least that one does," she says. The way she speaks is both coddling and condescending and you get the odd feeling like she sees you as a Barbie to dress up and play with, with no free will or mind of your own.

You pull on the dress. It's tight across the chest and the shoulders and your hips in all the ways you've never really thought about clothes being tight. Instinctively you tug down on the hem, only to find it's a minidress, the hem making it barely halfway down your thigh. As with the underwear, your chastity device bulges lewdly in the front, much to Miss Wail's pleasure. You feel the satin against your bare ass and even though you have to admit it, it feels... *good*.

Last, but not least in your emasculation, is the blonde wig. This Miss Wail helps fix atop your head, adjusting the long, wavy locks so that they frame your face and run down the back of your neck. It smells perfumed, the aroma of wildflowers clinging to the air around you.

Miss Wail looks at you and clasps her hands together. "How nice," she says with an appraising stare. She twirls her finger. "Show off for me."

Awkwardly, you turn with small, halting steps, and when your back is to Miss Wail, you feel a rush of air as she slaps your ass hard. You jump and squeal in surprise, eliciting a deep chuckle from the mistress.

"Now, what else does a sissy doll need?" she asks, looking the dungeon over as if deep, deep in thought. But based on the gleam in her dark eyes, you sense she already has something in mind.

Her gaze stops on the male bent over the whipping bench.

"Oh yes," she says. "A boyfriend. Since you aren't exactly a ten—no offense, dolly—I think this male here will do very nicely." She steps over to the whipping bench and begins undoing the straps, snapping her fingers until the slave lifts himself from his kneeling position; his eyes are downcast and he has an air of resignation, as if he's been through Miss Wail's tortures many times before.

Then something happens you could've never guessed: Miss Wail reaches into a tiny pocket in her latex catsuit and pulls out a silver key on a ring.

"Looks like it's your lucky day," she says to the slave. She taps the key against his chastity device a few times and then begins to unlock him, bringing him out of his metal prison; the male is modestly sized down there and even though it looks like he's been caged for a long, long time based on how scrunched up and pale his cock is, he starts to spring back to life instantly, a single touch from Miss Wail making him grow.

And as he does, you realize he's a bit more than "moderately" sized.

"Let's play a game," says Miss Wail, her ruby red lips curled into a cunning sneer. She points a finger at you. "You, dolly, have just been on a date with your sweetheart. It was grand: a nice dinner, a movie, blah, blah, blah. But now that he's put in to show you a nice night, dolly, it's time to put out. And a good sissy *always* puts out. Go and get him hard and decide if you're going to give him your mouth or that sissy pussy of yours."

When you hesitate, Miss Wail claps her hands together loudly.

"Go on! Get to stroking! Unless you're done trying to be my sissy?"

You have no choice but to become condemned to the manor—and likely a much worse fate than the one you're facing—or to do as Miss Wail commands. You take a step towards the male, unable to even look him in the eye. You grasp his cock in your hand. It's warm and semi-soft and with grating humiliation you begin to stroke him clumsily.

"You've got a minute to get him hard and make your choice," warns Miss

Wail. "And right now you seem to be giving him the dead fish grip. How utterly pathetic."

You take a breath and try to focus on the stroking, doing your best to imagine it as your own cock. Even though your goal is to get this man hard, you can't believe it when he actually starts to grow stiff in your grasp, his cock inflating to its full seven or so inches. The fat head throbs against your fingers with each tug and you can feel the blood pulsing through his veins, the newly-released male's breaths getting shorter and shorter as your strokes fill him with long-denied pleasure.

"Okay, okay, you don't want him to pop too quickly," says Miss Wail as she pulls your hand away from the slave's crotch. "No one likes a premature climax to the night." She looks to you. "Well? What will it be? Are you going to give him your mouth or your 'special' place?"

Offer your mouth (Page 279)
Offer your "special" place (Page 134)

21

You clear your throat. Here you go.

"Hello there," you say to the mistresses, as prim and proper as you can manage. "I'm a scout for, uh, slaves. You know, these sorry sods. I'm here to both assess the stock here and suggest a few new charges to anyone interested..." You observe their placid stares for a moment before you add: "Perhaps that might include yourself?"

The dark-haired mistress looks you up and down and then laughs to herself.

"Christ, you must not be very good," she says snidely. "You're dressed like a bible salesman."

The fair-skinned mistress joins in on the laughter. "He does look like that! Like a... what do you call those people again?"

"A Mormon?" asks the dark-haired mistress.

"Yes!" screeches the fair-skinned mistress. She looks back to you. "You look like a Mormon!"

As the women jokes and laugh, the tall mistress squints down at you, as if trying to read your mind. She puts her hands on her hips, her pencil skirt clinging to her willowy frame.

"How long have you been a slaver scout for?" she asks, arching one eyebrow. "I don't recognize you."

Feeling the pressure, you scramble to uphold your lie.

"I'm actually visiting for the week. Family, actually, but I also knew the manor wasn't far away so I decided to take a quick trip up and see if I can't, ah, make some connections." You hold out your hand and conjure up a fake name. "I'm Will Daniels. Pleased to meet you...?"

Ugh, what a name. But at least you came up with something. The mistress does not take your hand. It looks like she's about to say something when the dark-haired mistress butts in.

"Hey, I need a new slave," she says to you. "I'm thinking strong, not too strong, hairless, good at oral... got anything?"

"Uh..." Your mind goes blank. You haven't prepared for this at all. "If you have some contact info, I'm sure I could—"

"No no no, me first," says the fair-skinned mistress, laughing as she pushes her dark-haired friend out of the way. The two bicker and smile at each other. "I want a slave who can take pain. A *lot* of pain. I'm thinking needles, knives—"

"I was talking!" says the dark-haired mistress. She looks at you. "So, he should be handsome too, and he..."

She's soon interrupted by the fair-skinned mistress again and the bickering resumes, the cacophonous conversation making your ears ring. All the while, the tall mistress studies you carefully, seemingly suspicious. You feel grateful that you don't have to talk to her longer than you have to.

"Do you ladies have cards?" you ask, feeling dumb for the question before it's even out of your mouth.

The tall mistress snorts with laughter but says nothing.

"Uh, no," says the dark-haired mistress. "Do mistresses where you're from usually have cards?"

You pause. "Some do," you say, hoping you haven't lost your domineering audience.

"Well, we don't," says the fair-skinned mistress. She says it meanly, but there's a hint of concern that maybe she *should* have a card.

You try to think of how you can get yourself out of this mess.

"If you would just give me your names, I'm sure I can get in touch with you later," you say, feeling a bead of sweat run down the back of your head.

"That's Miss Hecate," says the tall mistress, hiking a thumb towards the dark-haired mistress. "And that's Miss Ember."

"And yourself?" you ask, more out completeness than any real desire to keep talking to this judgmental, willowy, tall woman.

"I'm Miss None-of-your-business," she says.

"Right," you say with an awkward laugh. "Well, I'm going to continue my observations inside, but I will be sure to follow up with you later, Miss Hecate, Miss Ember."

You start towards the basement door, feeling like you might faint as you make your way down the stone steps. Even though Miss Hecate and Miss Ember have resumed their teasing bickering, you can feel the other mistress staring daggers at you and pray she does not decide to interrogate you further.

You step through the open basement door and into a knot of grimy hallways, assaulted by the noise of wailing slaves and the vicious laughter of mistresses having entirely too good of a time. You hear paddles land on bare flesh as well as the heavy jangle of thick chains. This is not a place for the faint of heart.

But as you scope it out, you notice a room off to one end of a hallway; it's dim and small, but you can see a schematic on the wall that seems to be a layout of something that looks like it might just be the manor. You could check it out more closely or you could try exploring the rest of the basement.

Check out the room with the curious schematics on the wall (Page 69)
Explore the rest of the basement instead (Page 70)

22

Posing as a "scout" for new slaves sounds absolutely nuts to you. Instead, you take the bustle the exiting mistresses as a distraction for you to hide behind a half-built pair of wooden stocks off to the side of the stone steps leading down into the basement. The mistresses continue their ascent onto the verdant green expanse of the backyard, tugging their male slave behind them.

"Come on, you piece of shit!" the fair-skinned mistress yells at him. She shotgun spits at him, the spittle raining down on his hair and his face. He cringes underneath her severe yelling.

"Faster! Faster!" shouts the dark-haired mistress, moving around to the back of the male to kick him in the ass with her boot. He stumbles forward, the bindings around his arms and legs making him look like the fetish approximation of a dog, or a horse.

The slaves working in the backyard look over at the scene and rush back to their taskings, slotting wooden beams into joints and pulling rough lengths of rope to help lift ominous structures into the air; one slave runs a flag up a flagpole. It's a black flag with a pink female symbol embroidered upon it.

"You! Get over here!"

For a second, you think it's you they're yelling at and your heart begins to pound wildly. But you realize that they're talking to another male, one of the worker slaves who is carrying a set of heavy-looking short wooden stairs. It's the tall mistress doing the yelling and she snaps her fingers, ordering him over.

"On your knees!" she says, directing him to kneel in front of the bound slave on the leash. She turns to the other mistresses. "Do you think he's got enough lube or does he not some more spit?"

The dark-haired mistress gurgles a mouthful of spit and then slowly lets it drip down from her pursed lips, letting the wet glob fall onto the bound slave's forehead. It oozes down his face, getting in his eye and winding its way down to his mouth. The mistress snaps her fingers angrily, a signal that must be known to the bound man because he opens his lips to slurp up the wad of spit.

"Get him hard," the mistress says snidely, pointing to the kneeling slave, despite the fact that he's wearing a chastity device. "Do a good job and we'll let you keep your balls."

Illustrating her point, she reaches her long-nailed fingers between his legs and snatches his balls on them, squeezing hard. The bound male winces and dances in agony—as much as his bindings will allow, anyway. You wonder if the threat she made is real or simply just bluster... though you don't want to find out.

You start to creep towards the basement as the bound male jams his face towards the kneeling slave, lashing his tongue against the man's thighs and the skin between his leg and crotch, all the way up to the kneeling slave's tight chastity device. There is a bizarre look on the kneeling slave's face, one of disgust and pleasure wrapped in one. What is their game here? Is it just to make the kneeling slave uncomfortably hard in his chastity cage before he is sent back to toil in the backyard?

Just as you're about to reach the stone steps leading to the basement door, the tall mistress turns, spying you. She narrows her eyes.

"Hey. You."

This time it's definitely you that's being addressed.

Your mind begins to race with what options you might have to get out of this new predicament. The tall mistress gives the bound male a kick with her chunky sneakers as he continues to suck lewdly on the kneeling slave's chastity cage. She strides up to you.

"Explain yourself, male. Now."

You could try the tactic the tired, burly slave slyly suggested and pose as a "scout" here to talk to mistresses about new possible slaves...

...or you could pose as a new slave yourself: Mistress Merciless's slave. Given the status she seems to have at Matriarch Manor, perhaps you could say you're just here to check in on progress before going back up to her room to report on it. It's a risky gambit, but it *could* work.

Try to act like a scout for new slaves this time (Page 57)
Pretend that you're Mistress Merciless's new slave (Page 59)

23

You clear your throat. Here you go.

"Hello there," you say, as prim and proper as you can manage. "I'm a scout for new, uh, chattel. You know, slaves." The word tastes strange on your tongue. "I'm here to both assess the stock here and suggest a few new charges to any interested..." You think of what word would be best to describe the women here without giving yourself away. At the last second, a candidate jumps to mind. "...parties."

The tall mistress squints down at you, as if trying to read your mind. She puts her hands on her hips, her pencil skirt clinging to her willowy frame. Behind her, her accomplices continue to tease and torment the two slaves.

"How long have you been a slaver scout for?" she asks, arching one eyebrow. "I don't recognize you."

Feeling the pressure, you scramble to uphold your lie.

"I'm actually visiting for the week. Family, actually, but I also knew the manor wasn't far away so I decided to take a quick trip up and see if I can't, ah, make some connections." You hold out your hand and conjure up a fake name. "I'm Dan Wilson. Pleased to meet you...?"

Ugh, what a name. But at least you came up with something. The mistress does not take your hand.

"Miss Sandra," she says, still giving off an uneasy aura. "You don't need to know more than that."

You nod. Bit by bit you seem to be gaining at least a modicum of trust from Miss Sandra, although you can't help but notice the unfolding scene behind her. Now the dark-haired mistress has climbed on the back of the bound man and is swaying her weight from side to side, trying to get him to topple over, all while the fair-skinned mistress spanks the kneeling slave's buttocks, forcing him to shove his crotch in the bound male's face. They're having a wickedly good time of it and it's hard not to feel at least a little terrified by how callous and cold they can be.

"How's that one been?" you ask, pointing to the bound male. "Anything to note?"

The tall mistress turns back towards the slave and snorts. She shakes her head.

"Nope. Worthless pond scum, that's it. He thinks we're going for a walk but really—"

She pauses and gives you a strange look.

"Hmmm... if you're a slaver scout, what are you doing lurking out here?" she asks. "If I had to guess it seems like you're hiding. Why aren't you inside?"

You wrack your brain to come up with an answer...

Say that you were secretly observing the slaves, assessing their work (Page 61)
Deflect and compliment the mistress (Page 63)

24

You run your hand through your hair and take a breath.

"Hello Miss," you squeak out, feeling suddenly very dizzy. How in the world is this going to work? "I apologize for catching you by surprise, but I am a new slave under the, ah, care of Mistress Merciless. She asked me to come out here to check on the progress of the, uh, construction. I am to leave a report for her in her chambers so that she can review it at her earliest convenience."

The tall mistress plants her hands on her hips and looks at you curiously, like you've suddenly grown a second head. She has the look of a waify model, the sort that has spent more than a few glamorous weekends walking up and down the runway. She shakes her head slowly.

"You have *got* to be kidding me," she says under her breath, rolling her eyes.

You get ready to explain yourself further, your voice catching in your throat as you scramble to bolster your story any way you can.

But then the tall mistress speaks again, cutting you off before you have the chance to say anything to incriminate yourself.

"How many slaves does that woman need?" she asks, more to her than to you. "Well, I hope you took careful notes. Goddess knows that Merci has no patience for half-assed work."

You hold back a sigh of relief.

"Although..." she continues.

Your held breath becomes a panicked note of fear. You subtly clench your fists by your sides, trying to ward off your fear of what she might say next.

"Why the hell are you wearing clothes?" the tall mistress asks. "How fucking new are you? Get those off."

With the tall mistress watching, you strip down to just your chastity cage, the mistress's mouth slipping into a wide, mean grin as you do. Behind her you can see her fellow mistresses now have both the slaves on the floor; they're making the one who was kneeling do pushups in the dirt, while they're forcing the bound male to attempt to roll over from his back and onto his bound arms and legs. They laugh and shout as the men struggle to perform for them.

Once you're naked, the mistress stomps your clothes into the dirt, really making sure that she steps all over them until her white athletic sneakers are speckled with mud and bits of grass. Looks like you won't be wearing those clothes any time soon.

"Now look what you did," she says with a sneer. "You got my shoes all filthy. Clean them."

Knowing you have no choice but to commit to your lie that you're a new slave, you get down on your hands and knees on the backyard's lawn. The ground is soft but cold, and little stones in the dirt dig into your shins. You crane your head down and stick out your tongue, licking the white leather of the tall mistress's sneaker. Broken blades of grass and streaks of dirt are wiped away, tasting bitter and gritty in your mouth. The mistress observes you as you work, turning her sneaker one way and then the other so that you don't miss a single soiled spot.

When she's satisfied with one sneaker, she shows you the other, smirking as your tongue slowly goes dark with the licked up mud and filth. *It could be worse*, you think, grateful for when she finally lets you ease your licking. She bends down and pinches your ear, hard, pulling you back to your feet.

"Come on, slave, I'll show you to the third floor," she says, dragging you cruelly behind her. It feels like your ear is going to be ripped off with how hard she's tugging on it but you stay as silent as possible, knowing you have stumbled into the good fortune of getting up to the third floor with little more cost than a dirty tongue and a gritty throat.

Or so you hope.

As she marches you up a back set of stairs and through the long, elegant hallways of the second floor with their wooden moldings and carpet-covered floors, you fight back the urge to scream from her nails plunging deep into the soft flesh of your ear. Eventually she deposits you by a somber staircase leading up, but not before she wipes her sneakers clean on your bare thighs and stomach.

"Her room's up there," says the tall mistress. "Do what you've been told and then get back to the party. I don't want to see you outside again."

Even though the mistress sounds annoyed, there is a curious undertone to her voice, as if she wouldn't dare stop a slave of Mistress Merciless from completing his task.

Continue on to the third floor (Page 92)

25

"Oh, not lurking," you say with as much of a smile as you can muster. "Observing. But I can't just walk around with a clipboard, going up and down the line of slaves, can I? They won't act natural that way. I have to observe in as much of a non-invasive way as possible."

Miss Sandra frowns, her eyes narrowed at you. You don't know if she's disappointed in your tactics or if she simply thinks you're full of shit. She lets out a rolling sigh, the smell of coffee and cigarettes on her breath.

"And what did you observe?" she asks. It feels like there's a smirk hiding right under her placid frown.

You tilt your head to the side, pretending to be lost in thought, trying to decide what someone who would be a "slaver scout" would say. You tighten your lips into a flatline and exhale through your nose.

"Good work, but it could be better," you say. "Not a lot of observation out here either... at least not that I can tell."

Miss Sandra doesn't seem terribly interested in the observation of the slaves. She is quick to jump in with another question: "Any undervalued slaves you'd recommend a mistress pick up?"

You aren't quite sure what she's getting at, but you figure there must be some kind of auction or slave trade process that the mistresses of Matriarch Manor use. You look over the slaves, thinking which you might consider "undervalued"... but also not sure what will happen to any slave you single out.

Only one comes to mind. The burly slave who tried to help you. For a moment you consider mentioning him, only to realize that if you doom him to a terrible fate, he's just as likely to rat you out. Instead you point at the whiny slave from before.

"Him?!" Miss Sandra says in shock.

You nod. "Yes, he's... well, he's not a labor slave, but he seems to have a keen mind. After all, he's probably done the least amount of work of any of the slaves out here."

That much you believe to be true.

But Miss Sandra seems to think you're getting at something else and says,

"Ah. I see. Well, I can change that. Nice to meet you... Dan, was it?"

You nod, holding back your anxiety.

Miss Sandra walks away, towards the whiny slave. Her intentions do not seem kind. With her out of the way, you are free to walk into the basement without obstacle. Inside, you find a twisting maze of hallways, prison cells, and stations set up for humiliating acts of torture. The sounds of cracking whips and moaning slaves fills the air and you steel yourself for any more questions you might get about what you're up to.

As you slowly walk down the hallways of the basement, you see a small, dimly-lit cubby room. It seems to have a layout of some kind tacked on the wall. This seems to be the room that the burly slave mentioned and you could go check it out right now.

Or you could explore the rest of the basement.

Check out the room with the schematics on the wall (Page 69)
Explore the rest of the basement instead (Page 70)

26

"Well, Miss Sandra," you begin, stuttering slightly. "I didn't want to interrupt the festivities. Plus, I wanted to watch and learn from a true professional like yourself. Your dominance over these men... it's truly inspiring."

Miss Sandra chuckles at your flattery, her icy blue eyes twinkling with amusement. "Oh? Is that so?"

"Yes, I mean it," you continue, doing your best to keep your voice steady. "You're an excellent example of what a true mistress should be. Even I, in my own profession, can see how worth you are of respect and adoration."

The tall mistress tilts her head and smiles wickedly. "Oh? Prove it."

"Prove it?" you ask anxiously.

"Yes, you know," says Miss Sandra, a sharp edge in her voice. "Show me you mean it."

Your heart beats wildly in your chest as you think of a way to "prove" what you've said. Finally, an idea strikes. You kneel before her and bow your head low in submission.

"May I..." you swallow hard, "...may I lick your boots? Just to show you how even someone in my position can respect and honor your, uh, strength."

Laughter rings out from behind Miss Sandra as the other mistresses stop what they're doing and turn their attention towards you. The bound male slave continues to suck on the kneeling slave's chastity cage but both are now trying to see what's going on.

"Hmm," Miss Sandra muses aloud, stepping back so that her chunky sneaker is right under your bowed face. "I suppose that would be acceptable."

With a gulp, you extend your tongue and tentatively lick the dusty leather of her boot. The taste is unpleasant but you force yourself to continue licking up towards the laces, the leather scraping your tongue. You hear low chatter and hushed whispers, trying your damnedest to show such "admiration" in a way that still carries at least a sliver of the dignity you imagine a slaver scout should have—if such a thing is even possible.

Miss Sandra allows you to continue. She adjusts her sneaker this way and that way, letting you lick nearly every last inch of the top of it while she stands above you with her arms folded across her chest, her willowy stance swaying back and forth. You can't quite see her from where you are on your hands and knees, but you feel like she is grinning or maybe even chuckling to herself, an altogether uncomfortable feeling as you wait for her to tell you that you've done enough licking.

But she doesn't. She lets you keep going, seemingly content to let you endlessly lick her chunky white shoe. Your mouth is soon filled with leather tastes and sock smells and the earthy aroma of not just the backyard lawn but also something mustier that reminds you of old, forgotten concrete. You need to think of some way out of this, and fast.

But while your mind struggles to find a path to disengaging without insulting the mistress, the mistresses behind Miss Sandra go from whispering to gut-busting laughter as the sight of a supposed slaver scout licking their friend's sneakers becomes too much for them. As if they and Miss Sandra are in on some grand inside joke, she too begins to laugh and pulls her foot back to point an accusatory finger at you.

"What a crock of shit!" she roars. "You have no idea what you're doing, do you, Mr. Slaver Scout? Oh my, this is just too, too much, total utter ridiculousness…"

Panic sets in as you scramble back on your hands and knees only for strong hands to grab hold of you from behind. You've messed up, big time.

"This man is an imposter!" announces Miss Sandra

"Looks like we've got ourselves a new toy!" one of the mistresses from behind calls out gleefully.

As more mistresses are alerted and gather around you with sinister smiles on their faces and begin to drag you towards the manor's basement level, you fear you may be enslaved for a long, long time to come.

THE END

27

Before the young mistresses notice you, you duck into an empty cell that is lined with hay, pressing yourself against the stone wall. You hear their continued laughter and the dull thudding sounds as they beat and torment the poor male at the end of the leash.

"Walk, pig! Come on, show us how a real animal walks!" one of the mistresses calls out.

There is the swift sound of rushing air and then you hear the male let out a deep "Oomph!" before what you're sure is him tumbling to the floor. The women clap and shriek in joy.

"Look at him go! What a moron! Get up, moron! GET UP!" one of the mistresses yells.

Your heart races in your chest. They are moving slower than you guessed they would have, taking their time as they continue down the hall. You push yourself further back against the stone wall of the cell, able to smell old sweat, leather, and even... semen. A morbid part of you wonders what would've possibly gone on in this cell. How long are males kept in here?

Then it dawns on you... males must not just be disciplined in these cells, but live here too, kept like livestock in the basement of Matriarch Manor, taken out to be used and abused by the domineering women who live and visit the grand house.

The mistresses continue on and you can see from your risky hiding space that the male they're dragging forward is bruised, with spit dripping off the sides of his body and onto the gritty basement floor. You wonder where they could be off to. A cell to deposit him for a night? A room designed for even more sadistic torment?

After what feels like an eternity, the mistresses have finally passed down the hallway. You no longer hear their cruel laughter or the pained cries from their slave.

Once you've caught your breath, you exit the empty cell. Looking down the hallways, you notice there is a dim cubby room of some kind with a large diagram on the wall. You're pretty sure that it has a diagram of the manor itself, perhaps offering a way to figure out where Mistress Merciless's room is... and where the keys to your chastity device might be.

You also consider what else might be in the basement to use to help you get your freedom, though you shudder to think what might happen if you run into more mistresses on the prowl.

Check out the room with the diagram of the manor (Page 69)
Explore the rest of the basement instead (Page 70)

28

As the young mistresses get closer, they finally see you. They stop dead in the tracks, yanking the leash of the bound male so hard he nearly falls over; the taller mistress gives him a kick in the haunch for no reason other than to indulge her malice. The fair-skinned mistress glares at you.

"What are you doing here?" she demands to know. She adjusts her tailored blazer and tight, black slacks.

You fumble with your words, trying to think of a lie...

The mistress with the dark hair strides forward. She has a pixie-ish face and taut curves that jiggle ever so slightly under her maxi dress. You catch a waft of pleasant jasmine perfume.

"She asked you a question," the dark-haired mistress says, jabbing a finger in your face.

"I, um... I'm a guest," you say, unable to think of anything more convincing than that. Your mind races. Do they even allow male guests at Matriarch Manor?

The fair-skinned mistress snorts. "A guest. What are you doing down here then?"

The tall mistress seems bored by this questioning, more content to kick at the male slave on all fours, treating him like her personal sandbag. She starts to get into a rhythm with it, her chunky white athletic sneakers striking the male over and over in the thighs and stomach and between his legs, making him flinch and moan in pain. The dark-haired mistress looks back and gives the male slave a nasty stare.

"Shut up, pig!" she screeches.

You force your mind to continue its lie. "I got lost is all," you manage, trying not to let your nerves show. "I was enjoying the festivities upstairs and then went to find the bathroom and..."

The fair-skinned mistress looks to her friends and the three of them burst into shrill peals of laughter.

"You got lost and wound up here...?" she asks you with a predatory smile. "Who invited you, by the way?"

Your mind is blank. There's only one mistress you know at Matriarch

Manor.

"Mistress... Merciless," you say.

The tall mistress now has the male slave on his back and is grinding her sneaker into his face, a wide-eyed, vicious look on her heart-shaped face as she rubs the grime and filth off it onto the man's cheek.

"Well then!" says the dark-haired mistress, reaching over to an empty prison-like cell. She pulls the barred door open. "Why don't you just go in there and wait and we can have her come help you find your way."

Before you even have the chance to slip away, the fair-skinned mistress and her tall companion are closing in on you, nudging you backwards into the empty cell. The dark-haired mistress slams it shut!

"Enjoy your 'party'," says the dark-haired mistress. She blows you a mocking kiss as the women head off to alert Mistress Merciless, dragging their pathetic slave behind them.

As you sit back on the hay-lined cell, you listen to the sounds of screaming, crying men intermingled with the medley of slapping, spanking, caning and worse. That fate will soon be yours, you fear, once Mistress Merciless finds you locked in one of Matriarch Manor's basement cells. To think, you could've simply lived a horrible year in chastity and then been free, but now you are sure to suffer a far, far worse fate...

THE END

29

You step into the dim cubby. A diagram on the wall dominates this small space, with maps of the manor's floors. It's all too much to try to memorize—a Salon, a Pantry, a Kitchen, a Playroom, an Observation room and more; rooms labeled as the Red Room, the White Room, the Black Room; rooms belonging to all manner of mistresses, from Mistress Frost to Mistress Consuela to Mistress Ravage. But in this overwhelming sea of names and rooms and winding passageways, one name jumps out at you. Mistress Merciless.

She is located all the way on the third floor, far from here. You take a breath wondering how you will ever make it all the way up to her room. Looking around the small room, you now notice a few more ominous items that you missed before: a small, beaded whip, a long metal sounding rod, a pinwheel with sharp metal spikes. Taking your attention off these devious implements, you look back at the diagram, determined to find some way up to Mistress Merciless's room.

That's when you notice some sort of service elevator, not far from where you are now. You also notice there are a set of stairs also close to your location, but if you're reading the schematics correctly, it means you will have to pass through the ground floor Salon on your way to the upper floors. Then again, the elevator may stop there anyway.

As you mull over your choices, wondering which is least fraught with peril, you see a post-it note on the wall in feminine handwriting: "REMINDER! Stop dressing slaves! All manor slaves MUST be naked except for chastity and possibly a collar or cuffs! I'm sick of seeing males walk around in clothing they don't deserve! -MW"

You realize that to fit in you're going to have to get rid of your clothing. You reluctantly strip down to just your gleaming steel chastity cage, the chill of the basement making your teeth chatter... or maybe that's just your nerves. You stash your clothing in a nearby empty cell, burying it under as much hay as you can manage. It's a good thing you came to Matriarch Manor without your keys or wallet, perhaps knowing deep down you might not want to be bogged down by your personal belongings.

Try your luck with the elevator (Page 71)
Take the stairs and navigate through the Salon (Page 73)

30

As long as you keep your head down and your eyes to yourself, you're able to wander through the basement without drawing much attention. But of course, there's a grim reason for this: the prison cells and harsh-looking discipline stations built into the basement's stone walls are occupied with cowering slaves and wide-eyed mistresses engaged in all manner of sadistic play, far too busy wielding whips and canes and shockers and other awful implements to take much notice one more lowly "slave" scampering through the hallways.

In one station you see a slave in heavy wooden stocks, being taken from behind by two dildo-wearing mistresses taking turns, high-fiving each other as they see who can ride him the fastest. In another, you see a slave who is up on his tippy toes, his arms fastened to chains hanging from the ceiling as he tries to keep himself balanced, lest he risk getting his ass caned. In yet another, there are two slaves facing away from each other, their balls tied together while a pair of mistresses whips each one, forcing them into a savage game of tug-of-war. And then, perhaps most chilling so far, is a cell that looks like a crumbling, tiled bathroom with a toilet in the center. You see a mistress squatting atop this toilet and see a male below, his head locked into the porcelain throne.

You shudder to think what fate he's suffering.

Deep into the basement, you come to an intersection. One way leads to something that looks to be a dingy office of sorts with harsh bright lighting. The other way leads to a steep stone staircase that leads up.

Take the stone stairs leading up (Page 146)
Check out the basement office (Page 147)

31

Without your clothing, you feel truly exposed as you slink into the elevator. It looks antique, with wood-and-brass doors, incandescent lighting, and other classical mid-century flourishes that make you feel like you've gone back in time. There are four hefty knob-like buttons to the side of the doors: B, M, 2F, 3F.

You press the button for the third floor. Nothing happens.

You press the chunky button again, just in case, but alas the elevator doors do not close. As your eyes search the antique elevator, you come across a small, almost imperceptible slot underneath the column of knob-like floor buttons. Damn. It looks perfectly sized for some kind of ID or key card. Shelving your disappointment, you press the button for the second floor and get ready to be disappointed again.

To your relief, the elevator doors slide shut and the elevator car rumbles its way up. You hold your breath as it trundles to the M level... only for it to stop there. You can hear loud sounds of feminine conversation and thumping music through the elevator's wood-and-brass doors and realize you are about to be face to face with Matriarch Manor's party!

Quickly, you conjure up a story that you are an elevator attendant. Those used to be a thing, right? You think so, but what did they actually *do*? Press buttons? Open and close doors?

The doors open, all on their own. Standing there is a single mistress. She is lithe, with a mischievous look on her lily white face, her long, fiery red hair tumbling down her back. She is wearing a black leather catsuit that hugs her trim figure and that's adorned with decorative silver spikes and tons of straps and buckles that remind you of a cross between a motorcycle rider and a punky goth. Her stiletto boots clack as she struts onto the elevator.

Before she can bark a command at you, you scramble all fours, flattening your back to create a makeshift bench for her to rest on. For a moment she remains standing and then she presses her floor and plops down on your back with her full weight—which while isn't terribly much, is set down so callously upon you that you nearly crumble to the elevator floor.

The elevator doors slowly close and it continues its way up.

The redheaded mistress runs her fingers through your hair, pulling at it like she was plucking leaves off a tree.

"I love these parties but they can get tiring," she says, though you know she can't be talking to you so much as she's at you, thinking through her own thoughts loud.

The elevator seems especially sluggish as it makes its way to the next floor. How in the world are you going to exit so you can keep looking for the third floor and Mistress Merciless's room?

The redheaded mistress snatches your hair tighter. With her other hand, she grabs at your bare ass, enjoying how she can squeeze the flesh in her claw-like grip; it's enough to make you wince in pain.

"I've been saying for years that they need to spread the party out more," she continues with a dramatic sigh. "Have a few rooms, one with all the dancing and drinking, one a bit more low key, maybe another that... bah, I don't know. I'm not a party planner. That's why the Manor has a Board."

The elevator comes to a snail-like stop and the doors open. You don't have a great vantage point from your bench pose, but you can see an elegant hallway with a patterned runner across hardwood floors. The walls have wooden embellishments and there are light sconces, pieces of hanging artwork, and even a few sculptures set up to give a feeling somewhere between a mansion and a museum. The redheaded mistress stands, the leather of catsuit squeaking.

"Come on, slave, I need to blow off some steam," she says.

Apologize and make an excuse that you're acting as an elevator attendant right now (Page 76)
Go with the mistress (Page 78)

32

Fortune favors the bold. That's what they say, isn't it?

You decide to navigate the basement hallways looking like a slave on a mission, keeping your head down and your posture weak as you pass by cells stuffed with slaves, mistresses taking out their aggressions on helpless males, and a few scenes that you don't know what to make of but which fill you with a deep dread and morbid curiosity.

Thankfully you've followed the layout correctly and reach a utilitarian wooden staircase that ascends up into the M-level of the manor. Sounds from the party are very loud now, and you feel yourself on a thin line between the moaning, groaning tortures of the basement and the rampant jubilance of the party upstairs. With your heart in your throat, you walk up the wooden steps, ready to seek out the second floor staircase at once.

The party in the manor's Salon is nothing like you've ever seen.

Unlike the winding basement, this level of Matriarch Manor is mostly open space, but the exquisite, intricate decorations make it feel like there are many rooms in one, the large space partitioned off by shimmering sheets of satin, hanging lamp chains, erected wooden structures that remind you of the architecture of far off lands, and tinted glass screens that veil the activity beyond from the knot of women and slaves at the Salon's center. The women—mistresses—you can see appear to be having a grand time as they guzzle champagne and snack on appetizers, using the nearby naked males as everything from living benches to garbage cans, not even thinking twice as they spit unwanted food into their mouths and order them to their hands and knees. It's a chilling sight to see how natural dominance seems to come to these women and it has you thinking you need to be done with this terrifying place as soon as humanly possible.

You scan the room for Mistress Merciless, not wanting to run into the one person who would recognize you here. Fortunately you don't see her, but with all the mistresses packed into the large, loud, open space, it's just as likely she's somewhere and you simply missed it.

You also look for a stairway leading to the second floor. You thought you'd understood where it should be based on the layout plans in the basement, but now that you're up in the chaotic sprawl of the party, everything seems different, shuffled around somehow. You keep your head down and try to orient yourself, wandering through the crowd as your blood runs cold.

"So what did you do then?" you overhear one mistress ask another.

"What do you think I did?" responds the other mistress. "I got a bigger dildo and I said: I'll give you something to cry about."

Shrill cackles erupt from the mistresses and you continue to look for the stairs. You overhear another conversation:

"Is it true do you think? Is the male brain really wired for submission?"

"Oh, absolutely. All the alpha, beta crap in the wildlife only happens for males, not for females. They *literally* have wiring that says someone is supposed to be their master. Why do you think it's so easy to tame them?"

You keep searching, getting nervous that you'll never be able to find a way out of the party before Mistress Merciless runs into you. Yet another conversation blooms to the side of you:

"So, like... did he eat it?" a woman asks as if she doesn't want to know the answer.

"He sure did. It was either that or stay with his mouth stuffed like that for the whole day."

"Ohmigod. I can't, I just can't with all this."

Finally! You spot the stairs just fifteen feet away, right past a curtain of silk streamers that hang down from the ceiling. You rush towards it...

...only to be stopped by a mistress in a white leather corset, with fishnets, matching white leather boots, and something that looks like a military cap on her head. Her skin is the color of rich mocha and her curled, highlighted hair hangs down to her squared-off shoulders; unflinching deep hazel eyes stare you down.

The way she's standing in front of the stairs, you think for a second that she's there to guard them, but you're dissuaded from this notion when she speaks.

"Well, well, well... what do we have here? A lost little slave boy? I was just looking for a lost little slave boy." Her grin is mean and wolfish.

In a moment of terror, you try to pretend you didn't hear the mistress and attempt to walk by her. She snatches you by the shoulder and shoves you back, making you stumble on your heels and nearly fall over. She jabs a sharp nail into your chest.

"I'm talking to you, slave," she says, her voice thick with resentment.

"I-I'm sorry mistress," you say.

She shoves you again and again you almost fall.

"You sure are," the mocha-skinned woman says. Your senses are overwhelmed by a mix of shea butter and flowery perfume, the smell descending on you like a cloud. "Stand up straight when I talk to you!'

You snap to attention, not even realizing you were slouching to begin with.

"Hands at your side! Chin tucked in!" she barks, commanding you like an irate, impatient drill instructor.

As you try to follow her orders, they just keep on coming—"Eyes down! Hips squared! Feet straight! Stomach tucked in!"—and the mistress chortles spitefully at the sight of you scrambling to keep up. When she's finally got you exactly as she wants you, like some little doll she's posing, she leans in clothes and whispers in your ear.

"I don't care where you're going or whose slave you are, you don't just walk away from me when I'm talking to you," she says, seething.

"Yes, Miss," you squeak out.

"That's Miss Onyx to you!"

"Yes, Miss Onyx!"

"That's better, you pathetic worm. Now, let's see what other lessons you can learn..."

Let Miss Onyx have her way with you (Page 96)

Regretfully tell Miss Onyx you are required on the second floor (Page 95)

33

You bow your head and quietly say, "I'm sorry Miss, but I'm to stay in the elevator as the attendant."

She wrinkles her nose and for a second you think she's about to launch into a tirade. But then she says: "What a waste. We really need a slave to press some buttons and be a bunch for a sixty-second elevator ride?" She groans and rolls her eyes, but at the very least it seems like your deflection has worked!

"Great, now I'm going to have to find another tongue slave," she says, looking up and down the second floor hallway, like she might find just such a slave kneeling there. Then she exits the elevator, ignoring you completely.

You watch her trim, leather-encased form strut down the hallway, hips swaying and ass swinging like a pert little pendulum. A little part of you thinks maybe being a tongue slave for her wouldn't have been so bad...

...but alas, if you're ever going to get out of your chastity—and out of Matriarch Manor—you're going to have to focus on finding Mistress Merciless's room and, hopefully, the keys to your freedom.

The doors of the elevator begin to close again, the mistress's arrival ruining your shot at finding a way up to the third floor. It begins to go down and you feel a lump in your throat as you wonder who's summoned it.

It stops at the Salon M-level and you brace yourself, trying not to imagine the imposing form of Mistress Merciless on the other side. Two young mistresses enter, both in beige jodhpurs that seem to be painted on their legs with matching white blouses, along with tall riding boots. They both have the vibrant glow of youthful innocence to them, and both have flushed cheeks from what you guess are more than a few glasses of wine. One has short-cropped blonde hair that she's pushed back behind her ears, while the other has a long ponytail of fine, silky hair.

"Floor, Misses?" you say stiffly as you try to act your part as elevator attendant.

The mistresses giggle.

"Basement," the blonde says. Then she tentatively adds: "Slave."

You press the button for the second floor and the elevator doors close.

The mistresses look at each other excitedly and then back to you as the elevator trundles its way into the manor's basement floor.

In a flash, the ponytailed mistress closes the gap between you and her. She puts her hand on your chest and from her breath you can smell she must be quite drunk.

"You look fun," she purrs, her mistress friend sidling up next to you. "This is our first manor party and we are dying to have some more *fun*."

The blonde slips a hand between your legs, petting your chastity cage. "We sure are. And if you play with us, we might even make it worth your while..."

You try to puzzle out why these women simply don't command you "play" with them, still unable to wrap your head around whatever protocol seems to be in place for Matriarch Manor that allows some women to demand whatever they want while others almost seem to be seeking permission. Although perhaps it's not you they're seeking permission from, but whoever they think you've submitted yourself to...

The ponytailed mistress's hand moves to your nipple. She flicks it playfully, making it harden as the elevator comes to a thudding stop. The doors open, revealing the labyrinth of the basement's cells and stations.

"Well?" the blonde asks. "How about it? Can you join us... slave?"

She steps off the elevator with a sultry stride, keeping her clear eyes locked on yours. The ponytailed mistress slips two fingers into the ring at the base of your chastity cage, urging you forward and tilting her head to the side. She gives you a puppy dog pout.

"Why won't you join us, slave?" she asks petulantly.

These drunk, young mistresses seem incredibly eager to have a slave to play with. And while you don't know what their definition of "play" is, this is probably the kindest you've been treated since you arrived at the manor. How exactly would they make it worth your while?

With a joyous rush, you imagine them—somehow—being able to take you out of your cage! Your cock surges as you imagine the freedom you'd feel and then even go as far as to consider the remote possibility these young vixens would let you fuck them. A pipedream, perhaps, but one that makes you try to get rock hard nonetheless.

Go with the young mistresses (Page 84)
Politely decline and stay on the elevator (Page 86)

34

You scamper after the mistress, continuing on your hands and knees. She doesn't stop you nor tell you to stand. Thankfully, the carpeted runner takes most of the impact off your hands and knees, though you do have a sinking feeling that maybe it was a mistake to follow an unknown woman to an unknown location. In front of you is the sight of her thudding stiletto boots and her leather-clad legs... not to mention the hypnotic swing of her pert bottom in the leather catsuit, her ass swaying back and forth, back and forth, back and forth.

You feel yourself getting hard in your chastity cage, the unkind steel denying even a hint of an erection. Imagine having to put up with this for a year! You'd go insane, you're sure. A hint of smoke and honey floats up your nostrils, the mistress's perfume, you figure.

Eventually, she stops in front of a door that's painted crimson red. She knocks, waits, and then opens the door. Inside is a room that is decorated in crimson red to match the door, with an Asiatic flair. Silkscreen prints hang on the walls, depicting scenes of women luxuriating in lush meadows and serene forests while naked males toil endlessly, some of them contorted down onto their bellies with their faces pressed between the spread legs of the women. Furniture with red leather padding is spread across the room, though most of it seems arcane to you, at least from your all-fours positioning, anyway.

But one piece of furniture is not arcane: a hefty-looking queening throne set into the center of the room. This item has a padded seat for, presumably, a mistress to comfortably rest her haunches, while an opening down below has been created for someone, surely a slave, to lie down and put his head, giving him ample access to the woman's crotch and backside.

Your suspicions are soon confirmed as the redheaded mistress closes the door behind you and starts unzipping her leather catsuit at the crotch. She straddles the queening throne, her lily white bottom presented like some kind of exotic pale fruit and her tender red pussy laid bare so that you can see the thick, strawberry blonde hair of her bush. The way she's sitting is so casual and so nonchalant that it's as if she's done this a hundred times before, not even needing to command a male slave on what to do. There is something truly demanding about it all, like she sees you nothing more than a thing to use...

...nevertheless, the sight and the heady smell of the redheaded mistress makes your caged cock stir. You could see yourself getting under there and servicing her with your lips and your tongue, or you could attempt to extricate yourself from this situation while you still have the chance.

Slip into the queening throne and service the mistress (Page 81)
Apologize and make up an excuse that you're required elsewhere (Page 80)

35

"Uh, Miss...?"

"Miss *Chambers*," the redheaded mistress says, practically seething. "Haven't you learned your mistresses yet?"

This is already not going well.

"Yes, venerable Miss Chambers, I would delight in servicing you to the best of my abilities, but I must... I am needed elsewhere, I'm now just remembering." Your lie feels thin and like it might fall apart at any minute.

Miss Chambers looks over her shoulder at you, her bare bottom hanging in the padded cradle of the queening throne. She scoffs.

"You're 'needed elsewhere'?" she asks, equal parts annoyed with you and frustrated to have something get in the way of her needs. "What are you, daft? Why didn't you say something earlier?"

"I, well... it slipped my mind, Miss, and it was only once—"

She cuts you off, uninterested in the trifling details. "You brainless dolt," she says. "Where are you 'needed' anyway? Who is more important than me right now?"

You need to come up with something to tell her, but you haven't seen enough of the party or the manor to have many options.

Make up an excuse about the basement (Page 104)
Make up an excuse about the backyard (Page 106)

36

Having all these beautiful, domineering women shoved in your face all day as you've explored and spied upon Matriarch Manor has you more pent up than you've felt all week in your new chastity device. Even though you suspect it's against your better judgment to crawl down and get your head into that queening throne, the sultry sight of the redheaded mistress is too much for you and you give into your animal instincts, getting down on your back and slotting your head into the throne's under-cavern. As you push your head into it, you realize how it's designed with hidden springs to take the weight of your head while keeping you right under the mistress's exposed pussy and ass. You feel your cage tuck at your balls as your cock tries to grow, pulling the entire steel device with it in a cruel bit of torment to turn your denial into domination by the inanimate thing.

"Show Miss Chambers how much you respect her," she says, settling further down onto the throne so that her bottom nearly makes a seal with your face. With how she's sitting, your mouth is flush with her pussy lips, but if she were to shift a little bit, you'd be tongue-deep in her asshole.

You lift your tongue up tentatively, touching it to Miss Chamber's lips. They are puffy and warm and already wet. The taste of her is sweet and fragrant, reminding you of heavily ripe summer fruit tinged with musky perfume and an undercurrent of feminine sweat. To you, it's one of the many aromas of sex, and for you it only inflames your denied lust even more, your cage's ball ring continuing to pull on your testicles so hard you feel like they might pop off at any moment.

The mistress gives a sigh as you dip your tongue into her tenderly. She leans down further on you and your lips touch hers; there's a moment when you think she's about to suffocate you, but she lifts up just before your nose dips into her as well, letting you lick her in a crisscross pattern up and down her pussy. As you reach her clit, you hesitate to attend to it, old habits of teasing women with your mouth coming back to you. What you do instead is nuzzle your face deep against her, pushing you tongue as deep as it will go into her, looking for that elusive G-spot you know too well. Your nose butts against her clit as you search for it and Miss

Chambers sighs again, the sigh lustier and more lewd this time.

She swivels her hips to pull your tongue out of her, rocking back so that her clit is directed down to your mouth. You know what she wants and in your sex-haze you want nothing more than to give it to her.

You gently wrap your lips around her clit and give her teasing little licks on either side of it, searching for the spots and the rhythms that make Miss Chambers begin to squirm. Surprisingly, they aren't hard to find—either you're a lot better at oral than you remember, or Miss Chambers is the kind of woman who luxuriates in pleasure, able to find it in all manner of moments. Once you've figured out the way she enjoys her worship, you don't dare deviate from that pattern. It's like practicing the piano, you think, but a whole hell of a lot more rich and heady and lewd.

"Ohhh, yes, yes yes yes," she hisses, keeping her body perfectly still for you to keep sucking and licking on her. Your jaw starts ache and your tongue feels like it's about to come off at the base, but—as with that piano practice—only practice makes perfect and you want to give this exuberant, sultry woman all the perfection in the world right now.

You can feel her body tighten above you and can even hear the queening throne squeak ever so slightly as she squeezes its outer sides with her legs. With metronome precision, you *lick lick lick lick*, terrified that the constant, repetitive motion is going to psych you out and cause you to falter.

Just as you think you can keep it up no longer, the mistress gives a loud moaning squeal of joy and gushes wetly on your face, her juices running down your cheeks and your chin, tickling you behind the ears. That ripe summer fruit and feminine musk taste floods your senses and you instinctively reach down to your crotch before you remember the damned chastity cage. You want to stomp your feet and bang your fists in frustration, but Miss Chambers isn't done with you yet.

As she calms down from her orgasm, she swivels her forward, pulling her pussy away and presenting you with her twitching, puckered asshole.

"Clean," she says imperiously. "No tonguing. You haven't earned that privilege, slave."

Although you're relieved to not have to jam your tongue up this woman's ass—or are you?—you can't help but wonder what part of your service kept you from earning that "privilege". You run your tongue up and down the redhead's ass crack, the taste markedly different from her pussy. It's not foul, thankfully, but it is intensely musky in a completely different way, reminding you more of heavy oils and dank weed and something else that's just on the tip of your tongue.

So to speak.

You do your best to clean every last little wrinkle and crevice of her ass crack, not even pausing your lavishing attention until your mouth is dry and Miss Chamber's buttocks is wet with your spit. It's around then that she stands up off the queening throne with all the pomp of getting off the toilet. She stretches catlike, pushing her hands up towards the ceiling, and yawns.

"That was nice," she says, twisting one way and then the other, a few small bones in her lower back popping with a satisfying sound.

Then without warning, she bends down and throws a lever attached to the outside of the queening throne. You feel a little jolt on either side on your neck and as you try to pull your head out from the throne's under-cavern, you realize your head has been locked inside!

"But I'm not done with you yet, slave," she says, grinning down at your wet face and tired tongue.

Her green eyes give you a testing look, as if daring you to fight against your fate. Seeing that you are staying calm, she tests you further.

"Maybe I'll even use you as my toilet," she suggests with a quirk of her full lips. She tosses her long, fiery hair back over her shoulder, eagerly looking for a reaction. "Technically I'm not *supposed* to in this room, but I won't tell if you don't."

As she continues to stare down at you, you find yourself at yet another crossroads. You could accept your fate—and all that might come with it—or you could try to beg for your freedom, pleading with the mistress that your job well done deserves freedom.

The choice is yours.

Beg Miss Chambers for your freedom (Page 98)
Accept your fate (Page 100)

37

You clench your teeth and unclench your fists as you make the decision to follow them. Their youthful exuberance is infectious, it's true, but it's their promise to make it "worth your while" that truly captures your interest. You step off the elevator with a sense of trepidation, but also excitement. Perhaps these young mistresses could be the key to your freedom.

"Good boy," the ponytailed mistress purrs, her fingers brushing your bare skin. She leads you down a dimly lit corridor, her friend following closely behind. You can't help but watch as their hips sway in time to an unheard rhythm, their matching outfits accentuating every curve and dip of their bodies.

Their attention is intoxicating; they hang on your every, servile word as though it were gospel, their eyes sparkling with genuine interest. They flirt openly with you, dropping innuendos and double entendres into casual conversation until even you find yourself blushing. Their laughter echoes off the cold stone walls of the dungeon-like basement; a stark contrast to the grim surroundings.

After what feels like hours of wandering aimlessly through the labyrinthine basement, one of the girls stops suddenly in front of an open cell door. She peers inside curiously before calling out excitedly to her friend.

"Look what I found!" she exclaims, holding up a bundle of clothing for all to see. It's only then that you realize that those are your clothes—the ones you stashed away earlier in hopes of fitting in.

The girls exchange a glance before turning back towards you, twin smiles spreading across their faces like wildfire. "Now this," the blonde says triumphantly, "is interesting, isn't it, slave?"

Your heart sinks as you watch them examine your clothes with great interest, poking and prodding at them as though they were some sort of exotic artifact. The reality of what this discovery means slowly begins to dawn on you: they've found evidence of a male trespasser in Matriarch Manor.

"Oh my god, this is such a score!" the ponytailed mistress squeals in delight.

"Yes," agrees her friend, "We should alert the other mistresses. They can lock down the manor, or something, and find out who these belong to." She turns towards you then, her expression hardening slightly as she adds: "You better hope they don't belong to you, *slave*. I mean, like, what are the odds but why don't you just get in there..."

They push you gently into the cell and close the door behind them with an ominous clang. The lock clicks into place with a finality that makes your stomach churn.

"And we'll find out for sure later. We'll be back soon, ta ta," the blonde says as they walk away hand-in-hand. Their laughter grows fainter and fainter until all that's left is silence and darkness.

You collapse onto the floor, reeling from this sudden turn of events. You'd imagined countless outcomes for this evening, but being trapped in a cell by two young mistresses while they go try to find the owner of the very clothes *you* stashed is not one of them. As reality sets in once more, you can't help but feel a sense of dread creeping up on you. You have failed.

If only you'd been able to better control your impulses or hidden your clothes better, maybe you'd be a few steps closer to your chastised freedom now, instead of waiting for the inevitable moment when those two young vixens cash you in for their social standing at the manor and you face the icy wrath of Mistress Merciless herself.

THE END

38

Despite the temptation, you resist your baser instincts and give the young mistresses a sad look.

"I'm sorry Misses, I must stay here to attend to the elevator," you say.

They return your frown with even poutier looks, the ponytailed mistress letting go of your chastity so she can join her blonde friend. Part of you aches to go with them and to feel their supple hands on your body again and it takes everything you have not to rush out of the elevator and into the basement.

"That's too bad," says the ponytailed mistress. "We would've had so, so much fun."

The blonde gives you a little wave. "Bye bye, slave boy," she says before she blows you a kiss.

Watching the elevator doors close is one of the most painful things you've had to do so far. You sigh and press the second floor button, the elevator resuming its slow trundling upwards. As it passes by the M level, you brace yourself for yet *another* guest getting on but, to your relief, it continues on up.

At the second floor the doors open and once again you are relieved to see there is no demeaning, demanding mistress waiting for you there. Thank god!

You step out of the elevator and begin to explore the second floor.

Slinking through the hallways, you take in decorative art pieces—vases, erotic sculptures, and vintage devices set on pedestals under glass cloches— as well as paintings that hang from the walls, depicting scenes both placid and perverted. The floor under your feet threatens to creak with each step, but the carpeted runner helps to muffle sound... as does the thumping of your heartbeat in your ears, making your head feel full and dizzy.

There many doors in these intersecting hallways, though as you start trying knobs to see if any might be open, you find the majority of them are locked tight. Maybe those ones are bedrooms, maybe not; after all, it seems like Matriarch Manor houses endless spaces devoted to female supremacy and you try not to imagine what might be behind some of these ominous, unmarked doors.

A few do stand out however. Around the bend, there is a door that is completely black, so black in fact that at first you think the door is actually open, leading into a dark space beyond. But as you near the black door, you see that it's actually a trick of the light—or maybe the paint that's been used—that make it appear to actually suck up the light from the incandescent wall sconces that line the second floor's hallways. There is no etching on this door's frame, though it does have a silver knob, unlike the other doors, as well as a thick, gleaming lock plate. From the looks of it, it seems to be unlocked.

Down from the black door is its opposite, an all-white door that almost blinds you when you see it. It seems to be painted with a glossy hue and when you lean in close you can see there is a fine pattern etched onto the gloss of the white door's paint. The rounded etched shapes look like horns or teeth and for some reason you can't explain, they leave you with a familiar, uneasy feeling. Looking close, you see it hasn't been closed all the way.

You wonder if you might find something of use in these rooms. More information on the manor? A master key for your chastity device? That sure would be nice. Or perhaps just a hiding spot for a bit to collect your thoughts as you wander near-naked through the second floor's hallways, the sounds of the party below still hanging in the air and reminding you that at any time you could run into wandering mistresses, with little excuse for why you're up here alone.

Go through the white door (Page 27)
Go through the black door (Page 25)
Look for the third floor (Page 88)

39

Forgoing the safety—or the danger—of any of the rooms on the second floor, you continue looking for the stairs. The hallways of the second floor have a strange way of doubling back on themselves even though you know the manor can't be all that large, and on more than one occasion you find yourself wondering if you've already been done a particular hallway or if they simply look so similar that you can't tell the difference.

As you set about methodically looking for the third floor stairs, you take in some of the decorations set out in the hallways. There's a black metal chastity device in a domed glass display case, much like the one Mistress Merciless forced you into for the year, but upon closer inspection you see that the inside of it is lined with terrifyingly sharp spikes designed to punish even the slightest of erections.

In another display case, you see a thick, curved dildo with a tube running out from its base and a squeeze pump that reminds you of a turkey baster. It's not until you get a closer look and read the display case plaque that you realize what this dildo does: "Semen Pumper: A realistic dildo with a reservoir for actual or synthetic semen. When desired, the pump can be activated to squirt the semen liquid into the body of the slave into which the dildo is inserted. This creation, credited to Mistress Wail, has proved an effectively way to emasculate and feminize unruly male slaves."

You turn your attention to the framed works of art on the walls. Many of them are oil paintings and while at first you think they depict classical pieces of art, you notice that in each seemingly traditional piece is a man hidden away in a position of submission, such as the 18th Century-looking government hall with only female officials who have men huddled underneath the tables, desperately trying to pleasure their female superiors or the medieval-style castle that has numerous tall, narrow prison cells built into its outer walls, where naked men stand with forlorn looks on their face, left to the harsh sun and night chill.

Part of you is starting to feel like you never should've come to Matriarch Manor.

Who built this place? Who are these dominant women? You've always been aware of the power the mistresses of Matriarch Manor have over the town—and how they've used this place as a kind of headquarters—but you've never had to deal with them, not really. When you'd hear rumors that men disappeared in the depths of the manor or the mistresses using some twisted legal ruling to put men under their boots, you shrugged it off. It wasn't *you* who was suffering, so why bother?

But now, being deep in the manor yourself, you are left with endless questions about these women and the true power they yield. You even think that perhaps you got off *lucky* with just a year sentence in chastity for what you said and did to Mistress Merciless on that drunken night. From what you've seen so far, it could've been a lot, lot worse.

It's while you're lost in your thoughts that you stumble upon the stairs leading to the third floor! You almost can't believe it. Part of you wants to run down the hall and up the stairs, shocked that you haven't already been discovered on the second floor already. But another part of you tells you to take your time and not to screw things up now, even though you can still hear the wafting sounds of the party, fully aware how mistresses could be making their way the stairs to this floor at this very moment.

Quickly dash to the stairs (Page 90)
Take your time (Page 92)

40

You can't wait any longer. You've been seeking a way to the third floor and now you have your chance!

You dash down the hallway, realizing too late that the carpeted runners on the hardwood floors don't really absorb that much sound... nor do they stop the floor from creaking loudly as you rush across it. You try to slow your gait but it's too little, too late. A nearby door—the jet black one with the sliver knob and large lock plate—flies open. A mistress steps out, grabbing you before you can wriggle away, and yanks you inside. She slams the door shut.

You're so stunned that you think you're going to faint. You're in a dungeon-like space decked out in hulking, intimidating black furniture. There's a half-covered low cage to one side, an X-shaped cross with pulleys where the arms and legs would go, a harness of some sort hanging from the ceiling, and, against the far wall, a padded whipping bench with a bound slave set face down upon it. His back is red with welts and his ass is even redder, no doubt the work of the many-tailed purple flogger that is lying on the floor behind the bench. From what you can tell, the man has been crying.

A heavy smell hangs in the still, stagnant air of the dungeon space. It smells like a mix of leather and rubber, or diesel maybe, and it's so thick you can taste it on your tongue.

Then you turn your attention to the mistress.

She would be stunning if she wasn't glaring hatefully at you right now. With her sable, wavy hair, ruby red lips, and strong bone structure, there is something positively classical about this woman, as if she's stepped out of the elegant era of 1940s and 50s Hollywood films cast in brilliant, gripping technicolor. She has a figure to match this old world beauty that's complete with curvy hips, full teardrop breasts, and a pleasant backside that is made only more alluring by the sleeveless red latex jumpsuit she's wearing. Her eyes are hardened shards of black glass with long, inky lashes and perfectly manicured brows, and you can't believe that in that moment the only thing you can think is that you want those gorgeous eyes to give you a softer look than the angry stare you're being subjected to.

Somehow, you aren't surprised when she speaks with a posh English accent.

"And what the bloody hell are you doing running down the hallway?" she asks.

You try to think of an excuse but your mind is completely blank. It's a terrible time to be tongue-tied.

She snaps her fingers angrily in your face.

"Hello? Hellllloooooo? Is anyone in there? My goodness, the slaves just get dumber and dumber here don't they?" she asks in the direction of the male bound over the whipping bench. He whimpers something in the affirmative that makes the posh mistress laugh. "Don't worry, you pathetic bitch. No one will ever be as dumb as you."

Following her gaze, you see there's more than just the pink-red blows of the flogger on the male's back and ass. At some point, the mistress has also written something in pink Sharpie marker across one tortured cheek: Property of Miss Wail.

That name seems familiar, but you aren't sure why.

"Well?" Miss Wail asks, turning back to you. "Are you going to speak or am I going to have to flog the words out of your unruly husk of a body?"

Try to escape from Miss Wail (Page 93)
Spill your guts to Miss Wail (Page 36)

41

You head up the stairs leading to the third floor. A thin, royal blue carpet with an intricate design covers the steps, thankfully muffling your footsteps. The sounds of the party feel much farther away now and by the time you reach the landing of the third floor, they are but a distant din. Unlike the second floor, the third floor seems to be made of just one wraparound hallway that—as far as you can tell—goes along the outer walls of Matriarch Manor, with doors leading to rooms on the outside, no doubt giving those that the rooms belong pleasant views of the outside.

The air up here is still and slightly stuffy, and you can smell a mix of perfume, incense, and flowers as you creep through the wraparound hallway. It's unnerving that there's just a single hallway up here, giving you few options should you hear anyone coming up the stairs or out from their room; the one solace is that between every set of solemn wooden doors is an archway that looks to lead to a small, shared space of some sort, each sitting under slanted glass panels, like those of an atrium.

You survey the rooms on the floor. All but one has a name carved into its wood, and that lone door out instead has ornate designs carved into it from top to bottom, the images depicting a swirling sprawl of astrological symbols. Two doors down from it is the room you've only imagined so far: the one belonging to Mistress Merciless herself, the mistress's name written in a stiff, imposing font. Between the ornate door and Mistress Merciless's room is the only shared atrium space that isn't completely cast in shadow. Peering through the archway, you see that it's set up to be some kind of lounge space, with a low sofa and a hexagonal tea table and erotic sculptures displayed in the center of the cubby.

Investigate Mistress Merciless's room (Page 202)
Check out the lounge space (Page 203)
Go through the ornate door (Page 204)

42

You make a run for the door, cutting across the dungeon space in just a few quick strides. You grasp the door's silver knob in your hand, turn, and realize the door has been locked from the inside. You look for the latch to unlock it, but you can't make heads or tails of the door's large, smooth locking plate. Your breathing goes shallow and your heart starts to race.

Miss Wail grabs you roughly by the upper arm and spins you back to her.

"And where do you think *you're* going?" she asks. She has the purple flogger in her hand down and cracks in the air right next to you. It's deafeningly loud. "I don't know who you think you are or what you think you're doing, but I will *not* be interrupted by some... slave."

The way she says that word, "slave", is disdainful and haughty. She cracks the flogger again.

"I'm so-so-sorry!" you whimper.

"Not yet you aren't, no," she says. "Hands over your head, worm."

You raise your shaking hands like it's a stick-up. With the flogger still in one hand, the mistress squeezes at your sides and your belly and your chest with the other hand, making curdled looks of disappointment. She turns you around to keep pinching at your lower back and buttocks with all the routine judgment of picking out which piece of meat to cook for the night.

"Hmph. Look at you, so weak," she says as she snatches your chin in her hand, pulling her face to yours. Even though her gaze is stern and cold, that elegant face makes your heart flutter. "Do you think you're weak, slave?"

There's no denying—you certainly *feel* weak. You do your best to nod your head in her tight grasp. Miss Wail smiles and then looks around the room, thinking.

"Yes, I have just the spot for a weakling like you," she says in that posh accent of hers. Then she marches you over to where the harness hangs from the ceiling, letting go of you for a moment before she flicks a control switch on the wall.

The harness descends until it's just touching the ground. It's made from sturdy leather straps with a solid platform base, the straps crisscrossing one another to form a diagonal pattern that reminds you of Chinese finger traps. Miss Wail snaps open several of the straps and instructs you to step inside. Once you do, she snaps the straps back into place and then she flicks the control switch once more.

You hear a motorized winch start to whirr and very slowly the top part of the standing harness cage is pulled back up to the ceiling, the straps slowly tightening around you. Then the platform you're standing on begins to lift as well and your weight acts to tighten the straps further, the crisscrossed leather pressing hard against your bare flesh. You can feel every little part of you squeeze through the straps: the flab on your torso, your buttocks, the bulge of your thighs, your shoulders.

"There we go," says Miss Wail, as she turns the harness so that you're facing the rest of the room—and so she's facing you. "A hanging slave sausage in his nice leather casing."

Without warning, she brings the flogger down on you, the rawhide tails smacking against your exposed skin. You flinch and whimper, much to Miss Wail's delight.

"I can't wait to see the pretty patterns that I'm going to make after I've made all that flesh look rosy and pink," she says, bringing the flogger down again, painting a different part of your exposed body with thudding, striking pain. The force of the blow is enough to make the hanging harness slowly start to turn, giving Miss Wail new targets to flog.

You feel blows on the backs of your legs and back and the sides of your hips, only now and again turning back around to see the glamorous form of Miss Wail in her red catsuit, poised and ready to strike again. Each crack of the flogger makes you feel further and further away from freedom as you come to realize you've squandered your chance to escape your chastity... and very likely squandered your chance to escape Matriarch Manor.

The night will be long and will be at the mercy of Miss Wail and anyone else she desires. As you twirl in your strappy harness cage like a bound piece of meat, you wonder if you could've done things differently.

But it's too late for that. At least you have the sight of the voluptuous, imperious Miss Wail to help soothe you as you feel your skin sizzle with the blows of the flogger.

The mistress raises the flogger high above her head and grins at you, her teeth gleaming white.

"Brace yourself, worm. This one is going to hurt."

THE END

43

Still trying to hold the impossible posture dictated by the mocha-skinned Miss Onyx, you say: "Miss Onyx, I am required upstairs and I fear that I am gone too long I will be in serious trouble."

"You think I give a *shit* about your trouble?" she says, striding around you. Her white leather boots clack on the Salon's floors, their sharp toes knocking away stray balloons and little piles of glittery confetti.

You watch her with your downcast eyes, only able to see her from the waist down. Her body is toned, with an hourglass figure, her full, plump ass held tight by her meshy fishnets. You can see the strong muscles of her legs as well, along with the colorful pink nails she dons as she keeps her hands resting on her cinched hips. As she walks, that cloud of shea butter and flowery perfume grows and grows, starting to cling to you too.

"No, I understand Miss but—"

"Shut up, I haven't asked you a question, slave," she says. As she passes behind you, you feel a hot swat on your ass and you jump much to Miss Onyx's delight. She swats you again and you jump even more, your body beginning to tremble with fearful anticipation.

"I like my meat afraid," she says. The next time she touches you, it's not to slap you but to rub your lower back and ass, her nails drawing along your bare skin to make you shudder. "Where are you supposed to skitter away to, little scaredy-meat?"

"The second floor, Miss Onyx," you say.

"'The second floor, Miss Onyx'," she repeats back, using a high-pitched tone to mock you. "I *guess* it's bad sport to get in the way of other mistresses' needs... however, you won't get in trouble if I don't say you're in trouble. I can't believe I'm going to say this, but I'll leave it to you, scaredy-meat. Go do whatever miserable, droll task you've been assigned upstairs or go upstairs... with me."

Go up to the second floor by yourself (Page 14)
Change your mind and offer to go up with Miss Onyx (Page 119)

44

Miss Onyx grins, her hazel eyes gleaming with wicked delight. She orders you to the floor, and you comply instantly, falling onto hands and knees. Her leather-clad foot comes down on your back, pressing you flat against the ground.

"All right then, slave," she purrs in a voice like smoldering velvet. "We're going to start with something simple: boot worship."

She presents her shiny white leather boot for your inspection. The smell of polished leather fills your nostrils as she nudges it towards your face. Heart pounding, you take a deep breath and lower your head to begin your humiliating task, only hoping that it will soon be over so you can continue to seek your freedom from chastity. Miss Onyx's laughter peals out over the din of the party as you lick her boot clean like a slavish dog. You feel heat rising in your face at the shame of it all, but also an odd sense of satisfaction—at least you're doing something right today.

As the minutes pass, the tasks Miss Onyx sets for you become more complex and degrading. She makes you bark like a dog while crawling around on all fours; fetch drinks for her by carrying the wine glass base in in your mouth; eat food from a dish on the floor without using your hands that tastes as if it's been spit out, maybe more than once.

All around you, women are laughing and pointing. Some come closer to watch or participate, their voices echoing in your ears over the thunderous pounding of your heart. Your excitement is palpable; this utter subservience feels strangely liberating in the most perverse of ways, yet at the same time you know you need to find some way to bring this to a close soon. The Salon is simply too exposed for this to continue.

The longer this goes on, however, the more people start to notice, until Mistress Merciless herself strides over. As she steps into view from behind a satin curtain, her eyes narrow slightly as they land on you and your heart sinks. Why did you let Miss Onyx take control in such a risky place?

Although at first you don't see Mistress Merciless since you're too busy contorting yourself into yet another degrading position for Miss Onyx's amusement. But when Mistress Merciless's cool voice cuts through the mirthful chatter like a whip crack, everything suddenly goes silent.

"What's this?" she asks in a tone that sends shivers down your spine.

Miss Onyx looks up from where she's been lounging on a plush divan and shrugs nonchalantly. "Just having some fun with this lost little slave boy," she says dismissively.

Mistress Merciless takes a step closer and suddenly she's standing over you; her powerful presence casting an impressive shadow across your submissive form. "I recognize this one..." she murmurs thoughtfully. "Last weekend, yes? Too many whiskeys? I bet you're regretting that now."

For one heart-stopping moment, there's silence as everyone waits for Mistress Merciless to make a decision about what will happen next. Then her lips curl into a cruel smile that chills your blood.

"I think we'll keep him," she announces casually—as if deciding to adopt a stray dog rather than claim a human being as property—and laughter ripples through the room once more at her words

Your heart sinks deeper as realization dawns. There will be no escape from Matriarch Manor now. You're trapped here forever under these women's ruthless control, property of Mistress Merciless herself... forever bound to serve within these shadowy walls and forever subject to their sadistic whims and alluring torments...

It's terrifying...

It's degrading...

And yet...

A part of you feels okay that there will be no more stress and struggle over what to do and how to act. All you need now is to do what you're told and to do it well. But before you can fall deep into some inner debate about whether freedom or confinement is the better fate, Miss Onyx is commanding you down on your back so that you can take turns tasting her and Mistress Merciless's boots, ordering you to say which boot sole you prefer.

It's going to be a long night and a long life at Matriarch Manor.

THE END

45

"No, please! Don't!" you beg.

Miss Chambers's eyes sparkle in the warm light of the room with its crimson walls, those red walls seeming positively bloody now.

"Don't?" she repeats back. Her look hardens and her shoulders square. You can tell this is *not* what she wanted to hear. "That's not a word in your vocabulary, slave," she spits out. "Neither is 'no'. Neither is anything else if I fucking don't want it to be. I thought we were having fun but here you are, getting mouthy on me. You know if I want to I could—"

She stops herself and you aren't sure if you want her to finish that thought. Which is just as well, since a different thought seems to capture her attention then as she marches over to a rattan basket in the corner, tossing the top off it to fish out a pair of handcuffs. You can't see her as she returns to you because walks behind the queening throne, but you sure do feel it when she secures the handcuffs first on one wrist and then yanks your hand up so she can secure the handcuffs to your other wrist. Only when you try to move them do you realize she's also tethered you to the throne itself, keeping your hands low and far away from ever finding the lever she used to lock your head in place.

Your heart begins to pound awfully hard. This isn't good.

What's even worse is when she sits on the queening throne again, this time with her body turned the other way so that catsuit-clad legs straddle yours. You see her unzip the crotch of her catsuit, pussy hanging ominously above your head.

"You're going to drink every last drop of what I'm about to give you," she says with grim determination. "Or else I will beat your balls until they are purple. Do you understand me?"

You say nothing and Miss Chambers slams her fist against the queening throne.

"Do you UNDERSTAND me, slave?" she asks in a terrifying shout.

You nod pitifully.

"Speak! I want to hear you!"

"I understand you," you say, your voice wavering. You can't believe this is about to happen.

She slams her fist once more against the queening throne, softer this time.

"And you're going to do what?" she asks like a chiding schoolteacher.

"I'm going to... uh, drink every drop," you say.

"You sure as fuck are," she says.

As you wait for Miss Chambers to empty her bladder onto your face, you try to think how you could've played this better. A kinder word? A more ingratiating offer? You have no idea. But when the first drop of hot, salty piss hits your cheek, you sure wish you'd navigated a better path through Matriarch Manor.

THE END

46

Not trusting that this is a mistress you can win over with only a silver tongue, you nod as much as the queening throne will allow, hoping beyond hope that this will somehow earn her favor. If her goading was truly just a test, then she should back off... right?

Nope. Miss Chambers dances in excitement as you nod, a sadistically blissful look on her face.

"That's wonderful!" she cries out with a happy squeal. If not for the circumstances, you sure wouldn't mind seeing such a pleased smile on the woman's gorgeous lily white face. But alas. She double checks the lever on the side of the queening throne and then says, "You stay *right* there— hah!—because I'm going to get some friends. I know of a few other ladies who have been dying to give this a try..."

With a teenage excitement that betrays her mid-20-something appearance, she fixes her black leather catsuit and then rushes off out of the room, letting the door slam behind her.

You are left to consider what's going to happen when she returns.

Of course, you could try to escape. You'd just have to find the lever, free yourself, and then make sur you don't accidentally run into Miss Chambers as you slip through the second floor hallways. It's not *impossible*, but if you're caught it's sure to be a terrible predicament for you.

Then again, being her and several other mistresses' toilet doesn't exactly sound wonderful either.

Try to get away from Miss Chambers (Page 101)
Remain where you are (Page 102)

47

You're no fool—you know a good opportunity when you see one. Wasting no time, you search frantically the outside of the queening throne for the lever Miss Chamber's flipped, eventually finding something thin and metallic. You push and then pull it, and you hear another clicking sound as the pressing bolts that secured your head inside the queening throne retract back into the seat's base. Slowly, you pull your head out, relieved and more than a little bit dizzy when you stand up.

As you're collecting yourself, you see that someone's dropped something that looks like a business card under one of the room's squat red leather stools. The thick layer of dust suggests it's been there for a long time. You lean over and on the card you see simple lettering that reads: "Mistress Merciless of Matriarch Manor." Scribbled in the corner is some feminine writing.

"3F gives no F's!"

You have no idea if that's Mistress Merciless's writing or not, but it does confirm that she's on the third floor of the manor. Leaving the card where it is, you stand up and creep towards the room's door, listening to make sure no one is on the other side. When you're sure the coast is clear, you slip out into the hallway.

It's empty. You carefully step down the hallways, peeking around corners before you make any turns, hoping that you will stumble upon the third floor stairs before Miss Chambers comes back.

Just when you think you're never going to find them, you see a staircase at the end of the hall, leading up into a private, quiet landing. Your violin-string-tight nerves tell you to run, but you wonder if it's better to take things slow and take your time getting to the stairs. They aren't all that close, that's for sure.

Rush towards the stairs and the third floor (Page 90)
Take your time (Page 92)

48

You don't fight your fate, but are you sure you're ready to accept it?

Eventually Miss Chambers returns, alone, her eyes sparkle in the warm light of the room with its crimson walls, those red walls seeming positively bloody now.

"They'll be here soon," she says in a chilling voice. "But for now, I think I might just have to get started without them. But first…"

She pads over to a rattan basket in the corner, tossing the top off it to fish out a pair of handcuffs. You can't see her as she returns to you because walks behind the queening throne, but you sure do feel it when she secures the handcuffs first on one wrist and then yanks your hand up so she can secure the handcuffs to your other wrist. Only when you try to move them do you realize she's also tethered you to the throne itself, keeping your hands low and far away from ever finding the lever she used to lock your head in place.

Your heart begins to pound awfully hard. This isn't good.

What's even worse is when she sits on the queening throne again, this time with her body turned the other way so that catsuit-clad legs straddle yours. You see her unzip the crotch of her catsuit, pussy hanging ominously above your head.

"You're going to drink every last drop of what I'm about to give you," she says in a bizarrely happy, saccharine tone. "Or else I will beat your balls until they are purple. Do you understand me?"

You say nothing and Miss Chambers slams her fist against the queening throne.

"Do you understand?" she asks again, still in that sweet-as-pie voice that sends a chill through your body.

You nod pitifully.

"Ahem. I can't hear you," she says.

"I understand you," you say, your voice wavering. You can't believe this is about to happen.

She knocks menacingly on the queening throne again, each knock more severe and harsh than the last.

"And you're going to do what?" she asks like a chiding schoolteacher.

"I'm going to... uh, drink every drop," you say.

"You sure are," she says.

As you wait for Miss Chambers to empty her bladder onto your face, you try to think how you could've played this better. A kinder word? A more ingratiating offer? You have no idea. But when the first drop of hot, salty piss hits your cheek, you sure wish you'd navigated a better path through Matriarch Manor.

THE END

49

"It's... the basement," you say, trying to hide your panicked improvisation. "I was supposed to be there..."

You look around frantically for a clock, but find none.

"...I think by now, Miss Chambers. I'm sorry, I do not know the exact time."

"Nor do you need to," she says, still frustrated. "You slaves only need to know two times: now and later. I doubt your little brains could handle much more."

She sighs through her nostrils.

"The basement... another thing I'm sick of," she says, rolling her eyes. "They get their way with everything." Her green eyes dart over to you. "Though I really suppose it's rotten for you, slave. A lovely meal of pussy or being one of those wretched things in a cage. Oh well."

You stand there for a few seconds too long, trying to process what she's saying. Perhaps there is more to the basement than even you suspected.

"Well?" she snaps. "Why are you still here? Go get to your precious 'basement duties' or whatever it is and stop wasting any more of my time... unless you *really* want to know how awful those cells can be!"

Her voice goes to a roaring pitch and you give a slight bow as you slip out of the room and back into the second floor hallway. As you wander, your curiosity tugs at you. What's the true purpose of the basement, anyway?

You know you shouldn't dwell on it but you can't help but think there's a chance that all the chastising—and chastity releasing—goes on down there, out of sight of the finer, nicer rooms of the rest of Matriarch Manor. Probably not, but you could twist the logic around for why it would make sense.

As you're lost in your thoughts, you find yourself looking down the hall at a somber set of stairs that lead up to what must be the third floor. Yes! You can feel yourself getting closer and closer to Mistress Merciless's chambers.

Do you rush over to those stairs before anyone exits one of the second floor's many locked rooms or comes around a bend and finds you standing there? Do you creep over to them carefully and take your time?

Unable to decide, you turn, only to find yet *another* option: an almost invisible fake section of wall that's actually a narrow door. A small plaque next to it reads "Basement Access".

Give into your curiosity and explore the basement (Page 70)
Rush up the stairs (Page 90)
Take your time going up to the third floor (Page 92)

50

"The backyard," you say, clearing your throat. "I need to help with the work being done to get everything ready for, uh, later."

Miss Chambers gives you a knowing smirk.

"Nice try," she says, her voice full of smug disdain. "So close to lying your way out of this room and yet you had to mention the one thing I know far too much about. I helped handpick the slaves working in the backyard today and I know, for a fact, that they have been working there nonstop since this morning... and I know you aren't one of them."

You freeze. Fuck.

Miss Chambers continues: "That tells me a few things. First of all, you do *not* need to be in the backyard right now, but more pertinently... you are a LIAR. And a lying slave in Matriarch Manor is an untrained slave. Who are you? Which mistress do you belong to?"

You have no answer for her question, fumbling over a couple of half-baked attempts that fail to impress Miss Chambers. She laughs, her annoyance turning into spite.

"Oh, you are so, SO fucked, slave," she says as she runs her tongue along her teeth several times, a gesture that seems to signify some kind of unbridled excitement. She gets off the throne and zips her catsuit back up. "You could've just enjoyed being beneath me and that would've been that, but now... oh, you are going to pay. I promise you."

As the mistress closes in on you, you instinctively back away, bumping into the silkscreen artwork hanging from the wall. You reach helplessly for the doorknob, but it's way too far away to even offer a chance of escaping.

"Any final pleas you'd like to offer?" asks the mistress with a snide laugh.

"I'm sorry!" you say, knowing it's too little, too late.

"Oh not yet you're not. But I promise you, you will be."

THE END

51

What the hell, the throne it is.

You jam yourself under the tall throne's seat, barely squeezing into the tight space. In your contorted position, you can barely do more than look down at the floor—which you now see is patterned a sandy gold to mimic sand—as you hear the door swing open. A woman in low, clacky heels enters with a huffy, annoyed sigh.

"Where *is* he?" she says in a thick Latin accent.

The mistress stomps around the room in a full circle, revealing that she is a slighter size, and is wearing a white-and-pink houndstooth skirt, a white blazer, and a thin pink blouse underneath. You can't see her face but you can see her long, straight black hair that goes almost all the way down to her waist. Your heart thumps in your chest and you hope beyond hope that she doesn't see you.

She seems just about to leave when she pauses. Slowly, she turns around and then—to your horror—she bends down, her long black hair streaming down as you see her sharp, commanding face with its aquiline nose, bow lips, and fiery eyes.

"You don't look like who *I'm* looking for," she says in her thick accent. "But I'm sure someone is looking for you if you're hiding like that. Looks like I am about to cash in."

As she smirks to herself, you realize that you have accidentally trapped yourself under this throne with no easy way to get away—if such a thing would even be possible. The mistress reaches for a hidden button on the wall and presses it firmly, a soft chime ringing throughout the beachy, bright space.

"Stay right there," she says. "We'll figure out what to do with you soon enough."

Whatever she has in mind, you know it won't be good.

THE END

52

Figuring there's nowhere to hide in the open room anyway, you might as well face the music—and try to see yourself through. Just as the door opens, you gather yourself up into a tall standing position with as upright a posture as you can manage, doing your best imitation of a slave ready to serve.

You hear a huffy, annoyed sigh and the sound of clacky heels as a Latina mistress enters. She's of slighter size, and is wearing a white-and-pink houndstooth skirt, a white blazer, and a thin pink blouse underneath. Her hair is long and black and straight, falling all the way down to her waist, and the face that waterfall of hair frames is tanned and bossy. She has an aquiline nose, rosy cheeks, and bright pink lips that pop against her crisp white blazer.

"Oh, that was fast," she says in a thick Latin accent as she looks at you.

She steps forward to inspect you. Her hands trace your skin, nails drawing along your chest and then to your sides and your back as she walks around you in a slow circle. You feel the dig of her nails in your ass as she grabs both cheeks sharply, forcing you to jump at her grasp. She laughs. It's a deep, throaty laugh—a smoker's laugh, you think—and as your eyes dart around the room to the display cases full of dildos and strap-ons, you realize your ass is exactly what this mistress might be interested in.

She completes her circle and looks up at you with a tipsy smile. "You'll do," she says with a nod, going back to lock the door. Beach sounds continue to emanate from the speakers in the corners of the ceiling as the mistress strips off her blazer and kicks off her short heels, herself becoming even shorter now.

"How many times have you taken it up the ass, slave?" she asks nonchalantly. "You know, estimated. Ten, twenty, fifty, that kind of thing."

Why oh why did you have to come into *this* room?

You chew your lower lip and say in a near-whisper: "Never, Miss..."

Her eyes widen and the gleam of her teeth shows in a sharkish grin. "Never? Oh my god! A virgin! It's my lucky day," she says. Then she adds: "And no Miss. It's Domina. Domina Huitaca. Go on, try it, slave."

"Domina Weet-a-ka," you try, fumbling over the pronunciation.

The domina gives a mocking laugh. "That's such an uptight way to say it. Relax. *Huwee-ta-ka*, almost like there is an 'f' at the front. Try it again."

Feeling the embarrassment of a student struggling to learn another language, you go through several more rounds of trying to pronounce the domina's name to her liking while she disrobes. She oh-so-casually takes off her skirt and then her thin blouse, leaving her in just a stunningly white matching bra and panty set that seems preternaturally bright against the domina's tanned, golden skin. Her curves are taut and lithe and you can see the flex of muscles in her arms and stomach and legs. An athlete maybe? Or just someone who enjoys staying fit and trim so she can relax proudly on the beach.

Finally, you get her name right, much to the domina's pleasure. She claps her hands together in a way that is both praising and insulting.

"Good, good!" she croons in her thick Latin accent. "Now try to say something. Say: 'Domina Huitaca, may we pick out a dildo together so you can take my virginity?' She struggles a bit with that last word—virginity—overpronouncing the syllables; in a way that only makes it feel more ominous to you, as if any other kind of virginity than being fucked in the ass doesn't even matter to the domina.

This is the moment of truth. If you continue with the domina's command, there will be no turning back—she'll soon have you bent over and on the other end of a fake cock for who knows how long. And if you *were* going to try to somehow weasel out of this situation with some convincing and a lot of luck, this is the moment to try.

Repeat after Domina Huitaca and let her have her way (Page 110)
Try to weasel out of this situation (Page 115)

53

"Domina Huitaca," you say, knowing there's no turning back now. "May we pick out a dildo together so you can take my virginity?"

The domina's eyes light up with delight. "Yes we can!' she exclaims.

She puts her arm in yours, like she's leading you out to the dance floor, and takes you on a tour of the phallic items in the room's display cases. There are big black cocks with realistic balls, pretty pink ones that are ribbed and abstract, ones that wobble when the Latina knocks on the case, ones that seem to have little motors built into the base to allow for vibration, ones with nubs, ones with ridges, ones with big, reddened heads that you swear have some kind of tubing inside. Some are already attached to harnesses while others seem too girthy to fit into any harness, making you wonder what in the world they could be used for. It's an entire line up of fake cocks, and although you're hoping to find—just one!—that is tiny and unintimidating, they're all at least modestly sized, which is a hell of a lot more than you've ever been subjected to.

After the first tour, Domina Huitaca takes you on another go around.

"It's time to decide," she says gleefully. "Or else I'm going to decide for you."

The thought of that sends a shiver down your spine.

Glumly, you choose the dildo you think will be the most merciful: it's purple and shiny and seems to be the smoothest of them all, if perhaps a touch thicker than some of the others that have far more ribbing and veins on them.

Domina Huitaca opens up the display case and takes it out, along with a harness. She holds onto the dildo and hands you the harness.

"Put that on me," she orders you.

You have to get down on your knees to reach, but once you're there you position the leather harness over the domina's crotch, making sure it's level to her guidance before you wrap the straps around the back, fastening and buckling them across her ass, which you can feel is taut and firm enough to bounce a quarter—or even a whole fist—off of. Being so close to her, you can smell the domina's natural scent mixed with a bright, citrusy perfume, creating a kind of sun-kissed lusty feeling in the air.

She hands you the dildo.

"And that," she says.

It takes you a minute to figure out how to slot the dildo through the harness's center ring, but once you do, you find yourself face to face with the bobbing, smooth purple cock that will soon be going in your ass.

Domina Huitaca jiggles the cock by its base as if testing it, looking down approvingly at how the dildo and the harness fit snugly on her trim frame. She snaps her fingers and points at the bench. She doesn't order a verbal command, expecting you to do as ordered without a single word from her.

You stand and resign yourself to the bench. Once you've sussed out how to rest your legs against its padded kneelers, you find yourself in a semi-folded over position, with your hands and head resting on a padded cushion and your legs spread wide with your ass jutting out. The domina ties down your ankles and wrists with nylon straps, following up those bindings by securing your thighs and your upper back to the bench, keeping you from being able to do much more than wriggle about helplessly.

"Since this is your first time, I'm going to be very generous with the lube," she explains, squirting a copious amount of the cold, viscous liquid down on your ass. "Say 'Thank you, Domina Huitaca'."

You blush as you're forced to thank the domina while she readies you for an assfucking. "Thank you, Domina Huitaca."

She pauses at your pronunciation and then sighs. "You'll get it eventually," she says with casual boredom. Then she takes up a position behind you. "Oh wait! I almost forgot!"

The domina pads over the door and flicks a switch on the wall. From the ceiling, two mirrored panels descend to cover the wall in front of you and the wall behind you, creating a mirrored chamber hallway; you imagine that if you were sitting on the throne facing the door, you'd be able to look to your left and right and see a scene that stretches out to infinity. What you can see instead is your own nervous face staring back at you, as well as the back of the Latina domina's body as she takes her position again behind you, standing up on a lower footrest of the bench so that she and her fake cock can reach your buttocks.

"No looking away," she says in her thick accent. "I want you to watch."

You stare horrified, transfixed, as the Latina domina spreads your cheeks wide. It's an utterly humiliating view to see such an intimate part of you so exposed, but that humiliation doesn't come close to comparing to the feeling of the purple cock pushing against your asshole. The domina teases you with its tip, spanking it against you in motions so routine for her that you wonder just how many asses she's taken in her life. She wiggles the dildo's tip against your hole, the lube allowing it to sneak inside again and again. Each time it does, you feel yourself getting just a little bit more open and watch in the mirrors as the Latina's pert, golden buttocks tighten while she pushes herself further inside.

It feels... odd. Not good, but not like all the awful stories you've read about either. The pleasure is perverse in its discomfort, a kind of needy, filling sensation that grows the longer the domina is inside you. You claw at the bench's padded rest and curl your feet, your body trying instinctively to dislodge this foreign phallus, but fighting it is useless—Domina Huitaca isn't going anywhere.

She begins to roll her rips against you, stretching your hole out further. The way she moves her hips imagine that she must be *sublime* in bed. It's just then that the dildo butts up against your insides in away you've never before, like the domina has just thrust against some magic little button that makes your balls feel especially full and a hot tendril of pleasure worm its way up your cock. You groan, unable to hold it in.

"That's right, slave," says Domina Huitaca. She exaggerates the roll of her hips, moving them in a slight circle to pull the dildo nearly all the way out before sinking it back into you. You groan again, closing your eyes. "You like me fucking your prostate? Look at me!"

You open your eyes to see the domina staring at you gleefully in the mirror. As she catches your stare, she pumps herself in all the way, her body pushing up against yours and somehow the pressure of the phallus on you squeezes out a hot drop of precum through your caged cock. You grunt through clenched teeth. The sensation is wonderful and tortuous and emasculating.

A wicked smile plays on Domina Huitaca's lush pink lips as she watches your reactions in the mirrors. "You're enjoying this?" She asks, her voice a husky murmur. Her eyes sparkle with mischief and unspoken promises of what's yet to come.

"Answer me," she commands, slowing her rhythmic thrusts to a halt. The lack of movement leaves with only the sensation of being intensely full.

"Yes, Domina Huitaca," you admit begrudgingly, the words heavy on your tongue.

"That's it," she praises, resuming her movements with a renewed vigor that has you gasping for breath. "Love my dick. Take my dick."

The mirrors reflect every detail of your assfucking: the way the lights dance on her caramel skin highlighting her lithe curves; the way her breasts bounce slightly each time she thrusts into you; the way her eyes never leave yours in the mirror.

The dildo inside you is relentless and unapologetically firm. It pushes past your limits, finding spots within you that make stars burst behind your eyelids as you fight to keep your eyes open and not give into the wild sensations of being fucked like some street alley slut. Domina Huitaca controls everything, from your position to the speed at which she takes you. It's degrading and exciting all at once, stripping away any semblance of control you thought you had and, quite oddly, letting you savor a moment of truly letting go.

Your caged cock throbs is also letting go, trying to grow in the tight metal prison and leaking out precum as Domina Huitaca pumps you over and over. Soon the cage is warm and slick with your secretions, and you find yourself wishing that there was some way to get it off you so that you could pump your own cock in time with the Latina's thrusting. You start to rock your own hips against the bench in a futile effort to rub your denied cock against the cage, grunting and whining as both of your bodies become sheened with sweat.

"You're doing so well," coos Domina Huitaca between grunts. Her fingers dig into your hips as she drives herself deeper into you. "Such a good boy for me. Such an ass slut."

Sweat trickles down from your forehead onto the bench beneath you as Domina Huitaca continues to mercilessly ride your ass, her breath growing ragged and heated. She's focused on your body now and not your eyes, her small, strong hands gripping your ass as she pounds away, continuing to milk you in your cage to the sound of your bodies slapping together.

"Good boy," she repeats again and again like a mantra until it's all that fills the room.

You soon realize there's more to the domina's fucking than you thought: either something in the harness or the dildo itself is somehow rubbing against her too, her exaggerated hip rolling allowing Domina Huitaca to pleasure herself as she stretches you wider than you've ever known. She looks at herself in the mirror and grins, enjoying the view of her mastering you. It's then that the thrusts become slower and more intentional and seconds later the domina is moaning and falling over you, her long hair draping down the sides of your sweaty torso as she braces herself for her trembling, full body orgasm.

It passes like a thundercloud and when it's over, she remains on your back, heaving breaths while she looks at you glassy eyed in the mirror. Despite the milking and curious sensation of being so full down there, you're still denied—if anything you feel even *more* denied now, like you were brought to the edge of true pleasure and left to stare at it through the grill of a cage. It makes you frustrated and moody just to think about.

Domina Huitaca pulls out slowly then steps back to admire her work, leaving you panting on the bench with shaky legs bound in place by nylon straps. Your reflection in the mirror looks dazed and wrecked, with cheeks flushed with exertion, lips parted in silent gasps, and sweat-soaked hair plastered on your forehead. With one last triumphant smirk reflected towards you in the mirror, Domina Huitaca unstraps the harness, tossing it and the dildo into a discrete bin in the corner of the room.

"You did so well for a virgin!" she cries out happily, returning with a hand towel that she uses to clean the lube and sweat from your body. The Domina does so in a way that is tender yet distant, like you're just some piece of furniture she's caring for, something she's used and now knows she's responsible for tidying up. The hand towel goes in the room's bin with the harness and dildo,

She gathers up a handful of your hair in her fingers and pulls your head up, speaking to you through the mirror panel hanging from the ceiling. She smirks.

"I'm keeping you for the night," she says in her thick Latin accent. "Your ass is mine. I don't care *whose* slave you are, you're not leaving this room."

But the way she says it, she doesn't sound so sure she can even do such a thing. Maybe it's the exhaustion speaking from the ordeal you just went through but you think there might be a chance to try to change her mind... although given the domina's fiery temperament, it seems just as likely that rejecting her demand will infuriate her, dooming you to an even worse fate.

Give in to the domina (Page 138)
Politely decline her command (Page 140)

54

You decide this has gone on long enough. It's time to get out of here before you're stuck in this room all night.

"Domina Huitaca," you say, still not getting her name quite right. "I'm terribly sorry but I think I may be in the wrong room."

The smile on the domina's face fades. "Wrong room? What is that, wrong room?" she asks, obviously annoyed.

"Ah, I mean, well..." Your mind spins in a tizzy as you try to make up a lie. "I was told to come to the second floor, but I think I misheard the room to go to, I'm very sorry. It was supposed to be..." Your mind goes blank for a second, just barely recovering in time. "...darker? Warmer? I believe I was told it would be a bedroom. You look around as if in confusion, feeling the shakiness of your lie grow out of your control."

The domina tilts her head to the side, her hair spilling over one shoulder.

"This is the bullshit," she says. "You are lying."

It feels like there's ice in your veins as the domina so effortlessly calls you out.

"No Domina Wee-taka, I—"

"*Huitaca*," she stresses, looking even more angry. "Who told you to come to this floor?"

Your hands fidget at your sides. "One of the mistresses downstairs," you say.

"Which one?" insists Domina Huitaca.

"I, uh, I don't remember..."

"Why don't you name *any* mistress who is downstairs right now?" she asks, putting even more pressure on you. "Or just the name of any mistress?" You don't answer. "Oh, having trouble thinking, are you?"

Domina Huitaca scoffs as you mumble over your words, pouncing on your every attempt to weasel out of this room with another sharp, pointed question, until you're reduced to nothing but an inarticulate, barely intelligible, shrinking violet of a man.

"I tell you what," she says, her Latin accent very thick now. "I give you a fighting chance."

You raise your eyebrows, waiting to hear whatever offer she's about to make you. The domina widens her stance and puts her hands on her hips, slightly moving her weight from one foot to the other. It's a decidedly athletic pose, like that of a tennis player or a wrestler and it's then that you realize she *literally* means she's going to give you a 'fighting" chance.

As this realization dawns on you, you let out a tiny laugh. You don't mean to, it's just that she's so small compared to and so slight that even with the muscle that is lurking beneath that golden skin, you can't imagine her overpowering you in any way. The domina narrows her eyes at you.

"What's so funny, slave?"

You don't push your luck. "What're the rules?" you ask to change the subject.

"Pin me to five, and you can go," she says, continuing to bounce her weight from foot to foot. "If I pin you, then, well… you'll see."

"Deal," you say. Adrenaline courses through you as you squat and ready yourself. You've never wrestled before, not really, but how hard can it be?

"We go on three," announces the domina. She's smiling merrily now and it feels a bit like she's easing into her element, her bouncing getting more and more limber. "One… two… three!'

You lunge clumsily at her, feeling like a sluggish bear as you swipe and miss the Latina's small frame. She darts around behind you and juts a foot between your legs, twisting to make you lose your balance. You stumble sideways, catching yourself at the last moment with a stuttering step.

But the domina is already pushing forward with her next move, clotheslining you with her sinewy arm. It's like being hit in the stomach with a metal rod and you bend forward, gasping for breath as she tries to flip you over onto the ground. Planting your feet and bending your knees, you manage to resist her pull, but the pain in your stomach throbs. You paw helplessly at her body, grabbing her sides and her ass and then—to your shock—one small, shapely breast. It's enough to make you pull your hand away in misplaced shame and the domina takes advantage of your modesty, throwing her full weight forward.

This time you can't hold your footing and you tumble onto your ass, Domina Huitaca shoving your shoulders down towards the ground. Her thumbs press into sensitive pressure points that jolt you into coherence.

She begins her count: "One, two…"

You kick our legs wildly and then with all your might shove her off of you, the two of you rolling towards one of the walls with its embedded display cases. You wind up on top of the domina, your caged cock pressing against her crotch, your hands holding firm onto her upper arms. Bewildered by the warm feel of her underneath you, you stare at her in stunned silence, the Latina's face growing sharp with taunting mischief.

"Say my name," whispers the domina.

"Domina Huitaca," you say, actually managing to get it right this time.

"You'll never be a winner with that attitude," the domina says.

Before you can puzzle out what she means, she's taking advantage of your lapse in focus, snaking her legs around you and whipping you onto your back again. Her hands snatch your wrists and she presses your arms to the ground, coiling herself around you like a snake. As you thrash and try to free yourself, Huitaca tightens herself around you even more, sinking her mouth towards your neck and sinking her teeth into your skin. It's not enough to draw blood, but it shocks you nonetheless.

She starts to count again: "One, two, three, four..."

You push up with all your might once more, but the domina is too tightly coiled around you! Just as you're getting an inch or two off the ground, she slams you back down, her fingernails digging into your forearms and her teeth once more biting your neck. You feel her hot tongue lash against your skin.

"Just let this happen," she hisses, squeezing your legs in hers. "One. Two. Three. Four..."

Part of you desperately wants to fight her off with everything you've got, but some hidden little sliver of you is actually *enjoying* this, liking the way the domina's warm body feels against your own. You can sense your body giving up and can feel your muscles loosening as you let the domina complete her count.

"...five. I win," she announces.

She sits up so she's perched on your chastity cage, her face flushed with exertion. A bright pink smile spreads across her lips. "On your belly," she says. When you don't obey immediately, she shouts it again in her thick accent: "ON YOU belly!"

The Latina lifts herself off you and you whimper to yourself as you flip over onto your stomach, feeling defeated and mastered in a way you never knew possible. It seems unthinkable that this small woman was able to pin you down so easily—and that you, somewhere deep, deep down, let it happen.

Then you hear her stand and open up one of the display cases. There's a pang of fear at the bottom of your stomach.

The Latina plops back on you, sitting now on the backs of your thighs. Something begins to buzz above you and as Domina Huitaca presses the vibrating dildo between your ass cheeks, you know exactly where it's headed.

"Had you just not be a liar I would have used lube," she explains, as if this is all your fault. "Now you have to take my dick dry."

As you sit with your face buried in the sand-patterned floor of the beach-like room, you only hope that the dildo is a lot thinner than it feels as it starts to press unrelentingly against your hole.

It's going to be a long night.

THE END

55

"I'll go... with you," you say to Miss Onyx, deciding that you'd rather have the favor of this demanding mistress instead of annoying her—or worse, making an enemy out of her. As soon as you do, her eyes light up with anticipation and she wastes no time snatching you by the hair to pull you up towards the second floor.

Even though the second floor's hallways and sea of unmarked doors seem indistinguishable from each other—aside from a few—the mistress is able to find her way perfectly, making sure turns and striding down the halls with purpose. You do your best to keep up, her grip on your hair threatening to become a savage tug should you slow down too much. Your feet stumble and your arms flail to keep your balance, but even with all the chaos of stumbling down the second floor's hallways, you still manage to ogle the mistress from behind, admiring her strong frame and hourglass curves, the sight of her in the white leather corset and fishnets enough to make you drool.

Betraying you, your cock throbs in your chastity device, a failed erection pushing against the device's tight steel.

Miss Onyx stops at a nondescript door. No room number, no identifying markings. Yet somehow she's sure this is exactly where she needs to be. She throws the door open and tosses you inside, slamming the door behind you both.

You're faced with a luxurious bedroom decorated with fine, bright silks, plush colorful throw pillows, a huge four poster bed, a couple of nailhead leather armchairs, and a large steamer trunk set against a window veiled by sheer curtains. From the look of the light outside, it's getting later, making you think for a second about the toiling slaves in the backyard and how they're faring in the falling darkness and chill of the night.

But there's little time to think before Miss Onyx is shoving you back onto your heels. The imposing mistress has little trouble bullying you backwards and it's not until you reach the bed and fall back onto it that she stops her shoving. She takes a step forward, between your legs, and you can feel the mesh of her fishnets against your skin and can smell her flowery perfume quite strongly now. Miss Onyx bends down towards you and in a husky whisper asks:

"Heads or tails?"

You blink dumbly, not understanding the question.

"I'm sorr—"

She cuts you off with an authoritative wagging finger.

"Shh! Answer. Heads... or tails?"

As you've lurked your way through Matriarch Manor, so many of your choices at least had *some* meaning behind them, but this might be the first one that feels truly arbitrary. Heads? Tails? A 50/50 coinflip decision? You feel a tickle of sweat down your neck. Miss Onyx seems to be delighting in the look of confusion on your face, soaking up the panic of you playing *her* game without having any idea what the rules are.

Choose Heads (Page 121)
Choose Tails (Page 124)

56

You pick Heads, letting your intuition guide you.

"Heads, Miss," you squeak out in a tiny, unsure voice.

The mistress gives you a cold, predatory look. "Heads it is," she says.

She holds up a hand, wiggling her fingers towards you to show off the pink, dazzling nails. Her hands are larger, maybe even larger than yours, and as her fingers dance about, you can see the fine, strong muscles in her forearm flex and relax.

"Do you like my manicure?" she asks you with a surprising hint of self-consciousness.

You nod, and not just to placate the mistress, either. The shiny, gel-like nail coloring with its sparkly patterning just below the surface really is nice, complimenting the mistress's creamy mocha skin perfectly. The mistress pushes her hand towards you, offering the top of it towards your lips.

"Give my hand a kiss," she orders you.

You reach over and kiss the top of her hand, tasting her lotion and inhaling the intense flower fragrance she's wreathed in. Her skin feels warm underneath your lips.

"Good. It's important to show respect by kissing a tool of discipline before it's used."

You knit your brow, trying to understand what she means when the first slap catches you on the side of the cheek. It's firm and hard, enough to make your head whip to the side. Before you can even figure out what's going on, she bats you with the other hand, her slap cupped and sharp. You shrink away.

Miss Onyx glares at you. "Don't you pull away from me, meat," she says, seething. "Bring your face back here."

You look up sheepishly at her as she hovers over you, her hands at the ready. The last thing in the world you want to do is bring your face close enough to be slapped again, but from her haughty, unkind stare you are sure that if you don't, she's sure to think of an even worse punishment. Slowly, you lean forward, bracing yourself.

"Tilt your chin up," she commands. "Come on, I'm not going to tell you again, meat."

You notch your chin upwards, a tight grimace on your face and your eyes narrowed in fear.

"You're very poorly trained, you know that? Every slave should be ready to present himself to a mistress at her slightest command. Open your eyes."

You force yourself to give Miss Onyx a wide-eyed stare. It's torture to hold the vulnerable position, knowing at any moment she cou—

Her palm cracks against your cheek three times in rapid succession.

"Look at me!" she snaps, forcing your attention.

You stiffen your head and turn straight towards her. Your cheek stings, hot little prickles alighting across your skin.

"I'm going to slap you now," she says. "You are not to look away from me."

Somehow knowing it's coming is even worse than it being a surprise. Miss Onyx raises her hand and takes aim, bringing it down swiftly on your other cheek. The blow isn't so hard that you're even in danger of being knocked to the ground or even away, but it is jarring and disorienting, making it a struggle to keep your eyes focused on Miss Onyx's bossy, bitchy face. She slaps you again and again and again, sometimes on the same cheek, sometimes switching sides, her hands making a dull thudding noise as they strike your face. You feel the blows in your teeth and your skull and even down to your elbows, your eyes starting to water from her nonstop face slapping. After fifteen or twenty slaps she finally pauses and you feel the tears run down your cheek, your view of Miss Onyx blurry and hazed.

"What's the matter?" she asks cruelly. "*You're* the one who picked Heads."

Your stomach churns as you try to imagine what Tails would've gotten you instead.

Miss Onyx snaps her fingers. "Face up, slave!"

With your lips trembling and your fallen tears hanging off your jaw, you tilt your face back to Miss Onyx. The stinging in your cheeks had passed the point of pain and slipped into numbness, but as Miss Onyx makes you wait you can feel the rush of blood under your skin bringing sensation back as well, preparing you for another round of humiliating torment.

She makes you wait. And wait. And wait.

It isn't until your eyes clear and you see the snarling, gleeful grin on Miss Onyx's face do you realize there's more to this discipline than you'd guessed. When she sees the confusion bloom in your eye she says:

"Ask me to slap you, slave."

Your heart beats hard in your chest. Does she really expect you to ask for pain? But the look she gives you tells you that's *exactly* what she expects.

"S-s-slap me, Miss Onyx."

"Is that how a slave asks a mistress for something?" she snaps back, disappointed.

Oh, god. She wants you to say *please*.

"Please slap me, Miss Onyx," you say, your expression sinking into despair.

"As you wish," she says.

A slap comes from the left and then the right, where she begins to strike you in a perfect rhythm, seemingly enjoying the sound of her own palm as she cracks it against your right cheek. Five slaps, then ten, twenty. Your tears start anew and then, without realizing it, you start to blubber and cry and soon you're sobbing, all while Miss Onyx paddles your face with a heartless, icy look.

You aren't sure when she stops. But by the time she's done, your vision is nothing but a spinning blur and your face so hot you could cook an egg on it. It's like someone shattered your world and put all the pieces back together again in the wrong way, everything around you seeming too bright and too muted and somehow *off*.

It takes you more than a few seconds to realize that Miss Onyx's hand is held out for you to kiss again.

You plant a kiss on top of it, but Miss Onyx doesn't pull away; she's not ready for you to stop showing your "respect" for the hand that left you with a sharp ringing in your ear. You kiss the sides of it and the fingers, then the fingertips, craning your head all around to cover every inch of her hand with a slavish kiss, still so dizzy you can barely remember why you've come to Matriarch Manor or even your own name.

Through the nightmare haze of your demeaning instruction, Miss Onyx asks you a question.

"Whose slave are you?" Her voice sounds very far away. Thinking that you don't—or maybe, in that moment, *can't*—understand her, she adds: "Who put you in your chastity device?"

Make up a mistress name... if you can (Page 142)
Admit that Mistress Merciless put you in chastity (Page 144)

57

You pick Tails, letting your intuition guide you.

"Tails, Miss," you squeak out in a tiny, unsure voice.

The mistress gives you a cold, predatory look. "Tails it is," she says.

She steps over to one of the nailhead armchairs and takes a seat, making sure to not cross her legs. She pats her fishnet-clad legs, the muscled thighs underneath jiggling ever so slightly with each pat. You can see her hands are strong and recently manicured, with pink, dazzling nails.

"Over here," she says. "Over my knee. Don't make me wait."

You hoist yourself off the bed and shuffle over towards Miss Onyx; you don't like the feeling of what's about to happen. It takes you a bit of maneuvering to be able to drape yourself over the mistress's thighs, feeling the strong muscles of her legs push against you. She pulls you to one side, adjusting you, and you feel your upper chest, neck, and head hanging off her, the blood starting to pool in your face. She holds her hand down towards you.

"Do you like my manicure?" she asks you with a surprising hint of self-consciousness.

You nod, and not just to placate the mistress, either. The shiny, gel-like nail coloring with its sparkly patterning just below the surface really is nice, complimenting the mistress's creamy mocha skin perfectly. The mistress pushes her hand towards you, offering the top of it towards your lips.

"Give my hand a kiss," she orders you.

You reach over and kiss the top of her hand, tasting her lotion and inhaling the intense flower fragrance she's wreathed in. Her skin feels warm underneath your lips.

"Good. It's important to show respect by kissing a tool of discipline before it's used."

You knit your brow, trying to understand what she means when the first slap catches you on the bare ass. It's firm and hard, enough to make you yelp. Before you can even figure out what's going on, she spanks you again, her slap cupped and sharp. You flail on her legs.

Miss Onyx digs her bright pink nails into the flesh of your ass cheeks.

"Don't you scramble away from me, meat," she says, seething. "Or I will make your ass into hamburger."

You try to turn your head, seeing her angry, snarling face. She has her hand raised, ready to spank you again, and while the last thing you want in the world is to stay bent over her knee, you don't dare reject the woman's unkind, haughty demands, sure she'll just think of an even worse punishment. Slowly, you release your ready-to-flail tension, taking deep breaths in hopes that you can calm yourself.

"Stick your ass out," she commands. "Come on, I'm not going to tell you again, meat."

You push your butt out, offering it to her like some perverse Christmas ham. You feel your body start to quiver.

"You're very poorly trained, you know that? Every slave should be ready to present himself to a mistress at her slightest command. Arch your back."

You force yourself to arch your back and give Miss Onyx even easier access to your thrust out buttocks. It's torture to hold the vulnerable position, knowing at any moment she cou—

Her palm cracks against your ass cheek three times in rapid succession.

"Don't squirm!" she snaps, forcing your attention.

You soften your body and relax as best you can. Your cheek stings, hot little prickles alighting across your skin.

"I'm going to slap you now," she says. "You are not to try to wiggle away."

Somehow knowing it's coming is even worse than it being a surprise. Miss Onyx raises her hand and takes aim, bringing it down swiftly on your other cheek. The blow isn't so hard that you're even in danger of bruising or being shoved off her somehow, but it is jarring and disorienting, making it a struggle to keep yourself calm as you hear Miss Onyx's stern breathing. She slaps you again and again and again, sometimes on the same cheek, sometimes switching sides, her hands making a dull thudding noise as they strike your ass. You feel the blows down your legs and in your belly and even all the way to your feet, your eyes starting to water from her nonstop spanking. After fifteen or twenty slaps she finally pauses and you feel the tears run down your cheek, your view of the room's hardwood floor going hazy.

"What's the matter?" she asks cruelly. "*You're* the one who picked Tails."

Your stomach churns as you try to imagine what Heads would've gotten you instead.

Miss Onyx snaps her fingers. "Ass out, slave!"

With your lips trembling and your fallen tears hanging off your jaw, you push your ass up to Miss Onyx. The stinging in your cheeks had passed the point of pain and slipped into numbness, but as Miss Onyx makes you wait you can feel the rush of blood under your skin bringing sensation back as well, preparing you for another round of humiliating torment.

She makes you wait. And wait. And wait.

It isn't until your eyes clear and you hear Miss Onyx's low chuckle that you realize there's more to this discipline than you'd guessed. When she notices your slight head turning and blooming confusion she says:

"Ask me to spank you, slave."

Your heart beats hard in your chest. Does she really expect you to ask for pain? But the way she's asked you tells you that's *exactly* what she expects.

"S-s-spank me, Miss Onyx."

"Is that how a slave asks a mistress for something?" she snaps back, disappointed.

Oh, god. She wants you to say *please*.

"Please spank me, Miss Onyx," you say, your heart sinking.

"As you wish," she says.

A spank hits the left cheek and then the right, where she begins to smack you in a perfect rhythm, seemingly enjoying the sound of her own palm as she cracks it against your flesh. Five slaps, then ten, twenty. Your tears start anew and then, without realizing it, you start to blubber and cry and soon you're sobbing, all while Miss Onyx paddles your ass in a heartless, unending beat.

You aren't sure when she stops. But by the time she's done, your vision is nothing but a spinning blur and your ass is so hot you could cook an egg on it. It's like someone shattered your world and put all the pieces back together again in the wrong way, everything around you seeming too bright and too muted and somehow *off*.

It takes you more than a few seconds to realize that Miss Onyx's hand is held out for you to kiss again.

You plant a kiss on top of it, but Miss Onyx doesn't pull away; she's not ready for you to stop showing your "respect" for the hand that left you with a sharp ringing in your ear. You kiss the sides of it and the fingers, then the fingertips, craning your head all around to cover every inch of her hand with a slavish kiss, still so dizzy you can barely remember why you've come to Matriarch Manor or even your own name.

Through the nightmare haze of your demeaning instruction, Miss Onyx asks you a question.

"Is that really all you can take?" she asks. "Are you squeezed dry, with nothing left to offer me but you begging me with apologies of how weak you are? Or will you take as much as I'm willing to give you?"

Break down and beg for her to stop (Page 128)
Take the spanking as best you can (Page 130)

58

It *is* all you can take. In your sniffling, shameful state, you cry out: "Please! Please stop! I can't take anymore!"

Miss Onyx isn't pleased. She grabs your hair in her hand and yanks your head up, forcing you to look at her at an angle that feels like it's going to make your neck snap. There's a nasty snarl on her lips and fire in her eyes and you realize you have made a terrible choice in denying the mistress her fun.

Without warning, she lets loose a half-wad of spit, the flinging bolas of saliva catching you in the corner of your eye and on the outside of your cheek. For a second you go to wipe it away but can see from the way she glares down at you that such behavior would only earn you another shotgun spray of spit, if not worse.

"You're SORRY?" she roars. "Who trained you? I need to know which mistress would let their slave be such an unruly piece of trash."

You try to think of a mistress name—anyone but Mistress Merciless, knowing you'd only doom yourself if you uttered that name in this moment—but nothing comes to mind.

"Mistress.... Mistress..."

You struggle to come up with a mistress name, trying to think if there are any you heard during your time in Matriarch Manor so far that would pass muster with Miss Onyx. Nothing comes to mind. You conjure up a name—any name—from the depths of your dizzy thoughts and pray that it's convincing.

"Mistress Amber," you say. Your voice also sounds far away, like it's coming from a completely different person.

Miss Onyx raises an eyebrow. "Mistress Amber?" she asks with suspicion in her voice. She laughs to herself and you feel your world turning upside down. "Not sure I've met her. What does she look like?"

You're still so disoriented you have a hard time thinking of how to describe anyone, let alone some fictional mistress.

"Tall..." you say, having to clear your throat. "Blo... brown hair. A, uh... a face, a tall face."

Miss Onyx does not seem convinced. "Mistress Ember, you said?"

"Amber," you stammer. "Miss... Mistress Amber..."

"You said Mistress Ember," she pushes you with a playful grin.

Did you say Mistress Ember? You're having trouble remembering, not sure if Miss Onyx is simply playing games with you or if you've lost the thread of your own lie. You feel slightly nauseous and wanting some fresh air.

You go to stand. "I'm... I..."

The room spins.

"I should see what Miss Amber is, uh, what she's doing..." You brace yourself on one of the bed's poster rails, also now feeling so very thirsty too.

"Don't you mean Mistress Umber?" taunts Miss Onyx.

Now you're sure she's messing with you, toying with you the way a cat plays with a mouse that's already dead but doesn't know it. She takes a step toward you, crowding your precious space and making you feel even more suffocated. You trip backwards and fall onto the bed again.

"Lying is a serious offense at Matriarch Manor," she says, her voice devoid of all playfulness and any slivers of joy that might've been in there before. "We're going to figure out *exactly* how you managed your way in here and then you're going to wish you really did belong to the mistresses. The price for trespassing here is even worse than lying."

Just as you're racing to think of a way to salvage your lie, Miss Onyx slaps you across the face again. It's far, far harder than the other slaps were and you feel a trickle of blood at the corner of your mouth. The ringing in your ear sharpens.

The next thing you know, Miss Onyx is picking up a landline phone.

"Yes. Yes. I'm in the Silk Room and I'm here with an outside male posing as a manor slave. Yes, right now. No, he's not going anywhere. Excellent. We'll be here."

After Miss Onyx hangs up the phone, she gives you a dirty, menacing look.

"Poor, poor meat. You're about to be devoured by the manor."

THE END

59

You shake your head no. "I'll take it Miss," you manage, even though you're terrified to utter the words.

"Yes, you will," says Miss Onyx.

Even though you can't see what's reaching for, you know she's reaching for *something*. You hear some hidden compartment—maybe in the armchair, maybe from somewhere else—click open and then hear a sound like a dulled sword being unsheathed. Soon the mystery comes to an end as Miss Onyx puts something long, thin, and black in front of your tear-streaked face.

"Kiss," she says condescendingly.

You kiss the doubled length of black leather, smelling oil and diesel and sweat and, you think, even some blood.

"This is going to hurt much much worse than my hand," she announces. Her tone is flat, more like she's reading ingredients off a bag of chips than telling you that you're about to feel awful, unimaginable pain. She pulls the double length strap away and you can feel it whiffing back and forth above your bare ass, gritting your teeth as you wait for its first bite.

When it does land, it's nothing like you've ever felt in your life. It's dull, yet cutting, heavy yet so light it seems to slice open your skin. And the noise— oh god, the noise of it, deafeningly loud and terrible, like the largest pair of hands you can imagine clapping right in your ear. You yelp and scream and jerk your body against Miss Onyx's legs, knowing you shouldn't try to pull away but having no idea how you can possibly tell your body *not* to obey that deep, instinctual need for escape. Needless to say it hurts. But what hurts even more is the aftermath, which feels like Miss Onyx just sprinkled acid on your ass cheeks that continues to bite and wind its way through your flesh, the heat of it making you want to reach down and try to dig out those nasty little bitey sensations, even though such a thing is beyond impossible.

Miss Onyx gives you a few moments to relish the pain before she hits you again with the strap. This time you cry, loudly and unabashedly. Miss Onyx doesn't seem to mind, herself seemingly relishing in your agony.

"That's right, take it you bitch," she says in a voice that drips as much acid as the doubled strap makes you feel across your tortured ass.

She brings the strap down again two more times in rapid succession and if there's one thing worse than feeling the acid heat of the heavy leather stripping your behind, it's feeling it twice without any relief. You scream until you're hoarse and buck against her, the mistress's fishnet scraping your skin. She keeps you over her knees with a firm hand on your mid-back, nails slightly digging into you as if to tell you to get yourself under control. When she releases you, she pulls the strap along your skin, letting its hard corner exfoliate you and torment the already tormented flesh. You hiss, stomping your feet against the hardwood, and as Miss Onyx laughs you can guess this is exactly the sort of reaction she was hoping for.

"Are you done yet, meat?" she asks you, her own breathing nearly as heavy as yours. Through the pain, you realize she may be beginning to tire herself out from all the pain she's giving you.

Once more, you shake your head no—you've committed to this position and you might as well see it through, even though you truly do worry that she might soon be making minced meat from your ass. How much longer can she really go? Not much longer, you pray.

Miss Onyx chuckles deeply.

"Hah. Well. Color me impressed, scaredy-meat. You're actually holding your own. Up! Get up!"

You rise suddenly, blood rushing down from your head and feeling more than a little dizzy. She shoves you towards the bed, face first, and you fall over it, grateful for the smooth, luxurious silky feeling beneath you.

"I'm going to be right back," she tells you. "And then we'll see how resilient you really are."

Believing she has thoroughly spanked you into submission, Miss Onyx walks right out of the room, letting the door slam, going to who knows where. It takes you a moment to realize you're in the room all alone.

You could stay put and wait for her to see if you can somehow sway her favor towards you somehow.

Or you could make a run for it. It's bound to be risky, but are you really sure you can last under this treatment for that much longer?

Stay put (Page 132)

Make a run for it (Page 137)

60

Maybe it's how achingly sore and brutalized your ass feels or maybe it's just something terrifying about Miss Onyx herself, but you stay exactly where you are, unable to bring yourself to get up off the bed. Laying your head against the bed's fine silks, you hear your own heartbeat and your breathing, both washing you in a soothing white noise that lets you take your mind off the stinging welts rising up all over your backside.

Your chastity cage presses into your body, pinching slightly. Your quest for freedom seems hopeless—the manor is too big, too rife with opportunities for you to fail. You let out a long sigh and further cement the idea that you'll just stay in this bedroom and see what happens.

You don't know how long it is before Miss Onyx returns, maybe five minutes or ten, maybe more. But when does, she isn't alone. There are three other mistresses with her, all of them tipsy from the party downstairs. Their voices are shrill and they're ecstatic to see you lying across the bed with your ass in the air.

One of them dumps out a bag of implements right near your head: a plastic-tailed flogger, an acrylic paddle, a short leather bullwhip, and a rattan cane. All of them meant, you realize, for you.

"We'll take turns," Miss Onyx tells the other mistresses. "Each person gets fifteen seconds to give it as hard as they want. First one to get it screaming wins."

You. You are the "it" here, and it's *you* they want to scream. You've made a terrible mistake.

You claw at the bedspread as one of the mistresses picks up the rattan cane.

'Ready," says Miss Onyx, ignoring you completely. "Set. Go!"

You see stars in your eyes as the cane cracks against your already beaten buttocks. The pain of it makes you jerk against the bed like an electrified ragdoll, your motions sending the mistresses into fits of guffawing laughter. The cane cracks against you several more times in the fifteen seconds the mistress has and when she's done, your legs are trembling madly and your entire body is shaking wildly. She tosses the cane dismissively on the bed and you see another domineering hand pick up the acrylic paddle. It's clear and it reminds you of plastic stationery sets from when you were younger.

But any nostalgic memories are swept away when the paddle lands on you. It hurts in such a different way than everything so far, landing with a flat, heavy, *deep* kind of blow that spreads across your entire ass at once. It's like falling backwards onto an unforgiving concrete floor, over and over, the pain jolting up into your belly to make you heave and clutch at the bedspread even tighter. You bury your face in the bed. You want to scream. You should scream. But your entire body is just one agonized knot, incapable of coherent thought or action.

You feel the paddle being tossed back on the bed, landing uncomfortably close to your face. As you look up, you see someone pick up the plastic-tailed flogger.

"Ohhhh that is a *nasty* piece of work," you hear Miss Onyx say.

And as you find out several seconds later it is. It really, really is.

As those two dozen or so thin plastic tails slice across your too-sensitive ass cheeks, you begin to wail. At least now they'll stop, you think as your throat aches with your pained scream. But they don't.

In fact, they're just beginning.

THE END

61

You sheepishly turning around tells Miss Wail what you've decided on. She steps over and guides you instead to the whipping bench, bending you over its padded—and still warm—top.

You couldn't have imagined taking this slave—or any man, for that matter—into your mouth, but the one thing you didn't consider is that would've been a case of you *having* some control instead of *someone else* having it. Miss Wail hikes up the hem of your dress so that it is pulled up past your waist and then you hear her inch the slave over to stand between your spread legs.

"Get ready, dolly," she says gleefully.

You feel the man's rough hands on your hips as he brusquely pulls your underwear down. You feel a cool gust of air as your ass cheeks are spread and then realize that the slave himself is blowing a cool stream of air down on you, making your asshole twitch involuntarily. Your face burns with shame and you bury it into the padded leather of the whipping bench.

"Oh she's getting shy!" croons Miss Wail. "I think she's going to need you to loosen her up slave. On your knees, tongue out."

Your eyes bolt open. The slave spreads your cheeks open wider and you seize up as you feel his tongue run up your ass crack, the tip of it tickling your hole in a swirling, teasing motion. Your mind is torn between thinking how in the world this slave can so easily take such orders from Miss Wail and the twisted fact that your hole is actually *relaxing* and opening up from the slave's ministrations. You suck in tight, anxious breaths while he continues to tongue you, hating how it's beginning to feel the slightest bit good.

"There we go, she's definitely loosening up now," Miss Wail says, chuckling darkly. "I think she's ready."

The slave pulls his tongue away and the next thing you feel is something warm and hard and pulsing on your ass. He begins to inch the tip into you, your hole too open and relaxed to fight it, and you can feel him push himself in, inch by inch, and even though your hole tries to tight to force him out, all it does is encourage him further, the slave sinking more and more inside. You thrash, but Miss Wail is there to hold you down, leaning over to whisper in your ear.

"Do you really want me to tattle on you, dolly? Or are you going to be a good girl?"

You let your flailing go and Miss Wail pats you patronizingly on the head.

"Go ahead slave," she tells the other male. "She's ready for you."

He pumps himself into you from head to balls, going slowly until the slickness of his spit and your mixed sweat allows him to go faster and faster. You feel his free balls bump against your caged ones, the dull pain of it making you grunt and flinch and curse yourself for being stuck in your chastity device. The male grips your hips and ass as he pumps, seemingly annoyed with how your squirming is making it hard for him to get his rocks off. Miss Wail sees this too and lets out a shrill cackle.

"She's fighting you!" says Miss Wail to herself. "Show her who's boss!"

The slave, either on his own volition or as directed by his mistress, slaps your ass so hard it stings, making you yelp. His pumping speeds up.

"You've got two minutes," Miss Wail tells him. "Taking too long is just as bad as being premature."

He picks up his pace and you hear the sound of his body slapping against yours, his cock bumping against your prostate and—despite everything—making *you* try to get hard, your cock growing hopelessly against its steel cage. You grunt and claw at the bench, pushing away to nowhere while you're relentlessly fucked in the ass by the slave.

"Squeal," Miss wail says to you. "Squeal like you like it."

Your mind is in too many places to know what she means, but you let out a high-pitched, whiny cry, the sort that you've heard too many times in cheesy porno clips. It's debasing and degrading and makes you want to curl up into a little ball and disappear, but it makes the man behind you speed up his thrusting even more. His little sighs and grunts fill the room along with your bodies slapping and you know he must be getting close.

"It's time, slave. Cum now or never cum again," Miss Wail commands.

That's enough to do it. The male slave *explodes* inside of you, jetting hot streams of cum into your ass. It is thick and seemingly neverending, and now that the male's started to cum, he is holding you fast to pump every last drop of his pent-up seed into you. Finally, once his balls are drained dry, he pulls out, letting him leak out of you while Miss Wail laughs and laughs to herself.

"Well, well! That was quite the show."

She takes you from the whipping bench helping you clean up, and then puts her male slave back where you just were, not even bothering to lock him up again. She straps him down and turns back to you.

"When you're ready, I suppose you should be on your way," she says, handing you a small towel to help clean yourself.

You take a few minutes to collect yourself and once you have, Miss Wail commands you carefully take off your sissy wear and leave folded nicely on the bench. She blows you a dramatic kiss as you leave the space, giving you one last reminder before you head off to the third floor.

"Remember—if you mention a single word of me allowing you to go upstairs, I will make you *severely* regret it."

And with that, you go off to the third floor staircase.

Go up to the third floor (Page 92)

62

You've taken all you can and you know an opportunity when you see one. You stand up off the bed, feeling shaky legged and terrified that Miss Onyx will come back any second. But you steel yourself and stumble towards the door, listening against it first for footsteps and chatter before you pull it open and step out into the hallway.

Your ass stings and your skin feels bathed in fire, but you push forward, determined to push your way towards where Mistress Merciless's bedroom should be on the third floor. You move slowly through the second floor hallways, hoping not to run into anyone else. You turn the corner and see a staircase leading up. The floor above seems quiet and, in a strange way, sacred.

You could take your time getting to the staircase, but there's always the risk someone might find you and, in your still-disoriented state, it might be very hard to come up with any convincing excuses for why you're walking around the second floor.

Or you could make a dash for it and hope that you don't get anyone's unwanted attention...

Make a dash for the stairs (Page 90)
Take your time (Page 92)

63

The Latina domina's fiery temperament is too much for you and you decide that no, you can't risk saying anything. And, when you stay quiet, Domina Huitaca makes sure it stays that way when she gets another hand towel from behind one of the room's display cases and ties it around your head as a makeshift gag, shoving it deep between your teeth. It causes you to drool and slowly wet the towel—and the padded bench below you—but if that bothers the domina, she doesn't say so. Instead, she's busy lubing you up again and doing her own tour of the beachy room's dildo display cases, taking her sweet time to pick out a thick cock that is curiously close to her own skin tone.

Now that you've been fucked once in the ass, it takes the domina far less work to get the second cock into you. She rides you even harder than before, sprinkling in slaps and spanks and even spitting on your twitching, exposed asshole a couple of times just because she can.

Though you're having the built up denial in your balls slowly milked out through Domina Huitaca's fucking, that's clearly not her goal. She goes through almost half a dozen orgasms with a whole host of fake cocks, until the room smells like lube and pussy and ass, all of it mingling with the beachy sea salt and citrus aroma being pumped into the room by some unseen air fresheners. In between fuckings, Domina Huitaca takes a rest on the throne—while you stay strapped to the bench like a piece of meat. It's during one of these rests that there's a quiet chime coming from the panel next to the room's door.

With a huffy sigh over being disturbed, the domina goes to answer the chime. She presses a rectangular button below a small speaker you hadn't noticed before.

"Yes? I'm busy," she says, annoyed.

A female voice responds, crackling through heavy background noise. "Yes Huitaca, just letting you know that we're running late with your slave. He should be ready soon and will meet you in the Beach House. Apologies for the inconvenience."

Domina Huitaca looks back at you with a stony stare. Then she presses the intercom button again.

"You can cancel that," she says.

The woman on the other end asks, "Are you sure?"

"Yes," says Domina Huitaca. "Positive."

Whatever rays of playfulness were breaking through the Latina's bossy attitude are gone now, replaced by a woman who looks enraged that she was duped. Slowly her lips sink into a severe frown and her fists clench at her sides.

"You think I'm a fool?" she asks you.

You say nothing, having no idea what you *can* say in this moment. She slaps your ass so hard you feel it all the way in your throat.

"You think I'm stupid?" she roars.

She stomps towards the display cases, pulling out the biggest, blackest, fattest dildo there is.

"You're going to talk."

Your mouth drops open at the size of the dildo. It's impossibly large and there's absolutely no way that *thing* can go into you without tearing you a new one. Your heart pounds hard and your sweat goes cold. Your intentions at Matriarch Manor aren't worth that, no matter what the consequences for them.

"No no no, I'll tell you everything!" you cry in a pathetic begging voice.

Domina Huitaca grins. "I know you will—after I'm done with you."

You shut your eyes and bury your face into the bench's padded cushion, bewildered at the thought of what it's going to feel like to have that massive phallus thrust up your ass. Unfortunately for you, you're soon about to know all too well.

THE END

64

You let a beat of silence pass as you decide to try to change the domina's mind. You know it's a long shot, but what other choice do you have? This woman seems like she'll never stop if you let her have her way with you for the rest of the evening.

"Domina Huitaca," you say, being very careful with your pronunciation. "Thank you for allowing me to serve you—and for you taking my, uh, my virginity..."

"But?" she asks sharply.

You shake your head. "This is not a 'but'. It's simply that, as a slave, I have other duties to the manor. Other tasks to perform, others to serve. I am afraid that if I were to spend the evening with you—as lovely as I'm sure it would be—I would be failing my duties to Matriarch Manor."

Several more beats of silence pass, The domina stares you down, refusing to even blink, but you hold her gaze somehow, even as your eyes begin to water. You do your best to make you look a sorry one without overdoing it; just a slight hint of remorse, enough to—hopefully—sell her on this being as hard an outcome for you as for her.

Finally, the domina sighs. "It's cute you think you have a choice at all," she says, patting you on the back. "I could keep you in here all night, fuck you with every last dildo there is, send you downstairs bow-legged and limping, and you know who would get in trouble for your 'duties' not being done. You. Not me, you."

You hang your head, breaking eye contact with the domina. Then, to your surprise, she pats your head affectionately.

"That was nice," she says, undoing your straps. "You didn't fight me. I hate a slave who fights me. You put me in a very, very good mood... which is why I am going to let you go."

You whip your head up and give the Latina a look of shock in the mirror.

"Really?" you say before you can stop yourself.

The domina chuckles to herself. "You're cute, you know," she says as she helps you to your feet. "I would've had *so* much fun breaking you."

She walks you to the door. It's unbelievable. Are you really about to escape the room? Your ass feels sore as you walk, reminding you that even if you do escape, you certainly paid a price for it.

Domina Huitaca opens the door.

"Goodbye, slave," she says.

Even though there's a hint of wistfulness in her voice that tempts you ever so slightly to change your mind, you step into the hallway while you have the chance and bow your head, pretending to pad off like you have somewhere urgent to be. You hear the door shut. Will the domina get herself another slave to fuck? Will she make him her toy for the night? Will she come looking for you in a few minutes, wondering exactly where or who has called you?

You turn through the maze of the second floor's hallways as you think over these questions, stumbling upon the sight of the third floor in the distance. You could run down the hall and get to those stairs right now, ensuring Domina Huitaca doesn't change her mind and come for you—or you can take your time to go slow and steady to the third floor.

Make a break for the stairs (Page 90)
Go slow and steady (Page 92)

65

"Mistress.... Mistress..."

You struggle to come up with a mistress name, trying to think if there are any you heard during your time in Matriarch Manor so far that would pass muster with Miss Onyx. Nothing comes to mind. You conjure up a name—any name—from the depths of your dizzy thoughts and pray that it's convincing.

"Mistress Amber," you say. Your voice also sounds far away, like it's coming from a completely different person.

Miss Onyx raises an eyebrow. "Mistress Amber?" she asks with suspicion in her voice. She laughs to herself and you feel your world turning upside down. "Not sure I've met her. What does she look like?"

You're still so disoriented you have a hard time thinking of how to describe anyone, let alone some fictional mistress.

"Tall..." you say, having to clear your throat. "Blo... brown hair. A, uh... a face, a tall face."

Miss Onyx does not seem convinced. "Mistress Ember, you said?"

"Amber," you stammer. "Miss... Mistress Amber..."

"You said Mistress Ember," she pushes you with a playful grin.

Did you say Mistress Ember? You're having trouble remembering, not sure if Miss Onyx is simply playing games with you or if you've lost the thread of your own lie. You feel slightly nauseous and suddenly in need of fresh air.

You go to stand. "I'm... I..."

The room spins.

"I should see what Miss Amber is, uh, what she's doing..." You brace yourself on one of the bed's poster rails, also now feeling so very thirsty too.

"Don't you mean Mistress Umber?" taunts Miss Onyx.

Now you're sure she's messing with you, toying with you the way a cat plays with a mouse that's already dead but doesn't know it. She takes a step toward you, crowding your precious space and making you feel even more suffocated. You trip backwards and fall onto the bed again.

"Lying is a serious offense at Matriarch Manor," she says, her voice devoid of all playfulness and any slivers of joy that might've been in there before. "We're going to figure out *exactly* how you managed your way in here and then you're going to wish you really did belong to the mistresses. The price for trespassing here is even worse than lying."

Just as you're racing to think of a way to salvage your lie, Miss Onyx slaps you across the face again. It's far, far harder than the other slaps were and you feel a trickle of blood at the corner of your mouth. The ringing in your ear sharpens.

The next thing you know, Miss Onyx is picking up a landline phone.

"Yes. Yes. I'm in the Silk Room and I'm here with an outside male posing as a manor slave. Yes, right now. No, he's not going anywhere. Excellent. We'll be here."

After Miss Onyx hangs up the phone, she gives you a dirty, menacing look.

"Poor, poor meat. You're about to be devoured by the manor."

THE END

66

"Mistress Merciless," you say. Your voice also sounds far away, like it's coming from a completely different person.

Miss Onyx raises an eyebrow. "You're one of Merci's slaves?" she asks, slightly unbelieving.

You speak the words as if levels deep in a backwards dream: "Mistress Merciless put me in this chastity."

Miss Onyx tilts her head to one side and then the other, her curly, highlighted hair bouncing back and forth. Her cold eyes drill into yours and somehow you can tell she's looking for the truth in you, perhaps having used the disorienting, dehumanizing face slapping to draw you into a state where you'd be less likely to lie... or just less likely to lie convincingly.

"What do you think of Mistress Merciless?" she asks you.

The words come all too easily: "She scares me, Miss."

Miss Onyx chuckles at that. She runs her tongue against her teeth as she thinks, perhaps mulling over some choice with no gratifying outcome. After a few moments of deliberation, she gives you a tight-lipped smile.

"Oh if you were anyone else but Merci's, we could've had *so* much more fun," she says with a tinge of regret in her voice.

She backs away from you and takes a seat in one of the leather armchairs with a dramatic sigh. You are, seemingly, free to go.

You stand, afraid for a minute that you will collapse, but then find your footing. You turn to the mistress and bow your head like a waiter who has just delivered the last course of a meal. She waves you away.

"Tell Merci I said hi," she says.

You go out into the hallway while you have the chance, still not completely sure what happened. Does Miss Onyx respect—or fear—Mistress Merciless enough to not lay another hand on her slave without permission? And if it so, what does that mean for Mistress Merciless's demeanor, given how cruel and controlling Miss Onyx was without a second thought?

You move slowly through the second floor hallways, hoping not to run into anyone else before you find a way to finally get to the third floor. You turn the corner and see a staircase leading up. The floor above seems quiet and, in a strange way, sacred.

You could take your time getting to the staircase, but there's always the risk someone might find you and, in your still-disoriented state, it might be very hard to come up with any convincing excuses for why you're walking around the second floor.

Or you could make a dash for it and hope that you don't get anyone's unwanted attention...

Make a dash for it (Page 90)
Take your time (Page 92)

67

You like the look of the stone steps. They offer promise and opportunity—not to mention a way out of this suffocating, claustrophobic basement. But as you climb up them, there is a cacophony of noise... and not party noise, either. It sounds like clanging dishes and thrashing metal and as you reach the stop of the steps, you realize they lead into a bustling kitchen.

Under the kitchen's bright lighting, there are a dozen slaves preparing food and pouring beverages, working with a terrified precision as dictated by a warden of a woman who struts up and down the kitchen's gleaming stainless steel stations. She shrieks at the males taking too long and swats the ones who seem to be doing a fair enough job just for the hell of it.

The woman, who seems barely drinking age herself and younger than pretty much all of the male slaves, delights in her power over them. She is wearing a long, black pencil skirt with a fluttery hem, clacky black patent leather heels, and an open blazer over what appears to be no shirt or bra whatsoever. Her skin is ghostly pale and her chestnut hair is short with loose curls that bounce with every step she takes. The woman's black-frame glasses add to her sultry, secretariat look, as does the clipboard in her hand that she takes frequent notes on as she observes the labor of the kitchen slave staff.

You avoid making eye contact with her as you try to figure out if you should leave or not when she shouts:

"You! Slave! Did they send you up for maid duties? Why aren't you dressed yet?"

You turn and see the young mistress is staring daggers at you through her black-frame glasses. The way she looks at you, you sense that neither here in the manor nor outside of it has she *ever* let a man displease her without paying for it.

You could let this domineering kitchen mistress continue to think you're the "maid" that was sent up and take your chances in hopes of finding some other path to your freedom... or you could turn tail and run.

Pose as the slave on "maid" duty (Page 173)
Turn tail and run (Page 172)

68

You tiptoe over to the dingy office, squinting your eyes against the overly bright fluorescent lights. It's a small office, with furniture that looks like it's from the 1960s: there's a metal desk, a roller chair, shelves bolted into the walls, and several filing cabinets, not to mention fetish posters tacked up on the walls depicting scenes of women in exotic leather and latex garb taking chained and naked male slaves to task. Part of you wonders whether these scenes happened somewhere in Matriarch Manor, perhaps this very basement, and have to turn away before you're overcome with dread that they still might happen to you if you don't find a way to free yourself and get out of this manor.

Sitting on the desk you see a paper cup. It's filled with coffee that looks to be piping hot. Someone was here, very recently, and they're probably coming back.

In a mad scramble, you fish through the desk drawers, finding stacks of papers and bizarre-looking metal devices, and then you pull open the drawers of the filing cabinets, growing disheartened as you find nothing but more and more paperwork. But then, as you pull open the bottommost drawer of the last filing cabinet left to search, you see an oversized keyring with one single key. Looking closely on it you see it says: "Chastity - Master".

Adrenaline pulses through you. Is this it? Is this the literal key to your freedom?

You could try to free yourself now, even though the piping hot office sits in the corner of your eye like a grim warning, or you could take the master key with you and hope that it actually works once you're somewhere safer. Whatever you do, you'd better make up your mind fast.

Unlock yourself now (Page 148)
Take the keys with you (Page 149)

69

A bird in the hand is worth two in the bush, you think to yourself, knowing that if you don't unlock yourself now you might not even get the chance again. With your hands shaking, you raise the key to the tiny padlock of your cage, fumbling to get it to slip in. You panic for a moment, thinking it doesn't fit, and then the key goes in. You turn it, gently, and there's a pleasant, soft click as the padlock opens. Yes! Amazing! It worked!

You put the master key back where you found it and pull off your chastity device, feeling the cool, dingy air of the basement on your newly freed cock. You can't believe how good it feels to have the device off you, to be able to move without the metal digging into your skin and to not worry about the pinch of the cage's hinging. You touch yourself, unable to help it, and a thrum of pleasure rips through your body. Oh, if you were just about anywhere else you think you'd jerk off right then and there.

But the basement office is no place for *that* kind of gamble. You stash your chastity cage at the back of one of the filing cabinet drawers, stuffing it behind mounds of old-looking paperwork, and then you take a big, deep breath.

It's time to get the hell out of there.

You step out of the office and hear footsteps on stone. Because of how echoey the basement is, you have no idea where they're coming from. You could run back in the office and try to hide or you can press forward, looking for a way to escape through the maze-like basement hallways.

Hide in the office (Page 151)
Go back through the basement hallways (Page 154)

70

It's tempting, but you decide to take the master key with you, holding it tight to your body. Hopefully it will work once you get outside, but at least this way you won't have to worry about being the only chastised male in all of Matriarch Manor.

You pad through the hallways, trying to look like you're on your way somewhere important while still maintaining a somewhat somber, respectful air. Out of the periphery of your vision, you can see the slaves in their cells—there seem even more now, as if they've been stashed away after being used upstairs—and still half of the stations in use by mistresses who seem much more drunk and more rowdy than they were before. You even pass by one station that smells strongly of metal and fire, only to turn and see a light branding iron in one of the mistresses hands!

A dozen steps and a hallway later, you hear a male scream that rises to a pained pitch and then becomes suddenly, grimly silent. You stop in your tracks, fighting off the shudders of terror, when you hear a man whispering your way.

"Psst! Hey! Hey you!"

You look before you can stop yourself and see the poor wretch in his cramped, hay-lined cell. He looks like he has flogger marks on his belly and his arms, along with dirt speckling his face, including on the very tip of his nose. It's the look of someone who has been through hell and back and he looks back at you with big, pleading eyes.

"That's the key, right?" he whispers. "The master key?"

You all of a sudden regret stopping. You take a step away.

"Hey!" he whisper-shouts. "Come on! Free me! I won't tell anyone!"

Cursing yourself, but not wanting to have a shouting slave give you away, you lean in and whisper back:

"It's just for the chastity cages, not for the cells," you say, wondering whether you should've come up with some lie for why you're carrying it. The gears in your head begin to turn as you start to prepare one, just in case.

"Nah man, it's not," he insists. "They use it for everyone. I've seen them! Come on, you can't just leave me in here! I've been here so long..."

His pleading tone is enough to make you wonder just how Matriarch Manor has managed to keep him—or the other slaves—locked away for long, seemingly against their will. You know they have immense political power in town and that, based on Mistress Merciless's actions, they aren't afraid to wield it when they're displeased. Could this extend to keeping manor slaves? Do they have dirt or other leverage that forces these men to stay here and serve them? Are they really *that* powerful and their leverage *that* strong?

You take a small step backwards, not sure whether to give into the slave's begging or to leave him behind.

Apologize and keep going (Page 162)
Be kind and free the slave (Page 161)

71

Rattled by the sound of footsteps, you run back into the office and look for a place to hide. Your eyes flit about the narrow room, and you see there are really only two options—under the desk and behind the door—with the first almost ensuring that whoever was here will find you when they return. You duck behind the door and keep it closed, a tendril of fear running down your spine.

Maybe this was a mistake.

The footsteps get louder. And louder. And then they enter the basement office.

"Where is that damn thing," you hear a female voice say, followed by the sound of the filing cabinet drawers being pulled open and shut again. "Which cabinet was it? I thought she said all the way on the left."

Her heels click on the cold stone floor as she paces, trying to find what she's looking for. Did you actually put the master key away in the right place? You sure thought you did. Peeking around the edge of the door to check where she's searching, you see that she's tall and statuesque, draped in a tight leather dress that hugs every curve of her body. Her hair is a fiery red, cascading down to her shoulders in waves. You hear a jingling as she finds the key after all, quickly darting back behind the door as she starts to turn around. How are you ever going to get out of here?

"Who's there?" she calls out, her voice carrying an edge of authority that makes you freeze in place. You hold your breath, praying she doesn't see you.

But it's too late. Looking down, you see that the door is not flush with the floor and that there's a large gap at the bottom that is casting light on your bare feet. You hear the woman's heels click over towards you and then she pulls the door open, revealing you. Her gaze locks onto yours, and a cruel smile curves her lips. "Well now," she purrs, "What have we here?"

Before you can even think about running, she's grabbing your wrist in a grip that's surprisingly strong for how delicate she looks. Tugging you out from behind the door, she pulls you out of the office and towards the empty prison cells lining the basement walls, only then noticing you aren't in chastity.

"And what are you doing without a cage?"

You watch dumbfounded as she uses the master key—which you thought was just for chastity devices—to unlock the empty prison cell. Damnit, how useful that knowledge would've been five minutes ago! She brusquely shoves you into the cell, which is small and sparse with a tattered mattress in one corner and a bucket in the other. She slams the door shut, the lock clicking into place immediately. Even though the cell door's bars are old and rusty, they look sturdy enough to keep anyone from escaping.

The mistress twirls the keyring around her finger playfully.

"I'll say, I wasn't too happy to have to come and fetch this key but I never expected to find a chastity-less slave while I was out it. I think some of the manor mistresses are going to have quite a few questions for you. But that can come later. In the meantime, enjoy your quarters," she says, taunting you by ringing the key against the bars.

You watch her—and your only chance at escape—walk down the basement's stone hallway, shouting and begging for her to come back and that you can explain, if only she'd give you a chance. Then she turns the corner and she's gone, leaving you in the cell to rot.

You fall down to the stone floor and lean against the cold, unforgiving wall. Your head drops and you look at your cock, freed from one prison and yet finding itself in another. You're so disappointed with how close you were to success that you don't even feel like touching yourself after a week of straight denial.

And yet you do so anyway, languidly stroking your cock as you think that this may be the last chance you get for a very long time. You try to think of your favorite jerk off material—porn clips with busty blondes in lewd positions, amateur clips of hot chicks getting railed into screaming orgasms—but again and again it's the mistresses of the manor who enter your thoughts, somehow invading your mind and your privacy even then, until you finally manage to push them away for long enough to cum into the cell's metal bucket that looks like it's used for much worse.

Depressed, you lie down on the mattress, soaking in the least satisfying orgasm of your life. Your stomach grumbles and your body trembles from having no clothing or blankets to help you stave off the basement's subterranean chill. You wait. And you wait. You try to go to sleep but the basement lights never even flicker, their too-white hue wrenching your eyelids open every time you attempt to shut them. You get up and jerk off, again, this one even less satisfying than before. It feels mandatory, like work, like you *have* to take advantage of this freedom before it's gone again and you swell with resentment at Matriarch Manor and Mistress Merciless, cursing her and the rest of the mistresses that they can so easily bully men like you into sexual denial and then—without even blinking—shove you into a cell without trial or representation.

But that's what they've done. And they aren't afraid of the repercussions of doing so, either. That thought might be the most frightening of all, as it slowly dawns on you just how much power and influence Matriarch Manor must have to act so indiscriminately.

Perhaps you'd better start getting ready to make your pleas to the mistresses once they come to get you from your cell—and you're sure they are going to extract a high toll to let you go that's sure to be a hell of a lot worse than a year of chastity.

THE END

72

Figuring there's no way to escape the basement office if someone walks in there—not to mention barely any place to hide—you pad down the hallways, trying to remember the turns you took to get to the intersection. Everything feels heightened now and on edge, and as you pass by some of the occupied cells with slaves in them, you see them look at you curiously, their eyes darting from your face down to your crotch.

Fuck, maybe you should've left your chastity device on until you were out of the manor.

You pick up the pace, practically speedwalking as you pop around corners and cut down corridors, stepping deeper and deeper into the belly of the basement and its many stations designed for the humiliation and degradation of male slaves. While the mistresses might have been occupied with their tormenting before, they can't help but be drawn to you as they too seem to notice that there's something different about you than the other slaves. At first it seems like they don't even pick up on it, but as you pass by more and more busy mistresses, you begin to hear worrying whispers.

"Is he out of chastity?"

"Can they do that?"

"Who is letting their slave walk around like that?"

"Someone's in trouble!"

"Imagine if he somehow got himself out?"

Sweat begins to run down your back and your palms feel cold and clammy. How long before one of these mistresses decides to stop you to ask what exactly you're doing out here? Worse still, you keep losing your way in the basement, doubling back on sections you've already walked through and causing even *more* of the mistresses and slaves down here to see that you're the only free male in all of Matriarch Manor. You need to get out of here, now.

But how? You could try to make a run for it, moving even faster as you desperately look for a way out, or you could try your best to stay calm to not raise any more suspicion.

That's when you see it: the basement door leading to the backyard. It's fully open now and you can hear chattering outside and also feel the cold breeze blowing in. The air smells so sweet, tinged with woodsmoke and grass. Your muscles twitch, begging you to let them fire off in a mad sprint to the outside.

Stay calm and go slowly (Page 156)
Make a mad dash for the outside (Page 157)

73

You calm your breath and take slow steps towards the open door. The entire time your heart is pounding and your eyes are searching your periphery, looking at the cells that line the way outside. Most are empty, but one or two seem to have a slave huddled in the corner, sleeping or cowering away the evening.

Freedom is twenty feet away. You count the steps it takes. 1, 2, 3, 4...

The tension of the moment is maddening as freedom looms fifteen feet away, then ten, then...

...the door closes from the outside. You look around, confused, and as you turn all the way around you see a half-dozen mistresses in crisp uniforms have gathered behind you. They're wearing something like combat boots mixed with riding boots, their distance from you suggesting they've been taking slow, quiet steps to keep you from noticing they were there.

But now that they see you, they drop their ruse.

"Where do you think you're going, little slave?" one asks.

The time for being calm is over. You turn and run towards the basement door, wondering just what your odds are of getting away from the manor once you're outside. But as you pull on the basement door, it refuses to budge, either barricaded or locked somehow from the outside. You yank on the door desperately, cursing under your breath.

"No, no no no no, god please no," you say, feeling the world fall out from under your feet.

The next thing you feel is the grip of the uniformed mistresses as they pull you away from the door.

"God can't help you now," another one of the mistresses says. She's holding a leather strap in one hand that she brings down on the back of your knee, the sting of the blow making you crumple down to the floor.

The mistresses gather around you, two on each side to grab you under the armpit and drag you away while the others follow. Your heels drag on the basement floor.

You don't know where you're going. But you know it won't be good.

THE END

74

It's time to listen to your body. You dash towards the open door, mistresses turning from their stations to stare in disbelief at you. Their questions rise to a fever pitch and soon they are all shouting at each other, asking what's going on, some even claiming that there is a runaway slave—or worse—at the manor. But you only hear them for a few seconds before you're out in the backyard, the cold air chilling your skin.

You take in your surroundings. Just as when you arrived, there are slaves still toiling to finish some of the backyard preparations but there are also dozens of mistresses out here, sipping on warm coffee and munching on snacks. They huddle in groups and around the firepits of the backyard, warming themselves by the orange flames. It's only because of the setting sun that no one seems to immediately notice you aren't wearing a chastity device and you quickly step to the edge of the backyard to catch your breath.

Then you peer down the narrow path that led you from the front of the manor to the backyard. You notice now how there is another path leading from it, this one into the woods surrounding Matriarch Manor. All you have to do is nonchalantly head down there and you can escape, unlocked and free...

...and completely naked. Once the sun has completely set, there is sure to be an even more vicious chill in the air. Luckily for you, you didn't bring your wallet or keys, stashing both at your place nearly three miles away, so you *could* get home completely naked, but it sure won't be a fun journey.

As you're pondering the trek, you notice a rack of luxurious fur coats that have been brought out for the mistresses to don should the cold be too much for them. Maybe you could, ah, "borrow" one? No one's noticed you lurking at the edge of the backyard yet—or at you aren't in chastity—so who's to say that they'll notice you carrying a coat off to the manor's side path?

Then again, you've already come this far. Do you really want to risk it all just to have a cozier walk home? Well, a cozier walk and less chance you're stopped by someone who sees a naked man stumbling through the woods, that is.

Escape while totally naked (Page 158)
Grab a jacket (Page 159)

75

Forgoing the warmth of a nice, comfy fur, you peel away from the direction of the backyard, the party back there already starting to reach a shrill, drunken fever pitch. Though as you do, you wistfully look back at the rack of coats that have been set out for the mistresses to wear to keep warm—if only you could have one too.

You trod off down the first path you can find away from the manor, stepping onto a dirt path that goes along the main road you walked along to get here. It snakes and curves, but you generally are able to follow it, the setting sun making you pick up your pace lest you risk being lost naked and in the dark in the woods around Matriarch Manor. Now and again you turn back towards the manor's lights to help orient yourself and even this far away you can hear the occasional laugh or crack of something—wood? A whip? Something you can't even imagine?—that signals the party is still going strong and is sure to be for quite some time.

You continue home, your mind filled with strange fantasies about the domineering women you encountered at Matriarch Manor. It's weird to think how these women who were so terrifying before now make your cock stiffen with excitement. Who knows: Maybe one day you'll return…

CONGRATULATIONS! YOU FREED YOURSELF AND ESCAPED
MATRIARCH MANOR!

76

Fuck, it's cold out! Sure, it's only a few miles back to your place, but what if the temperature drops even more? What if you get lost? What if someone sees you wandering through the woods and roads on your back? You can't take these risks, not when there is a bounty of warm fur coats just a few feet away.

You hang along the edge of the backyard, staying in the inky darkness as much as possible, and slot yourself between the tree line and the nearest rack of coats. They look *so* warm and even smell performed, the pleasant smell of mossy oak and juniper filling your nostrils. You reach out to grab a coat and tug on it gently.

It doesn't give. You tug more firmly this time, and yet it still stays tight on the hanger. You try another and the same thing happens, causing you to take a look to see if the coats are somehow tied to their hangers. As far as you can tell, they aren't; there just seem to be so many of them that it's hard to get any one out without moving the entire pile to one side, something you're not ready to do.

You'll just tug harder. One strong pull, that's all it should take. You listen to the backyard gathering rise and fall with conversation and clapping and shouting, trying to time your pull so that it will be muffled by the sounds. Your pulse is in your ears now and your body is quaking from the cold.

You count in your head, telling yourself you'll pull on the third swell from the outdoor chatter.

Someone screams and then an entire gaggle of women shout and clap at some unseen spectacle.

Three.

There's a loud whistling sound, followed by the crack of a whip and the blood-curdling scream of a man. More laughter. Someone blows dramatic kisses.

Two.

A cracking sound floats across the backyard, followed by another, then one more. Women ooohh and aaahhh and then there's the sound of tears and an incredulous scoff and something else that sounds an awful lot like a chains jangling.

One. It's time.

You tug on a coat hard, determined to grab it this time, and then you stare in horror as the entire rack starts to career towards you. You try to push it back, but the shift in weight is too sudden and the more the rack leans towards you, the faster it falls, the coats offering nowhere to push against. Your hands slip through the sea of furs and the rack tackles you to the ground.

Well, at least you're warm as the women start to gather around you, trying to figure out what's going on.

"Oh Christ, these slaves get more and more clumsy every month," one mistress says, snapping her fingers to get some of the larger slaves over to lift the rack over you.

As it's lifted, the women see you don't have a chastity device.

"Holy shit," one says. "Why isn't he caged?"

Just then, women burst out of the basement, huffing and puffing.

"We have an escapee!" one of them shouts. "A male without a chastity device! We just saw him!"

"He's right here," says a mistress with her hair tied up in a neat and proper bun. Her dark eyes glance down at you. "You have a lot to answer for, my poor little slave."

Before you can summon the strength to stand and run off into the woods, slaves—fellow men—are picking you up and holding you fast by the arms, dragging you back to the basement to be questioned...

Goddamnit, you were so close! If only you hadn't gotten greedy at the end.

Alas.

THE END

77

Feeling empathy after all you've been through this day, you give in and decide to free the slave. Part of you hopes the key won't even work, that it truly is a master key just for chastity devices—that's what it says, doesn't it?—but it fits in the cell lock perfectly and with a quick turn you hear the cell door open, freeing the slave.

You step back, making sure to hold on tight to the key lest the slave betray you and run off with it, leaving you with nothing.

"Heh, relax," he says, stretching his legs as he clambers out of the cell. He looks around, making sure the stations nearby are unoccupied. "I know what you're up to. I'm not gonna take the key. But I can get you away from here, if you want. You know, as a thank you."

"I was on my way out already," you say, still feeling untrusting.

The slave smiles sadly. He has sandy brown hair and tired, light eyes. You could see him outside the manor working in customer service or sales, trying his luck to make people happy. That's how it certainly feels right now as he gives you a repentant, apologetic look.

"Sure you were," he says. "Except you were going the wrong way. Come on, I've been here a long time and I've never seen you before—I know you don't know where you're going. Let me help you. You won't regret it."

How about it? Will you trust this slave and follow him down a promise path of freedom or will you keep going your own way, leaving this man you just released alone to do whatever he might with the knowledge that you possess not just a chastity master key but a master key for all the cells in the basement and who knows what else?

Trust the slave (Page164)
Go your own way (Page 166)

78

It's time to listen to your gut. You give the slave a sad, sorry look as you step away, his whispering shouting continue until it's far beyond you. You keep waiting for him to start shouting for real, but you don't hear anything—or at least you don't think you do, unable to separate the cries of slaves in the basement with what might actually be an attempt at intelligible speech and dire calls for help from the basement mistresses. That's when you see it: the basement door leading to the backyard. It's fully open now and you can hear chattering outside and also feel the cold breeze blowing in. The air smells so sweet, tinged with woodsmoke and grass. Your muscles twitch, begging you to let them fire off in a mad sprint to the outside.

But you keep your measured march as you go towards the open door, ignoring the last set of cells and occupied stations. No one calls out to you or asks what you're doing and before you know it, you're out in the backyard, the cold air chilling your skin.

You take in your surroundings. Just as when you arrived, there are slaves still toiling to finish some of the backyard preparations but there are also dozens of mistresses out here, sipping on warm coffee and munching on snacks. They huddle in groups and around the firepits of the backyard, warming themselves by the orange flames. It's only because of the setting sun that no one seems to immediately notice you emerging from the basement and you quickly step to the edge of the backyard to catch your breath.

Then you peer down the narrow path that led you from the front of the manor to the backyard. You notice now how there is another path leading off from it, this one into the woods surrounding Matriarch Manor. All you have to do is nonchalantly head down there and you can escape, free...

...and completely naked. Once the sun has completely set, there is sure to be an even more vicious chill in the air. Luckily for you, you didn't bring your wallet or keys, stashing both at your place nearly three miles away, so you *could* get home completely naked, but it sure won't be a fun journey.

As you're pondering the trek, you notice a rack of luxurious fur coats that have been brought out for the mistresses to don should the cold be too much for them. Maybe you could, ah, "borrow" one? No one's noticed you lurking at the edge of the backyard yet, so who's to say that they'll notice you carrying a coat off to the manor's side path?

Then again, you've already come this far. Do you really want to risk it all just to have a cozier walk home? Well, a cozier walk and less chance you're stopped by someone who sees a naked man stumbling through the woods, that is.

Escape while totally naked (Page 158)
Grab a jacket (Page 167)

79

"Alright," you say. "Sure. Thanks man, I appreciate it."

The slave nods and you follow him back the way you came, You also follow his mannerisms, walking with his same gait and his same shameful-yet-purposeful look that seems to ward off the curiosity of the surrounding mistresses as they engage in play in the basement's discipline stations. You make a right, and then another right, and you find yourself grateful for the slave's assistance since this feels completely like the wrong way to you.

It's when you make a third right that you think something might be wrong.

"Hey," you whisper, once you're in a stretch of hallway with mostly empty cells and sleeping slaves. "Aren't we going in a circle? Three rights? You sure this is the way?"

"I'm sure," says the slave. His voice is no longer a whisper now and he turns back to you with a dark smile on his face. He takes a big breath in. "Guards! Mistresses! There's an escaped slave down here! Come quick!"

Chatter begins to spread throughout the basement, followed by a low chiming sound that seems to be some sort of alarm. Rages surges through you at the slave's betrayal.

"You son of a..." you say, getting ready to sock him in the face. But the slave is ready for you, getting the first blow to your stomach and making you crumple down the ground in pain. He gives you another kick, just above your chastity device, and he shouts again.

"Mistresses! I'm over here! I've subdued him!"

Laughing wildly to himself, the slave tackles you, holding you down with all his strength.

"You stupid fool!" he says in your ear. "You moron! You're so screwed and I'm gonna be *so* rewarded!"

His laughter is unhinged and feral, as is his strength which keeps up with even your mightiest attempts to shove him off you. You kick your feet and flail at him and even try to spit in his face, but he's more animal than man in that moment, keeping you pinned down until a half-dozen uniformed mistresses swarm over the two of you. They have more serious bindings than you've seen so far at the manor, with sets of handcuffs and ankle cuffs for you that keep your feet only two inches apart and that lock your wrists behind your back. The women hoist you to your feet and shout you into submission, their shrill yells making you cower and bow before them.

One of the mistresses tears the key away from you and slaps you in the face with a gloved hand, the impact dizzying you. She slaps you again and shouts in your face so loud you start to cry. The other mistresses jeer and deride you, poking you roughly in the sides and in the thighs and take turns shoving your head one way and then the other. It's all so chaotic and disorienting that you feel whatever resolve you'd built up over the evening instantly crumble... and soon you're crumbling too, falling down to your knees while the women start to kick you, using you as their personal sandbag in some unspoken competition to see who can get you to groan and whimper the loudest.

Through the haze of pain and shocking treatment, you see the same mistress who took the key from you turn towards the other slave. She gives him a tight, prim smile.

"Very good, slave. You've served the manor well. I think a reward is in order."

The slave looks deliriously pleased, practically bouncing up and down where he stands in excitement.

The mistress snaps her fingers and starts to walk down the hallway. "Come with me," she tells him in a bored tone. "I'll let you clean the grit from my feet and, if you do a very good job, I'll even let you lick the shit off my asshole."

You're sickened at how ravenous the slave looks as he follows the mistress away, his tongue almost wagging out of his mouth in perverted joy. What kind of a "reward" is that?

Not that you have much time to think about it. The women continue kicking you until they're forced to stop and catch their breath. You think then that your torment is over, surely, but then the leather straps come out, each one identical to fit the mistresses' uniforms. They start to bring their leather straps down on you in a rain of stinging pain, and even with your hands up to try to block the blows you can feel the heat of each strike, the straps catching you on the forearms, and the back and the chest and even in your armpits.

You start to scream for mercy, knowing that they aren't going to stop anytime soon.

Always be careful who you trust.

THE END

80

"I'm sorry," you say. "I need to do this alone. It's not your fault, just what I have to do."

The male slave shrugs but wastes no further time on you, heading in the direction you just came. At the next bend he pauses and peeks around the corner and once he's deemed it safe, he continues on, out of sight. You wonder if he was right—if he really *was* going to help you, but you can't think of it right now. Maybe you'll see him again... whatever he was trying to do by escaping the cell but not wanting to be freed from his chastity.

You continue on.

But as you work your way through the basement's labyrinth, you start to hear chatter—a *lot* of chatter. It sounds urgent and worried and then it's followed by a low chiming bell that, to you, sounds like an alarm.

Did the slave narc on you? Or was he caught? Fuck. There's no way to know if your cover is blown. You could keep going the way you've been going, nice and steady, or maybe it's time to cut and run before you're found walking around with the basement's master key.

This is a tough choice, for sure, made all the harder by the fact that you feel so, so close to escaping Matriarch Manor.

Remain calm and go slow (Page 169)
Find an exit as soon as possible (Page 171)

81

Fuck, it's cold out! Sure, it's only a few miles back to your place, but what if the temperature drops even more? What if you get lost? What if someone sees you wandering through the woods and roads on your back? You can't take these risks, not when there is a bounty of warm fur coats just a few feet away.

You hang along the edge of the backyard, staying in the inky darkness as much as possible, and slot yourself between the tree line and the nearest rack of coats. They look *so* warm and even smell performed, the pleasant smell of mossy oak and juniper filling your nostrils. You reach out to grab a coat and tug on it gently.

It doesn't give. You tug more firmly this time, and yet it still stays tight on the hanger. You try another and the same thing happens, causing you to take a look to see if the coats are somehow tied to their hangers. As far as you can tell, they aren't; there just seem to be so many of them that it's hard to get any one out without moving the entire pile to one side, something you're not ready to do.

You'll just tug harder. One strong pull, that's all it should take. You listen to the backyard gathering rise and fall with conversation and clapping and shouting, trying to time your pull so that it will be muffled by the sounds. Your pulse is in your ears now and your body is quaking from the cold.

You count in your head, telling yourself you'll pull on the third swell from the outdoor chatter.

Someone screams and then an entire gaggle of women shout and clap at some unseen spectacle.

Three.

There's a loud whistling sound, followed by the crack of a whip and the blood-curdling scream of a man. More laughter. Someone blows dramatic kisses.

Two.

A cracking sound floats across the backyard, followed by another, then one more. Women ooohh and aaahhh and then there's the sound of tears and an incredulous scoff and something else that sounds an awful lot like a chains jangling.

One. It's time.

You tug on a coat hard, determined to grab it this time, and then you stare in horror as the entire rack starts to careen towards you. You try to push it back, but the shift in weight is too sudden and the more the rack leans towards you, the faster it falls, the coats offering nowhere to push against. Your hands slip through the sea of furs and the rack tackles you to the ground.

Well, at least you're warm as the women start to gather around you, trying to figure out what's going on.

"Oh Christ, these slaves get more and more clumsy every month," one mistress says, snapping her fingers to get some of the larger slaves over to lift the rack over you.

As it's lifted, the women see holding the master key to the basement.

"Holy shit," one says. "Why does he have the master?"

Just then, women burst out of the basement, huffing and puffing.

"We have a theft!" one of them shouts. "A male just took the master key! We just got a report of it!"

"It's right here," says a mistress with her hair tied up in a neat and proper bun. Her dark eyes glance down at you. "You have a lot to answer for, my poor little slave."

Before you can summon the strength to stand and run off into the woods, slaves—fellow men—are picking you up and holding you fast by the arms, dragging you back to the basement to be questioned...

Goddamnit, you were so close! If only you hadn't gotten greedy at the end.

Alas.

THE END

82

It's time to listen to your gut. You walk with a measured step, saying to yourself that you've made it this far in the basement by not rushing. Even as the chatter and unnerving alarm grows louder, you chew on your lower lip as you continue on, praying whatever it is, it has nothing to do with you.

Please please please please, you think.

That's when you see it: the basement door leading to the backyard. It's fully open now and you can hear chattering outside and also feel the cold breeze blowing in. The air smells so sweet, tinged with woodsmoke and grass. Your muscles twitch, begging you to let them fire off in a mad sprint to the outside.

But you keep your measured march as you go towards the open door, ignoring the last set of cells and occupied stations. No one calls out to you or asks what you're doing and before you know it, you're out in the backyard, the cold air chilling your skin.

You take in your surroundings. Just as when you arrived, there are slaves still toiling to finish some of the backyard preparations but there are also dozens of mistresses out here, sipping on warm coffee and munching on snacks. They huddle in groups and around the firepits of the backyard, warming themselves by the orange flames. It's only because of the setting sun that no one seems to immediately notice you emerging from the basement and you quickly step to the edge of the backyard to catch your breath.

Then you peer down the narrow path that led you from the front of the manor to the backyard. You notice now how there is another path leading off from it, this one into the woods surrounding Matriarch Manor. All you have to do is nonchalantly head down there and you can escape, free...

...and completely naked. Once the sun has completely set, there is sure to be an even more vicious chill in the air. Luckily for you, you didn't bring your wallet or keys, stashing both at your place nearly three miles away, so you *could* get home completely naked, but it sure won't be a fun journey.

As you're pondering the trek, you notice a rack of luxurious fur coats that have been brought out for the mistresses to don should the cold be too much for them. Maybe you could, ah, "borrow" one? No one's noticed you lurking at the edge of the backyard yet, so who's to say that they'll notice you carrying a coat off to the manor's side path?

Then again, you've already come this far. Do you really want to risk it all just to have a cozier walk home? Well, a cozier walk and less chance you're stopped by someone who sees a naked man stumbling through the woods, that is.

Escape while completely naked (Page 158)
Grab a coat (Page 167)

83

You take off running like a bat out of hell, your feet pounding on the floor as your pulse races. You turn down the hallways blindly, desperately searching for an escape as the chatter turn to shouting and the grim alarm seems to get louder.

That's when you see it: the basement door leading to the backyard. It's fully open now and you can hear chattering outside and also feel the cold breeze blowing in. The air smells so sweet, tinged with woodsmoke and grass.

Freedom is twenty feet away. You count the seconds it takes. 1, 2, 3, 4...

The tension of the moment is maddening as freedom looms fifteen feet away, then ten, then... the door closes from the outside. You look around, confused, and as you turn all the way around you see a half-dozen mistresses in crisp uniforms hot on your heels. With your heart pounding in your ears and the chaos of the basement, you couldn't hear them at all, but somehow they caught up to you, perhaps because you were making much more noise than you thought.

"Where do you think you're going, little slave?" one asks.

The time for being calm is over. You turn and run towards the basement door, wondering just what your odds are of getting away from the manor once you're outside. But as you pull on the basement door, it refuses to budge, either barricaded or locked somehow from the outside. You yank on the door desperately, cursing under your breath.

"No, no no no no, god please no," you say, feeling the world fall out from under your feet.

The next thing you feel is the grip of the uniformed mistresses as they pull you away from the door.

"God can't help you now," another one of the mistresses says. She's holding a leather strap in one hand that she brings down on the backside of your knee, the sting of the blow making you crumple down to the floor.

The mistresses gather around you, two on each side to grab you under the armpit and drag you away while the others follow. Your heels drag on the basement floor.

You don't know where you're going. But you know it won't be good.

THE END

84

Fuck this. Of all the things up the stone stairs from the basement, you *never* imagined that you'd find a chaotic kitchen ruled by a bitchy kitchen mistress with no patience.

"Uh, sorry, wrong way," you say, trying to slink back down the steps.

The kitchen mistress doesn't even blink. She looks beyond angry now and shouts again, so much louder this time that she catches the attention of slaves working at other stations in the overly bright kitchen.

"STOP!" she roars "How DARE you walk away from me!"

You can keep going for the stairs—and hope she doesn't follow you down to the basement—or you can stay, subjecting yourself to the kitchen mistress's wrath in hopes of avoiding a more terrible fate later...

Stay in the kitchen (Page 177)
Try to go back to the basement to check out the office (Page 147)

85

You're in a gambling mood today. You give the kitchen mistress a low apology, eliciting a long, angry sigh from her. But once she's done looking angry, she has two large helper slaves of hers bring over a garish maid's outfit, shouting at you as she directs you to put it on. It's tight in all the least comfortable places and once you think you've got it on, the kitchen mistress tugs and pulls at the fabric, adjusting it until she's huffily satisfied with the way you look. She shoves you towards a pair of swinging doors that seem to lead out into the thrumming party.

"Get out there and go entertain!" she barks.

With so many slaves and mistresses in the thick of the party, you feel confident that you've got at least some time before you start to stick out and shuffle out into the fray, looking for an opportunity to be useful. You have no experience being this kind of "slave" or even really submitting for that matter, but there's a kind of crackling energy in the air that fills you with excitement as you pass by so many gorgeous women decked out in high fetish fashions and elegant attire. Most seem to be deeply engaged in their own conversations, or "playing" with some poor male who is quivering beneath them, but despite that a few look your way... and not with malicious or angry looks either.

If anything, you'd say most of the looks you're getting are appraising as these women try to decide if they should engage with you, many of them looking you up and down long enough to even make you feel good about yourself, in a very specific kind of way, of course.

This is not the kind of attention you're used to. Not that you're bad looking or anything, but you're far more used to a night out at the bars or in your wilder moment the clubs, with you and men like you doing most of the looking while the women present laugh and dance and drink their nights away. But clearly in Matriarch Manor things are different. Here, women have the power and men are the objects of ogling and taunting stares. At first it's a giddy feeling to have so much attention, but your mind quickly makes an important connection:

Just as men in bars and clubs ogle women, they also make moves on them and try to exert power *over* them. That very same thing has already happened to you at the manor, and it's sure to continue.

You're weaving through a claustrophobic pocket of the party when someone grabs you by your chastity device, yanking you over, cock and balls first, to where she's enjoying a glass of something big and brown that smells like overproof whiskey. Keeping a firm grip on your cage she gives you a tipsy, heated stare.

"When I say 'Jump!' you sissy', you say 'How high?'," she tells you.

"What?" you ask, not following.

"Jump!" she shouts.

Does she really want you say 'How high?' and to jump for her. You look down at the poofy skirt of your maid's uniform, wondering just how firm of a grip the mistress has on you.

"Jump!" she shouts again. Her nails dig into your balls and you dance from foot to foot in pain.

"How high?" you squeak out.

"As high as you can!" she orders.

You look up at the mistress. She has the tall, thin look of a gymnast, and if it wasn't for her slate gray tailored suit which frames full, heart-shaped hips and such a round ass it threatens to rip the fabric, you'd swear she was. Her blazer practically hangs off her sharp shoulders and despite having the warm, olive skin of somewhere in the Mediterranean, her short black hair is streaked with platinum blonde hair dye, the contrast no more evident than with her full, dark eyebrows. She gives you a smile with plump purple lips, watching you expectantly.

You jump before you can let yourself worry about it too much. A little voice inside tells you this is a terrible idea. Squatting down, you then launch yourself up, feeling a rush of relief as the mistress brings her clawed grasp up with your jump. Your floofy maid's uniform flutters about, the skirt rising up before sinking back down as you land.

She lets go of you, sparing your balls.

"That's as high as you can jump? No wonder why you're a sissy bitch," she says in an icy tone. She laughs, a laugh that encapsulates all the mean better-than-you girls you've come across in high school, college, and beyond. "Get on your knees, sissy, you're too pathetic be standing with me."

Just your luck that you had to wind up entertaining a mistress on the bossy, haughty end of the spectrum.

You lower yourself to your knees, the dyed blonde mistress now towering above you. She stares down at you derisively.

"That's better," she says, her dark plum lips spreading wide. She takes a long sip of her strong whiskey. "Exactly where you belong."

The tip of her open-toed heels slides under your chastity device and you feel the mistress's toes tickling your balls. It's both a pleasant and surprising feeling, and you tense yourself for a sudden kick to your crotch.

"How small are you down there, loser?" she asks, looming over you.

It takes a second to catch on that she's asking how big your cock is. You tell her the number. It's never been a point of shame for you, but as the mistress laughs raucously to herself, you feel the weight of her grinding humiliation.

"Oh my GOD," she shrieks. "You could've told me anything! No WONDER why you're dressed up like you have a clitty instead of a dick!" She pushes against your device with her foot, continuing to give into her laughter. "Why did you pick a number so small? Oh wait—is it even smaller and you thought *that* was an improvement? That is SO sad. Did you tell me a fake number? Oh it really is a clitty, isn't it?"

You shake your head no. "That's how bi—that's my size, Miss," you admit, the shame of her words pelting you like hot chips of charcoal. The look in the woman's face as you admit this is full of disregard for you, a gleeful, nasty look that both makes you want to throttle the bitch and have her grace you with her favor, and the only thing you loathe more in the moment than your humiliation is that bizarre duality of wanting and not wanting her.

"Rub your clit on my leg," she says after another sip of whiskey. "Come on! I wanna see if I can get you to cum."

You hesitate. So far, *most* of your humiliations in the manor have been things done to you but this is different. This is you having to take action to make a fool out of yourself.

The mistress thwaps you in the balls and you double over, clutching your crotch.

"Hump my leg!" she demands tipsily over the bassy thump of the party's music. "Or else... or else I'm going to *really* make you feel like a sissy and cut your balls off!'

A drunken threat, for sure, but you don't want to find out just how much she can torment you if she wants to. So you crawl towards her, positioning your legs around her awkwardly and pushing your cage against her shin. It's not a great angle, but really there's no angle you can imagine working for humping someone's leg.

You start to rock your hips. Even your shy starting motions make the mistress burst into even more laughter, the sound of it grating on your ears. Your cock is anything but hard right now, but you're forced to hump against her leg like you've got a massive hard-on, all to the sounds of her—and increasingly, other mistresses—laughing and pointing at your maladroit efforts.

"Wait wait wait," says the mistress, barely able to breathe now from all her laughter. "Take that stupid uniform off. I need to see if you're as pathetic and stupid as I think."

Under her severe instruction, you strip the maid's uniform away, and with each piece you remove the mistress—and those gathered around her—laugh louder and point more cruelly at your body, making all kinds of comments about how you're not a "real" man and how you should be punished for even thinking you can pass as an actual maid.

When you're naked, except for your chastity device, the mistress wrinkle her nose, making a disgusted face. "Ewww, maybe you should've left the uniform on," she says, deriding you. She flaps her hand, as if beckoning you to go away.

"I'm done," she announces, either having grown bored of her antics or simply wanting to humiliate you further.

As she engages with the other mistresses in the group, you slink away, actually feeling a little bit dejected, bizarrely enough.

You could continue to serve the mistresses in hopes of finding one more likely to show you favor or you could try your luck with the antique elevator at the other end of the Salon, the one that seems to be letting mistresses out into the party every few minutes. Maybe you would fare better on another floor...

Try your luck with the elevator (Page 179)
Continue to serve the Salon mistresses (Page 181)

86

"I'm sorry Miss, yes, I'm the maid," you respond, trying to sound as humble and apologetic as possible. You don't dare meet her gaze, instead focusing on the shiny floor beneath your feet.

The kitchen mistress scoffs, her lips pulling back into a sneer of contempt. "Forget being a maid," she spits. "We'll find someone with a half a brain for that."

She steps closer to you, her high heels clicking ominously against the tile floor. You can feel the heat from her body, a stark contrast to the cold fear coursing through your veins.

"You think you can just turn your back on me?" she asks, her voice dripping with venom. "That you're above the rules? That's not how it works here."

Before you can react, she delivers a swift kick to your balls. Pain sears through your leg and you stumble backward, barely managing to stay upright. A tiny gasp escapes your lips, the only outward sign of your discomfort.

"That's for trying to scurry away," she hisses. She turns toward the rest of the kitchen slaves who have stopped their work to watch the spectacle. "And this..." she continues, delivering another cruel kick to your balls, "... is just because I don't like you."

You fall onto one knee this time unable to suppress a grunt of pain. The kitchen mistress smiles in satisfaction at your predicament.

"Now," she says with an icy calmness that sends shivers down your spine. "I think it's time we put you in your place."

She motions for two of the larger kitchen slaves to come forward. You try to get up but they hold you down effortlessly, their hands like iron bands around your arms.

With a playful twinkle in her eyes that belies her ruthless demeanor, the kitchen mistress picks up a wooden spoon from one of the tables and approaches you.

"This is what happens when someone thinks they're above their station," she declares before bringing down the spoon hard against your bare backside.

The impact stings more than you can imagine and involuntary tears spring into your eyes. But more than the physical pain, it's the humiliation that cuts deep. Again and again she strikes until your backside is throbbing and red-hot with pain. All the while she maintains an air of nonchalance that makes it all so much worse. She finally stops after what feels like an eternity but instead of comforting relief all you feel is dread knowing that this probably isn't over yet. As if reading your thoughts, she nods towards a stack of dirty dishes on one end of the kitchen.

"You're going to wash those," she orders tersely before releasing you from her minions' grip.

Barely able to stand due to pain and exhaustion, nevertheless you shuffle towards the dirty dishes obediently under her watchful gaze.

Sweat trickles down your forehead as you submerge your hands into the hot soapy water and start scrubbing away at plates encrusted with remnants of rich food too fancy for common palates like yours.

Minutes turn into a half hour and then a whole hour with you bent over a sink washing dishes while enduring taunts and sarcastic remarks from the little dictator whenever she passes by, noticing that a number of the other slaves set to work in the kitchen are chains to their stations. Finally you hear a dreadful sound of heavy clunking metal as the kitchen mistress has her two doting, obedient large slaves bring over just such a chain for you.

"These parties go on very, very late, slave," she says with an air of pride. "Sometimes until five or six in the morning. You will be working a full shift until then."

The slaves secure your ankle to the dishwashing station and the kitchen mistress strikes your ass again with the wooden spoon, purposefully hitting the spot she'd been wailing on earlier.

Despair overwhelms you as you realize you are not only not going to get your freedom from chastity, but that your very freedom from Matriarch Manor is no more. Your back aches. Your legs ache. Your hands feel tender and weak from the constant rush of scalding hot dish water. Everything about the station seems designed to be uncomfortable and after so long hunching over it, with barely a foot of chain length to help stretch your feet, you wonder how you'll ever make it through the night... or what will transpire once the mistresses of the manor realize you are a trespasser.

It's going to be a horrible, horrible night for you.

THE END

87

You wander over to the elevator, the party having taken an even darker, more intense turn. Now there are mistresses playing wicked games with the slaves right in the middle of the Salon dance floor, ranging from relatively tame by-the-balls tug-of-war to using slaves as their own personal pincushions in an attempt to break them. You avert your eyes, terrified you will get sucked into the swirl if anyone sees you looking for too long. The only silver lining in all of this is how distracted the mistresses are, allowing you to get over to the antique elevator without much attention. Its doors are open and, lo and behold, the elevator is blissfully empty!

You hop inside and study the floors—B, M, 2F, 3F—trying to pick a floor to explore.

You hit 3, but the button doesn't seem to work, the elevator emitting a low buzz. Is it broken? Somehow blocked off? Instead you hit 2F and the doors slowly start to close.

Just as they're about to seal shut, they jolt open and you find that you're face to face with two young mistresses enter, both in beige jodhpurs that seem to be painted on their legs with matching white blouses, along with tall riding boots. They both have the vibrant glow of youthful innocence to them, and both have flushed cheeks from what you guess are more than a few glasses of wine. One has short-cropped blonde hair that she's pushed back behind her ears, while the other has a long ponytail of fine, silky hair.

"Floor, Misses?" you say stiffly as you try to act your part as elevator attendant.

The mistresses giggle.

"Two," the blonde says. Then she tentatively adds: "Slave."

You press the button for the second floor, grateful they didn't choose another floor, and the elevator doors close. The mistresses look at each other excitedly and then back to you as the elevator trundles its way into the manor's basement floor.

In a flash, the ponytailed mistress closes the gap between you and her. She puts her hand on your chest and from her breath you can smell she must be quite drunk.

"You look fun," she purrs, her mistress friend sidling up next to you. "This is our first manor party and we are dying to have some more *fun*."

The blonde slips a hand between your legs, petting your chastity cage. "We sure are. And if you play with us, we might even make it worth your while..."

You try to puzzle out why these women simply don't command you "play" with them, still unable to wrap your head around whatever protocol seems to be in place for Matriarch Manor that allows some women to demand whatever they want while others almost seem to be seeking permission. Although perhaps it's not you they're seeking permission from, but whoever they think you've submitted yourself to...

The ponytailed mistress's hand moves to your nipple. She flicks it playfully, making it harden as the elevator comes to a thudding stop. The doors open, revealing the second floor's nondescript hallways.

"Well?" the blonde asks. "How about it? Can you join us... slave?"

She steps off the elevator with a sultry stride, keeping her clear eyes locked on yours. The ponytailed mistress slips two fingers into the ring of your chastity cage, urging you forward and tilting her head to the side. She gives you a puppy dog pout.

"Why won't you join us, slave?" she asks petulantly.

These drunk, young mistresses seem incredibly eager to have a slave to play with. And while you don't know what their definition of "play" is, this is probably the kindest you've been treated since you arrived at the manor. How exactly would they make it worth your while?

With a joyous rush, you imagine them—somehow—being able to take you out of your cage! Your cock surges as you imagine the freedom you'd feel and then even go as far as to consider the remote possibility these young vixens would let you fuck them. A pipedream, perhaps, but one that makes you try to get rock hard nonetheless.

Go with the young mistresses (Page 184)
Regretfully decline (Page 186)

88

Just a little longer, you tell yourself, feeling confident that if you could just ingratiate yourself to the *right* mistress, there might be another way out from this predicament.

You busy yourself as you thread through the crowd, keeping your head bowed any time you see a stern mistress or hear some angry ranting. You think that maybe now that you're without your maid uniform, you should go back to the kitchen—just in case the kitchen mistress sees you—but you push on, desperately looking for any mistress with a hint of kindness to her.

That's when you see the young woman sitting in the corner. She's on a designer velvet chair with a deep seat and an artsy high back, and she's tapping away at her phone with an intense look of concentration and, most importantly, a kind smile on her face. Her cheeks are flushed from alcohol and her face—a golden pixie's face with choppy black bangs that bring out her smudgy makeup—is sparkling with delight and anticipation. The mistress wears a pink ruffled Lolita dress with an oversized belt and shoulder sleeves, the cutesy dress matching a pair of pink combat boots and a playful heart-shaped purse, like she's going for some kind of gothic-punk version of Barbie dress-up. She seems smaller than she is tall, with a trim figure with modest curves hidden by the ruffles of her dress.

You pad over to the mistress and get down on one knee. It seems a tad chivalrous—and a little foolish—but it's what comes natural to you. The mistress doesn't seem to notice, still entranced by the glow of her phone. Her fingers tap across the screen wildly and you wonder if you should interrupt her to ask if she needs anything.

Cautiously, you clear your throat and ask in a mild voice: "Miss, is there anything I can get you?"

She glances up from her phone for a second at you and then goes right back to what she was tapping out. Just as you're starting to feel like a complete dolt for getting down on one knee to try to ingratiate yourself to this woman, she does something you never would've guessed: she reaches down and hikes up the ruffle hem of her poofy pink Lolita dress, pulling the whole thing up so that it's well above her knees. What you see under the hem of that dress are her pale, soft legs and her completely bald, pink pussy.

Reaching a hand over the pulled-up hem, she points a pink nail between her legs. The implication is quite clear.

Not being prepared for *this*, you slowly inch your way between her legs. Once you're there, she drops the hem again and you hear her quick tapping resume once more. You press your face towards her pussy.

Your heart pounds in your chest as you push your face closer to her sweet spot. The air is filled with the intoxicating aroma of her arousal, a mix of musk and a hint of vanilla. Your lips quiver at the anticipation of feeling her against your tongue. You can feel the heat emanating from between her thighs, a stark contrast to the AC-driven chill in the room. With the first experimental lick, you find yourself immersed in her taste, an inexplicable blend of tangy sweetness that makes you want to delve deeper. Her skin is silky smooth against your tongue, which now darts to explore every fold and crevice.

She doesn't seem to pay you any mind, lost in whatever was keeping her entertained on her phone. Does she really not think about you down there? Or is she so used to this—are all the mistresses of the manor so used to the service of slaves—that she really can see you as nothing more than a living vibrator, fated to deliver her pleasure? You ponder these questions as you continue worshiping her pussy, your humiliation growing... alongside your arousal.

The more you taste her, the more intoxicated you become. Her essence fills all your senses. The sound of her soft moans becomes musical notes in your ears, harmonizing with the rhythm set by your darting tongue. Each stroke stokes you brown lust and each muffled whimper from the woman makes your cock surge against its metal cage. You curse yourself for being stuck in that goddamn stupid device, not even able to get hard!

Then her thighs tighten around your head as if holding onto for dear life, one left lifting to wrap herself around you. You're pressed hard against her wet lips now, struggling to breathe. Do minutes pass? A half hour? You lose track of time as you lash your tongue up and down her, taking turns between suckling on her clit and dipping your tongue deep between her sweet, vanilla musk folds.

You can feel as she nears climax. Her legs tense and her thighs press harder against your head, squeezing your ears against your skull. But even in her orgasm, the woman is so obviously otherwise occupied with *whatever* she's doing on her phone that her moaning is muffled like it's an inconvenience and her wild gushing against your face is done with all the boring routine of blowing her nose.

She stills and then comes the harsh reality as she pushes you away like a used and discarded napkin. You try to limber away, but your legs are so sore from their held position that you stumble anyway, falling back on your ass as the woman's ruffled dress scratches across your wet face.

Looking up, you see the woman *still* is staring at her glowing screen, oblivious that you're even still there. It's at that moment, when you're still tasting her on your lips and trying to catch your breath, that you hear a dreadfully familiar voice.

"Well, well, well. If it isn't my drunken friend from the bar. How's chastity life treating you? Had I known you were interested in coming to the manor, I would've invited you myself, you naughty party crasher you."

You know that voice. It's Mistress Merciless. The mistress whose leg you're humping looks over at Mistress Merciless and you follow her gaze.

It's Mistress Merciless alright. Although you could try to play dumb and convince her you're someone else. It might ward her off from taking an undue interest in you, or it might incite her further. With how small and foolish and dumb you're feeling, it's hard to think straight on what the better choice is.

Admit you are who Mistress Merciless thinks you are and talk to her (Page 187)
Pretend to be someone else (Page 189)

89

You clench your teeth and unclench your fists as you make the decision to follow them. Their youthful exuberance is infectious, it's true, but it's their promise to make it "worth your while" that truly captures your interest. You step off the elevator with a sense of trepidation, but also excitement. Perhaps these young mistresses could be the key to your freedom.

"Good boy," the ponytailed mistress purrs, her fingers brushing your bare skin. She leads you down the hallway, her friend following closely behind. You can't help but watch as their hips sway in time to an unheard rhythm, their matching outfits accentuating every curve and dip of their bodies.

Their attention is intoxicating; they hang on your every, servile word as though it were gospel, their eyes sparkling with genuine interest. They flirt openly with you, dropping innuendos and double entendres into casual conversation until even you find yourself blushing. Their laughter echoes off the wallpapered hallways, adding to the second floor's metered elegance.

After what feels like hours of wandering aimlessly through the labyrinthine second floor, one of the girls stops suddenly in front of an open cell door. She peers inside curiously before calling out excitedly to her friend.

"Look what I found!" she exclaims, holding up a folded-up note that was tucked behind one of the second floor hallway's works of art. She unfolds it. It seems to be a map of the manor, the sort designed for those lurking around. *You* certainly didn't draw it however... but who did?

The girls exchange a glance before turning back towards you, twin smiles spreading across their faces like wildfire. "Now this," the blonde says triumphantly, "is interesting, isn't it, slave?"

Your heart sinks as you watch them examine the map with great interest, poking and prodding at them as though they were some sort of exotic artifact. The reality of what this discovery means slowly begins to dawn on you: they've found evidence of a male trespasser in Matriarch Manor.

"Oh my god, this is such a score!" the ponytailed mistress squeals in delight.

"Yes," agrees her friend, "We should alert the other mistresses. They can lock down the manor, or something, and find out who this belongs to."

She turns towards you then, her expression hardening slightly as she adds: "You better hope it doesn't belong to you, *slave*. I mean, like, what are the odds but why don't we just make sure you don't go anywhere..."

They push you through one of the second floor's many identical doors, locking it behind them as the blonde mistress goes to a phone sitting on a nightstand next to a bed with fine silk sheets.

"Yes. Hi. We uh... we think there's an intruder in the manor. Oh, because we found a map. Yes, we're with a slave now. There is? Interesting. Okay, give us a call back. We'll be here."

The mistress looks at you. "Funny, it seems like there has been trouble with an errant slave tonight," she says, sending shivers down your spine. Could *that* be you? Your head is spinning now, having never imagined there would be another slave trying to lurk through the manor. Goddamnit!

"They're going to do a headcount of the slaves. Someone will be up soon to get your information,," the blonde says. "In the meantime... why don't we have some fun?"

But fun is the last thing on your mind as the mistresses shimmy out of all of their clothing, stripping down to just their underwear. They take seats in plush, nailhead armchairs, spreading their legs, making it more than a little obvious what will be expected of you.

In a different situation, this might be bliss to you. But now you simply must service them as you wait for this "headcount" to reveal the truth behind who you are and why you're sneaking around Matriarch Manor.

If only you'd never went with these women and they never found the map, maybe you'd be a few steps closer to your chastised freedom now, instead of waiting for the inevitable moment when those two young vixens cash you in for their social standing at the manor and you face the icy wrath of Mistress Merciless herself.

THE END

90

Despite the temptation, you resist your baser instincts and give the young mistresses a sad look.

"I'm sorry Misses, I have other tasks I attend to," you say.

They return your frown with even poutier looks, the ponytailed mistress letting go of your chastity so she can join her blonde friend. Part of you aches to go with them and to feel their supple hands on your body again.

"Are you *sure*?" asks the ponytailed mistress. "We'll have so, so much fun. Promise."

"Totally promise," says the blonde mistress. "What else do you have to do, anyway?"

Thinking on your feet, you say: "I, uh... I'm needed on the third floor. Some routine cleaning, but I must ensure the Mistresses are well taken care of, you understand."

The two women look at each other curiously.

"The third floor?" asks the ponytailed mistress. "I've been wanting to see what's up there..."

"Me too..." says the blonde.

"We could go... together," offers the ponytailed mistress, still amazing you with how moderate she's being in her attitude towards you. Both of them, really. They truly must be new to Matriarch Manor based on what you've seen so far this evening.

Now you are faced with another grueling choice. You *could* go with these women to the third floor, let them "play" with you, and have earned your way an easy pass to get up there without anyone catching you...

...or you can decline them again and continue on your way, hoping beyond hope that you make it up there without incident.

Decline them once more and say you have other duties to attend to (Page 194)
Give in and go with them (Page 245)

91

Who are you kidding? Try to get one over on Mistress Merciless in Matriarch Manor? You're more likely to grow wings and fly away. Knowing you've been caught, you sigh.

"Hello, Mistress," you say, trying to show deference to the tall, raven-haired woman with the glowering stare.

She's just as haughty as when you encountered her last weekend and just as cocky. Of course then, when you were several drinks deep, you took that attitude to be the spoiled snotty air of privilege. That's why you said what you said and made the scene you did... even if you could admit in the sober light of day that it was excessive. But now, having seen the manor with your own eyes, you know there's more to her attitude than unearned privilege: there's power in it too, real power from Mistress Merciless having real status at Matriarch Manor. These women—and the slaves, for that matter—respect her, even fear her. Had you only known all this before you got into a shouting match with her at that bar, you wouldn't be in this mess right now...

"Hello... slave?" she purrs, a smirk on her crimson lips. "Is that what this is about? You've come to join Matriarch Manor as a slave, have you? I wish you'd said something earlier. I could easily arrange for that."

A group gathers to watch Mistress Merciless talk down to you, no one on the outer ring of fashionably dressed mistresses daring to interrupt or even speak too loudly. Under their hush the music continues the thump along, as do the more distant sounds of sadistic torment and cold, icy laughter.

"I'm sorry for introducing, Mistress," you say, wishing you'd rehearsed something to say should you run into Mistress Merciless. "I was just hoping that you could, you know... find it in your heart to release me from this, uh... from the..."

Mistress Merciless scoffs. "From your chastity? THAT'S why you're here?" The mistress puts her hands up on her leather-clad hips, her red-and-black catsuit in its harlequin pattern making her pert bottom and heavy breasts seem exaggerated, while somehow managing to make the mistress's waist look teeny-tiny. The catsuit has one of those patterns that's dizzy to look at for too long and even though you keep pulling your eyes away, the bold body of Mistress Merciless keeps you coming back for more.

"Yes...?" you squeak.

The mistress's face breaks open in a loud, booming laugh. "Well, my my! That is bold! I... I don't think I've ever had a male just *ask* for his freedom. If nothing else, you're a funny one, I'll give you that, you little shit."

You bow your head and stare at the Salon floor, studying the parquet wood. You don't want to overplay your hand but are you actually... getting through to the mistress? You push your luck further.

"Even just coming out of my device sooner would be wonderful, Mistress. A year is such a very long time..."

"I know it is," says Mistress Merciless. She squats down and tilts your chin up with a single finger, forcing you to look at her severe, cruel face. "That's why I put you in there. So you would have 'such a very long time' to think about how utterly rude you were."

You swallow and put on a sorry, despondent look, drawing from your own feelings of exhaustion to try to sell the mistress on your remorse. But Mistress Merciless only smirks.

"Do you think I'm weak?" she asks.

"No," you're quick to say. And it's true. You certainly do *not* think Mistress Merciless is weak.

Mistress Merciless nods to herself. "Well, male, I'll tell you what. If you do what I tell you to, right here and right now with no dithering or hesitation, I'll cut your sentence down to a month."

A month. You could do a month, right? It's certainly better than a year, twelve times better in fact. But what will the mistress require of you?

You nod in agreement. If you *really* don't want to do whatever she says, you can just decline... right?

Mistress Merciless raises her brows. "Really? Just like that? You don't even want to hear it before you agree?" There's both approval and incredulity in her voice; if nothing else, she seems amused with you. "If you insist. Here's my offer..."

Several of the watching mistresses lean in, eager to hear what Mistress Merciless is about to say.

"I've had a bit too much champagne to drink and the ladies room is so very far away. If *you* get down on your back and offer to be my toilet so I don't have to leave the party, I promise to let your out of chastity after just a month. Still interested?"

Bring yourself to agree to be her... you know (Page 196)
Draw the line. Enough is enough (Page 200)

92

You tilt your head down and say, "I'm very sorry Mistress, I think you've mistaken me for someone else."

You look up at Mistress Merciless through the veil of your fallen bangs, hoping that between being undressed and keeping your voice a little deeper—it was deeper, right?—she'll believe she's mistaken you for someone else.

And for a second your gambit seems like it's working. Mistress Merciless tilts her head to the side as she studies you, shifting her weight from one foot to the other in her red-and-black harlequin catsuit, the diamond-like pattern making the mistress's full bust and round, generous hips look even more like an hourglass figure. She taps the toe of her heeled boot against the Salon's parquet floor, thinking.

Then she speaks and you realize how foolish your lie was.

"Do you think I'm a moron?" she asks.

You stay with your head bowed, feeling your chest tighten. Damnit.

"Helllooooo, that's a question," says Mistress Merciless impatiently. She reaches out the sharp toe of her boot and pokes you under the chin, lifting your head as she raises her leg, forcing you to look at her. She looks displeased with you.

"Answer, worm," she says. "Do you think I'm a moron?"

You shake your head as much as the toe of her boot will allow. She juts it hard up against your jaw.

"Speak."

"No, Mistress, I don't," you manage, squirming as the sharp leather pokes into you.

"Then why are you treating me like a moron?" she asks. "You think I wouldn't remember your face? Your voice? Your dumb, stupid, slumpy posture? After what you said and did to me last weekend? You've got to be absolutely mad if you think I'd forget *you*, you little shit."

Fear courses through you and the entire party seems to slow down, the crowd now moving in slow motion and even the music sounding like it's being played on a tape deck with dying batteries. You try to swallow, but the mistress's boot is dug in too deep; the spittle hangs at the back of your throat, causing you instead to try to clear your throat with an awkward cough.

Mistress Merciless sets her foot down and gives a disappointed sigh. "I have to say, I was rather curious what you were doing in the manor when I saw you but now... oh, now I am very much in a bad, bad mood. No one likes to be treated like a moron." She turns to some of the mistresses who have gathered to watch the unfolding scene. "Do they?" she asks them. They shake their heads, confirming Mistress Merciless's annoyance. "No, they don't," she says back to you, determined not to let your attempted lie go.

"Well, maybe you males do," she then adds. "I have no idea what goes on in those little cashew-sized brains of yours."

"I'm sorry Mistress," you say, wanting desperately to rub your neck where the mistress's show poked you but not wanting to irritate her further. "I just... I..." Your mind is a blank. Had you thought this far ahead, maybe you wouldn't have lied at all.

Mistress Merciless rolls her eyes and groans. "Just shut up already," she says. "And get down on your hands and knees. I'm tired. I need a rest."

When you hesitate to do as she commands, the mistress snaps her fingers and points at the floor, stomping her foot to make her point. You scuttle into an all-fours position and barely by the time you've adjusted yourself, Mistress Merciless is sitting on your back, putting her full weight on you. The woman isn't heavy by any means, but she is tall and imposing and has no problem letting you have to deal with her relaxed weight. She wiggles from side to side as you struggle to brace yourself for her.

"Stop moving!" she shouts, slapping you on the ass and making you flinch. She tries a slap on the head instead, knocking your skull to one side and you squeeze your entire body to keep your back as rigid and straight as possible. Moments later, a slave comes over with a tray of champagne flutes. Mistress Merciless takes one and begins to talk with the mistresses around her, several of whom grab their own slave to sit on. These other men seem to be having a much easier time acting as human furniture, but you are sweating and wincing before long.

The minutes pass by as if they're hours and the conversation happening above you turns into a blur. Occasionally Mistress Merciless reaches a hand down to claw at your skin or to pinch a bit of flab on your body and, when she does, those moments feel awash with glaring, panicky color, her motions threatening to break your concentration and send both of you crashing to the floor. You try to lock your arms and squeeze your hips, eventually finding a position that puts all the strain on your poor joints as the mistress laughs and excitedly gestures and leans back now and again.

It feels like an entire night has passed by the time she stands up and you breathe a massive sigh of relief, which is quickly undercut by you wondering just how long she intends to treat you this way. Will she let you go? Is there still some small chance to get your chastity device off? Honestly, in this moment you simply want to be free of the manor and to never, ever return.

Mistress Merciless has other plans for you, though.

She gathers up a fistful of your hair and drags you with her as she walks, commanding you to stay on all fours. You stumble along, your neck stretched as she keeps her tight grip on you, and your limbs bump on the hardwood Salon floor. Your body aches and your muscles scream for a good stretch as Mistress Merciless guides you over to a slightly quieter corner of the room. She shoves you behind a frosted screen that partitions this corner off and as you look around your surroundings, you realize this nook is outfitted in comfortable velvet upholstery, with luxurious lounge chairs, a plush shag carpet, and even sound absorbing panels on the walls to create an especially secluded, oasis-like feel to the space.

"Listen to me and listen carefully," she hisses. "I have not decided what to do with you yet. If I wanted, I could have you thrown in the basement and 'sentenced' to as many months or years of hard labor as I wanted. Sure, we'd have some legal hoops to jump through, but you'd be amazed at what some campaign contributions and, ahem, 'donations' to state law enforcement will buy you when it comes to operating autonomously."

You quake under her words, trying to inch yourself away from the looming lady, only to bump into a velvet armchair. She continues, unconcerned with your mounting terror.

"Oh yes, I still need to think about *your* fate," she croons wickedly, twisting the knife of your grim anticipation deeper in. "And you know what, worm? I do my best thinking when I'm seated. Rest your head on that chair!"

She points to the velvet chair behind you and you wriggle backwards, huffing and puffing as you try to get your head back on its seat. As you do, you can see the mistress unzipping the crotch of her harlequin catsuit, exposing her pussy and ass. She straddles your body. Then she lowers herself, planting her backside right on your face! It is warm and sweaty and oh-so-musky, the weight of her pressing cruelly on your skull. You whimper in discomfort and the mistress pokes the point of her heel into your leg to silence you.

"Ah, that's better. Your face makes quite the cushion. Maybe we *should* keep you in the manor—the ladies could take turns sitting on your stupid dumb face. It's certainly a lot better than having to listen to you mewl and whine, that's for certain!'

You make a muffled sad sound beneath her that must come off as comical to Mistress Merciless, the mistress laughing at the pathetic noise.

"Don't just lie there! Lick my asshole. Walking around in this suffocating, tight catsuit, I'm pretty sure there must be a few spots that I missed with the toilet paper!"

Utterly revolted, you stick your tongue out, gingerly touching it to the mistress's ass crack. If her ass was warm and sweaty, her crack is ten times so, the taste of it so thick it's almost like pungent oil in your mouth. You search with your tongue until you find her hole, wondering if she was being serious or simply trying to psych you out. You like, horrified with yourself, and you feel the mistress's hole relax, along with the heavy weight of her backside on your head. She lets out a sigh.

"Yes, like that worm, get that tongue in there. Go on, deeper. Deeper."

Mistress Merciless coaches as you to slide your tongue deep into her hole and up her ass, commanding you with a kind of callous nonchalance as she soon has you licking and sucking at her filthy rim. It is the most demeaning thing you've ever done in your life, even more demeaning than jerking off to the most outlandish porn videos you can remember. But in a bizarre, unexpected twist, you feel your cock start to grow in its cage. It's denied an erection, of course, but it pulses against the hard steel and you can feel your cock throb achingly and your balls go blue with sick, perverted lust.

Who *are* you? And who has Mistress Merciless made you into with your chastisement?

You tongue her hole even more deeply, no longer needing her coaching as your taboo excitement takes over. You start to get into a rhythm—tongue in as deep as it will go, pull out and tickle her rim, lay the flat spade of your tongue on her, tongue back in—that actually seems to please the mistress, her sighs slowly turning into deep, throaty moans.

"Well, well... maybe we found a calling for you after all," she says in a husky, breathy voice. "Asslicker. Who knew you being so full of shit would have such... thematic resonance." She laughs to herself but then quiets again, losing herself to your ministrations. You can feel when she moves her hand between her legs to play with her pussy and pick up your rhythm, adjusting it so you speed along with her dancing, teasing fingers. By now, your entire mouth is coated with the taste of ass and your face is beginning to feel numb, the world all around you muffled by the mistress's sweaty cheeks. Somehow though, you don't stop your worship—you don't even *think* to stop—licking her dutifully and actually enjoying how you're able to bring this terrifying, imperious woman a modicum of pure joy.

When she comes, she presses herself down on you even harder, bearing down with a deep lusty grunt that leaves your tongue snatched by her twitching hole like some twisted trick. You feel the trickle of her wetness as she gushes onto you, the warm liquid splattering against your chin and down your chest. Then the mistress unclenches her body, sucking down deep, heaving breaths as she collects herself.

She stands up, drying herself off with a black hand towel she's picked up from the arm of the chair. She tosses it to you in a move that is both dismissive and, in a strange way, thoughtful.

"Clean yourself up," she says. "And then decide if you're going to leave this manor and go home or if you're interested in something more... long term." She zips up the crotch of her catsuit. "I think I know which one you'll choose, you pathetic little asslicker."

You watch her hips sway as she walks back into the thick of the party, the diamond harlequin pattern dancing in your vision like a sultry pendulum.

Yes, you know which one you'll choose too.

THE END

93

Somehow, you summon strength to decline the flirty, sultry mistresses for a second time. The three of you exit at the second floor and you turn off from them the first chance you get with a low bow, still nervous that you might run into them again. You go slowly through the hallways, trying to listen for where they are so you can stay far away, when you stumble upon a staircase leading up. It is quiet and slightly ominous and although you'd like the luxury of deciding if you should head up it immediately or not, you know it's better to be up there than to risk the mistresses running into you again... assuming they haven't around found somewhere to play—and someone to play with.

You head up the stairs leading to the third floor. A thin, royal blue carpet with an intricate design covers the steps, thankfully muffling your footsteps. The sounds of the party feel much farther away now and by the time you reach the landing of the third floor, they are but a distant din. Unlike the second floor, the third floor seems to be made of just one wraparound hallway that—as far as you can tell—goes along the outer walls of Matriarch Manor, with doors leading to rooms on the outside, no doubt giving those that the rooms belong pleasant views of the outside.

The air up here is still and slightly stuffy, and you can smell a mix of perfume, incense, and flowers as you creep through the wraparound hallway. It's unnerving that there's just a single hallway up here, giving you few options should you hear anyone coming up the stairs or out from their room; the one solace is that between every set of solemn wooden doors is an archway that looks to lead to a small, shared space of some sort, each sitting under slanted glass panels, like those of an atrium.

You survey the rooms on the floor. All but one has a name carved into its wood, and that lone door out instead has ornate designs carved into it from top to bottom, the images depicting a swirling sprawl of astrological symbols. Two doors down from it is the room you've only imagined so far: the one with a carving that suggests it belongs to Mistress Merciless herself, the mistress's name written in a stiff, imposing font. Between the ornate door and Mistress Merciless's room is the only shared atrium space that isn't completely cast in shadow. Peering through the archway, you see that it's set up to be some kind of lounge space, with a low sofa and a hexagonal tea table and erotic sculptures displayed in the center of the cubby.

Investigate Mistress Merciless's room (Page 202)
Check out the lounge space (Page 203)
Take a look at the room with the ornate door (Page 204)

94

You take a deep breath and let it out in a tired sigh. You can't believe that you're about to agree to this, but who could blame you, really? A year in chastity is ridiculous—absurd!—and there's no way you think you can survive that long without being able to touch yourself or even get hard without the cage painfully punishing you. What's a few minutes of filthy, awful humiliation in exchange for getting released in only a few short weeks?

At least that's what you tell yourself. You know the reality will be much, much harder to stomach. Literally.

"Okay," you say in a tiny voice.

Mistress Merciless cups her hand around her ear and leans in. "What was that? I couldn't hear you," she says.

"Okay," you say, louder.

"Okay, what?" asks Mistress Merciless. Oh boy, does she really want to drag this out.

"Okay, I will... your... I'll..."

You think that maybe, with all your bumbling speech, Mistress Merciless will step in and finish your thought for you. But no, she is determined to let you twist in the wind until she's satisfied with what you've said.

"I will... be, uh... your, you know... your toilet. I will be your toilet."

It hurts to say the words out loud, to feel the gravity of them and how they doom your next few minutes to come. A smile curdles on Mistress Merciless's face. She points a finger towards the floor.

"On your back. Chop, chop. I'm just *full* of piss."

Your body starts to tremble as you lay down on your back. You can feel the bass through the Salon's floor and notice, for the first time, the huge room's high ceilings that are covered in black and red and purple and pink balloons. There's a whole sea of them up there and you find yourself trying to look for patterns in the chaotic mess of balloons, anything to take your mind off what's about to happen.

Then your view is taken away as Mistress Merciless straddles your head, the heels of your boots nearly piercing your ears. Now you're looking up at her harlequin catsuit from below and you can see there's a black zipper that runs from crotch to ass. The mistress squats slightly as she opens up that zipper, the tension of the leather releasing to reveal Mistress Merciless's creamy skin and the wild, dark bush above her pussy. A wave of disorientation washes over you as she squats down further, the leather spreading more, and then you are face-to-pussy with the domineering woman, her pink, petaled lips almost being offered to you to lick and worship.

You can't process what's about to happen. You try to think of anything else, of being far, far away on a beach somewhere or in a bar or anywhere but under this mistress's squatting haunches.

"Open your mouth," commands Mistress Merciless. "I don't expect an untrained toilet to get every last drop, but if I don't think you're trying your hardest, the deal is off."

Your eyes shoot open. *What?*

But you don't even have time to process that latest twist of the knife as Mistress Merciless says: "Here it comes!"

You open your mouth wide and shut your eyes tight. The first few drops that fall are tepidly warm. It's an odd feeling, like warm rain or being splashed with tea that's been left to sit out. They splatter on your lips and cheeks, none even falling into your mouth; that doesn't happen until the drops become a stream that Mistress Merciless takes a moment to aim, catching you on the upper lip at first before the mistress adjusts her hips. A few of the drops run up your nose and you instinctively panic, leaning your head up and causing the mistress's aim to be off once more.

"Keep your head down!" she hisses as the stream grows stronger, rushing into your mouth. It's more than tepidly warm now and bitter—so bitter—unlike anything you could've imagined. This was a mistake. The worst mistake. An absolutely asinine mistake. You've never had to consider swallowing while drinking something so warm and bitter like this before, and it's surprisingly hard. Your throat doesn't want to open and your muscles don't want to move. Still, you manage to gulp down the awful hot, salty-bitter tea-ness of it, taking a second to close your lips to do so and getting splashed right in the face again.

Your panic grows. You can't do this. There's no way anyone can do this. Will Mistress Merciless stop? She'll have to stop, right?

No. She does not stop.

"Open your eyes!" she commands and you wrench them open just a little bit, now feeling that the little splattering drops have gotten onto your nose and even your forehead. The sight of her raining piss down on you is flinch-inducing and dig your fingers hard against the floor as you try to hold onto your sanity, swallowing and gulping and guzzling as much of her as you can, all while trying to get some breaths in there too.

How much can there be?

Mistress Merciless seems to be controlling her own muscles well, keeping you from being totally overwhelmed but prolonging your agony in the process. The other mistresses are leaning way in now, and several of them have their phones out to record your humiliation. With an awful feeling of self-disgust, you feel your belly begin to get full. It's a sickening sensation and you want to quit, to make this torture end right this very second. But if you do that, then all of your degradation will have been for nothing. You keep your mouth open and accept your role as Mistress Merciless's toilet.

Even with your best attempts to drink and swallow, you still find your mouth filling faster than you can empty it and soon you begin to overflow. Warm rivulets run down your cheeks and to your neck, pooling under your head to wet the back of your hair. You want to cry. No human should have to be subjected to this—even if you made the choice yourself to be where you are now.

Soon you can't even swallow anymore and everything is just overflowing, causing a spreading puddle that causes the mistresses at the edge of the watching circle to take a few small steps back. Not Mistress Merciless though. She keeps emptying her bladder, onto you now instead of in you, chuckling darkly at the frantic look on your face. Finally, after what seems like a dehumanizing eternity, the stream slows to a trickle and you're able to swallow whatever was left in your mouth, choking and coughing at the warm, bitter pungency of it.

Mistress Merciless squats down even farther, her pussy now just inches from your lips. From somewhere unseen, someone hands her a stack of cocktail napkins. She dabs herself dry and to add even further humiliation to your hideous, disgusting situation, she drops the wadded up napkins in your mouth.

"There we go," she says to you, a huge grin on her face. "I feel *much* better. You though... you look like you've seen better days."

She gingerly steps away from you, leaving you lying on the floor of the manor's Salon. Slaves are already stepping forward to mop up the mess. You sit up and feel a disconcerting fullness in your belly, your hair dripping down your back. Slaves keep their eyes away from you, in fear that the same thing might happen to them, and the party's mistresses look at you with pure revulsion. In that moment, you are less than. A thing. An object. Something to be used for such a foul act and then ignored. Mistress Merciless is already disappearing into the party again, totally uninterested in you.

Thankfully, a slave eventually hands you a towel to wet and dry your body off, but you can still feel the mistress's dried piss clinging to your skin, the stink of it wafting all around you. People—mistresses and slaves included—get out of your way as you're directed to the slave's bathroom down in the basement to wash yourself off, accompanied by a uniformed mistress who looks exceedingly unhappy about her job.

There is a grim finality to the evening as you shower in a mildewy, tiled stall that barely has lukewarm water, the mistress watching the entire time with a disdainful look on her face. No matter what she would've thought of you before, she certainly thinks less of you now.

Once dry from your shower, you are permitted to find your stashed clothes and to leave the manor, your hair still wet. In three weeks you will return to—hopefully—have your chastity removed, but even after you are free, you know that you will be forever changed, reduced to lower depths you never thought your life would reach.

Forever and ever, you'll always wonder: Was it worth it?

THE END

95

Nope. No way, no how. There are some lines you just won't cross and this is one of them.

You shake your head at Mistress Merciless. "I... no, I can't do that," you say.

Mistress Merciless smirks. "I guess you *do* have some self-respect after all," she says, chuckling to herself. "I'll be honest though, I kind of wanted to see how low you would go and how much of a piece of shit you'd let me treat you."

This sparks off a conversation among the watching mistresses that quickly descends into cacophony. Mistress Merciless leans over to share some thoughts of her own as the mistresses trade stories of just how low *they've* been able to get males to act and soon enough it's like you're not even there anymore.

Isn't she going to give you some other way to reduce your time in chastity? You clear your throat.

"Miss? Miss? Mistress...?"

Mistress Merciless snaps her head around and glares at you. "What?" she asks.

"Is there... something else I can do to get out of this thing sooner?"

The laugh from Mistress Merciless is loud, barking, and incredulous, like a shotgun blast right to your face. "No! I already *gave* you an option and you turned it down. Frankly, you should be thanking your lucky stars I don't have you detained for trespassing, you little worm! After all, Matriarch Manor technically sits in its own legal jurisdiction and we can do whatever we want with people trespassing on our land."

Your blood runs cold at this revelation and Mistress Merciless catches the look of worry in your eyes.

"Oh yes," she continues. "If I so wanted, I'd have you thrown in the basement and 'sentenced' to as many months or years of hard labor as I wanted. Sure, we'd have some legal hoops to jump through, but you'd be amazed at what some campaign contributions and, ahem, 'donations' to state law enforcement will buy you when it comes to operating autonomously. Shall I show you? Would you prefer to spend your chastity downstairs, with the other males and a few very, very creatively sadistic ladies?"

You shake your head frantically and Mistress Merciless gives you a cold, sharkish grin.

"Didn't think so. Now, get out of my manor and don't come back until next year."

She points a finger at the double doors leading outside.

"Go on, get out of here! NOW!"

You scramble to your feet and the crowd parts as Mistress Merciless stalks after you, finger still pointing at the doors of the manor. She walks slowly but without stopping, like some kind of horror monster right on your tail, and you struggle to pull open the doors and stumble out into the cold of the night, completely naked... except for your chastity cage. Mistress Merciless stands at the threshold, her brows knitted in anger.

"And stay out!" she shouts, slamming the door so loudly it echoes throughout the surrounding woods.

And then you're left all by yourself, to wander home in the twilight and chill of evening. It's going to be a miserable, frustrating year of denial and yearning.

Just 51 weeks to go.

THE END

96

You step over to Mistress Merciless's room, certain that it's going to be locked. Yet, when you turn the doorknob it gives in your grasp, granting you entry to the mistress's private chambers. What luck!

Luxury. That's the word that comes to mind. Pure and utter luxury. A massive Persian rug nearly covers the entirety of the bedroom, its tasseled edges the only evidence that the floors below are the same dark hardwood used in the rest of the manor. The walls are papered in gold-and-red silk, with regal designs that go all the way up to the slate-painted ceiling, from which hangs a crystal chandelier. The layout of the room has a canopy bed to one side, its crimson drapes open, along with two end tables on either side of it; across from the bed is a round dark wood table with two matching armchairs on either side of it, the setup placed next to a brassy vanity that is overflowing with jewelry and makeup and all sorts of small knick-knacks. On the same wall as the bedroom door is a heavy-looking armoire with silky materials hanging out from under one of its slightly ajar doors.

What catches you by surprise is that there is *another* door in this room, one that appears to lead into a private bathroom. It's the first room with a private bathroom you've seen so far, signifying the importance of Mistress Merciless herself.

You think about where a mistress like her might hide a chastity key. The vanity seems like a natural place, though the armoire might offer a more hidden—yet not obtuse—spot to keep a key to a device like yours. Then again, there might be more to the bathroom than you can see from here, with its own places to stash important items. Those are your best guesses and a good start for your search for freedom.

Look through the vanity (Page 212)
Open up and search the armoire (Page 213)
Go into the bathroom (Page 214)

97

You step through the archway to check out the atrium lounge space. With heavy carpeting and fabric panels on the walls, all sound seems to be absorbed in here, making for a peaceful, relaxing space. The low sofa looks ridiculously comfortable and you could imagine yourself sitting for a breather... if you didn't have far more important things to do.

Out the slanted glass windows, you get a half-view of the backyard. Much work has been done since you last saw it and you also notice that mistresses have begun to filter out there with drinks in hand and slaves following dutifully behind, ready to hold their beverages or act as impromptu seats for them. Most of the mistresses are wearing at least a light jacket, and from the occasional whip of tree branches of fluttering of fallen leaves, you can only imagine how cold the near-naked slaves are below as they scuttle across the backyard lawn. You make sure not to get too close to the glass though, as the setting sun is surely making it easier to spot people in the windows of Matriarch Manor; all you need is to be spotted now, when you've finally reached the third floor.

Sweeping your gaze around, you see that the rooms of the third floor all have balconies... including the one belonging to Mistress Merciless. What's more, there's a ledge between the atrium lounge and her balcony, one that you could probably traverse if you opened up the side windows of the space and kept your footsteps calm and sure.

Of course, a less daring approach would be to return to the wraparound hallway—provided the door to Mistress Merciless's room is even unlocked.

Return to the third floor hallway (Page 205)
Go out on the ledge (Page 206)

98

You decide to check out what's beyond the ornate door with its astrological etchings. Something about those designs draws you in, as does the fact that it looks nothing like the other doors on the third floor. As you step inside, you realize why that might be.

This large, double bedroom-sized space seems to be set up like some kind of a colorful playroom. The walls are beach pink, there are endless S&M toys strewn across the floor, and there are both many pieces of curious fetish furniture and metal carts full of lube and condoms and medical supplies, all of it so out in the open that you're left exactly who this room is intended for. Whatever the answer, it's clear that the people who come here know exactly what they're getting into and are less interested in theater than they are in indulging themselves in perverse pleasure.

Closets with louvered doors sit along one wall and a simple utilitarian bathroom is accessible from the opposite wall, though there seems to be nothing of interest in there than a toilet, sink, and a narrow shower stall.

This room feels both recently used and about to *be* used, existing as if in a perpetual state of use where mistresses come and go constantly, with slaves in tow. Perhaps it's some kind of elite playroom, you think, a place where pretentions drop and all manner of curiosities are explored.

You could leave—it's probably the saner option, who knows—or you could stay and search the room further. Maybe you'll get lucky and find that this playroom isn't just used for domination, but also for the locking— and unlocking—of male slaves.

Search the playroom (Page 262)
Leave (Page 263)

99

Stepping back into the hallway, the first thing you notice are excited female voices... and they're getting louder! They seem to be coming up the stairs or from around the corner. Whatever the direction, you don't have long before they reach your location.

You could duck back into the lounge space or try one of the doors, either the ornate one with its intricate etching or the one to Mistress Merciless's room.

Whatever your choice, you'd better make it quickly.

Dart back into the lounge (Page 208)
Duck into Mistress Merciless's room (Page 202)
Go in the room with the ornate door (Page 204)

100

You steady yourself and take a nice, big breath. Then you open up the side window of the atrium lounge, feeling a gust of chilly air come in from the outside. You duck under the window frame and step onto the ledge, wondering how you *ever* thought this was a good idea; the ground below looks like it's thousands of feet away and the ledge now seems as thin as a strand of spaghetti. With one hand sliding along the outer wall of Matriarch Manor, you take slow steps along the ledge, inching yourself towards the balcony of Mistress Merciless's room.

You want to run, but you don't, doing your best to shove out thoughts of you slipping and falling to your demise. The balcony is ten feet away. Then eight. Then five, four, three...

You reach over and grab the balcony railing. Your heart feels like it's going to explode. When you considered crossing the ledge, you never considered having to get over the balcony railing and now that you have to, your entire body is quivering in panic, your mind spinning as you wonder if people below can see you.

It's all too much for you and you literally throw yourself over the railing, landing head and shoulders first on the balcony. You wriggle your legs over and curl up into a terrified ball, the chilly air pricking at your skin. You listen for sounds from below, but there's only the chatter of the growing outdoor gala interspersed with the low howl of the wind.

You get to your knees. That's as much as you can manage right now as you reach for the balcony door. What if it's locked? You dumbass, you didn't think of the locks! You're so sure you're going to be stuck out here and forced to either wait for capture or—even worse, in a way—go back across the ledge that can't believe it when the balcony door swings inward.

You clamber inside and shut the door behind you, grateful for the chance to breathe in peace. Once you've calmed down, you're able to take in the majestically opulent room that belongs to Mistress Merciless.

Luxury. That's the word that comes to mind. Pure and utter luxury. A massive Persian rug nearly covers the entirety of the bedroom, its tasseled edges the only evidence that the floors below are the same dark hardwood used in the rest of the manor. The walls are papered in gold-and-red silk, with regal designs that go all the way up to the slate-painted ceiling, from which hangs a crystal chandelier. The layout of the room has a canopy bed to one side, its crimson drapes open, along with two end tables on either side of it; across from the bed is a round dark wood table with two matching armchairs on either side of it, the setup placed next to a brassy vanity that is overflowing with jewelry and makeup and all sorts of small knick-knacks. On the same wall as the bedroom door is a heavy-looking armoire with silky materials hanging out from under one of its slightly ajar doors.

What catches you by surprise is that there is *another* door in this room, one that appears to lead into a private bathroom. It's the first room with a private bathroom you've seen so far, signifying the importance of Mistress Merciless herself.

You think about where a mistress like her might hide a chastity key. The vanity seems like a natural place, though the armoire might offer a more hidden—yet not obtuse—spot to keep a key to a device like yours. Then again, there might be more to the bathroom than you can see from here, with its own places to stash important items. Those are your best guesses and a good start for your search for freedom.

Look through the vanity (Page 212)
Open up and search the armoire (Page 213)
Go into the bathroom (Page 214)

101

You rush back into the muted lounge space, trying your best to crouch down behind its low sofa. The voices get louder and you can soon tell there are two of them, both female, excitedly talking to each other.

"Oh my, oh my that was... epic," one says, a slight slur in her words from a night of loud music and drinking.

"Not bad," says the other, her tone crisper and more coherent. "But I've seen wilder manor parties, just you wait. And the outside 'Cool Down' tonight looks like it's going to be insane. I heard they're going to make the slaves do a gladiator fighting thing. Last one standing gets out of his cage for a day or hour or something, while all the rest are going to be soooooorrry."

"I forgot about the Cool Down! Ohmigod, this is the best day ever. Let's go take a look to see how it's coming along."

"Right over here, we can look out the cubby windows."

Now, along with the voices, you hear footsteps. And they're headed your way. You cower deeper down, wishing the sofa were higher.

"Come on, let's—OH GOD!"

You hear a shriek followed by a shocked, confused laugh.

"A slave! You, get out of there! Now!"

You reluctantly pick your head up to see two mistresses from the party standing there, one with pale skin and alcohol-flushed cheeks who looks East Asian wearing a silk Chinese dragon print dress with a short collar and a split hem and the other who looks Middle Eastern with her hair up in a ponytail, big hoop earrings, and a front-knotted pink crop top blouse with long, flounce sleeves and cut off denim booty shorts.

"Kayla, what the hell," says the East Asian mistress.

"Looks like we have a stowaway, Tiffany," says Kayla with a dazzling, devilish smile. She flicks her finger up at you. "You! I said: Get up!"

You shakily rise from behind the sofa, cursing yourself for thinking you could easily hide away in the lounge. Kayla gives Tiffany a sly, wicked look. Then she fishes out a box of cigarettes from the front pocket of her cut-off denim shorts and sits down on the sofa. She snaps her fingers and points to the floor in front of her.

"Over here, slave," she says.

"What are you doing Kayla?" asks Tiffany.

"Enjoying a smoke break," Kayla says. "Come on, join me."

As Tiffany takes a seat next to Kayla, you come around from the sofa and look towards the lounge's archway.

"Don't even think about it," says Kayla, holding her cigarette in her mouth as she lights it. She takes a deep inhale and lets it go towards the glass ceiling of the atrium lounge. She hands the cigarettes and her lighter to Tiffany, who takes them with some hesitation, the look on her face suggesting she's still trying to figure out what Kayla's up to. Kayla points to the ground. "Kneel."

You get down on your knees as the women smoke in silence, Kayla not taking her emerald green eyes off you. She takes a long drag of her cigarette and blows the smoke in your face, the blue-white cloud stinging your eyes and your nostrils.

"Tiff, did you mean what you said before? That you wanna become an official Matriarch Manor mistress?" asks Kayla.

Tiffany nods as she sucks on her cigarette. The blush in her cheeks is very pink now, giving her a faux-innocent glow. "I do. One day."

"Well, I'm going to teach you something," says Kayla. "Something that was taught to me when I started my application: Harden Your Heart."

Tiffany raises an eyebrow at Kayla. "Meaning...?"

"Meaning that a lot of women *try* to join the manor but they just can't do it. And the reason is usually something like they feel bad for one of the slaves or they think they can't go as far as other women or they just get too soft-hearted in general. That's why you've got to harden your heart if you're gonna be here. Watch."

Kayla takes a long, long drag of her cigarette, holding the precious nicotine-laced smoke in her lungs before she lets it roll down onto you in a heavy cloud. Her cigarette has begun to ash. She holds it out towards you and says, "Slave, give me your tongue."

"Kayla..."

Kayla shushes Tiffany. "Just watch," she says. "Slave. Tongue. Now. Or I report you for lurking up on the third floor."

You reluctantly loll out your tongue, looking in horror as Kayla flicks the ash of her cigarette onto it. You go to pull your tongue back in, but the mistress stops you.

"Hold it there until I say so," she says. Then she ignores you, returning to her conversation with Tiffany.

"See the thing is, if you view the slaves as 'men' or even as 'people', you're already going the wrong way. They aren't men or people and they aren't deserving of the way you'd respect an actual person. They're *things*. Things to use, to abuse. And the only way to really internalize this notion for yourself is, well, you gotta fake it till you make it. Go on, try ashing your cigarette in its mouth."

Tiffany, wanting to impress her friend, takes as long of a drag as Kayla did, coughing for a slight spell before her cigarette has a long column of flaky ash threatening to fall from its tip. She holds it over your tongue with a somewhat apologetic look on her face. Then she taps it and the column of ash tumbles onto your tongue. It's very warm for a second before it's cooled by your saliva, your ashy spit coating your tongue with the burned, charcoal taste of the cigarette. You can feel your mouth watering from being held open and your tongue start to ache as you continue to keep it held out for the mistresses' use.

They continue to chat, taking turns ashing their cigarettes on your tongue until there's a gratuitous pile of the saliva-wetted filth. It slides towards your mouth and the edges of your tongue, forcing you to make a scoop-like shape to hold it all in. All the while, the smell of smoke grows and the air gets thick with the blue-white haze that stings your eyes and your nostrils and makes you want to desperately get some fresh air.

When Kayla is done with her first cigarette, she gives you a terrible, snarling smile. "This is going to hurt," she says, more a promise than a warning. Then you watch helplessly as she brings the smoldering tip of her cigarette to the flat of your tongue, crushing it out on your tender flesh while you clench your fists shut and try to fight through the pain. She grinds that cigarette down and leaves it on the pile of ash, still not permitting you to swallow. She looks at Tiffany expectantly.

"Your turn," she says.

Apprehensive, Tiffany follows Kayla's lead. She sucks down her cigarette as quickly as she can, blowing the smoke right at you per Kayla's instruction, and then, like she's stomping on a roach in the kitchen, she smushes the cigarette butt onto your tongue, catching you on the tip and making you grunt in pain. Kayla laughs delightedly. When Tiffany's managed to push the cigarette to just a small nub, she drops it next Kayla's discarded smoke. Only then does Kayla flash her emerald green eyes at you and say:

"You may now swallow, slave."

It's just as bad going down your throat as sitting on your tongue, maybe even worse. Your throat feels chalky and gritty and you cough as you try to choke down the mistresses' waste, unable to believe they've just used you as a human ashtray. As you stay doubled over, coughing, you hear the flick of a lighter.

They aren't done with you yet.

"And here's the thing," Kayla says to Tiffany as they both start on their second cigarette. "You see what we just did? You see how he *listened* to us? He didn't have to do that. He could've refused, could've suffered the consequences, could've kept his pride. But he doesn't *have* pride. Because he's a sub-human piece of garbage. Aren't you, slave?"

Kayla thrusts out her lit cigarette towards you. She's not interested in your mouth anymore. She hovers it over your skin, just an inch away from your shoulder, then your chest, and then your nipple.

"Go ahead, nod your head like a dummy or I'm putting my cigarette out on you right now," she says.

You bobblehead nod and Kayla snorts, all while Tiffany watches with a mix of shock and awe.

"Put your cigarette out on him," she says to Tiffany. "The slave's going to choose a place for you to do it. And if I don't like where he picks, I'm going to choose a different one."

Tiffany leans forward with her lit cigarette. She seems unsure. You're unsure too, trying to figure out what part of your body you could offer up that would placate these women, thinking how this is not how this evening was supposed to wind up. What will these women do to you after they've had their fun? Will they let you go, or will they drag you downstairs for more torment?

Somehow you don't think freedom is what they have in mind.

Slowly you turn around, showing your back and buttocks; it feels like it'll be less painful that way and at least you won't have to watch.

"Oh look, he's offering you his balls," says Kayla snidely. "Go ahead, Harden your heart and teach this thing what it really is."

As you wait for the cigarette to land, your body trembling, you regret coming to Matriarch Manor at all. Maybe you could've found a happier fate, but you know that deep down in your heart, these mistresses have no intention of letting you go.

THE END

102

The vanity seems like a logical place to start, with all its tiny little items and small drawers for hiding things. You start to dig through the vanity drawers, pushing through piles of makeup tubes and little cases, your hands and fingers picking up all sorts of pigments as you search. Heavy perfume wafts up from the vanity, something earthy and wild and cloying. You try not to look at yourself in its tri-fold mirror as you search, unable to stand the sight of your chastised self, and so you turn your attention to the vanity's many drawers, pushing aside piles of earrings and rings and necklaces, getting excited every few seconds that one of the pieces of jewelry is actually a key.

But no, there are no keys in here. The closest thing you find is a small brooch shaped like a bee and you curse yourself for thinking the mistress would keep something like a chastity key in this mess of a vanity. Just as you're letting out a huffy sigh, you notice a slip of paper under a heavy pearl necklace. It's been folded several times before and on it is a four-digit code that reads: "0714".

What could this code possibly be for? You look down at your chastity device dumbly, as if there's suddenly going to be a combination lock down there instead of a padlock, but of course there isn't.

Still, the code *could* be useful. You take the piece of paper, not trusting your memory after all you've seen at Matriarch Manor so far. Then you close up the vanity drawers. The armoire feels far, far less interesting after the bust that the vanity was; if there wasn't a key in the vanity, there sure won't be one in the armoire. That leaves the private bathroom to check out, if you're still feeling curious, or can resign your search, hoping to find some other way out of your chastity.

Go into the bathroom (Page 214)
Resign your search (Page 219)

103

You start with the armoire, thinking that its proximity to the door will at least let you hear if anyone's coming—hopefully. Opening it up, you see it is absolutely stuffed with outfits and shoes and just piles of clothing, all kinds. There are dresses and blouses and jeans and heels and boots and things you don't even know the names of, all of it carrying a clean, lightly perfumed smell that makes you think of heady patchouli and woodsmoke, a kind of earthy, mossy smell that is luxurious yet wild.

You begin to despair. There is no way you're going to be able to search through all of this clothing without making a mess of the armoire, giving away that you've been here. You consider it for a second, dumping everything out so you can completely search the heavy piece of furniture, but think better of the idea; sure, you'll need to get of the manor eventually and it won't matter what you've left behind then, though why start making scenes when you haven't even found the key to your chastity cage yet?

As you're stuffing the clothing back in, a pair of jeans slip out and fall on the floor. As they do, you see something white and plastic sticking out of one of the small pockets. There's a moment of excitement as you think you've found your key, but instead it's merely a keycard, a white plastic rectangle with red and black stripes on it. In the corner it reads: "Private Elevator".

Thinking it might come in handy, you hold onto it, wishing you still had clothing of your own to stash it in.

You could keep searching Mistress Merciless's room, looking through her vanity and checking out her private bathroom. Or you could take your "prize" and go, resigning yourself to the fact that this search might be a lot more complicated than you thought.

Explore the bathroom (Page 214)
Investigate the vanity (Page 217)
Resign your search (Page 216)

104

Mistress Merciless's private bathroom. Surely there are some secrets to discover in there, right?

You step into the dim marble space and flip on the warm lights overhead. It's a luxury bathroom alright, with a deep jacuzzi tub, a standing shower, a black porcelain toilet with one of those Japanese bidet attachments on it, and a double sink that is littered with all manner of makeup and perfumes. Just to be safe, you close the bathroom door; it's not like you'd have anywhere to run to if someone came into the room while you were searching the bathroom, but at least you'd have the chance to hide—or think of an excuse for why you're there.

You rifle through the double sink's small vials, finding nothing more than tubes of lipstick and containers of concealer and poofy makeup brushes the kick up a colorful cloud of feminine smelling powder dust. Then you go through the medicine cabinet, which are stuffed with more elegant perfume bottles and makeup containers—along with some feminine odds and ends you'd rather not think too hard about—but ultimately none of it is what you're seeking.

As you give the bathroom another once over, you notice something odd about the toilet: there are painted metal eyebolts at its base. Looking closer, you see there is a small length of chain tucked away behind the toilet, but you can't possibly imagine *why*. Regardless, your instincts tell you it's not for anything wholesome. And as you're inspecting the toilet, you see something blinking on its glossy black surface. It's a red mote of light, flashing slowly right under the porcelain, and it's not until you turn around that you realize the light belongs to a security camera tucked into the corner, veiled by shadow.

Your eyes go wide. Is this room being recorded? Why? By who?

You go to leave. The doorknob will not open.

From a hidden speaker you hear a crackling female voice: "I don't know who the hell you are, slave, but that is Mistress Merciless's private bathroom. And she has been notified of your trespassing."

You try the knob again, turning it with all your might... but it still refuses to open.

"You stay right there," continues the crackling voice. "You will be dealt with soon enough."

You fool! Of all the things you could've done, you put yourself not just in Mistress Merciless's private chambers, but her private bathroom too, putting so many obstacles between yourself and a clear path of escape. Now, instead of just a year of chastity, you will have to contend with the mistress's wrath as she discovers you're also a trespasser and who knows what she'll do to you once she discovers that.

Well, you'll find out soon enough.

THE END

105

An uneasy feeling prickles at the back of your neck and you decide to end your search, feeling like you've spent enough time in Mistress Merciless's room. At least you were able to find this elevator keycard, whatever help that might do you. You slip back into the third floor's wraparound hallway, giving the doors and archways one last look. That's when you see it in one of the darkened archway spaces: no slanted windows offering a view outside. You're not sure how you missed it before, but as you creep forward, you see that this space is fully covered and at the end of it there is a slender, antique-looking elevator. Next to the elevator is a black rectangular box with a blinking red light.

You can't help but walk up to that black box and press the elevator keycard to it. The light goes from red to green and you hear the whirr of motors as the elevator makes its way to you! You feel a lump in your throat and your heartbeat in your ears as the elevator reaches it, opening up its doors in near silence. Thankfully no one is inside. You step in and the doors close behind you, the elevator trundling its way down without you even pressing a button.

It continues for a minute and then stops with a slight jolt. You see then that this isn't just an elevator, it's a *double* elevator, with doors in front of you and behind. From behind you, you hear the sounds of the Salon party, the music thumping away and the women beyond laughing and shouting drunkenly to each other. Luckily, this elevator requires you push a button to exit, the button to the Salon staring at you like a knobby, unblinking red eye.

You turn around the other way. There is a matching red button but there is one difference: a keypad sits above this button, taunting you. You try to press the button. Nothing happens, save for a low buzz that emanates from somewhere in the elevator. Apparently you need some kind of a code to use this door... a code you do not have. You could exit into the Salon. To do so without drawing immense suspicion, you'll have to leave the keycard in the elevator too, unfortunately Or you could try a code at random. After all, there are only 10,000 possibilities. What could go wrong?

Exit into the Salon (Page 225)
Try a code at random (Page 222)

106

The vanity seems like the next best place to search, with all its tiny little items and small drawers for hiding things. You start to dig through the vanity drawers, pushing through piles of makeup tubes and little cases, your hands and fingers picking up all sorts of pigments as you search. Heavy perfume wafts up from the vanity, something earthy and wild and cloying. You try not to look at yourself in its tri-fold mirror as you search, unable to stand the sight of your chastised self, and so you turn your attention to the vanity's many drawers, pushing aside piles of earrings and rings and necklaces, getting excited every few seconds that one of the pieces of jewelry is actually a key.

But no, there are no keys in here. The closest thing you find is a small brooch shaped like a bee and you curse yourself for thinking the mistress would keep something like a chastity key in this mess of a vanity. Just as you're letting out a huffy sigh, you notice a slip of paper under a heavy pearl necklace. It's been folded several times before and on it is a four-digit code that reads: "0714".

What could this code possibly be for? You look down at your chastity device dumbly, as if there's suddenly going to be a combination lock down there instead of a padlock, but of course there isn't.

Still, the code *could* be useful. You take the piece of paper, not trusting your memory after all you've seen at Matriarch Manor so far. Then you close up the vanity drawers. A code and a keycard... it hardly seems like they could be related, but you've seen stranger things at Matriarch Manor so far. You could continue on into the private bathroom, but having not found any chastity key in either the vanity or armoire, you're beginning to feel discouraged. Maybe it's time to leave Mistress Merciless's room before you press your luck.

Check out the bathroom (Page 214)
Resign your search (Page 218)

107

An uneasy feeling prickles at the back of your neck and you decide to end your search, feeling like you've spent enough time in Mistress Merciless's room. At least you were able to find this elevator keycard and that four-digit code, whatever help that might do you. You slip back into the third floor's wraparound hallway, giving the doors and archways one last look.

That's when you see it in one of the darkened archway spaces: no slanted windows offering a view outside. You're not sure how you missed it before, but as you creep forward, you see that this space is fully covered and at the end of it there is a slender, antique-looking elevator. Next to the elevator is a black rectangular box with a blinking red light.

Who knows where this elevator might lead, even if it works at all. You could explore it to find out or you could go back and give into your curiosity to check out that ornate door that looks different from all the other rooms on the third floor.

Try to operate the elevator (Page 221)
Check out the room with the ornate door (Page 220)

108

An uneasy feeling prickles at the back of your neck and you decide to end your search, feeling like you've spent enough time in Mistress Merciless's room. You slip back into the third floor's wraparound hallway, giving the doors and archways one last look.

That's when you see it in one of the darkened archway spaces: no slanted windows offering a view outside. You're not sure how you missed it before, but as you creep forward, you see that this space is fully covered and at the end of it there is a slender, antique-looking elevator. Next to the elevator is a black rectangular box with a blinking red light.

Who knows where this elevator might lead, even if it works at all. You could explore it to find out or you could go back and give into your curiosity to check out that ornate door that looks different from all the other rooms on the third floor.

Try to operate the elevator (Page 241)
Check out the room with the ornate door (Page 204)

109

You decide to check out what's beyond the ornate door with its astrological etchings. Something about those designs draws you in, as does the fact that it looks nothing like the other doors on the third floor. As you step inside, you realize why that might be.

This large, double bedroom-sized space seems to be set up like some kind of a colorful playroom. The walls are beach pink, there are endless S&M toys strewn across the floor, and there are both many pieces of curious fetish furniture and metal carts full of lube and condoms and medical supplies, all of it so out in the open that you're left exactly who this room is intended for. Whatever the answer, it's clear that the people who come here know exactly what they're getting into and are less interested in theater than they are in indulging themselves in perverse pleasure.

Closets with louvered doors sit along one wall and a simple utilitarian bathroom is accessible from the opposite wall, though there seems to be nothing of interest in there than a toilet, sink, and a narrow shower stall.

This room feels both recently used and about to *be* used, existing as if in a perpetual state of use where mistresses come and go constantly, with slaves in tow. Perhaps it's some kind of elite playroom, you think, a place where pretentious drop and all manner of curiosities are explored.

Just as you're about to leave, you spot something shiny in one of the piles of play toys. You step over slowly, searching into the pile with cautious optimism, and out if it you pull out a ring of jangling keys. Your eyes trail down and you see that studding the pile are discarded chastity devices not too different from your own.

Your heart races. Could this be it? Have you found the keys to your freedom?

You could try them, right now, or you could take them with you and go back to the elevator bank to see where it leads.

Try the keys (Page 253)
Leave and go back to the elevator (Page 221)

110

You can't help but walk up to that black box and press the elevator keycard to it. The light goes from red to green and you hear the whirr of motors as the elevator makes its way to you!

You feel a lump in your throat and your heartbeat in your ears as the elevator reaches it, opening up its doors in near silence. Thankfully no one is inside. You step in and the doors close behind you, the elevator trundling its way down without you even pressing a button.

It continues for a minute and then stops with a slight jolt. You see then that this isn't just an elevator, it's a *double* elevator, with doors in front and behind. From behind you, you hear the sounds of the Salon party, the music thumping away and the women beyond laughing and shouting drunkenly to each other. Luckily, this elevator requires you push a button to exit, the button to the Salon staring at you like a knobby, unblinking red eye.

You turn around the other way. There is a matching red button but there is one difference: a keypad sits above this button, taunting you. You try to press the button. Nothing happens, save for a low buzz that emanates from somewhere in the elevator. It looks like you need a code for this door.

You look down at the slip of paper with its four-digit code. 0714. You punch the numbers into the keypad and there is a soft chime from somewhere in the elevator.

You have a choice, perhaps the most important choice you've made so far. Will you go through this front elevator door and out of the manor, with your personal freedom intact while your cock stays locked up in its cage? Or will you continue to roll the dice and explore the party in the Salon, still hoping to find some way to unlock yourself?

Keep in mind that if you check out the Salon, you'll want to leave the keycard behind and swallow the slip of paper with the code on it, just to be extra careful that no one figures out what you've been up to.

Exit into the Salon (Page 225)
Leave Matriarch Manor (Page 240)

111

Hey, you've always thought of yourself as lucky in life, so why would you expect your luck to run out now?

You decide to take a chance, a wild shot in the dark. You reach out to the cold, metallic keys and begin pressing them at random. 5-6-2-8, you punch in. You press the red button.

Immediately, a loud buzzing sound fills the elevator. Your heart races as panic sets in.

Suddenly, the once quiet elevator is filled with a blaring alarm that drills into your skull. Harsh red lights flash menacingly, matching the rhythm that is your frantic heartbeat. Sweat trickles down your forehead as you frantically try to press other buttons, but it's too late.

The elevator doors behind you slide open and you're met with the sight of several elegantly dressed mistresses turning their attention towards you. Their laughter dies down as they look at you with predatory grins, amused by your predicament once they figure out the source of the blaring alarm.

"Oh ho ho," one of them purrs, a wicked glint in her eyes as she saunters forward. Her long scarlet gown is cut daringly low and her stiletto heels click ominously against the marble floor.

"I think someone has been very naughty," another says from behind a patterned silk fan, her eyes going wide with malice.

Within moments, they surround you like vultures circling their prey. They claw you out from the elevator despite your feeble attempt to stay inside, the women not hesitating to slap and smack you to get you to obey.

"Trying to escape, are we?" snarls one of the mistresses.

Their laughter echoes through the room, even competing with the party's thumping music, like some cruel and unnerving musical sample as they shove you deeper into the party, allowing even more of the mistresses to gather around.

Before you can even think about escaping, two women grab a strong hold of your arms while another takes your chin in her hand and tilts it upwards forcefully. You meet her gaze and instantly feel yourself shivering under her icy stare. It's Mistress Merciless.

"I didn't think I'd be seeing *you* so soon," she hisses before delivering a sharp slap across your cheek to get you to stop squirming.

Your heart pounds erratically against your rib cage like a caged bird desperate for freedom as they lead you towards some kind of standing wooden contraption that looks like a mix between pillory stocks and a windmill. They throw you against it, several mistresses working in unison to strap you into the bizarre device. It forces your arms and legs away from your body, while keeping you bent over at an awkward angle. As you try to stand, you hear a click and feel a heavy wooden paddle smack you across the ass, the paddle whooshing away before clicking back into place. You double over in pain, cursing under your breath as the cacophony of the mistresses assaults your ears.

You try to stand again and again you hear the click and then the heavy, dull smack of the paddle, followed by its whooshing away. There must be some kind of reset mechanism in this contraption, making it so that unless you maintain the impossibly uncomfortable bent over position, your ass receives a nasty spank. You do your best to stay bent over, but without any way to support your weight except by your own core strength, it's only a matter of time before you need to alleviate your discomfort. This time you try to slowly rise up, yet alas the paddle is ready to spank you into submission once more.

Mistress Merciless bends down into view, her raven black hair fluttering as the paddle whooshes back into place. Her dark eyes search yours as she takes a sip from her champagne.

"I had let you off easy," she says. "A year in the cage, but total freedom. I guess I was wrong. You deserve a much more stringent punishment. And for your act of *trespassing* on private property, I will arrange to have you under house arrest... here. Your new home. For the next year."

"You... you can't do that," you stammer, unable to believe how fast the ground is falling out from under your feet.

"Oh, but I can!" she says. "Don't you know we *own* this town? You stupid, stupid male. It is going to be a horrible year for you."

The lactic acid builds in your legs and stomach and you shift to ease it, hearing the dreadful click once more as the wooden paddle cracks against your ass. You cry out, right in Mistress Merciless's face.

But all she does is smile.

THE END

112

It's not an easy decision to make, but you decide to take your chance wandering through the party in the Salon. The way you see it is there is no hope of you guessing a code at random to get out of this elevator and, with no seeming way to get back up to the third floor or any other floor, you're stuck taking the gamble with the mistresses in the party—not to mention, you're *still* locked up in your chastity, having not achieve your goal for the evening.

Sometimes you have to go deeper into the crevasse to escape.

With a heavy sigh, you push the button for the Salon. The elevator's doors slide open. In an incredible stroke of luck, the private elevator is tucked into a cubby separated from the thick of the party, allowing you to exit without being seen. Leaving the keycard behind on the floor of the elevator in the corner, where you hope no one will spot it, you slip off into the party, your eyes desperately looking for Mistress Merciless so you can stay far, far away.

As with all raging parties, lots of alcohol and not enough food seems to have turned the mood wild. Mistresses have put slaves up against the wall to use for whipping practice, while others have turned them into living, suffering furniture, with the lucky slaves "merely" being stools and human carpets, while the less fortunate ones are forced to hold burning candles between their teeth and in their asses. The entire room has a dizzying, aromatic smell to it that isn't quite perfume nor air freshening fragrance, the odor reminding you of women's department stores, ladies underwear drawers, and the scent of concrete after rain, all mixed into one.

You stick to the outer wall of the party, trying to figure out your next move. You haven't spotted Mistress Merciless yet—thank god—but that also means you don't know her whereabouts, making it that much harder to avoid her.

One option is to mingle in the Salon, trying your luck at winning the favor of a mistress or maybe learning more about where you might possibly get yourself unlocked, though such a prospect is becoming increasingly daunting.

The other option is to make it into the Salon's far kitchen to take shelter from the mistresses of the party. It seems very unlikely Mistress Merciless would be in there and, as you keep your eyes focused on the kitchen's swinging doors, you see a staircase at the end of it leading downstairs.

Ultimately, you figure it comes down to whether or not you think it's worth taking the risk of being in the Salon or if going into the basement is likely to be a better bet. Neither choice feels great, but standing on the outside of the party's throng is sure to get you noticed sooner rather than later.

Mingle in the Salon with the mistresses (Page 227)
Go through the kitchen and investigate the staircase (Page 231)

113

With so many slaves and mistresses in the thick of the party, you feel confident that you've got at least some time before you start to stick out and shuffle out into the fray, looking for an opportunity to be useful. You have no experience being this kind of "slave" or even really submitting for that matter, but there's a kind of crackling energy in the air that fills you with excitement as you pass by so many gorgeous women decked out in high fetish fashions and elegant attire. Most seem to be deeply engaged in their own conversations, or "playing" with some poor male who is quivering beneath them, but despite that a few look your way... and not with malicious or angry looks either.

If anything, you'd say most of the looks you're getting are appraising as these women try to decide if they should engage with you, many of them looking you up and down long enough to even make you feel good about yourself, in a very specific kind of way, of course.

This is not the kind of attention you're used to. Not that you're bad looking or anything, but you're far more used to a night out at the bars or in your wilder moment the clubs, with you and men like you doing most of the looking while the women present laugh and dance and drink their nights away. But clearly in Matriarch Manor things are different. Here, women have the power and men are the objects of ogling and taunting stares. At first it's a giddy feeling to have so much attention, but your mind quickly makes an important connection:

Just as men in bars and clubs ogle women, they also make moves on them and try to exert power *over* them. That very same thing has already happened to you at the manor, and it's sure to continue.

You're weaving through a claustrophobic pocket of the party when someone grabs you by your chastity device, yanking you over, cock and balls first, to where she's enjoying a glass of something big and brown that smells like overproof whiskey. Keeping a firm grip on your cage she gives you a tipsy, heated stare.

"When I say 'Jump!', you say 'How high?'," she tells you.

"What?" you ask, not following.

"Jump!" she shouts.

Does she really want you say 'How high?' and to jump for her. You glance down at your chastity device with a panicky look.

"Jump!" she shouts again. Her nails dig into your balls and you dance from foot to foot in pain.

"How high?" you squeak out.

"As high as you can!" she orders.

You look up at the mistress. She has the tall, thin look of a gymnast, and if it wasn't for her slate gray tailored suit which frames full, heart-shaped hips and such a round ass it threatens to rip the fabric, you'd swear she was. Her blazer practically hangs off her sharp shoulders and despite having the warm, olive skin of somewhere in the Mediterranean, her short black hair is streaked with platinum blonde hair dye, the contrast no more evident than with her full, dark eyebrows. She gives you a smile with plump purple lips, watching you expectantly.

You jump before you can let yourself worry about it too much. A little voice inside tells you this is a terrible idea. Squatting down, you then launch yourself up, feeling a rush of relief as the mistress brings her clawed grasp up with your jump.

She lets go of you, sparing your balls.

"That's as high as you can jump?" she asks in a bitchy tone. She laughs, a laugh that encapsulates all the mean better-than-you girls you've come across in high school, college, and beyond. "Get on your knees, loser, you're too short and stupid to be standing with me."

Just your luck that you had to wind up entertaining a mistress on the bossy, haughty end of the spectrum.

You lower yourself to your knees, the dyed blonde mistress now towering above you. She stares down at you derisively.

"That's better," she says, her dark plum lips spreading wide. She takes a long sip of her strong whiskey. "Exactly where you belong."

The tip of her open-toed heels slides under your chastity device and you feel the mistress's toes tickling your balls. It's both a pleasant and surprising feeling, and you tense yourself for a sudden kick to your crotch.

"How small are you down there, loser?" she asks, looming over you.

It takes a second to catch on that she's asking how big your cock is. You tell her the number. It's never been a point of shame for you, but as the mistress laughs raucously to herself, you feel the weight of her grinding humiliation.

"Oh my GOD," she shrieks. "You could've told me anything! You're not getting out of *that* thing any time soon." She pushes against your device with her foot, continuing to lose herself to laughter. "Why did you pick a number so small? Oh wait—is it even smaller and you thought *that* was an improvement? That is SO sad. *Did* you tell me a fake number?"

You shake your head no. "That's how bi—that's my size, Miss," you admit, the shame of her words pelting you like hot chips of charcoal. The look in the woman's face as you admit this is full of disregard for you, a gleeful, nasty look that both makes you want to throttle the bitch and have her grace you with her favor, and the only thing you loathe more in the moment than your humiliation is that bizarre duality of wanting and not wanting her.

"Try to hump my leg," she says after another sip of whiskey. "Come on! You're so small down there you can probably get it up in that cage, I wanna see if I can get you to cum."

You hesitate. So far, *most* of your humiliations in the manor have been things done to you but this is different. This is you having to take action to make a fool out of yourself.

The mistress thwaps you in the balls and you double over, clutching your crotch.

"Hump my leg!" she demands tipsily over the bassy thump of the party's music. "Or else... or else I'm going to cut your balls off!'

A drunken threat, for sure, but you don't want to find out just how much she can torment you if she wants to. So you crawl towards her, positioning your legs around her awkwardly and pushing your cage against her shin. It's not a great angle, but really there's no angle you can imagine working for humping someone's leg.

You start to rock your hips. Even your shy starting motions make the mistress burst into even more laughter, the sound of it grating on your ears. Your cock is anything but hard right now, but you're forced to hump against her leg like you've got a massive hard-on, all to the sounds coming from her—and increasingly, other mistresses—laughing and pointing at your maladroit efforts.

It's then that you hear a dreadfully familiar voice.

"Well, well, well. If it isn't my drunken friend from the bar. How's chastity life treating you? Had I known you were interested in coming to the manor, I would've invited you myself, you naughty party crasher you."

You know that voice. It's Mistress Merciless. The mistress whose leg you're humping looks over at Mistress Merciless and you follow her gaze.

It's Mistress Merciless alright. Although you could try to play dumb and convince her you're someone else. It might ward her off from taking an undue interest in you, or it might incite her further. With how small and foolish and dumb you're feeling, it's hard to think straight on what the better choice is.

Admit who you are and speak with Mistress Merciless (Page 187)
Pretend to be somebody else (Page 189)

114

The kitchen and the stairs beyond it is. You hope you aren't making a mistake.

With purpose, you stride your way towards the swinging kitchen doors and push your way through, immediately blinding by the kitchen's bright lighting. Inside there are a dozen slaves preparing food and pouring beverages, working with a terrified precision as dictated by a warden-like woman who struts up and down the kitchen's gleaming stainless steel stations. She shrieks at the males taking too long and swats the ones who seem to be doing a fair enough job just for the hell of it.

The woman, who seems barely drinking age herself and younger than pretty much all of the male slaves, delights in her power over them. She is wearing a long, black pencil skirt with a fluttery hem, clacky black patent leather heels, and an open blazer over what appears to be no shirt or bra whatsoever. Her skin is ghostly pale and her chestnut hair is short with loose curls that bounce with every step she takes. The woman's black-frame glasses add to her sultry, secretariat look, as does the clipboard in her hand that she takes frequent notes on as she observes the labor of the kitchen slave staff.

You avoid making eye contact with her and pick up your pace as you speed towards the stairs going down. Just as you're about to reach the staircase, you hear a shout from behind.

"You! Slave! Where are you going?"

You turn back and see the young mistress is staring daggers at you through her black-frame glasses. The way she looks at you, you sense that neither here in the manor nor outside of it has she *ever* let a man displease her without paying for it.

Whatever your answer is, it had better be convincing.

Answer that you're not allowed to say where you're going (Page 232)
Apologize for the intrusion and return to the party (Page 233)

115

You bow your head in apology and say, "I'm sorry Miss, but I'm not permitted to say. I beg your forgiveness."

Her eyes flash with rage. To her, such an answer is simply unacceptable. She marches forward, getting in your face and nearly making you take a step backwards onto the stairs, which would send you tumbling down them with a broken neck. Up close you can smell the wine on her breath and can feel that even though she's small in stature, she presents the energy of someone twice her size. A tiny little dictator, that's what you think. The most frightening kind.

"This is *my* kitchen," she snaps, flicking her clipboard angrily. "No one goes through *my* kitchen without me knowing what it's for and why."

A little voice inside tells you to play this carefully, that you're dancing on the edge of a knife right now. The question is *how* do you play this? Do you push the little dictator mistress and once more tell her that you cannot say? After all, sometimes the best way to fight back against a bully is to stand your ground.

Or you could try a different route. There is one mistress who seems to have considerable standing in Matriarch Manor: Mistress Merciless. If there's one thing little dictators fear, it's an even greater dictator than themselves.

You clench your teeth as you try to decide.

Lie and say it was Mistress Merciless who sent you (Page 237)
Insist that you cannot say (Page 238)

116

"I'm sorry Miss, I went the wrong way..."

You try to turn and dart back out of the kitchen, but the little dictator mistress stops you, holding her clipboard out like a shield.

The kitchen mistress scoffs, her lips pulling back into a sneer of contempt. "You slaves were told again and again not to interfere with my kitchen operations. You think you're special? That you're above the rules? That's not how it works here."

She steps closer to you, her high heels clicking ominously against the tile floor. You can feel the heat from her body, a stark contrast to the cold fear coursing through your veins. Before you can react, she delivers a swift kick to your balls. Pain sears through your belly and legs and you stumble backward, barely managing to stay upright. A tiny gasp escapes your lips, the only outward sign of your discomfort.

"That's for coming through my kitchen without my permission," she hisses. She turns toward the rest of the kitchen slaves who have stopped their work to watch the spectacle. "And this..." she continues, delivering another cruel kick to your balls, "...is for disrupting our work here."

You fall onto one knee this time unable to suppress a grunt of pain. The kitchen mistress smiles in satisfaction at your predicament.

"Now," she says with an icy calmness that sends shivers down your spine. "I think it's time we put you in your place."

She motions for two of the larger kitchen slaves to come forward. You try to get up but they hold you down effortlessly, their hands like iron bands around your arms. With a playful twinkle in her eyes that belies her ruthless demeanor, the kitchen mistress picks up a plastic whisk from one of the tables and approaches you.

"This is what happens when someone thinks they're above their station," she declares before bringing down the whisk hard against your bare backside.

The impact stings more than you can imagine and involuntary tears spring into your eyes. But more than the physical pain, it's the humiliation that cuts deep. Again and again she strikes until your backside is throbbing and red-hot with pain. All the while she maintains an air of nonchalance that makes it all so much worse. She finally stops after what feels like an eternity but instead of comforting relief all you feel is dread knowing that this probably isn't over yet. As if reading your thoughts, she nods towards a stack of dirty dishes on one end of the kitchen.

"You're going to wash those," she orders tersely before releasing you from her minions' grip.

Barely able to stand due to pain and exhaustion, nevertheless you shuffle towards the dirty dishes obediently under her watchful gaze.

Sweat trickles down your forehead as you submerge your hands into the hot soapy water and start scrubbing away at plates encrusted with remnants of rich food too fancy for common palates like yours.

Minutes turn into a half hour and then a whole hour with you bent over a sink washing dishes while enduring taunts and sarcastic remarks from the little dictator whenever she passes by, noticing that a number of the other slaves set to work in the kitchen are chains to their stations. Finally you hear a dreadful sound of heavy clunking metal as the kitchen mistress has her two doting, obedient large slaves bring over just such a chain for you.

"These parties go on very, very late, slave," she says with an air of pride. "Sometimes until five or six in the morning. You will be working a full shift until then."

The slaves secure your ankle to the dishwashing station and the kitchen mistress strikes your ass again with the plastic whisk, purposefully hitting the spot she'd been wailing on earlier.

Despair overwhelms you as you realize you are not only not going to get your freedom from chastity, but that your very freedom from Matriarch Manor is no more. Your back aches. Your legs ache. Your hands feel tender and weak from the constant rush of scalding hot dish water. Everything about the station seems designed to be uncomfortable and after so long hunching over it, with barely a foot of chain length to help stretch your feet, you wonder how you'll ever make it through the night... or what will transpire once the mistresses of the manor realize you are a trespasser.

Unfortunately for you, that moment is about to occur.

"Merci!" cries out the kitchen mistress as none other than Mistress Merciless strides through the kitchen's swinging doors. She has an empty champagne flute in one hand, walking as if she's seven feet tall. Slaves bow their heads as she passes, while the little dictator mistress runs up to her excitedly.

"Amelia! You've done such a fantastic job so far tonight," Mistress

Merciless purrs darkly. "I simply can't believe it. The food, the drink, and everything has been absolutely splendid, all thanks to your singular focus and hard work."

The way Mistress Merciless speaks, she doesn't even think to reference the labor of the slaves, treating their contributions more like the output from a bunch of kitchen appliances without free will. She puts her empty flute right in front of a slave's prep station, interrupting his flow and forcing him to decide whether to move it and keep working or to get Mistress Merciless a refill. His choice is made for him when the kitchen mistress—Amelia— glares at him and claps her hands together.

"Chop, chop!" she snaps before pointing to the fridge. The slave scuttles off. "My apologies, Merci, you know what idiots slaves are."

"Oh, it's alright. Though I must say I am looking forward to all the poor wretches being back in their cells so we can have some peace later."

Both women laugh unkindly. Mistress Merciless surveys and the kitchen and that's when she spots you.

"A familiar face," she says to herself.

Amelia turns and follows Mistress Merciless's gaze. "Oh *that* one. Can you believe he was cutting through my kitchen with nothing to say for himself?"

"Was he?" says Mistress Merciless. She glides towards you menacingly, Amelia flitting behind. "Just couldn't stay away, could you?"

You try to bow your head, as if the mistress might forget you're there. She reaches a long-nailed, long-fingered hand out, the talon of one nail pushing your chin up to face her. With her mussed, wavy black hair and her smoldering eyes, she has that kind of imperious, bitchy-hot look to her, the sort you can't help but stare at but can't watch for too long. Now, as you're forced to look into her eyes, you feel your stomach caving in and your legs turn to Jell-O.

"Merci...?" asks Amelia.

Then you're forced to listen as Mistress Merciless recounts the events that led you to your chastisement, her retelling painting you as a loud, oafish buffoon. Amelia smirks and scoffs at the retelling and, when Mistress Merciless is done, adds:

"Looks like he's where he belongs now, huh?"

Mistress Merciless considers this.

"No, I'm not sure about that," she says. For the tiniest of seconds, you feel a ray of hope... only for the mistress to smother it with horrible darkness. "It's too bright in here. Too clean. Too... civilized." She snaps her fingers at two of the larger slaves that have come over proactively to do any bidding Amelia might need done. "Take him downstairs to the cells. Put him in... the sweatbox."

One of the large slaves grasps your shoulders while the other undoes your ankle binding. They shove you brusquely towards the stairs you were trying to get to before.

"Yes, we'll see how he does in a few hours down there. By then I bet he'll just be *begging* to wash some dishes in scalding hot water."

Amelia shrieks with glee as you're forced down the stairs and into the dingy, stone-walled basement. You try to plead with the slaves, but they ignore you, shoving you harder and more forcefully every time you open your mouth. The sweatbox is just that: a metal-doored cramped little cell that is unbelievably hot and humid. They throw you inside and latch the door shut.

Moments later you hear a voice through the suddenly opened metal door's tiny window grill. Mistress Merciless.

"Trespassers are not tolerated at Matriarch Manor," she says. Her voice has an ominous echo to it thanks to the harsh walls of the hot, cramped cell. "Now, I don't know *why* you came here, but I'm sure it wasn't for altruistic reasons. But I'm merciless, not heartless. Three hours in the box. Then you will tell me why you're here and what you hoped to accomplish... and then I will determine a suitable punishment."

The slit of the window grill is covered up again, casting you in total, steamy hot darkness. The heat worms its way under your skin and into your brain, making every second feel like it's taking hours to pass. There's no escaping it, no matter what position you take or how soft or deep you try to breathe. You feel the sweat pouring off your body, soaking your hair and coating every inch of your skin. It makes even the slightest use of your hands slippery, the feeling not helped by the cell's moisture-slicked stony walls. Through some kind of crack in the stone or sealed up ventilation shaft, you can hear the distant thrum of the party and the occasional burst of feminine laughter.

You go over what you're going to say to Mistress Merciless again and again, each revision ever more stripped of your attempt to excuse your actions as the madness of the sweatbox's heat grows. You can't go back in this cell. Not again, not ever—and so you're prepared to say whatever it takes and do whatever's necessary.

Your new life as a slave at Matriarch manor has just begun.

THE END

117

Knowing this might be an idiotic idea, you lean in close, acting as conspiratorial as possible, and you say in a near-whisper: "Mistress Merciless. She told me to go downstairs right away to retrieve something for her and to speak to no one, but I want to respect your kitchen, Miss. I apologize for the inconvenience and hope you can see it in your graciousness to let me pass."

The little dictator thinks about it. Just the mention of Mistress Merciless is enough to get her relax her shoulders and let a sigh out through her nose, it carrying more of that sharp, winey smell you detected on her breath earlier. Her eyes search the dark kitchen floor in thought.

"Fine," she says begrudgingly. "But if she asks you for something like that again, you find another way downstairs. I don't care if it takes you an extra ten minutes, that's your problem, not mine."

You don't dare press your luck any further by saying another word, giving her a deep bow and then rushing down the steps into the basement.

Caught between the sounds of the party and kitchen staff upstairs and the wails and cracks of heavy implements beating against tender slave flesh in the basement, you feel disoriented. But the feeling soon passes when you spy what looks like some kind of office across from the stairs. The door is open and it is, seemingly, empty.

Anything is better than risking the little dictator mistress coming after you and so you pad down the hall towards the basement office.

Continue on downstairs into the basement office (Page 147)

118

"I'm truly sorry Miss, but I'm not allowed to say," you respond, trying to sound as humble and apologetic as possible. You don't dare meet her gaze, instead focusing on the shiny floor beneath your feet.

The kitchen mistress scoffs, her lips pulling back into a sneer of contempt. "Not allowed to say? What kind of nonsense is that? In my kitchen, there are no secrets."

She steps closer to you, her high heels clicking ominously against the tile floor. You can feel the heat from her body, a stark contrast to the cold fear coursing through your veins.

"You think you're special?" she asks, her voice dripping with venom. "That you're above the rules? That's not how it works here."

Before you can react, she delivers a swift kick to your shin. Pain sears through your leg and you stumble backward, barely managing to stay upright. A tiny gasp escapes your lips, the only outward sign of your discomfort.

"That's for coming through my kitchen without my permission," she hisses. She turns toward the rest of the kitchen slaves who have stopped their work to watch the spectacle. "And this..." she continues, delivering another cruel kick to your other shin, "...is for disrupting our work here."

You fall onto one knee this time unable to suppress a grunt of pain. The kitchen mistress smiles in satisfaction at your predicament.

"Now," she says with an icy calmness that sends shivers down your spine. "I think it's time we put you in your place."

She motions for two of the larger kitchen slaves to come forward. You try to get up but they hold you down effortlessly, their hands like iron bands around your arms.

With a playful twinkle in her eyes that belies her ruthless demeanor, the kitchen mistress picks up a wooden spoon from one of the tables and approaches you.

"This is what happens when someone thinks they're above their station," she declares before bringing down the spoon hard against your bare backside.

The impact stings more than you can imagine and involuntary tears spring into your eyes. But more than the physical pain, it's the humiliation that cuts deep. Again and again she strikes until your backside is throbbing and red-hot with pain. All the while she maintains an air of nonchalance that makes it all so much worse. She finally stops after what feels like an eternity but instead of comforting relief all you feel is dread knowing that this probably isn't over yet. As if reading your thoughts, she nods towards a stack of dirty dishes on one end of the kitchen.

"You're going to wash those," she orders tersely before releasing you from her minions' grip.

Barely able to stand due to pain and exhaustion, nevertheless you shuffle towards the dirty dishes obediently under her watchful gaze.

Sweat trickles down your forehead as you submerge your hands into the hot soapy water and start scrubbing away at plates encrusted with remnants of rich food too fancy for common palates like yours.

Minutes turn into a half hour and then a whole hour with you bent over a sink washing dishes while enduring taunts and sarcastic remarks from the little dictator whenever she passes by, noticing that a number of the other slaves set to work in the kitchen are chains to their stations. Finally you hear a dreadful sound of heavy clunking metal as the kitchen mistress has her two doting, obedient large slaves bring over just such a chain for you.

"These parties go on very, very late, slave," she says with an air of pride. "Sometimes until five or six in the morning. You will be working a full shift until then."

The slaves secure your ankle to the dishwashing station and the kitchen mistress strikes your ass again with the wooden spoon, purposefully hitting the spot she'd been wailing on earlier.

Despair overwhelms you as you realize you are not only not going to get your freedom from chastity, but that your very freedom from Matriarch Manor is no more. Your back aches. Your legs ache. Your hands feel tender and weak from the constant rush of scalding hot dish water. Everything about the station seems designed to be uncomfortable and after so long hunching over it, with barely a foot of chain length to help stretch your feet, you wonder how you'll ever make it through the night... or what will transpire once the mistresses of the manor realize you are a trespasser.

It's going to be a horrible, horrible night for you.

THE END

119

It's a difficult choice, but after what you've seen at Matriarch Manor tonight, it's settled: It's time to go home. You punch the red button for the doors leading outside of the manor. They shudder open and you feel the breeze of the evening air tickle your near-naked body. It's going to be a hike getting home the way you are, but you'll find a way... anything is better than sticking around too long in this forsaken place.

You peel away from the direction of the backyard, the party back there already starting to reach a shrill, drunken fever pitch. Though as you do, you wistfully look at a rack of coats that have been set out for the mistresses to wear to keep warm—if only you could have one too, but there's no point in risking your escape now, not when you've made it this far.

You trod off down the first path you can find away from the manor, stepping onto a dirt path that goes along the main road you walked along to get here. It snakes and curves, but you generally are able to follow it, the setting sun making you pick up your pace lest you risk being lost naked and in the dark in the woods around Matriarch Manor. Now and again you turn back towards the manor's lights to help orient yourself and even this far away you can hear the occasional laugh or crack of something—wood? A whip? Something you can't even imagine?—that signals the party is still going strong and is sure to be for quite some time.

You reach down to feel your chastity cage. 51 weeks to go. It's going to be a long time not being able to touch yourself. Maybe you can come back to the manor and try your luck again or maybe, somehow, you can convince Mistress Merciless to let you out.

But that will come later. For now you need to get home and thank your lucky stars no one caught you lurking around the manor... and try not to feel like you failed your task.

THE END

120

You stroll up to the elevator, looking for the button to summon it. There isn't one. Just the black box with its "flashing red light. That's when you realize you must need some kind of keycard to access the elevator. Realizing you're in a cramped little elevator bank with no other way out, you go back into the hallway... only to hear voices coming down the way.

"Oh my, oh my that was... epic," one says, a slight slur in her words from a night of loud music and drinking.

"Not bad," says the other, her tone crisper and more coherent. "But I've seen wilder manor parties, just you wait. And the outside 'Cool Down' tonight looks like it's going to be insane. I heard they're going to make the slaves do a gladiator fighting thing. Last one standing gets out of his cage for a day or hour or something, while all the rest are going to be soooooorrry."

"I forgot about the Cool Down! Ohmigod, this is the best day ever."

You try to walk away from the voices, heading down the hallway... but they continue almost right behind you. You duck into the lounge space near Mistress Merciless's room, the one with the low sofa and the windows that overlook the manor's backyard.

"Let's see how Cool Down is going," says one of the voices. "Right over here, we can look out the cubby windows."

Now, along with the voices, you hear footsteps. And they're headed your way. You cower behind the sofa, wishing it were higher.

"Come on, let's—OH GOD!"

You hear a shriek followed by a shocked, confused laugh.

"A slave! You, get out of there! Now!"

You reluctantly pick your head up to see two mistresses from the party standing there, one with pale skin and alcohol-flushed cheeks who looks East Asian wearing a silk Chinese dragon print dress with a short collar and a split hem and the other who looks Middle Eastern with her hair up in a ponytail, big hoop earrings, and a front-knotted pink crop top blouse with long, flounce sleeves and cut off denim booty shorts.

"Kayla, what the hell," says the East Asian mistress.

"Looks like we have a stowaway, Tiffany," says Kayla with a dazzling, devilish smile. She flicks her finger up at you. "You! I said: Get up!"

You shakily rise from behind the sofa, cursing yourself for thinking you could easily hide away in the lounge. Kayla gives Tiffany a sly, wicked look. Then she fishes out a box of cigarettes from the front pocket of her cut-off denim shorts and sits down on the sofa. She snaps her fingers and points to the floor in front of her.

"Over here, slave," she says.

"What are you doing Kayla?" asks Tiffany.

"Enjoying a smoke break," Kayla says. "Come on, join me."

As Tiffany takes a seat next to Kayla, you come around from the sofa and look towards the lounge's archway.

"Don't even think about it," says Kayla, holding her cigarette in her mouth as she lights it. She takes a deep inhale and lets it go towards the glass ceiling of the atrium lounge. She hands the cigarettes and her lighter to Tiffany, who takes them with some hesitation, the look on her face suggesting she's still trying to figure out what Kayla's up to. Kayla points to the ground. "Kneel."

You get down on your knees as the women smoke in silence, Kayla not taking her emerald green eyes off you. She takes a long drag of her cigarette and blows the smoke in your face, the blue-white cloud stinging your eyes and your nostrils.

"Tiff, did you mean what you said before? That you wanna become an official Matriarch Manor mistress?" asks Kayla.

Tiffany nods as she sucks on her cigarette. The blush in her cheeks is very pink now, giving her a faux-innocent glow. "I do. One day."

"Well, I'm going to teach you something," says Kayla. "Something that was taught to me when I started my application: Harden Your Heart."

Tiffany raises an eyebrow at Kayla. "Meaning...?"

"Meaning that a lot of women *try* to join the manor but they just can't do it. And the reason is usually something like they feel bad for one of the slaves or they think they can't go as far as other women or they just get too soft-hearted in general. That's why you've got to harden your heart if you're gonna be here. Watch."

Kayla takes a long, long drag of her cigarette, holding the precious nicotine-laced smoke in her lungs before she lets it roll down onto you in a heavy cloud. Her cigarette has begun to ash. She holds it out towards you and says, "Slave, give me your tongue."

"Kayla..."

Kayla shushes Tiffany. "Just watch," she says. "Slave. Tongue. Now. Or I report you for lurking up on the third floor."

You reluctantly loll out your tongue, looking in horror as Kayla flicks the ash of her cigarette onto it. You go to pull your tongue back in, but the mistress stops you.

"Hold it there until I say so," she says. Then she ignores you, returning to her conversation with Tiffany.

"See the thing is, if you view the slaves as 'men' or even as 'people', you're already going the wrong way. They aren't men or people and they aren't deserving of the way you'd respect an actual person. They're *things*. Things to use, to abuse. And the only way to really internalize this notion for yourself is, well, you gotta fake it till you make it. Go on, try ashing your cigarette in its mouth."

Tiffany, wanting to impress her friend, takes as long of a drag as Kayla did, coughing for a slight spell before her cigarette has a long column of flaky ash threatening to fall from its tip. She holds it over your tongue with a somewhat apologetic look on her face. Then she taps it and the column of ash tumbles onto your tongue. It's very warm for a second before it's cooled by your saliva, your ashy spit coating your tongue with the burned, charcoal taste of the cigarette. You can feel your mouth watering from being held open and your tongue start to ache as you continue to keep it held out for the mistresses' use.

They continue to chat, taking turns ashing their cigarettes on your tongue until there's a gratuitous pile of the saliva-wetted filth. It slides towards your mouth and the edges of your tongue, forcing you to make a scoop-like shape to hold it all in. All the while, the smell of smoke grows and the air gets thick with the blue-white haze that stings your eyes and your nostrils and makes you want to desperately get some fresh air.

When Kayla is done with her first cigarette, she gives you a terrible, snarling smile. "This is going to hurt," she says, more a promise than a warning. Then you watch helplessly as she brings the smoldering tip of her cigarette to the flat of your tongue, crushing it out on your tender flesh while you clench your fists shut and try to fight through the pain. She grinds that cigarette down and leaves it on the pile of the ash, still not permitting you to swallow. She looks at Tiffany expectantly.

"Your turn," she says.

Apprehensive, Tiffany follows Kayla's lead. She sucks down her cigarette as quickly as she can, blowing the smoke right at you per Kayla's instruction, and then, like she's stomping on a roach in the kitchen, she smushes the cigarette butt onto your tongue, catching you on the tip and making you grunt in pain. Kayla laughs delightedly. When Tiffany's managed to push the cigarette to just a small nub, she drops it next Kayla's discarded smoke.

Only then does Kayla flash her emerald green eyes at you and say:

"You may now swallow, slave."

It's just as bad going down your throat as sitting on your tongue, maybe even worse. Your throat feels chalky and gritty and you cough as you try to choke down the mistresses' waste, unable to believe they've just used you as a human ashtray. As you stay doubled over, coughing, you hear the flick of a lighter.

They aren't done with you yet.

"And here's the thing," Kayla says to Tiffany as they both start on their second cigarette. "You see what we just did? You see how he *listened* to us? He didn't have to do that. He could've refused, could've suffered the consequences, could've kept his pride. But he doesn't *have* pride. Because he's a sub-human piece of garbage. Aren't you, slave?"

Kayla thrusts out her lit cigarette towards you. She's not interested in your mouth anymore. She hovers it over your skin, just an inch away from your shoulder, then your chest, and then your nipple.

"Go ahead, nod your head like a dummy or I'm putting my cigarette out on you right now," she says.

You bobblehead nod and Kayla snorts, all while Tiffany watches with a mix of shock and awe.

"Put your cigarette out on him," she says to Tiffany. "The slave's going to choose a place for you to do it. And if I don't like where he picks, I'm going to choose a different one."

Tiffany leans forward with her lit cigarette. She seems unsure. You're unsure too, trying to figure out what part of your body you could offer up that would placate these women, thinking how this is not how this evening was supposed to wind up. What will these women do to you after they've had their fun? Will they let you go, or will they drag you downstairs for more torment?

Somehow you don't think freedom is what they have in mind.

Slowly you turn around, showing your back and buttocks; it feels like it'll be less painful that way and at least you won't have to watch.

"Oh look, he's offering you his balls," says Kayla snidely. "Go ahead, Harden your heart and teach this thing what it really is."

As you wait for the cigarette to land, your body trembling, you regret coming to Matriarch Manor at all. Maybe you could've found a happier fate, but you know that deep down in your heart, these mistresses have no intention of letting you go.

THE END

121

The opportunity just seems too good to pass up: a safe trip to the third floor *and* some kind attention from the women of Matriarch Manor for a change? Yes, please!

"I... I think my cleaning could perhaps wait a little bit," you say, your voice nearly cracking.

As if on cue, the women both clap their hands together joyfully and squeal in delight. The elevator trundles to a stop on the second floor and the doors open. The women pull you along after them, they themselves not knowing how to navigate the maze of the second floor's hallways. After a bit of searching and some trial and error though, they find the staircase leading up to the third floor and take you up it.

A thin, royal blue carpet with an intricate design covers the steps, muffling all of your footsteps. The sounds of the party feel much farther away now and by the time you reach the landing of the third floor, they are but a distant din. Unlike the second floor, the third floor seems to be made of just one wraparound hallway that—as far as you can tell—goes along the outer walls of Matriarch Manor, with doors leading to rooms on the outside, no doubt giving those that the rooms belong pleasant views of the outside.

The air up here is still and slightly stuffy, and you can smell a mix made of perfume, incense, and flowers as the girls investigate the doors, curiously taking them in, along with the archways that separate the doors and which lead to a small, shared space of some sort, each sitting under slanted glass panels, like those of an atrium.

As the girls pull you through the wraparound hallway, you take in the doors too. All but one has a name carved into its wood, and that lone door out instead has ornate designs carved into it from top to bottom, the images depicting a swirling sprawl of astrological symbols. Two doors down from it is the room you've only imagined so far: the one belonging to Mistress Merciless herself, the mistress's name written in a stiff, imposing font. Between the ornate door and Mistress Merciless's room is the only shared atrium space that isn't completely cast in shadow. Peering through the archway, you see that it's set up to be some kind of lounge space, with a low sofa and a hexagonal tea table and erotic sculptures displayed in the center of the cubby.

You can't believe you've stumbled upon Mistress Merciless's room like this! But even though you're dying to peel away and investigate it, the mistresses instead pull you through the ornate, their curiosity trumping yours.

This large, double bedroom-sized space seems to be set up like some kind of a colorful playroom. The walls are beach pink, there are endless S&M toys strewn across the floor, and there are both many pieces of curious fetish furniture and metal carts full of lube and condoms and medical supplies, all of it so out in the open that you're left exactly who this room is intended for. Whatever the answer, it's clear that the people who come here know exactly what they're getting into and are less interested in theater than they are in indulging themselves in perverse pleasure.

Closets with louvered doors sit along one wall and a simple utilitarian bathroom is accessible from the opposite wall, though there seems to be nothing of interest in there than a toilet, sink, and a narrow shower stall. Perhaps it's some kind of elite playroom, you think, a place where pretentious drop and all manner of curiosities are explored.

"Jackpot, Jenna!" cries the blonde gleefully.

"Whoa... there's so much stuff here Sadie," says Jenna, the ponytailed mistress.

Jenna walks towards one of the piles, catching sight of something interesting. She starts to dig through the toys, setting aside colorful dildos and bizarrely-shaped vibrators.

Sadie squeezes a handful of your ass cheek, making you jump with surprise. "We are going to have so much fun," she says, getting ready to practically pounce on you. She pushes you back towards a low flat rectangle of purple latex padding, almost shoving you onto it. Jenna, come help me figure out how to use this thing."

"One second," says Jenna, seeming frustrated that she lost sight of whatever she was looking for.

Meanwhile, Sadie orders you to sit on the mattress-like padding as she pulls at its thick corner straps. Each strap is long and has fifteen or twenty slotted holes. Slowly it dawns on you that these are cuffs of a sort, Sadie slowly working out how to wrap the strap around one of your ankles and thread it through and cinch it nice and tight. She goes to work on the ankle strap and then has you lie down, having you stretch your arms out in a V shape so she can cuff those too. You're now left spread eagle on the latex mattress which, you have to admit, is actually kind of comfortable all things considered.

Sadie looks around, spying the closet doors. She steps over them and wrinkles her nose at the sight of a mound of dirty laundry. Opening the next set of closet doors over, she finds racks and racks of fetish outfits, squealing excitedly.

"These look *so* cool!" she says, tucking her hair behind her ears as she flips through the outfits.

You almost can't believe it when she starts to strip right in front of you, pulling off her crop top blouse and her light blue jeans so that she's down to just a skimpy thong and a satiny bra. Your cock tries to harden in its metal prison, the swell of you pushing up against the constricting, suffocating tube that's far too short to ever get a full erection in. You hiss a sigh but don't pull your eyes away from the blondie, greedily taking in her soft curves.

Then off to the other side, where Jenna is, you hear a jingling, jangling sound. As you loll your head over you see yet another thing you can't believe: the sure-shouldered woman with the long, silky ponytail is holding up a huge keyring adorned with small little keys—the same sort you remember Mistress Merciless using to lock up your chastity device. Your heart pounds excitedly. Could this... be it? Could you have, quite literally, *stumbled* into freedom?

Looking back at Sadie, you see she's pulling on a heavy latex dress. It's powder blue with white piping and it has an altogether too-short floppy, ruffled skirt.

Jenna steps over to meet Sadie. "What did you find?" she asks.

"Soooo many outfits. Here, look and pick something out! I can't believe how many there are..."

Jenna hands Sadie the keys. "See if one of these opens his thing up," she says nonchalantly.

"Ohhh you wanna do that thing we talked about?" asks Sadie, taking the keys.

"I wanna try it at least," says Jenna.

Sadie laughs and sidles over to you, shooting you mischievous glances as she fiddles with the keys. There are twenty or thirty on the ring and she goes through them one by one while Jenna also strips herself down to a matching black lace bra and panty set. From the closet, she pulls out a pink leather corset with a snap crotch, taking off her underwear before pulling it on over her full, sensual hourglass frame. Rather curiously, she leaves the crotch unsnapped.

One of the keys slides into your padlock and Sadie gives it a gentle turn. There's an oh-so-satisfying click as your padlock opens! Your heart pounds so hard as you try not to show your excitement. Is this really about to happen?

As Sadie pulls off your chastity device, Jenna joins the two of you, sitting on the opposite side. Your cock springs to life almost instantly, the sight of how fast it grows making both girls giggle.

"Wow, *someone's* eager," taunts Jenna.

Sadie slowly begins to stroke you, being careful not to grip you too hard. She keeps her eyes locked on you as she does and you can't but help let out a breathy sigh, amazed at how good it feels to be touched for the first time in a week—and even longer, by someone else's hand.

"We're going to play a game," she tells you.

You see now that both women have their eyes on you, staring at you with a look that grows more devilish by the second.

Sadie continues to slowly stroke you. "It's very simple. Do not cum."

You furrow your brow and look from Sadie to Jenna and then back. Why is she stroking you if she doesn't want you to cum?

"Miss...?" you ask before you can stop yourself, worried your question might earn you some retribution.

But all it gets you is a sly smile from Sadie. "Do not cum. That's the name of the game, that's the rule of the game, and it is, like I said, very, very simple."

She strokes you a little bit faster now.

"And if you cum," says Jenna, hooking one leg over yours to perch herself above your knees. "We're going to report you. Do you know what happens to a slave here who cums without permission?"

You shake your head, knowing you shouldn't show your ignorance, but too terrified now not to find out more. Sadie lets go of your ragingly hard cock and Jenna scoots up, holding your shaft by the base as she teases her pussy with your swollen cockhead. It feels so good—insanely good—and your mind spins as you wonder how in the world you're to be able to keep from ejaculating.

Sadie draws a finger across her neck. "Off with his head!" she says, her eyes wide with sadistic glee.

"Well, not the *head*," says Jenna as she begins to sit on your cock, sinking herself all the way down to the base of you. She reaches down and snatches your balls with her fingers. "But you get the idea."

Your heart feels like it's going to explode. They *castrate* slaves who cum here? And these women—is that what they're going to have done to you? Your mind flashes back to their flirty grabs in the elevator and their over the top antics. At the time, you simply thought they were young, horny girls who'd had too much to drink, but the truth seems to be far, far worse.

They set you up.

They were *looking* for a slave to do this too, trying to find someone who they could take somewhere to remove his chastity and put him in an impossible position. How are you not supposed to cum?? That's insanity!

Jenna begins to rock her hips back and forth.

"Please, don't do this!" you cry. "Please, anything else, there's no way I'm going to be able to keep myself from, from, you know... oh god, please, please, please!"

As you beg and plead with the women, Sadie stands up and plants her feet on other side of your face. She lowers herself down onto her knees, pressing her thong-clad pussy against your mouth to muffle your protestations. Jenna's rocking begins to move in intensely pleasurable circles, grinding against you while flicks your nipples with her fingers.

"We're gonna take your baaaalls, we're gonna take your baaaallls," taunts Sadie, the honey-musk of her pussy invading your senses. You try to say "no no no no" but all you do is move your lips against the wet fabric of her thong, making the blonde woman give a slight moan.

Soon, Jenna's rocking becomes pumping, the ponytailed woman in her pink corset bouncing up and down on your cock faster and faster. It's insane you haven't cum already, but somehow you've managed to keep the fear of the moment front and center in your mind. You have to fight every instinct not to pump yourself along with her, to keep your hips glued to the latex mattress and your legs untensed. But even with the most willpower you've ever exerted in your life, your cock and balls have a mind of their own, especially after a week of lock up. You can feel your balls starting to tighten and have to keep trying to relax yourself so that your entire body doesn't tense excitedly in anticipation of blowing your last load ever.

Jenna's bouncing is now wet and you can hear her body slapping against yours, all while Sadie pushes her pussy harder and harder against your face.

Through the thin microweave of the thong, you can feel the blonde's wild bush scrape and scratch at your face, the blonde hairs there now soaked with her excited juices.

"Do you think we get to take them ourselves?" Sadie asks Jenna. "Or just watch?"

"I heard they give you a choice," says a breathy Jenna as she continues her vigorous bouncing on your dick. "Both to do it and how to do it."

"I want a tiny guillotine," says Sadie, grinding herself so hard against you that your nose dips into her slit, right through the sopping wet thong.

Jenna laughs harshly. "I wanna try kicking them til they're done," she says. "I hate balls. They're so ugly. Oh! I think he's getting close!"

And you *are* getting close, despite your best efforts to hold off. It's simply too much grinding and rocking and too much of the heady, intoxicating scent of sex. You grunt underneath Sadie and then give a muffled cry of frustration, pulling wildly at your latex bindings.

"Do not cum," commands Sadie. "Do not cum." She says it in such a serious tone that both girls giggle.

"Do not cum," says Jenna, mimicking Sadie's tone.

"Do not cum," the girls say in unison. It soon becomes a chant: "Do not cum. Do not cum. Do not cum."

The worst part about the chant is that it actually brings you to the point of no return even *faster*, their rhythm making it easier for your body to get ready. You feel the need build in your balls and clench your fists shut, your toes curly. It's almost time, you're almost there, just a little bit more and you will have no choice but to explode...

"Do not cum! Do not cum! Do not cum!"

With an agonizing groan of uncontrollable lust, you cum, pumping your seed deep, deep into Jenna's warm, tight pussy. For a few seconds you lose yourself in the sensation, relishing just how very good it feels to let go, but as the women cheer and clap and laugh, reality settles back down on you. It no longer feels exhilarating to thrust your hips wildly against the woman straddling you but she nevertheless continues to ride you, milking out every last drop of seed from your balls. Sadie pulls herself off you and when she sees the frowning, sad expression on your face she bursts into laughter. Jenna joins her. The women can't seem to believe just how crushed and defeated you look, pointing and laughing at you, sharing jokes with each other between gasping breaths.

"Ohmygod ohmygod, I can't breathe," says Sadie.

"That was amazing," says Jenna, wiggling her hips a little more as she extracts the last rope strands of cum from you.

"Please," you mewl. "Please don't take my balls."

Sadie bursts into yet another fit of laughter.

"Ohmygod... he thought we were actually going to do it!" she cries.

Jenna claps her hands together and throws back her head, chest heaving with her laughs.

Wait. Were they... just taunting you? You look around, wide-eyed and confused, as you try to process what just happened. As you stare at the women, stunned, Sadie is already gathering up your chastity device, while Jenna is lifting herself off of you very carefully. Keeping a hand under her pussy, she waddles up to your face and sits down, the still-warm cum dribbling out of her and onto your nose, lips, and mouth. It is bitter and bleachy and salty, and she pushes down on you, forcing it onto your tongue and down your throat.

"Eat up," she says, her laughter finally dying down.

You feel Sadie fitting your cage back on, wiping her hands clean on your thighs as she works. "I can't believe he fell for it," says Sadie. "That was wild."

As you choke and gag on the cum you're being force fed while your cock is shoved back in its steel prison, you realize with more than a little bit of sadness that you just had an orgasm with two gorgeous women—and didn't really enjoy a single moment of it. It was ruined in a way no other orgasm has been ruined in your life, with total and utter fear, and you wonder if you'll ever be able to have such a wonderful set up with women like this again.

But things are about to get even worse.

"When he's done cleaning me, we'll take him down to the basement," says Jenna, shimmying her hips to squeeze out more of your seed. "Then we can try this with another slave. This time I think we should bring like, a pair of gardening shears or something to *really* get him panicking."

"But I get to go this time!" says Sadie with a pout in her voice. You hear the damning click of the padlock on your cage. "I want to know what it feels like."

"A terror-jaculation?" Jenna offers. "I don't even know how to describe it."

"Don't ruin it for me!" says Sadie.

"Oh relax! You'll experience your own. For me it was, like, you could feel him really, really trying not to cum and then when he did, there was like this wonderful hopelessness and loss of control to it."

"I said don't ruin it!"

"The only thing ruined here was his orgasm," quips Jenna.

The women laugh and laugh, reliving their cruelty and command over you all over again.

"I love Matriarch Manor," says Sadie as Jenna lifts herself off your cum-slicked face.

"Me too," says Jenna. "Me too."

The same can't be said for you.

THE END

122

You catch your breath and stumble through the chastity keys until you find the one that fits your device's lock. You nervously turn the key and then hear a soft click. Success! The lock comes off, followed by the device itself. You toss both into the pile of toys and chastity devices, letting out a happy sigh as you're able to touch your cock for the first time all week. In fact, you're so delirious with joy that you think about jerking off right there in the playroom, but not even your sudden bliss can make you do something as foolish as that.

It's time to get out of the manor. You could head back to the elevator now and see if you can get it to work or you could take your time navigating the third floor, looking for some other way back down and out of the manor. You're so close to true freedom, you can taste it!

Beeline for the private elevator (Page 254)
Take your time navigating the third floor (Page 256)

123

You traverse the wraparound hallway of the third floor until you find yourself back at the archway with the private elevator. You walk towards it and its black box with the blinking red light, pressing the elevator keycard to it. The light goes from red to green and you hear the whirr of motors as the elevator makes its way to you!

You feel a lump in your throat and your heartbeat in your ears as the elevator reaches it, opening up its doors in near silence. Thankfully no one is inside. You step in and the doors close behind you, the elevator trundling its way down without you even pressing a button.

It continues for a minute and then stops with a slight jolt. You see then that this isn't just an elevator, it's a *double* elevator, with doors in front of you and behind. From behind you, you hear the sounds of the Salon party, the music thumping away and the women beyond laughing and shouting drunkenly to each other. Luckily, this elevator requires you push a button to exit, the button to the Salon staring at you like a knobby, unblinking red eye.

You turn around the other way. There is a matching red button but there is one difference: a keypad sits above this button, taunting you. You try to press the button. Nothing happens, save for a low buzz that emanates from somewhere in the elevator. It looks like you need a code for this door.

You look down at the slip of paper with its four-digit code. 0714. You punch the numbers into the keypad and there is a soft chime from somewhere in the elevator.

It's time to go home.

You punch the red button for the doors leading outside of the manor. They shudder open and you feel the breeze of the evening air tickle your near-naked body. It's going to be a hike getting home the way you are, but you'll find a way... anything is better than sticking around too long in this forsaken place.

You peel away from the direction of the backyard, the party back there already starting to reach a shrill, drunken fever pitch. Though as you do, you wistfully look at a rack of coats that have been set out for the mistresses to wear to keep warm—if only you could have one too, but there's no point in risking your escape now, not when you've made it this far.

You trod off down the first path you can find away from the manor, stepping onto a dirt path that goes along the main road you walked along to get here. It snakes and curves, but you generally are able to follow it, the setting sun making you pick up your pace lest you risk being lost naked and in the dark in the woods around Matriarch Manor. Now and again you turn back towards the manor's lights to help orient yourself and even this far away you can hear the occasional laugh or crack of something—wood? A whip? Something you can't even imagine?—that signals the party is still going strong and is sure to be for quite some time.

You continue home, your mind filled with strange fantasies about the domineering women you encountered at Matriarch Manor. It's weird to think how these women who were so terrifying before now make your cock stiffen with excitement. Who knows: Maybe one day you'll return...

CONGRATULATIONS! YOU FREED YOURSELF AND ESCAPED
MATRIARCH MANOR!

124

Not willing to risk the elevator, you lurk around the third floor on your way downstairs. But as you go down the hallway, you see two mistresses marching a male slave around the corner! How did you not hear them coming? You look around, as if there might be somewhere you could hide—as if you even *could* hide—knowing that you've made a grave miscalculation.

"What do we have here?" purrs one of the mistresses. She has a Nordic look to her, with long blonde hair and creamy pale skin, wearing a black leather cami dress with a skirt that looks like a cross between a negligee and a flirty summer dress. Black tights are pulled all the way up to her mid-thigh, matched with matte black ballet flats.

"A slave... on the third floor. Without his chastity. Are you all alone, little slave?" asks the other mistress. She's wearing a hypersexualized fetish schoolgirl outfit, with a skin-tight blouse sans bra, an absurdly short, pleated skirt, and striped tights with chunky Mary Janes. Maybe it's the straight black hair or powdered face—or just the schoolgirl outfit itself—but she has a distinctly Japanese look to her, along with vicious eyes that make you queasy.

The male slave between them warns you of the fate you're facing. He is hooded with his hands tied behind him and his ankles hobbled, his body covered in a graffiti scrawl of lewd drawings and insulting names, like the girls having been drawing on him like an old desk in the back of a classroom. He does not seem to be able to see or hear anything, jumping at their slightest touch.

"I was just goi—"

"I think he *is* alone, Umeko," says the blonde, Nordic mistress. She nonchalantly claws at the male slave's side, making him squeal in fear, and then approaches you, keeping her blue eyes locked on yours as she knocks on the ornate door. Of course, there is no answer.

"I think you're right, Inge," says Umeko, the Japanese mistress. Not to be outdone by her friend, she too claws at the hooded male and smirks to herself as he jumps away from her, almost stumbling to the floor. Then she's upon you as well, opening the ornate door to the playroom. She looks inside. "Yep. He's all alone."

"And now why would you be all alone and without your chastity?" asks Inge, taking small steps towards you and forcing you to step backwards to not have her crash into you, until your back is pushed up against the hallway wall.

"Slaves aren't supposed to be unchastised," says Umeko like some taletelling uppity schoolgirl... which isn't a stretch to imagine with her outfit, the hem of her microskirt showing off the undercheeks of a round, plump bottom.

"That's absolutely right," Inge says to you with a sickly sweet smile. A pleasant, summery smell wafts off the blonde, something like freshly cut grass mixed with orange blossom water. It makes you think of hot days and bright, sunny mornings. "I think we're going to need you to explain your behavior... inside."

"Yes definitely, we're going to need an explanation," says Umeko, retrieving the male slave and pushing him into the playroom by holding his bound hands, like she's pushing a rickety wheelbarrow.

Once Umeko and the slave are inside, Inge turns and extends her arm towards the door of the playroom. "After you," she says smugly.

Very conveniently, Inge's arm is stretched out to block the shortest path to the staircase. Your only other option for escape is to run *all* the way around the wraparound hallway, by which point she's sure to have blocked the staircase. You have no choice but to go into the playroom.

You go back inside. The bright colors and piles of toys seem far more ominous now than they did a few minutes ago and already Umeko has the male slave bent over with his ass in the air while she sifts through an assortment of humiliating, colorful dildos. She stops what she's doing and leaves him there to wait in his uncomfortable position, joining Inge after Inge's closed and locked the playroom door.

"Now, slave... tell us. Why aren't you wearing a cage?" asks Inge. Her blue eyes flash with the kind of malice reserved for a mean child picking wings off flies and legs off spiders. You wish you were anywhere else right now.

Your throat is dry as you try to speak: "I... I was going to be fitted for a new one," you say, already kicking yourself for your lie and all the other questions that it might raise.

But surprisingly, the mistresses aren't interested in disproving your lie.

"I'm sorry to say, you're going to be late for that appointment," taunts

Inge.

"Very late," agrees Umeko.

The women look at each other and share a snide, sinister smile.

"Do you think this slave's the right one?" Umeko asks Inge before she looks over at the hooded male slave with his ass in the air. "I feel like we kind of wasted the last one. It won't be fun if we do it to him now."

"Who cares if he's right, he's here. No cage. What's he gonna say?," says Inge. "Are you ready?"

Umeko probes at her belly with her thumbs and, as she does, your pulse quickens. What are these two mistresses up to? Even though you have no idea, the playroom suddenly feels very stuffy.

"Yep," says Umeko. "I sure am."

Inge looks back to you. "On your knees, slave," she commands.

You pitifully sink to your knees. Umeko searches through the mounds of toys in the playroom, pulling out a thin length of silk that looks like a leftover scarf from one of the partygoers' outfits. She brings it back to where you're kneeling.

"Do you want to go first or me?" she asks Inge.

"After you," says Inge, with a playful flourish that makes both women giggle.

Umeko hands the silk scarf to Inge and then looks down at you with a smirk.

"We're going to do a... taste test of sorts," she says.

"A sniff test," offers Inge.

Umeko chuckles. "A fragrance tasting," she says back, both girls giggling again.

Then Umeko turns around and under her skirt you can see the undercheek of the woman's tawny, plump ass; a pair of sheer pink panties are wedged between those cheeks and you can feel the heat and sweat and musk radiating off her body. Umeko reaches back and flips up the short hem of her skirt and then, without any warning, rips a tremendously loud fart right in your face.

It's pungent and aggressive, like mulch in the sun mixed with fertilizer, the waft of it making you nearly crumple backwards. Inge laughs at your reaction and at Umeko as she uses her micro skirt's hem to fan the smell towards you so that it wafts up your nostrils and seeps down your throat until you're gagging.

"My turn," says Inge, taking Umeko's position. Her skirt is too long to easily flip up, so she hikes it up instead, showing you the neon green thong she has on underneath that separates the Nordic blonde's high, firm ass cheeks. Even though you know what's coming, it's still deeply startling as she too rips a loud, odiferous fart.

This one is both the same and different to Umeko's, giving off a higher, almost sweeter pungency, although certainly still as rancid and awful as the first. You cough and try to pull your head away, but Umeko forces you to inhale, keeping your head still with one hand while she pinches her nose shut with the other.

A few moments later your sight is removed by the silk scarf that Umeko ties tightly around your head, making sure not even the slightest, tiniest silver of light can slip through. Both women start to walk around you in a slow circle, talking in turns.

"We're going to start the 'tasting' soon..." Umeko says, her voice husky and mean.

"...and you're going to tell us what—who—you're tasting..." continues Inge, making a laugh-scoff sound at her own declaration.

"...get it wrong and you'll be sorry..."

"...very sorry..."

"...like kick you in the balls until you can't have babies sorry..."

"...twist your nipples off and make you eat them sorry..."

"...turn this into a *real* filthy tasting sorry..."

"Eww no," says Inge with a shocked, delirious gasp.

"Okay, okay, too far, but the point is..."

"...you won't like it."

The women continue to walk and you realize far too late that you should've been trying to keep track of where they are. Their footsteps stop. Seconds pass. And then, with an awful-yet-slightly-funny raspberry sound, one of the girls rips another fart in your face.

Someone nudges you brusquely in the leg. They're waiting for an answer.

You reluctantly breathe in the stink, no longer able to differentiate the women at all. You sniff again and again, cringing at how you're taking their reek into your mouth and nose and lungs. It all just seems so terrible that you have clue who just farted right in your face.

"Uh... Miss..." You wrack your brain, hoping for an answer. "Inge?"

"Hah. Nope," says Umeko from in front of you.

You feel something like a pillowy slap that hits you head-on in the face, feeling a mix of soft skin and thin fabric that has a cloying stink to it.

As you tumble backwards to the sound of the girls' laughter, you realize Umeko just shoved her ass right in your face, hard enough to knock you down. One of them—Inge, you assume—forces you back to your knees and then you hear the footsteps start up again as the girls go round and round.

Then they stop.

Again, you find yourself subjected to another humiliating fart, this one tailing off in a comical high squeak that you can tell both girls are trying not to giggle at. They give you even less time this go around, both nudging you in the sides with the toes of their shoes. You sniff and gag and choke, no more aware of who it could've been than the last time.

"Inge...?" you ask, playing the odds. "Miss Inge?"

"Uhhhh NOPE!" shouts Umeko at you. Both girls clap and howl, excited that you've once again messed up their game.

You brace yourself to be hit in the face again with Umeko's ass, wondering how a thing that should be so delightful is so terrible, when you feel a sharp kick in your balls from behind that makes you fall forward in stabbing agony. As you do, there's another kick, this one from the front that catches you in the stomach. You groan, much to the pleasure of the girls, and then either clap or high five each other, you're not sure.

"Last chance," says Inge. "One more mistake and you get a demotion."

Having no idea what she's talking about, the girls start again, going in a circle of footsteps that turns one way and then the other several times over, the footsteps stopping so abruptly you don't think *anyone* can be in front of you.

As with the last few times, there's a pause and then a deep, rumbling fart. This one is a single loud tuba toot, more noise than anything else that leaves you sniffing around like some sort of blind underground creature. There's a hint of pungency and terrible reek but it's barely enough to go by and you're left, once more, guessing.

Three times a charm, you think, settling on your guess.

"Miss Inge," you say.

Your heart drops as the girls burst into peals of wicked laughter.

"WRONG!" shouts Umeko from in front of you.

The footsteps lead away, towards one of the piles of toys in the playroom, and when they return, you feel the women yanking your arms behind your back, fastening them tightly. They throw you to ground and you land in a position that you think can't be all that different from how the hooded male slave is positioned. Then you hear a familiar sound—keys.

Are they going to unlock you? Is such a thing even possible? And if they do... what will they do after that?

But alas, it's not *you* they're going to unlock.

"Come on worm, time to get up!" Umeko says in a voice that trails away from you.

Inge snorts. "He can't hear you, remember?"

"Hah, right," Umeko says.

There's the sound of fabric being pulled away and jingling keys and then a male sigh of exertion.

"Good news," Umeko says, and not to you. "We found you a nice pussy that you're going to get to fuck!"

As Umeko's footsteps return towards you—joined by another, heavier pair—you realize the playroom had the kind of keys you were looking for all along. But to your horror, they're being used to unlock someone else... who is going to get to fuck *you*.

Inge whispers in your ear: "Be a good pussy or else we're going to bring every last slave up here to fuck you."

She shoves your head further down into the floor of the playroom and parts your ass cheeks, letting loose a hot wad of spit.

You were so close to freedom. So close! And now it's all gone...

THE END

125

Against your fears and perhaps your better judgment, you start to search the playroom. Oh boy, there are so many strange toys here: odd, double-ended dildos that look entirely too big for any person, strange, motorized milking machines, metal devices which might be used for pleasure or for pain, a rainbow assortment of plugs and clips and slender rods that are suspiciously sized, open and discarded ice tray molds with a purpose that completely escapes you, and more, all of it seeming more bizarre and extreme than anything you've ever stumbled across. Whoever plays here, they play hard.

It's as you're picking through a pile of used rope and binder clips that you spot a chastity device. Looking up, you see another a few feet over, and then a half-open trunk full of them. Digging madly through the trunk, you come across a ring of keys! Quickly, you flip through the keys, seeing that they either have numbers on them or little colored dots. Then, just as you are overwhelmed by all the options and possibilities, you come across one key that is a little larger than the rest and a slightly different shade of brass, like it's been painted over. Etched across it in laser engraving is the word "MASTER".

This is it. You can't believe it. You've found a master key for the chastity devices from Matriarch Manor. But before you can celebrate your victory, you hear voices—plural—in the hall. They sound like they're far enough away but getting closer.

You could try to leave with the keys now or you could try to hide, but the only suitable hiding place seems to be the louvered doors against the wall which, when you check, you see are full of dirty, stinky laundry.

Leave now with the keys (Page 263)
Hide in the stinky laundry (Page 269)

126

Not willing to risk staying too long, you decide to leave the playroom. But as you pull open the ornate door and step back into the hallway, you find yourself face to face with two mistresses marching a male slave in your direction! How did you not hear them coming? You look around, as if there might be somewhere you could hide—as if you even *could* hide—knowing that you've made a grave miscalculation.

"What do we have here?" purrs one of the mistresses. She has a Nordic look to her, with long blonde hair and creamy pale skin, wearing a black leather cami dress with a skirt that looks like a cross between a negligee and a flirty summer dress. Black tights are pulled all the way up to her mid-thigh, matched with matte black ballet flats.

"A slave... on the third floor. Are you all alone, little slave?" asks the other mistress. She's wearing a hypersexualized fetish schoolgirl outfit, with a skin-tight blouse sans bra, an absurdly short, pleated skirt, and striped tights with chunky Mary Janes. Maybe it's the straight black hair or powdered face—or just the schoolgirl outfit itself—but she has a distinctly Japanese look to her, along with vicious eyes that make you queasy.

The male slave between them warns you of the fate you're facing. He is hooded with his hands tied behind him and his ankles hobbled, his body covered in a graffiti scrawl of lewd drawings and insulting names, like the girls having been drawing on him like an old desk in the back of a classroom. He does not seem to be able to see or hear anything, jumping at their slightest touch.

"I was just goi—"

"I think he *is* alone, Umeko," says the blonde, Nordic mistress. She nonchalantly claws at the male slave's side, making him squeal in fear, and then approaches you, keeping her blue eyes locked on yours as she knocks on the ornate door. Of course, there is no answer.

"I think you're right, Inge," says Umeko, the Japanese mistress. Not to be outdone by her friend, she too claws at the hooded male and smirks to herself as he jumps away from her, almost stumbling to the floor. Then she's upon you as well, opening the ornate door to the playroom. She looks inside. "Yep. He's all alone."

"And now why would you be all alone?" asks Inge, taking small steps towards you and forcing you to step backwards to not have her crash into you, until your back is pushed up against the hallway wall.

"Slaves aren't supposed to be on the upper floors of the manor alone," says Umeko like some taletelling uppity schoolgirl... which isn't a stretch to imagine with her outfit, the hem of her microskirt showing off the undercheeks of a round, plump bottom.

"That's absolutely right," Inge says to you with a sickly sweet smile. A pleasant, summery smell wafts off the blonde, something like freshly cut grass mixed with orange blossom water. It makes you think of hot days and bright, sunny mornings. "I think we're going to need you to explain your behavior... inside."

"Yes definitely, we're going to need an explanation," says Umeko, retrieving the male slave and pushing him into the playroom by holding his bound hands, like she's pushing a rickety wheelbarrow.

Once Umeko and the slave are inside, Inge turns and extends her arm towards the door of the playroom. "After you," she says smugly.

Very conveniently, Inge's arm is stretched out to block the shortest path to the staircase. Your only other option for escape is to run *all* the way around the wraparound hallway, by which point she's sure to have blocked the staircase. You have no choice but to go into the playroom.

You go back inside. The bright colors and piles of toys seem far more ominous now than they did a few minutes ago and already Umeko has the male slave bent over with his ass in the air while she sifts through an assortment of humiliating, colorful dildos. She stops what she's doing and leaves him there to wait in his uncomfortable position, joining Inge after Inge's closed and locked the playroom door.

"Now, slave... tell us. Why are you up here?" asks Inge. Her blue eyes flash with the kind of malice reserved for a mean child picking wings off flies and legs off spiders. You wish you were anywhere else right now.

Your throat is dry as you try to speak: "I... I was supposed to pick something up for a mistress downstairs," you say, already kicking yourself for your lie and all the other questions that it might raise.

But surprisingly, the mistresses aren't interested in disproving your lie.

"I'm sorry to say, you're going to be late," taunts Inge.

"Very late," agrees Umeko.

The women look at each other and share a snide, sinister smile.

"Do you think this slave's the right one?" Umeko asks Inge before she looks over at the hooded male slave with his ass in the air. "I feel like we kind of wasted the last one. It won't be fun if we do it to him now."

"Who cares if he's right, he's here," says Inge. "Are you ready?"

Umeko probes at her belly with her thumbs and, as she does, your pulse quickens. What are these two mistresses up to? Even though you have no idea, the playroom suddenly feels very stuffy.

"Yep," says Umeko. "I sure am."

Inge looks back to you. "On your knees, slave," she commands.

You pitifully sink to your knees. Umeko searches through the mounds of toys in the playroom, pulling out a thin length of silk that looks like a leftover scarf from one of the partygoers' outfits. She brings it back to where you're kneeling.

"Do you want to go first or me?" she asks Inge.

"After you," says Inge, with a playful flourish that makes both women giggle.

Umeko hands the silk scarf to Inge and then looks down at you with a smirk.

"We're going to do a... taste test of sorts," she says.

"A sniff test," offers Inge.

Umeko chuckles. "A fragrance tasting," she says back, both girls giggling again.

Then Umeko turns around and under her skirt you can see the undercheek of the woman's tawny, plump ass; a pair of sheer pink panties are wedged between those cheeks and you can feel the heat and sweat and musk radiating off her body. Umeko reaches back and flips up the short hem of her skirt and then, without any warning, rips a tremendously loud fart right in your face.

It's pungent and aggressive, like mulch in the sun mixed with fertilizer, the waft of it making you nearly crumple backwards. Inge laughs at your reaction and at Umeko as she uses her micro skirt's hem to fan the smell towards you so that it wafts up your nostrils and seeps down your throat until you're gagging.

"My turn," says Inge, taking Umeko's position. Her skirt is too long to easily flip up, so she hikes it up instead, showing you the neon green thong she has on underneath that separates the Nordic blonde's high, firm ass cheeks. Even though you know what's coming, it's still deeply startling as she too rips a loud, odiferous fart.

This one is both the same and different to Umeko's, giving off a higher, almost sweeter pungency, although certainly still as rancid and awful as the first. You cough and try to pull your head away, but Umeko forces you to inhale, keeping your head still with one hand while she pinches her nose shut with the other.

A few moments later your sight is removed by the silk scarf that Umeko ties tightly around your head, making sure not even the slightest bit of light can slip through. Both women start to walk around you in a slow circle, talking in turns.

"We're going to start the 'tasting' soon..." Umeko says, her voice husky and mean.

"...and you're going to tell us what—who—you're tasting..." continues Inge, making a laugh-scoff sound at her own declaration.

"...get it wrong and you'll be sorry..."

"...very sorry..."

"...like kick you in the balls until you can't have babies sorry..."

"...twist your nipples off and make you eat them sorry..."

"...turn this into a *real* filthy tasting sorry..."

"Eww no," says Inge with a shocked, delirious gasp.

"Okay, okay, too far, but the point is..."

"...you won't like it."

The women continue to walk and you realize far too late that you should've been trying to keep track of where they are. Their footsteps stop. Seconds pass. And then, with an awful-yet-slightly-funny raspberry sound, one of the girls rips another fart in your face.

Someone nudges you brusquely in the leg. They're waiting for an answer.

You reluctantly breathe in the stink, no longer able to differentiate the women at all. You sniff again and again, cringing at how you're taking their reek into your mouth and nose and lungs. It all just seems so terrible that you have clue who just farted right in your face.

"Uh... Miss..." You wrack your brain, hoping for an answer. "Inge?"

"Hah. Nope," says Umeko from in front of you.

You feel something like a pillowy slap that hits you head-on in the face, feeling a mix of soft skin and thin fabric that has a cloying stink to it. As you tumble backwards to the sound of the girls' laughter, you realize Umeko just shoved her ass right in your face, hard enough to knock you down. One of them—Inge, you assume—forces you back to your knees and then you hear the footsteps start up again as the girls go round and round.

Then they stop.

Again, you find yourself subjected to another humiliating fart, this one tailing off in a comical high squeak that you can tell both girls are trying not to giggle at. They give you even less time this go around, both nudging you in the sides with the toes of their shoes. You sniff and gag and choke, no more aware of who it could've been than the last time.

"Inge...?" you ask, playing the odds. "Miss Inge?"

"Uhhhh NOPE!" shouts Umeko at you. Both girls clap and howl, excited that you've once again messed up their game.

You brace yourself to be hit in the face again with Umeko's ass, wondering how a thing that should be so delightful is so terrible, when you feel a sharp kick in your balls from behind that makes you fall forward in stabbing agony. As you do, there's another kick, this one from the front that catches you in the stomach. You groan, much to the pleasure of the girls, and then either clap or high five each other, you're not sure.

"Last chance," says Inge. "One more mistake and you get a demotion."

Having no idea what she's talking about, the girls start again, going in a circle of footsteps that turns one way and then the other several times over, the footsteps stopping so abruptly you don't think *anyone* can be in front of you.

As with the last few times, there's a pause and then a deep, rumbling fart. This one is a single loud tuba toot, more noise than anything else that leaves you sniffing around like some sort of blind underground creature. There's a hint of pungency and terrible reek but it's barely enough to go by and you're left, once more, guessing.

Three times a charm, you think, settling on your guess.

"Miss Inge," you say.

Your heart drops as the girls burst into peals of wicked laughter.

"WRONG!" shouts Umeko from in front of you.

The footsteps lead away, towards one of the piles of toys in the playroom, and when they return, you feel the women yanking your arms behind your back, fastening them tightly. They throw you to ground and you land in a position that you think can't be all that different from how the hooded male slave is positioned. Then you hear a familiar sound—keys.

Are they going to unlock you? Is such a thing even possible? And if they do... what will they do after that?

But alas, it's not *you* they're going to unlock.

"Come on worm, time to get up!" Umeko says in a voice that trails ever farther away from you.

Inge snorts. "He can't hear you, remember?"

"Hah, right," Umeko says.

There's the sound of fabric being pulled away and jingling keys and then a male sigh of exertion.

"Good news," Umeko says, and not to you. "We found you a nice pussy that you're going to get to fuck!"

As Umeko's footsteps return towards you—joined by another, heavier pair—you realize the playroom had the kind of keys you were looking for all along. But to your horror, they're being used to unlock someone else... who is going to get to fuck *you*.

Inge whispers in your ear: "Be a good pussy or else we're going to bring every last slave up here to fuck you."

She shoves your head further down into the floor of the playroom and parts your ass cheeks, letting loose a hot wad of spit.

It won't be long now, you think.

THE END

127

Desperate and with no other options, you pull open the louvered door and dive into the pile of filthy, stinky laundry, shutting the door behind you. You burrow beneath the soiled clothing, covering yourself with dirty panties and discarded nylons and pieces of stained lingerie, unable to tell if they're meant for women or cross-dressed men. A pervasive reek of sweat hangs in there, growing stronger the longer you're buried in the awful pile of laundry.

Your instincts prove to be right when the voices in the hall grow louder and then, with a dreadful click, the playroom door swings open. Two mistresses with a male slave in tow march in, laughing and toying with their prey. You watch them through the slats in the closet door.

One of the mistresses, a blonde, has a Nordic look to her, with creamy pale skin and wearing a black leather cami dress with a skirt that looks like a cross between a negligee and a flirty summer dress. Black tights are pulled all the way up to her mid-thigh, matched with matte black ballet flats. The other is wearing a hypersexualized fetish schoolgirl outfit, with a skin-tight blouse sans bra, an absurdly short, pleated skirt, and striped tights with chunky Mary Janes. Maybe it's the straight black hair or powdered face—or just the schoolgirl outfit itself—but she has a distinctly Japanese look to her. Between them, their male slave is hooded with his hands tied behind him and his ankles hobbled, his body covered in a graffiti scrawl of lewd drawings and insulting names, like the girls having been drawing on him like an old desk in the back of a classroom. He does not seem to be able to see or hear anything, jumping at their slightest touch.

"Ohhh we are going to have so much fun, Umeko!" says the blonde, Nordic mistress. She nonchalantly claws at the male slave's side, making him squeal in fear, and then searches through the playroom.

"I think you're right, Inge," says Umeko, the Japanese mistress. Not to be outdone by her friend, she too claws at the hooded male and smirks to herself as he jumps away from her, almost stumbling to the floor. She forces the male slave to bend over with his ass in the air while she sifts through an assortment of humiliating, colorful dildos, eventually despairing at not finding what she was hoping for.

"Here it is!" shouts Inge, dragging over a heavy white-and-pink leather-wrapped box from the corner of the playroom.

"Oh my god, they *do* have one," says Umeko excitedly. "This poor, poor bastard."

With a grunt of exertion, Umeko shoves the male over so that he falls onto his back with a loud "Omph!". Together, she and Inge push the heavy leather-wrapped box towards him and you can see it is some kind of homemade contraption, a near-perfect cube with white leather sides and silver studs along the edges, with pink trim and two openings. The opening at the top is simple and circular, but the second opening, on the side, seems to be rimmed with some kind of latex-like flap that zips closed.

What could this thing ever be used for?

Satisfied with the position of the box, Umeko tears off the male slave's hood. He gasps for fresh air, his eyes adjusting to the bright lights of the playroom. Then, barely giving him a moment of respite, Umeko is directing his head towards the zippered flap. The look on the male's face is one of exhaustion, despair, and resignation. His head disappears into the latex-flapped hole before Umeko pulls the zips down, making a tight seal around his neck. You see now that the inside of the box must have some kind of cushioning or sloping to it, because the only way the male is able to get his head inside is if he presses it against the box's top hole. It's a tight fit, too, the edge of that top hole pressing into the male's face.

As Inge pulls up her skirt and sits her panty-clad behind on the slave's face, it occurs to you what this contraption is used for.

These women might be here a long time. You could wait things out in the laundry pile for as long as it takes and hope that they don't need anything from it—they wouldn't... right?—or you could wait for a pause in the action and try to make a break for it, though you'd have to come back later to grab the chastity keys to see if they'll unlock your device.

Wait for an opportunity to make a run for it (Page 271)
Stay hidden in the laundry as long as it takes (Page 276)

128

You wait and watch the mistresses through the slats in the louvered doors. They take turns facesitting the slave, smothering him until he is flailing desperately for fresh air. Then, in an unthinkable even worse move, they begin ripping loud, obnoxious farts right onto his face. The girls are ecstatic with the lewd noises they're making and the way their slave thrashes about like a bug on its back, but they simply refuse to stop, trying many ways to sit harder on his face or steal more and more of his breath away. It's too much for you to watch and you try to ward off the own horrible smells you're dealing with from the dirty laundry by daydreaming about how you might eventually escape.

Soon the facesitting turns into standing on the white-and-pink box and smushing their feet into the slave's face, pinching his mouth and nose shut. The slave tries to beg for mercy but the mistresses will not hear of it. They push their charge even further, until they are exhausted... and inspired in another way.

"Hey, Inge..." says Umeko.

"Yeah?" asks Inge with an exhausted sigh.

"I have an idea." Mischief flashes in Umeko's eyes. "You ever use a slave to... you know?"

Inge raises her eyebrows. "No, I don't know. To what?"

"You know... not just smothering but, like... you know." She hikes a thumb towards the bathroom.

"Ohhhhh. This again?"

"What! I'm curious," says Umeko in a pouty tongue.

Inge rolls her eyes. "Well, like... I'm not going to stop you. But I'm not joining you."

A sly smile spreads across Umeko's face. "Wanna watch?"

Inge huffs a laugh and says, "Sure. What the hell."

You watch unbelieving as the women stand and pull the male slave from the white-and-pink box. He's forced to stand, looking dizzy and disoriented, and then is marched to the bathroom. Umeko slams the door shut. You don't want to think about what's going to happen in there.

Quickly, you clamber out from the closet and make a measured rush for the door. You open it quietly and then slip into the hallway, your heart pounding so very hard. What would've happened if they'd found *you*? Might you be in that bathroom on, on your back, waiting for...

You shudder and start down the hallway.

That's when you hear voices from behind. Thinking as quickly as you can, you dart into the lounge-like space with its slanted glass ceiling, see a low sofa, a tea table, and several armchairs. You quickly duck behind the sofa and pray the voices pass. But instead they only get louder. Oh, shit.

"Oh my, oh my that was even more amazing," one says, a slight slur in her words from a night of loud music and drinking.

"It was pretty great," says the other, her tone crisper and more coherent. "But like I said I've seen wilder manor parties. Want to go back to where we were before?"

"Sure. We can check in the progress on the Cool Down ceremony."

"Right over here, right? The cubby with the windows?"

Now, along with the voices, you hear footsteps. And they're headed your way. You cower deeper down, wishing the sofa were higher.

"Come on, let's—OH GOD!"

You hear a shriek followed by a shocked, confused laugh.

"A slave! You, get out of there! Now!"

You reluctantly pick your head up to see two mistresses from the party standing there, one with pale skin and alcohol-flushed cheeks who looks East Asian wearing a silk Chinese dragon print dress with a short collar and a split hem and the other who looks Middle Eastern with her hair up in a ponytail, big hoop earrings, and a front-knotted pink crop top blouse with long, flounce sleeves and cut off denim booty shorts.

"Kayla, what the hell," says the East Asian mistress.

"Looks like we have a stowaway, Tiffany," says Kayla with a dazzling, devilish smile. She flicks her finger up at you. "You! I said: Get up!"

You shakily rise from behind the sofa, cursing yourself for thinking you could easily hide away in the lounge. Kayla gives Tiffany a sly, wicked look. Then she fishes out a box of cigarettes from the front pocket of her cut-off denim shorts and sits down on the sofa. She snaps her fingers and points to the floor in front of her.

"Over here, slave," she says.

"What are you doing Kayla?" asks Tiffany.

"Enjoying a smoke break," Kayla says. "Come on, join me."

As Tiffany takes a seat next to Kayla, you come around from the sofa and look towards the lounge's archway.

"Don't even think about it," says Kayla, holding her cigarette in her mouth as she lights it. She takes a deep inhale and lets it go towards the glass ceiling of the atrium lounge. She hands the cigarettes and her lighter to Tiffany, who takes them with some hesitation, the look on her face suggesting she's still trying to figure out what Kayla's up to. Kayla points to the ground. "Kneel."

You get down on your knees as the women smoke in silence, Kayla not taking her emerald green eyes off you. She takes a long drag of her cigarette and blows the smoke in your face, the blue-white cloud stinging your eyes and your nostrils.

"Tiff, did you mean what you said before? That you wanna become an official Matriarch Manor mistress?" asks Kayla.

Tiffany nods as she sucks on her cigarette. The blush in her cheeks is very pink now, giving her a faux-innocent glow. "I do. One day."

"Well, I'm going to teach you something," says Kayla. "Something that was taught to me when I started my application: Harden Your Heart."

Tiffany raises an eyebrow at Kayla. "Meaning...?"

"Meaning that a lot of women *try* to join the manor but they just can't do it. And the reason is usually something like they feel bad for one of the slaves or they think they can't go as far as other women or they just get too soft-hearted in general. That's why you've got to harden your heart if you're gonna be here. Watch."

Kayla takes a long, long drag of her cigarette, holding the precious nicotine-laced smoke in her lungs before she lets it roll down onto you in a heavy cloud. Her cigarette has begun to ash. She holds it out towards you and says, "Slave, give me your tongue."

"Kayla..."

Kayla shushes Tiffany. "Just watch," she says. "Slave. Tongue. Now. Or I report you for lurking up on the third floor."

You reluctantly loll out your tongue, looking in horror as Kayla flicks the ash of her cigarette onto it. You go to pull your tongue back in, but the mistress stops you.

"Hold it there until I say so," she says. Then she ignores you, returning to her conversation with Tiffany.

"See the thing is, if you view the slaves as 'men' or even as 'people', you're already going the wrong way. They aren't men or people and they aren't deserving of the way you'd respect an actual person. They're *things*. Things to use, to abuse. And the only way to really internalize this notion for yourself is, well, you gotta fake it till you make it. Go on, try ashing your cigarette in its mouth."

Tiffany, wanting to impress her friend, takes as long of a drag as Kayla did, coughing for a slight spell before her cigarette has a long column of flaky ash threatening to fall from its tip. She holds it over your tongue with a somewhat apologetic look on her face. Then she taps it and the column of ash tumbles onto your tongue. It's very warm for a second before it's cooled by your saliva, your ashy spit coating your tongue with the burned, charcoal taste of the cigarette. You can feel your mouth watering from being held open and your tongue start to ache as you continue to keep it held out for the mistresses' use.

They continue to chat, taking turns ashing their cigarettes on your tongue until there's a gratuitous pile of the saliva-wetted filth. It slides towards your mouth and the edges of your tongue, forcing you to make a scoop-like shape to hold it all in. All the while, the smell of smoke grows and the air gets thick with the blue-white haze that stings your eyes and your nostrils and makes you want to desperately get some fresh air.

When Kayla is done with her first cigarette, she gives you a terrible, snarling smile. "This is going to hurt," she says, more a promise than a warning. Then you watch helplessly as she brings the smoldering tip of her cigarette to the flat of your tongue, crushing it out on your tender flesh while you clench your fists shut and try to fight through the pain. She grinds that cigarette down and leaves it on the pile of ash, still not permitting you to swallow. She looks at Tiffany expectantly.

"Your turn," she says.

Apprehensive, Tiffany follows Kayla's lead. She sucks down her cigarette as quickly as she can, blowing the smoke right at you per Kayla's instruction, and then, like she's stomping on a roach in the kitchen, she smushes the cigarette butt onto your tongue, catching you on the tip and making you grunt in pain. Kayla laughs delightedly. When Tiffany's managed to push the cigarette to just a small nub, she drops it next Kayla's discarded smoke. Only then does Kayla flash her emerald green eyes at you and say:

"You may now swallow, slave."

It's just as bad going down your throat as sitting on your tongue, maybe even worse. Your throat feels chalky and gritty and you cough as you try to choke down the mistresses' waste, unable to believe they've just used you as a human ashtray. As you stay doubled over, coughing, you hear the flick of a lighter.

They aren't done with you yet.

"And here's the thing," Kayla says to Tiffany as they both start on their second cigarette. "You see what we just did? You see how he *listened* to us? He didn't have to do that. He could've refused, could've suffered the consequences, could've kept his pride. But he doesn't *have* pride. Because he's a sub-human piece of garbage. Aren't you, slave?"

Kayla thrusts out her lit cigarette towards you. She's not interested in your mouth anymore. She hovers it over your skin, just an inch away from your shoulder, then your chest, and then your nipple.

"Go ahead, nod your head like a dummy or I'm putting my cigarette out on you right now," she says.

You bobblehead nod and Kayla snorts, all while Tiffany watches with a mix of shock and awe.

"Put your cigarette out on him," she says to Tiffany. "The slave's going to choose a place for you to do it. And if I don't like where he picks, I'm going to choose a different one."

Tiffany leans forward with her lit cigarette. She seems unsure. You're unsure too, trying to figure out what part of your body you could offer up that would placate these women, thinking how this is not how this evening was supposed to wind up. What will these women do to you after they've had their fun? Will they let you go, or will they drag you downstairs for more torment?

Somehow you don't think freedom is what they have in mind.

Slowly you turn around, showing your back and buttocks; it feels like it'll be less painful that way and at least you won't have to watch.

"Oh look, he's offering you his balls," says Kayla snidely. "Go ahead, Harden your heart and teach this thing what it really is."

As you wait for the cigarette to land, your body trembling, you regret coming to Matriarch Manor at all. Maybe you could've found a happier fate, but you know that deep down in your heart, these mistresses have no intention of letting you go.

THE END

129

You decide to wait, as long as it takes.

And it does take a long, long time.

As Inge sits atop the box, you see the male's limbs slowly start to wander. Then they start to flail and then thrash, his hands—now tied in front of him—scrabbling up to try to push Inge off the top of it as she steals his air away, the women laughing at the sight of his panicked movements. Inge lifts herself up and you hear the male slave suck in a tremendous gasp of breath before Inge seals herself on top of him again.

"Do it," urges Umeko. "Do it do it do it!"

Inge concentrates for a moment. Then you hear a loud ripping roar from the top of the box that's followed by more frantic motions from the male slave. It takes you a second to realize that Inge just farted right into the male's face, his only breath now fouled with whatever terrible stink she just bequeathed to him. The women clap and chortle derisively, Umeko prodding her own belly and—you realize—getting ready to have her own time sitting on the male's face.

In time, though, as Inge isn't done. She alternates a few more rounds of seeing how far she can push the male before giving fresh air and then fresh, humiliating farts that go from sounding comical against the leather-wrapped box to sounding dreadful and debasing. When she's had her fun, the two women arrange for a seat swap that gives the slave less than a second or two of breath, Umeko flipping the short hem of her schoolgirl skirt to press her sheer pink panty-clad ass down onto the male's face.

You can hear him whimper and beg for relief, but instead what Inge does is sit on the male's legs. She makes excited sounds as he bucks against her while suffocating under Umeko's behind, Inge enjoying the ride of the male slave fighting to breathe. Umeko's farts are louder and deeper than Inge's and now, when she lifts herself up to grant the male air, you hear him gag and sputter from whatever dreck he's sucking down into his lungs.

"Please, please no more!" he begs before Umeko silences him.

"Shhh!" she hisses. "You're a cushion. Cushion's don't talk!"

A sad whimper emanates from the box and the girls cackle at the pathetic sound of it.

Their smother-fart torture continues for another twenty, thirty minutes, the girls having endless stamina for making their slave linger on the cusp of unconsciousness and a gasping, stink-filled awake state. You watch, horrified, as they torment him, growing ever more fearful that they might discover you hiding in the closet. What would they do then?

After Umeko and Inge tire of facesitting the slave, they take turns standing on the box itself, putting their feet over his face to play with their weight on his head. He groans through their trampling, sometimes clear and other times muffled as they cover his mouth and pinch his nose shut with their toes. Umeko in particular takes sadistic joy in holding the slave's nose shut, twisting it back and forth between her long, tawny toes. It's only when both girls are winded and bored do they finally give it all a rest and relax with colorful markers that they use to doodle in more graffiti across the slave's body, drawing obscene genitalia and insults in all caps lettering and all kinds of other, idle shapes until they've covered almost every inch of the man.

"I have an idea!" exclaim Inge as she finishes putting the details of a lewd, hairy pussy above the man's chastised cock. "Let's take him outside and blast him with cold water til he's clean. We could have the mistresses take turns, plus we could grab some food. I'm starving."

"Me too," says Umeko. "Great idea! Let's go!"

Like two girls playing with their favorite doll, they roughly pull the male slave out from the smother box. He looks dazed and is barely able to stand, but that doesn't stop the mistresses from shoving and kicking him forward, forcing him out of the playroom like a poor, beaten zombie thing.

You give it five minutes. Then you oh-so-slowly creep out of the closet and retrieve the keys for the chastity devices. Freedom! Sweet, sweet freedom! You cobble together items from the dirty pile of laundry to wear once you're outside, having to settle on sweatpants and a lady's blouse, and then head out into the hallway.

You creep down to the second floor, dressed in your ridiculous outfit. Your heart hammers away in your chest, praying you don't run into any other mistresses—or even other slaves who might be wandering the hallways. You trace your path along the outermost hallways of the second floor, keeping a close watch on the windows as you try to navigate away from the growing party of the backyard and towards the sides of the manor. Eventually you find your way to windows that overlook the narrow path you took so much earlier; there are no bushes or hedges to break your fall this time, but the drop is only fifteen or twenty feet. Not the most comfortable, but not terrible.

You open up the window. Cool air blows inside. You worm your way out through the window, hanging down from the window frame with the ring of chastity keys around your wrist. Then you drop and tumble onto the manor's mossy, stone path, feeling it knock the wind out of you.

You look around, expecting someone to be rushing towards you... but you're alone. All the women who are outside have made their way to the backyard to take part in the evening outdoor festivities. Not wasting any time, you rush into the woods surrounding the manor and head far far away, doing your damnedest to navigate along the main road and back towards your home. It'll be a long walk, but you'll get there, and you thank your lucky stars you didn't bring your keys or wallet to the manor, now seeing how much harder it would've been to keep them on you.

When you're a quarter mile or so from the manor, you stop to catch your breath and stumble through the chastity keys until you find the one that fits your device's lock. Success! The lock comes off, followed by the device itself. You toss both into the woods, letting out a happy sigh as you're able to touch your cock for the first time all week. In fact, you're so delirious with joy that you think about jerking off right there in the woods, but think you'd rather save it.

You continue home, your mind filled with strange fantasies about the domineering women you encountered at Matriarch Manor. It's weird to think how these women who were so terrifying before now make your cock stiffen with excitement. Who knows: Maybe one day you'll return...

CONGRATULATIONS! YOU FREED YOURSELF AND ESCAPED
MATRIARCH MANOR!

130

You get down on your knees and that alone tells Miss Wail what you've decided on. She steps over and gathers up the blonde locks of your hair, pulling them behind your shoulders.

You couldn't have imagined letting this slave—or any man, for that matter—fuck you in the ass, but the one thing you didn't consider is that would've been a case of you *taking* it instead of having to *give* it. Miss Wail grips the base of the slave's cock and points it towards your lips.

"Open up, dolly," she says gleefully.

You force your lips open and wrap them around the male's fully erect cock. He is warm under your lips and on your tongue, tasting sweaty and tangy and undeniably like male musk and semen. You gag at the taste, but Miss Wail puts her other hand on the back of your head, keeping you from pulling away. You shut your eyes and try to imagine what you've seen in porn, swirling your tongue around the cock and licking its underside, also realizing that there is only one way this is going to end... with his cum in your mouth.

Unable to help it, you really do try to pull away this time, but Miss Wail keeps you in place.

"A good dolly follows through," chides Miss Wail. "You don't want to disappoint your man, do you?"

Fighting back the filthy taste of him, you continue to suck, wrapping your lips as deep on his shaft as you can manage and then drawing them towards his cockhead, also drawing away the sweat and grime with them. It leaves a terribly bitter taste in your mouth and brings up what you've always imagined it's like at some dirty gloryhole or gas station men's room. You truly feel emasculated—without masculinity, at all—in that moment as you bob back and forth on the slave's shaft, feeling him pulse excitedly inside of you.

"Tickle his balls," Miss Wail commands.

You reach a hand up to try to find his balls but have to open your eyes to find your way. The ultra close-up POV of sucking a cock makes you dizzy and full of shame, though you are able to find the slave's full, heavy balls quickly enough to shut your eyes again just seconds later. You massage the slaves balls and hear him make a lascivious groan.

"Oh my, oh *my*, you're doing a great job, dolly. I do think your man is already getting close!" Miss Wail says teasingly. Then, to her slave: "All that time in lock-up and you're going to release so soon? It's almost sad, isn't it?"

You hear the man stifle his breathing as he tries to control himself, his balls feeling so heavy in your palm. In that moment you realize another inevitability: the sooner he cums, the sooner this nightmare is over. You tug gently on his sack, knowing how much you've enjoyed that sensation in the past, and the man groans again, his head pulsing on your tongue. You bob your head back and forth faster, keeping the tip of your tongue firm on the underside of his shaft.

"Oh, ho, ho! It looks like dolly finally gets the game," says Miss Wail, having long ago figured out what was at stake for you. "But can she get you off before you've had a choice to enjoy it, slave?"

Miss Wail takes her hands away from the slave's cock and your head, and the slave grabs your head instead, holding you firm to try to control the rhythm of your cock worship. The sweaty taste of him clings to the roof and sides of your mouth and as he nears the back of your throat, your gag reflex triggers, almost causing you to violently pull away.

You manage to stay where you are and fight against his grip so that *you* control the oral, your tongue now lashing in a zigzag pattern against him. You can feel his balls tighten towards his body as you keep massaging them and then, in a desperate last bid to end this, press your lips firmly against him and create as much suction as you can, humming and moaning while your mouth is closed.

That's enough to do it. The male slave *explodes* inside of you, jetting hot streams of cum against the back your throat. It is thick and truly gagging, but now that the male's started to cum, he is holding you fast to pump every last drop of his pent-up seed down your throat.

Finally, once his balls are drained dry, he lets go of you so that you can fall back on your heels to sputter and cough up his filth, all while Miss Wail laughs and laughs to herself.

"Well, well! That was quite the show."

She brings her slave back to the whipping bench, not even bothering to lock him up again, and then straps him down. She turns back to you.

"When you're ready, I suppose you should be on your way," she says.

You take a few minutes to collect yourself and once you have, Miss Wail commands you carefully take off your sissy wear and leave folded nicely on the bench. She blows you a dramatic kiss as you leave the space, giving you one last reminder before you head off to the third floor.

"Remember—if you mention a single word of me allowing you to go upstairs, I will make you *severely* regret it."

And with that, you go off to the third floor staircase.

Continue on to the third floor (Page 92)

THIS IS THE END OF CONTENT FOR ESCAPE FROM
MATRIARCH MANOR. THANKS FOR READING!

CHECK OUT MORE OF M.L. PAIGE'S WORK ON THE
FOLLOWING FEW PAGES...

Michelle Lucia Wants to Say...

Thanks for reading! I hope you enjoyed the story. Want another story, 100% FREE? I'll make you a deal: if you sign up for my newsletter today, I'll send you an exclusive download link to my Tease & Denial Femdom Erotica Chastity Checkup! It's the story of a boyfriend put in his place by his domineering girlfriend--at the dinner table in front of her college bestie! It's filled with delicious humiliation and nasty surprises.

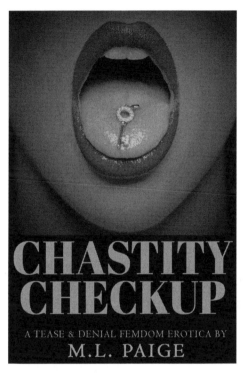

This 6,400-word ebook is no longer available anywhere on Amazon, so sign up today and grab your exclusive free copy! I promise your information won't be shared with anyone else and that I'll keep you in the know on new releases, special offers, and calls for advance readers.

https://sendfox.com/mlpaige

All you've got to do is follow the link and follow the instructions. Thanks again! Stay kinky, ~ Michelle Lucia

Also by M.L. Paige:

For a wild evening surrounded by Asian dommes...

Asian women rule and white men drool.

For the last year, Daniel Parker has been Kimiko Kishimoto's personal slave. She's teased, tormented, and trained him to please her in every way. But tonight Kimiko is taking Daniel to a special, secretive salon manor that hosts Asian dominatrixes and Asian women interested in experiencing the thrill of controlling white men. Daniel's never had to submit to anyone except Kimiko and the thought of being used and degraded by total strangers fills him with fear. Worse still, he knows he will have to compete with other slaves as they debase themselves to win Kimiko's praise and attention.

The stakes are also high for Kimiko. If tonight goes well, she will be welcomed into the salon as an official mistress, privy to the salon's many benefits and services. But she knows the salon's mistresses will be eager to put Daniel through his paces, subjecting him to extreme humiliation, dehumanization, and objectification as they try to prove him worthy...

For an immersive femdom harem of demanding sorority girls...

It's time for your interview with the sorority sisters of Phi Beta Chi. Lots of guys on campus have tried to become the submissive houseboy to the girls of Phi Beta Chi, and now it's finally your chance... but do you have what it takes? You'll have to "interview" with five different sorority girls to test your mettle, dealing with strict, sultry, devious, emasculating, and demeaning attitudes. Even if you do make it through the interviews, you may wonder if you're really ready for your new life as a sorority slave...

For a chastity, role-reversal tale...

Nathan's about to learn the true meaning of "happy wife, happy life." Nathan has been cheating on his wife Vera with a younger woman and he thinks he's been getting away with it. But what he doesn't know is that Vera is all too aware of his cheating ways and offers him an ultimatum: either suffer a bankrupting divorce or go into sexual chastity until Vera says otherwise. Choosing chastity, Nathan's life will be transformed from that of an unfaithful hubby to a pussy-whipped wimp, leaving Nathan denied and subject to Vera's every cruel whim...

These stories M.L. Paige's full catalog can be found on Amazon at:

http://amazon.com/author/mlpaige

Printed in Great Britain
by Amazon

48128845R00162